INVASIVE SPECIES

Michael Pickard

Second Edition

ISBN-13: 978-1530036035
ISBN-10: 1530036038

Acknowledgments

Sincere gratitude to Bill Crawford, Johanna Laemle, Rheta Pickard, The Writers of Glencoe, and Irwin Friedman for their unique insight, keen eyesight and prose hindsight.

1 - Selton (Kearney, NE)

Selton Serulia awoke in the dark, the two lumps on his head throbbing. He elbowed his way to sitting up, his backroots ripping clumps of grassy dirt from the soil. He'd read about Earthling emotions associated with their physiology. Feeling pain for the first time was intriguing but far from pleasant. Agonies traversed his body each time the lumps pulsed. They'd appeared on the top of his head as tender patches a few weeks ago – on the left and right sides running front to back. Since then, they'd grown bulbous, forcing him to wear a discarded piece of cloth on his head in public instead of his misshapen and stained fedora.

He had avoided touching them, afraid that if they were infected, he would make things worse. *Approaching recall is the worst time for my health to be in jeopardy.* But his self-control evaporated as the agony increased. He caressed the lumps, hoping that a gentle craniosacral massage would ease the pain. Instead, each stroke sent shock waves from his head to his toes. He felt like shouting. In the middle of the night in a sleepy rail yard in Kearney, Nebraska, latitude 40.693415, longitude -99.080660, no one would notice. Using his arms as leverage, he stood and staggered to the train underpass wall.

Desperate for relief, Selton placed one hand over each lump, positioned his fingers wide and squeezed. His mouth opened in a silent scream. The bumps burst open. Lit by halogen streetlights, swarms of thin filaments erupted from the lumps, forming patterns that sparkled, swirled and danced above his head. The filaments formed two distinct floating clusters, one drifting east, and the other west. That made no sense, given a consistent wind direction.

One lone filament lost touch with the upward currents and spun suspended in mid-air. Selton forced his body to jump. He caught the filament in his fist. Nothing he understood about his physiology matched this experience. *Is this an undisclosed symptom of ripening?* Selton staggered toward his bindle, a shoulder duffel bag containing his limited worldly goods, tucked behind an underpass beam. An empty jar from some previous adventure – homemade strawberry preserves, if memory could be trusted - was the perfect container to store the filament for subsequent analysis. Despite the still air in the bottle, the filament bounced from bottom to sides to top, as if seeking escape.

Selton's body yearned for a grassy area and sustenance. With the echo of pain and growing hunger, he dragged himself hand-over-hand along the underpass wall. His steps got smaller, becoming shuffles. As he escaped to bare sky, he fell to the ground and crawled on his belly over gravel and train tracks, arms and legs synchronized, until he reached a green patch of grass. With the last of his strength, he rolled over. While he looked up at the darkness, his backroots dug hungrily into the soil, craving nutrients that would flow up vascular pathways into his body. He knew from his parent's experience how tired Serulian soil was. The pH of Kearney's soil chemistry was as good as he'd ever experienced on any of his previous stops. *Given my parent's memories of Serulia's soil, anyplace on Earth would be better.*

Selton promised himself he'd figure out the cause of the filament phenomenon and its impact on his mission. After a good night's feeding. *If I am supposed to bring Earth's knowledge back to Serulia, then Dissemination Oversight better recall me soon.*

2 – Charlie (Washington, DC)

As a child, Charles Lindberg Keyson had a black thumb. His high school biology project in the backyard of the family's Virginia home never grew, despite precise watering and fertilizing. Charlie was certain Mother Nature nursed some vendetta against his need to be a gardener. Other students bought plants from local stores, repotted them and attempted to pass them off as their own work. Charlie accepted his F grade for the assignment.

His parents were sympathetic, suggesting that he direct his energies into other activities, perhaps ones involving other children. Instead, he sampled *A Study in Scarlet*, the first Sherlock Holmes novel, from his father's paperback collection and subsequently the remaining three novels and fifty-six short stories in sequential order.

As an adult, Charlie sat in his cubicle at the Environmental Protection Agency. Despite the passage of time, he never got over that failed biology project. In between his routine assignments, he'd search recent EPA case files on his computer, reviewing soil analysis reports submitted from multiple field agents. *I'm no pedologist, but I know there are multiple soil types.* Still, he was perplexed that nutrient content varied so broadly, with no discernable patterns. *Does measurement error contribute to the disparate results or are soils that variable*? He recorded the readings dutifully in his pocket-sized spiral notebook.

When Charlie attempted to discuss the topic with his colleagues, they scoffed. "Dirt is just dirt! Quit playing detective. You've been reading too many Quincy Grissom novels." *Don't they understand that being a field agent is just like being a private detective? They'd learn so much by reading him. Reminds me, my preorder of Grissom's latest adventure should be arriving soon.*

The one time he sent a recommendation for a formal study to his superior, his document was returned with prejudice. "I don't want to see any more of this crap" was written in red across the top.

Charlie's current assignment was reviewing the labeling on a variety of algaecides, antimicrobials, disinfectants, fungicides, herbicides, insecticides, insect growth regulators, rodenticides, and wood preservatives. The latest versions of these concoctions needed to adhere to EPA specifications, in particular, their active ingredients. *Unappreciated grunt work!* Charlie, the auditor, headed for the samples room.

Holding the bottles with rubber gloved-hands and reading the ingredients, some of them hazardous to bare skin, caused him to shiver in his rolling task chair. *This stuff can't be fatally toxic, or the lab guys would have detected it during testing. Leave it to government to mandate that one group tests products and another verifies labeling.*

His head swiveled from container to printed pages as he affixed colored stickers to each bottle and can. Green stickers meant the product passed, yellow meant more research and red meant failure. The sticker allocation reflected the department's expectations: sheets full of green ones, half a page of yellow, and only a handful of red.

After each evaluation, his eyes drifted upward, imagining between fluorescent lights the fictional details of a field case that would release him from this drudgery. *If I'm not verifying compliance, I'm updating the department's official website.* Since staring at a computer screen would have given him double vision and optic nerve distress, Charlie had violated department policy and printed out the materials he had to review and edit for changes. Departmental printers had been decommissioned due to funding cuts, so he engaged his boss's administrative assistant Jane Yong as co-conspirator, sharing her executives-only printer and grinding through reams of paper in the process. The sheets of allowable active ingredients in his hand were such a gift from Jane.

Above all, Charlie desired a field assignment. *An investigation with consequences.* Not just revised web pages or field manuals that no one would ever read. Not by choice, anyway. *So what if a particular pesticide has a revised docket that allows exemptions for unregistered use to temporarily address emergency conditions? I might care, but who else would?* A case in the field was a chance to make things better by his direct action and also avoid the current round of layoffs. *I could take charge in the field. Maybe if I do these jobs really well, eventually Director Stanton will give me the opportunity.* Charlie caught himself in his daydreams, picked up the next metal can, hoped it didn't leak and held it close to read the ingredients.

3 – Matt (Eureka, California)

Matt Thready Jr. slogged out of the English Literature lecture hall in the Creative Arts building on the campus of College of the Redwoods in Eureka, California. Rather than study in the hubbub of the school library or fight the distractions in his dorm, Matt headed for his quiet place, the Botanical Garden adjacent to the north-most parking lot in the western corner of campus. His parents had spent "tons of money" on Dartmouth, the four-year school of his choice, only to suffer shock when he flunked out after one semester. Excessive attention paid to girls and videogames had been his nemeses. "Prove to us you're a diligent student at a residential junior college and we'll reconsider a four-year university," they'd said. Success at Redwoods was his last chance to demonstrate that he'd "gotten his head on straight," to quote his father. Matt had decided that isolation was the simplest cure to avoid girls he'd feel motivated to date and video game machines he'd have the urge to play. In an effort to go cold turkey, he'd left his own video game console at home.

Matt walked through the parking lot and up the dirt path. The Botanical Garden was a curved ninety-degree swath of land with segments dedicated to a variety of small trees, bushes, and flowers. The cultivated vegetation was shielded from campus buildings by a stand of old-growth grand fir and red alder trees with a few trilliums growing beneath their shade. By ignoring the barely visible tip of the Creative Arts building, he could almost believe that he was out in the countryside, alone, and at peace.

Matt wandered through the garden, putting out his hand so the branches and fronds of California buckeye, deer fern, and Pacific reed grass rubbed against his skin.

His parents had been on campus during registration, at which time the school demanded a specialty. He'd selected Associate of Arts, Liberal Arts: Science Exploration, conveniently located at the top of the third column of choices. His father had smiled, irrationally commenting, "Humans in space will need financial planners." But the more classes he took involving flora -- Intro to Botany, Forestry – the more firm his decision: his future involved plants in the ground, not money management at some space colony.

Matt identified a good flat place and plopped down on the turf among wooly sunflowers, shrub western azalea, and huckleberry. Given how the garden had a calming effect, he entertained the possibility of a botanical career. *I should talk to somebody in the placement office about that.* He considered sharing that choice with his folks the next time they called, wondering how they'd react, especially his father. Matt fought off the urge to lie back and enjoy the natural peace and opened his textbook.

4 – Kwashay (Brooklyn, NY)

Kwashay Williams-Jackson sat in the small formal dining room of her mother's second-floor apartment in Brooklyn, New York, double-checking her calculus homework. A chicken and noodle casserole topped with crushed corn flakes baked in the oven, timed to be ready just a few minutes after her mother got home, as demanded.

She glanced at the ceramic cat clock on the wall above the sink. There was too little time before her mother got home to sneak into the pantry and use their home computer. *I can hear Mother scolding me for not getting permission.*

Kwashay's classmates had invited her to bowl with them that night, but she had to refuse, just like she'd refused every other one of their offers. In fact, she'd been surprised that they'd even bothered. She had the well-worn but accurate designation as "class bookworm," an appellation her mother would have endorsed.

"You have to work twice as hard as anybody else to get ahead," her mother had warned. "You'll have your chance to play once you make it." Her mother had "made it" as laboratory manager at Brookdale University Hospital just down the block, but Kwashay hadn't seen any "play" or pleasure in her mother's life, with the exception of a fistful of television shows to which her mother was devoted. Instead of rejecting her mother's directions outwardly, she went on fantastic expeditions in her mind, to places both factual and fictional. *London. Paris. Mars. The other side of a black hole!* After her homework was finished and verified, of course.

5 – Selton (Kearney, NE)

The first rays of light peeked out from between the low brick industrial buildings near the Kearney train yard. Selton rolled from side to side, loosening his backroots from the dirt, exhausted. The fitful awakening in the middle of the night had ineffectuated his taking nutrition.

In preparation for another day of reading at the local library, Selton sat up, extracting himself from the soil. Taking a glance over his shoulder, he examined the site of his previous night's feeding. Like all the others, brown circles with root entry holes formed a monochrome collage on a green background. *How delicious! Dissemination Oversight made a great choice with this planet!*

He stood up and grabbed a wall-mounted spray used to clean rail cars to wash the dirt from his body. After shaking off the excess water, he climbed into his clothing, faded and tattered. Perhaps one of the local merchants would donate alternative garb so that he could be more presentable in their public library, although no one had commented about his current outfit.

Selton gently ran a hand over the top of his head. The pain was a faded memory. His endodermis had already grown, partially covering up the ruptures. He whacked his fedora against his leg and mounted it on his head.

Since the Kearney, Nebraska Public Library wouldn't open for several hours, Selton took a casual stroll along First Street, choosing the sunny side to experience the full spectrum of the sun's rays. A child bicycled past, dropping newspapers at front doors. As Selton ambled toward the library, he recalled his earliest years. When his seed had grown into sentience, Selton had become aware of his preprogramming, facts encoded into his genetically modified organism.

He was from the botanical planet Serulia in the Seltus galaxy; his seed had been intentionally embedded into a meteorite that arrived successfully on Earth; his sole objective was to learn everything about the planet - or as much as he could consume - including how things work. The motivation for this extensive information gathering assignment wasn't disclosed. However, the signature on the preprogramming was "Dissemination

Oversight," from which Selton inferred that he would be recalled to disseminate the Earth information to other Serulians.

Like the rest of his species, Selton was flora, plant-life in Earthling parlance, with exceptional storage capabilities at the cellular level. His body's shape had been programmed to grow into a humanoid, seemingly a native resident on the outside but retaining his plant-like internals. The one external anomaly: the root system on his back, for taking sustenance each evening. Such feedings had kept his physiology firm and strong since his early days as a seedling.

Selton wondered what his journey had been like, sailing through the void of space. *It must have been lengthy and boring.* For a being whose primary purpose was absorbing knowledge, the idea of no stimuli during the ride was particularly disturbing.

Selton had grown into a young sprout barely in Earthling form when a hobo named Marathon Man came across him just outside Fort Worth, Texas, latitude 32.746534, longitude -97.322575. Marathon, as the others called him, had been traveling around the country with his teenaged son, Sprint, who he rescued from an abusive relationship with his mother. Marathon must have felt he needed to rescue Selton, the abandoned infant. He fashioned a luggable crib out of an old orange crate to which he affixed a handle.

Some of the other hobos argued that Selton would be too much trouble, or that Marathon didn't have the skills even though he was raising his son on the rails. He scoffed, "Every living thing got to live."

The first morning after Selton was adopted, Marathon Man woke up to find the crate tipped on its side, and the infant stuck in the ground with roots like a vegetable. Marathon was puzzled but accepting, and gave Selton the name Punkin.

Every morning, Marathon would drop his son and Punkin off at a local library. He'd go to the local Labor Ready storefront that offered short-term employment - recycling, sorting and the like - usually dangerous but requiring little skill.

His son and Punkin spent nearly all of their time together and grew up like siblings. Sprint started out as the big brother and babysitter. At the libraries, Selton learned about the existence of books. Each library they visited overflowed, shelf after shelf of reading material: picture books for the youngest residents, collections of short stories for the slightly older ones, thick tomes for the even older. And, one set of books that purported to contain all of the planet's information: an encyclopedia.

The environment couldn't have been better for his mission. Like infants who are born to suckle nutrition, Selton had to seek out knowledge and accumulate it. *I expect to share this back home on Serulia when my recall is eventually scheduled.* He taught himself to read with the assistance of librarians, Sprint and other patrons. The earliest books Selton encountered were simple, almost to the point of trivial. His mind was prepared for complex topics, not how Dick ran and that he should be observed.

Fact-based tomes were his focus. The smaller books for younger Earthlings did not satisfy his craving. Even the encyclopedia was insufficient. Selton learned to take books reserved for grown-ups from the restocking carts before they were placed on shelves too high to reach.

There was no plan, just opportunistic selection from unoccupied aisles and low shelves.

Almost as soon as he learned how to assimilate facts from books, Selton learned that he could invent information to be stored. Facts and figures didn't have to come from written sources. So, to document his journey, he invented a topic he titled his Personal Information Journal. And in Earthling style, he abbreviated it to PIJ. Information about cities he visited, other hobos he'd met, and the names of libraries and librarians became PIJed away for the future. *My Serulian brethren deserve to understand my process as well as my results.*

Selton grew more quickly than an Earthling. Soon, he was as tall as Sprint. When Sprint asked about it, Marathon told his son that Punkin had "an overactive pitueratary gland." In private to Punkin, Marathon would remark, "You're growing like duckweed."

6 – Charlie (Washington, DC)

Charlie completed the commercial product review successfully, meaning his Director didn't complain about the results. His next desk-bound project awaited him in his cubicle, a web site update. His boss had left him a stack of research reports from a variety of sources, government and independent. *Some college intern could do this work, and cheaper.* It took a while, but using a printed copy of the website's index, Charlie identified the sections of the EPA website that would be affected.

Jane surreptitiously printed out the corresponding web site pages Charlie requested. Soon he was hunched over his desk, his arms between two uneven stacks of paper. Making the changes, from a single line to inserting a whole new section, felt like it would take forever. *Field agents don't have nearly as much paperwork.*

Jane appeared beside his desk with her contagious smile. "I going down to Humane Beans for coffee." She coaxed a disobedient strand of straight black hair behind her ear. "Want something, Mr. Keyson?"

Charlie's eyes glanced up from the paperwork without moving his head. "No thanks."

"When I get back, maybe I help? You know, transcribe changes from you notes?"

Jane had a good mind and was clearly being wasted as an administrative assistant, even with her broken English. She could easily do the kinds of work Charlie was being assigned, which would release him to field duty. "You don't have to."

She put her hand on his. "I want. Besides, the sooner you finish project, the sooner Director send you out into field."

"From your lips-" He nodded his head towards the executive offices.

"What about my lips?" She caressed his hand.

He completed the modified idiom: *To Director Stanton's ears.* "Never mind." *Just my luck, the only woman who's shown interest in me recently works in my office.* Charlie remembered the intent but not the exact words of his father's lewdly worded aphorism about not dating coworkers.

"I put in good word for you. Hope it helps." She removed her hand from Charlie's. "I see you later."

Jane must have overheard Charlie's discussions with his Director, bordering on arguments, about whether he was up to handling a field assignment. The last time

Director Stanton caught him with printouts, he'd pointed out the window. "If you can't follow simple protocols here in the office, Charles, how can I trust you out there?"

With everything I've learned from Quincy Grissom, I'm better prepared than some of my peers. All I want is a chance.

7 – Matt (Eureka, CA)

Matt departed the Applied Technology building after one of those mentally demanding physics classes, where the books were snorers and the teacher's monotone voice didn't help. Most of the students were headed back towards the center of campus and the Student Union or Business Complex. Matt felt maybe some fresh air and another visit with nature out towards the Botanical Garden would help. Besides, lots of other students, especially females, opportunities for distraction, hung out in the Union between classes.

Fred, one of his classmates Matt was trying to avoid, ran up from behind. "Hey, you're going the wrong way."

Matt spun around, his long bangs whipping across his forehead. "I don't have class for half an hour."

"Weird schedule, man. Want to hang out? I'll skip Bio. Maybe we can find a couple of chicks in the cafeteria, get us some dates for the weekend?"

Fred's preoccupation with coeds was trouble. *Dating will just throw me off my academic game plan. Not again!* "I'm not going to be your excuse for cutting class."

"Come on! All the girls think you're cute. I can leverage that to get a date for myself."

My roommate at Dartmouth had said almost the exact same thing. "No thanks. I'll catch up with you later."

Matt thought ahead to his next class, Introduction to Surveying. He was responsible for field exercises: basic mapping, use of a compass and legal descriptions. He had all the necessary tools except one: transportation to the field site. Fred had a car. "Speaking of weekend, do you think you can drive me to Headwaters Forest Reserve? I've got to complete a field assignment."

"In exchange for a double date?" Fred folded his arms.

"Can't you just do it out of friendship, no strings attached?"

"If you were really a friend, you'd help me with my sex life."

Matt shook his head and walked away, leaving Fred standing alone. Over his shoulder, he saw Fred recover, sidling up to a female student who was headed towards the library.

Matt decided to use the lush forest adjacent to the east edge of campus for his surveying assignment. He'd already packed his compass and GPS device in his backpack, just in case.

Matt headed east to the woods, taking the sidewalk that led past the library and the gym. Using the track that surrounded the football field made the trek shorter. An accordion row of vertical trellises supported Chilean jasmine, five-leaf akebia, coral honeysuckle and climbing hydrangea vines, dividing the playing field from the adjacent woods.

As he came off the track on the far side, he saw a large sign announcing "Future Home of the Bates

Nanotechnology Center." The college was one of the world's richest men Armand Bates' alma mater, and his Bates Foundation frequently made donations to the school. Matt had heard from older students about changes in curriculum and instructors as a result. *Dad always says there's no such thing as a free lunch.* The future building would eliminate a section of woods just beyond the Emergency Response Training Center, at the far eastern edge of campus. Matt wondered how students would feel, making the hike to the new facility.

The densely wooded area was its own world. He picked his way among sturdy trees, recording GPS readings until he got to a clearing, latitude 40.690274, and longitude -124.192664. On the grass next to a tree was a mountain of sticks. Dozens and dozens, each about two feet long, no branches or knots, smooth along the surface. *They look like they came out of a factory, not from trees.* He examined one close up. The grass beneath it was a brown line. The ends of the stick were carved as if they were designed to fit together. Matt remembered playing with Lincoln Logs as a kid, where the ends had notches.

When Matt looked closer, the sticks were two different lengths, most of them longer. He picked up a second stick and connected the pair. The sticks vibrated, increasing in frequency. The forest blurred around him. His mind filled with images as if from a high-speed slideshow – his parents, his childhood as a baby and adolescent model, Little League as a shortstop, receiving his regional championship trophy for best score against the Road Warrior 3000 videogame, and faces of the dozens of girls he dated at Dartmouth.

Someone began speaking to him. His father! He'd know that voice anywhere. "You will build and operate this portal."

"Dad? Did you say Portal?" he asked in his own voice. Portal was a videogame he'd previously played. "You don't sound like GLaDOS." *No sign of an Aperture Science Handheld Portal Device either, just sticks.*

The glare of a brightly lit even-sided hexagon laying flat blocked out all scenery. Then a second one appeared hovering above it, connected by vertical supports at the corners. And then a third, a fourth and finally a fifth. Four layers tall, approximately eight feet. *This doesn't look like the game Portal at all.*

But his father wasn't done. "There are two towers."

A second hexagonal structure, the same height but larger, surrounded the first. *That explains the two sizes of sticks. What do you do, crawl in through the top?* The vision shone like a beacon. "The task is vital." Matt's mind accepted the assignment because there was no reason to resist. *Besides, this feels like a game.* Building these two concentric structures, one inside the other, like jail cells, was suddenly more important than anything, because the world will get better.

The vibrating sticks warmed to Matt's touch until they got so hot he had to drop them. The vision vanished as quickly as it had appeared, but the design was burned into his memory.

What in the hell was that? He looked around for his father, but he was alone. *Was I hallucinating?*

Matt reached down to the pile of sticks and picked up a single sample. "Maybe a TA in the biology department can help me identify this."

He stood up, grabbed his backpack and walked toward the main campus. One step, and the weight of the stick dragged his hand to his knees. *Huh?* Another step, and he was on his knees, the stick pinning his hand to the ground. *What's going on?* Matt wiggled his fingers, displacing soil until there was enough space beneath the stick to pull free. And that stick, the one at his feet, was now too heavy to pick up. A hearty kick moved the stick just enough so Matt could drag it back to the others. *This is freaky! These sticks really want to stick together.*

Having accepted the assignment, he approached construction of the prescribed portal with confidence. *Model car and airplane kits I built with my dad were a lot more complicated than this.* With the memorized vision as a blueprint, Matt picked up a longer stick and began construction in the clearing adjacent to the pile. The stick fought him, insisting on being placed north and south, forcing him to face east. The remaining sticks, five more for the outer hexagon and six for the inner, cooperated. *Maybe I misheard my dad. Did he say "operate"? How do you operate something that has no moving parts?*

Matt placed the twelve vertical sticks, the ones that would support the next levels. They leaned a bit, even when he pressed them firmly into position. *I hope it doesn't come crashing down.*

He checked his watch. He'd be late for class if he continued. For now, the start was both an accomplishment and a puzzle. He didn't push back about his new mission but wondered about it. *What's going to get better after I build and operate this thing?* Matt decided to keep the portal a secret. *If anyone else finds out, they'll just get in the way.* He left the incomplete structure and headed back to class.

I'll come back and finish it later. He shook his head. *All I need is another distraction.*

8 – Kwashay (Brooklyn, NY)

The next morning, Kwashay jumped off the bus and power-walked towards Brooklyn Technology High School, BTHS for short. Her dark blue uniform skirt flapped in the breeze. She was on the verge of another late arrival. This time it wasn't her fault. Not exactly. She had dawdled over breakfast, engrossed in the latest edition of *Scientific American*, the subscription a birthday gift from her aunt. Her mother had to shake her shoulder to tear her away from the article about nanobots in medicine.

She was looking forward to graduating in June, then enrolling in a good local college targeting her mother's choice of biomolecular science as her field of study. There were plenty to choose from in the New York City metropolitan area. NYU Polytechnic School of Engineering, a likely choice walking distance from BTHS, had already accepted her. Going to college locally would keep costs down. And she could continue to live with her mother.

In her peripheral vision, she saw a group of Boxers hanging out on the corner. That was her name for the aimless young men who wore their pants halfway down their legs exposing their patterned underwear. They preyed on schoolgirls, taunting and harassing them, sometimes even worse. *Damn this uniform.* Kwashay would have felt more comfortable if her legs weren't exposed. At least she was allowed a sweater over her starched white blouse. One of the ne'er–do–wells tipped his baseball cap and then put it on sideways. He looked goofy and dangerous all at the same time. If she were lucky, the Boxers would be elsewhere at the end of the school day.

Kwashay moved double-time up the stairs, the heirloom locket from her grandmother bouncing on its chain around her neck, just as the first bell rang. She'd have to run to get to homeroom. Her homeroom teacher was also her calculus teacher. Just before she exited the room after morning announcements, her homeroom teacher insisted that she come by after her lunch break.

Kwashay's attention to her class lectures was compromised by her impending conversation with her math/homeroom teacher. If he wrote up her tardiness, there would be a mandatory note to her mother. *That can't happen.*

Sure enough, he was upset about her pattern of late arrivals but had decided to punish her by assigning additional math problems, due the next day. She tried to stifle a smile. Math problems were a relief compared to a note home.

Her last class of the day was at the nearby NYU Polytechnic, where she was enrolled in an accelerated program for gifted students. Her mother had prodded her to get outstanding grades, which qualified her.

Kwashay enjoyed early dismissal from BTHS so she could get to NYU Polytechnic on time. At a strolling pace, she walked down DeKalb Blvd. along the south edge of Ft. Greene Park and past Brooklyn Hospital. Buildings became taller and more modern the further west she walked. A right turn put her on Flatbush Avenue, with heavy construction of new businesses and residences north of Long Island University, many framed by metal scaffolds. Especially in those areas, she appreciated the wide sidewalks. An ambulance screaming up the street caught her undivided attention. As a little girl, she would run to the window when she heard emergency vehicle sirens, which was frequently because of their proximity to her mother's hospital. Her mother promised her a ride in one but never made it happen.

Kwashay continued her journey only after the ambulance passed. Trees and shrubs planted in the raised median warmed the cold atmosphere. She crossed Flatbush at the light and followed Myrtle Avenue, forking off a pedestrian walkway straight to campus. The fifteen-minute stroll energized her.

Her class on Introduction to Cell and Molecular Biology ran late after students kept interrupting the professor with questions for which they should have known the answers. She frequently checked the clock on the wall. She knew that the buses ran less frequently the later she stayed. Her mother would be upset with a late arrival and no dinner ready. If her mother cooked, Kwashay's own dinner would be cold. And the Boxers and more dangerous folks would be emboldened by the night. When the professor said, "Dismissed," she ran down the hall past the custodian to the exit.

She was down the stairs and halfway to the corner when she spotted them, the same three Boxers that had acknowledged her that morning. She fingered her locket. *Maybe they didn't see me.* She pulled her sweater tight and picked up her pace. Instead of staying on Flatbush Avenue, she took an alternate route, east on Myrtle. It wasn't direct, but safer than coming into proximity of those young men. She looked over her shoulder after half a block. They'd vanished. She slowed her jog a bit, still anxious about time. She continued down Myrtle to St.

Edwards Street along the western edge of Fort Greene Park and took a shortcut across a field in the dark southwest corner.

That's when Kwashay tripped. She stumbled a couple of yards and caught herself by grabbing a tree trunk. The huge pile of rods behind her didn't look like anything she'd ever seen. Straight, dark. Too uniform to be branches off the nearby trees. Beneath each displaced rod was a corresponding brown mark, as if the grass beneath it had died.

Normally, her curiosity would have motivated her to stay and explore, but she had responsibilities at home. *Mama will be expecting dinner on the table.* Before she could take even a couple of steps toward the street, an emotional tug spun her around. She marched towards the pile and picked up one rod. Fairly lightweight despite its two-foot length. It didn't look or feel like metal or plastic, but not wood either. The puzzle absorbed her attention, as did the ends, which looked like fittings in a child's construction toy. *I have to catch my bus.*

Intrigued, she picked up a second rod and put the ends together, to see if they'd connect. As soon as they touched, the rods vibrated at increasing frequency. Her mind was invaded, scanned, her memories examined: a childhood dominated by reading and studying, skipping a grade in grammar school, her junior chess club trophy, winning the regional science fair for a genetics sequencing improvement, overcoming acne with expensive treatments her mother insisted she get, and her high school academic honors.

Her lips opened and a familiar voice spoke to her. "You will build and operate this portal." It was her mother's voice, coming out of Kwashay's mouth. A quick glance informed her that she was alone.

A brightly lit regular hexagon consumed her field of vision. It lay at an angle, viewed in perspective. Then a second one appeared hovering above it, connected by vertical supports at the corners. Third, fourth and fifth layers floated into place. Four layers tall, eight feet by her calculation.

It doesn't look like something a person can walk through. It's vertical.

But her mother wasn't done. "There are two towers."

A second hexagonal structure, the same height but bigger, surrounded the first. The vision shone like a Christmas display.

"The task is vital," said her mother.

It's just a hexagonal jungle gym. You can't operate it, you just climb on it. She tried to reject the order, despite her mother's insistence. *Preparing for finals and college are my priorities.* The mental demand was overwhelming and relentless, uncomfortably similar to her mother's insistent nature. Hands on her head, Kwashay fought back as hard as she could, but finally, emotionally fatigued, she acquiesced. Building these structures, one inside the other, became her duty. *Yes, Mama. I'll do it to improve the planet.*

The rods warmed as she concentrated on memorizing the three-dimensional blueprints. When the rods got too hot, she dropped them.

She shook her head as the image vanished. *What just happened? Visions, disembodied voices? I've gotten lots of demands from my mother, but nothing like this.*

Confounded by the experience, she decided to take one of the shorter rods with her. Maybe someone at NYU Polytechnic would be able to identify the material or do some kind of test on it. Their labs had spectrometers and other sophisticated machines that could be used in such an analysis. *BTHS barely has test tubes.*

She unzipped her backpack just enough to slide one rod into it. She hoisted the bag onto her back and took one step. The bag tugged at her shoulders, forcing her to lean back. A second step and the bag slammed to the ground, pulling Kwashay along with it. She landed butt first, legs flailing in the air. She straightened her skirt, loosened the backpack shoulder straps and climbed to her feet. Tugging at the backpack was useless. It was going nowhere. She checked her watch. The good buses had long passed, and she'd be really late for dinner if she didn't start for home immediately.

The air brakes of a bus arriving at the nearby stop hissed. Unable to lift the bag, she reluctantly ran to the stone retaining wall, jumped to the sidewalk and raced to the stop, where a bus sat with a door ready to close. She took a seat, straightened her locket chain and looked back in the direction of her bag, which held her textbooks, spirals with her class notes, and homework assignments, including the extra math problems. Her mother would expect that she'd have everything in her possession. Kwashay braced herself for a cold reception and a colder meal. As the bus pulled away from the curb, the three Boxers from earlier had taken a position near the bag, looking at the bus.

9 – Selton (Kearney, NE)

Based on his travel experience with Marathon and the other hobos, Selton's methodology for getting access to Earth's knowledge seemed straightforward: read books. All of them! And he'd learned that the best places to find large collections of books were libraries. He'd been fortuitously thrust into this approach, each day getting deposited at a local public library with Sprint.

Initially, the scale of these facilities overwhelmed him. The reality of buildings containing row after row of shelving filled with Earth knowledge boggled his mind. On each visit to a local library, he'd scurry to a random row, a random shelf and snatch a random title to ingest. The process worked well and the variety energized him.

Not so the travel. The hobo lifestyle was hardly glamorous. Marathon and his group were always on the move, looking for odd jobs with no training requirements and no long-term commitments. There were no creature comforts in a hobo village, although simple patches of green lawn satisfied Selton. At least, he seemed to have the inherent ability to know precisely where he was on the planet, according to a standard coordinate system.

When other hobos questioned Selton about his behavior, Marathon would intercede, saying, "Everybody got the right to live their life."

Soon, Selton seemed to be as old as Sprint, certainly as physically mature, and no longer needed him as a babysitter. Having long outgrown the orange crate, Punkin slept on bare ground under a thin threadbare blanket every night, even in the warmest climates.

Punkin also got smarter a whole lot faster than Sprint. When one of Marathon's group had a question, Punkin always had the answer, even though he seemed to be a teenager.

"You sound like some kind of professor or something," the questioner would comment.

Marathon began calling him Professor, Prof for short, since the nickname Punkin no longer seemed to fit. When their relationship matured, Selton asked Marathon why he became a hobo.

"Guess it run in the family. My dad was an abusive SOB. I ran away when I couldn't stand the beatings no more. I told the first hobos I met that I was in for the long run, which is why they named me Marathon Man. Later, when I heard about what the wife was doing to Sprint, I had to go back and save him. Like I saved you."

"Did I need saving?" Selton had asked.

"Darn right! I saw you were different from the first. Don't bother me none. I met lots of folks, every one unique. None with roots on their back, got to say. But I don't judge." Marathon gave his adopted son a hug, his fingertips tracing the tendrils. "Sorry. I been wanting to do that ever since I saw 'em."

After just a couple of years, the two young men changed roles. Selton looked after Sprint, keeping him out of trouble. Often, that took much more effort than ingesting shelves full of books. Sprint didn't join the other men in day work, even though his job as babysitter had ended. That left plenty of time for Sprint to wander the streets, panhandle, and attempt adult activities involving alcohol and females.

Marathon had taken the time to teach Punkin about hobo ethics. "Hoboes are people who travel to work. Tramps are people who travel and don't work. Bums are people who don't travel and don't work." Selton worked hard to keep Sprint from becoming a tramp and shaming his father.

Selton's timing didn't always match the rest of the American Gypsies, one-way hobos described themselves. In some locations, he wanted to stay and ingest books from a diverse set of both public and specialty libraries and was forced to depart early to stay with the group. In other towns, the group took up residence for a long time, well after Selton had completed his use of the local facilities. Those discrepancies of motivation and timing became a roadblock to Selton's mission. As Marathon got older, the likelihood of him settling down also loomed large. Although he loved Marathon like a father, Selton knew he had to continue his quest alone.

Under the pretense that he'd reached the age of consent, Selton announced his departure from the group at a railroad yard in Little Rock, AR, latitude 34.746483, -92.289597. Marathon made no objection, rubbing his open hands on his pants, although his feelings were clear by his slumped shoulders and hanging head. Before Selton walked away, Marathon rolled up his fedora and thrust it into Selton's hands, making for an awkward handshake. "Just in case, to keep you dry."

Selton accepted the gift and nodded. "You've been like a father to me." Although he'd read about human emotion from both a clinical and emotional perspective, it was the first time he witnessed a human being cry.

Selton wandered out of the village toward the parked trains. When he prepared to don his new headwear, he found that Marathon had stuffed some paper money inside. *Did "keep you dry" have a deeper hobo meaning?* Using lessons learned from his adopted family, he hopped the next train out. To avoid recreating the timing problem, he avoided joining other wanderers, although he was polite when their paths crossed. Besides, no group would compare to Marathon and his associates.

Selton's tactics were straightforward and repetitive. He would patronize a local library, consuming all of the new books within. Then, he'd ride the rails to another city and repeat the process.

One of his first destinations was Nashville, Tennessee, latitude 36.174465, longitude -86.767960. The young and undisciplined Selton continued to choose random books from all non-fiction disciplines. His internal physiology captured the information off the page directly with little processing. After only a few weeks, he realized that his overall storage capacity would constrain the amount of information he could retain if he continued using that technique. And, his directive had been quite precise: capture all of Earth's information.

As his only alternative, Selton began to extract and store only the facts from the books. The first implication was that he needed to erase everything he'd stored and start over. The loss of his personal information journal, or PIJ, was of more concern than the contents of books, which could easily be replaced from the same sources. *How sad to forget all of the people and places I've encountered.* The second was that processing information from various disciplines, book to book, required frequent reorganization of the information stored in his cells, which caused unproductive periods. His time on Earth would be long but finite, and so couldn't be wasted.

Selton decided to change his process and ingest information about one subject at a time, the origin of his more precise shelf-by-shelf process. This had the added benefit of more complete coverage of a library's contents.

Of course, reading books in sequence was a lot more obvious to librarians and other patrons.

Early in Selton's travels, almost all of the books were new, and so he needed to stay in those locations for longer periods of time. Although Selton didn't put down roots, in the Earthling vernacular, he did become very familiar with the customs and practices of those locations. Selton paid tribute to those localities by reading extensively about them, in terms of history and culture, to appreciate the nature of his new temporary home. Those concepts on the page came to life whenever Selton took the opportunities to interact ever so fleetingly with the Earthling natives, mostly during their celebrations and festivals, where he could be an anonymous part of the event, just one of the crowd. The filaments that exploded from his skull and danced overhead the previous night reminded him of the fascinating fireworks on Fourth of Julys from years past.

Selton's mission urged him on. While traveling through the south, he would peek out of the traveling train car at the expansive lush plantations to pass the time. He often resisted the urge to leap from the train and throw himself backside down in the fertile fields. *Dissemination Oversight is counting on me.*

Selton's memory of when he first identified fiction versus non-fiction was as clear as the day it happened. First, because he'd PIJed it away, but second, because it was the only time a librarian had made fun of him. He'd completed the Dewey Decimal System topic 999 for the first time, ironically extraterrestrial worlds, at a small neighborhood library in Raleigh, North Carolina, longitude 35.795611, and latitude -78.640339. But there were more books, organized alphabetically by author's last name.

He sampled some by an Earthling named Asimov and was astounded at the level of technology and space exploration depicted in those tomes. *This doesn't match Earth's historical record.* When he asked the obvious question about the disparity, the young male librarian laughed out loud, violating the facility's own rules about noisy behavior. "You've got to be kidding! This –" he grabbed the Asimov book from Selton's blue-gloved hand, "- is fiction. It's make-believe. Sheesh!"

It was also the first time Selton's otherwise filling torso felt empty, as if someone had scooped out his internals. *Is this one of those Earthling emotions? Embarrassment? Sadness?* It was not pleasant, and it took many more libraries and librarians for Selton's confidence in them as a sub-species to be repaired.

Despite Selton's understanding of fiction versus non-fiction, he never figured out the inherent value of poems. Their brevity didn't convey much information, and the short lines forced abrupt head and eye movement.

Selton's journey brought him to the East Coast of the United States. Despite his phenomenal absorption rate, he understood that the United States Library of Congress in Washington, D. C., longitude 30.286914, latitude -97.728168, was just too large, and his continued presence would become obvious. Instead, Selton decided to continue to see the world, at least the part bounded on two sides by vast bodies of water.

Selton's pattern was predictable traveling from town to town, seeking out collected books, making libraries his place of business and librarians his friends. And just as he knew he had to devour all of the information he could, the goal slipped from reach every year, as there were more things to learn, more things invented, more things evolving and changing. He could feel his cells bloating with the accumulated information. After finishing all of the new volumes in any particular library, he'd move on to the next one. There were always new books or new editions of old ones.

After decades of traveling, Selton didn't intend on stopping in Kearney, Nebraska even for a short visit. Some force beyond his comprehension pulled him off his freight train as it came into town. A few hobo compatriots who'd attached themselves to Selton when he left Salt Lake City en route to St. Louis pleaded with him to continue their journey south to warmth, but he refused despite himself. He accepted his feelings as perhaps reflecting his growth and maturity. *Settling down is what human beings call it. Even hobos do it when they get older.* He was in Middle America, almost exactly. Kearney's longitude of precisely -99.080855 put him smack dab in the middle of the United States, east to west. Kearney felt like his last stop before his mission leaders would recall him.

The hiss of a passing garbage truck pulled Selton from his reverie. He rounded the corner, looked both ways for traffic and took a diagonal path to the steps of the Kearney Public Library, his latest operational location. Books were waiting.

10 – Charlie (Washington, DC)

Charlie glanced up after finishing another in a seemingly endless sequence of web page updates. At least the last one was a complete page rewrite, which took some creativity. The benevolent clock showed five: quitting time. He buried his papers in the bottom drawer of his desk, out of his Director's sight. The rest could wait for tomorrow. Or even longer. He stood up, checked his pockets to be sure he hadn't left anything behind and took one step out of his cubicle.

Jane was standing a couple of feet away, as if waiting for an opportunity for conversation. "I wondering what you might be doing. For dinner?"

Jane was the only female co-worker who'd ever asked him out. Charlie viewed the propositions as distracting from work and borderline inappropriate. "I'm just going to grab a burger and veg out. Why do you ask?"

"I thought you like Korean cuisine for a change. I know great place, taste like Mama used to make." She dug the toe of her shoe into the carpet. "I no like going home to empty apartment."

"I wouldn't be very good company. My mind is mush." Even though he was having trouble focusing, his rule about dating female colleagues was absolute. *Work and dating don't mix.* "Maybe some other time. But thanks for asking."

"You're welcome, Mr. Keyson." Jane skulked away in the direction of her desk.

By the time the elevator finally reached the ground floor after innumerable stops for other departing workers, Charlie had rethought his dinner plan, a burger from Ollie's Trolley. Jane's comment about Korean food chafed his mind and excited his taste buds. *Maybe I should have accepted her offer. It was just dinner.* It was too late and too awkward to go back. *She's probably left.* Maybe there was some carryout Chinese place within walking distance.

Charlie saw Brad Lane, one of the senior people in his Director's group, with a few colleagues milling around him in the lobby. He approached and waited until there was a break in conversation.

Lane's back was toward Charlie. One of Lane's colleagues, a redhead, asked, "Did you hear about his new assignment?"

Charlie shook his head. Lane turned to face him.

The same colleague waved his arms. "This is big!"

Lane adjusted his wireframe glasses. "A Bates Energy power plant in Eden, North Carolina has been storing coal ash at their site. Except there was a problem."

"Problem?" said the redhead. "More like an ecological disaster. Coal ash is spilling into the Dan River."

"That's terrible." Charlie searched the other's faces for agreement.

The redhead smiled. The others were stoic.

Only Lane's showed remorse. "Seventy miles of the river have been coated in toxic waste. We should have been more diligent."

"A project like this is a career maker, pal." The colleague was dragging on Lane's arm. "Work this right, and you'll have your own department."

Lane's colleague sounded almost joyful about the disaster.

That's the kind of incident an agent could sink his teeth into. "I'm sure you'll do a great job." Charlie felt stupid asking, but that was the reason he'd approached the group in the first place. "Say, do you know of a good Chinese restaurant around here?"

All of the men in Lane's entourage except the redhead tapped away at their smart phones. Lane had an answer quicker than the rest. "Jenny's Asian Fusion on Water Street." He showed Charlie the number, which he typed into his feature phone.

"That'll do." Stopping for carryout was the perfect excuse to avoid getting packed on the Metro or standing on a crowded bus. At a comfortable pace, Charlie could cover the two miles to his place at SkyHouse Apartments in just less than forty minutes, not including the stop. In addition to the fresh air and exercise that would clear his mind, there was the bonus of a freshly prepared dinner.

Charlie left the Clinton Federal Building, home of EPA's Headquarters, and headed south on 12th St. SW, calling and ordering their special dinner entree to go while he walked. It would be ready at just about the time he'd arrive. Further south, nondescript office buildings housed equal numbers of government bureaucrats and lobbyists. Twelfth flowed into Maine, paralleling Water Street, the location of Jenny's restaurant. His order of Pad Thai Noodles sautéed with shrimp, chicken, egg and peanuts was ready when he arrived.

As Charlie continued his walk home, he was delighted that the foliage of the tree-lined streets and boulevards made this part of Washington much lusher than the concrete and steel and glass monuments that served as offices. He followed Maine Street's curve, bending around to the east. A few steps south on 4th, and Charlie was home.

Every time he approached Sky House, the irony struck him: he was living in the former Environmental Protection Agency headquarters, which had been adaptively reused as a pair of apartment buildings. *Like leaving the EPA and coming home to the EPA.*

Charlie grabbed the contents of his locked mailbox including a padded envelope. *The new Quincy Grissom novel!* He took the elevator, got off at his floor and opened his apartment door. "I'm home," he shouted. After hanging up his coat and loosening his tie, he threw the mail on the counter next to the small fish tank, home to one lone goldfish. "How ya' been, big boy?" Charlie sprinkled a bit of multi-colored fish food, but not too much. AquaLung scooted to the surface, devouring the treat.

Charlie ignored all of the mail except the padded envelope. He ripped open the pouch containing the next in his subscription to the Quincy Grissom series of private detective novels. "*Fraud Multiplied*. Sounds ominous." The front cover was the image of a calculator nearly buried by a jumble of overlapping multicolored credit cards. He read the back dust jacket headline: "What international danger lurks behind a series of petty credit card abuses? Quincy Grissom is in charge!"

Eating dinner while it was still mildly hot was first priority. Charlie consumed most meals in front of his television. He put his finger on the remote's power button and looked over at his roommate. "Let's see what's been going on in the world while I was editing web pages."

AquaLung flashed its tail, splashing as it dove to sample remnant bits among the faux coral.

The sprinkle of water reminded Charlie of the polluted Dan River. He put down the remote, stood up and returned to the counter. "You know, you're right. It'll all be bad news anyway. Probably give me indigestion."

Charlie prodded about half the contents of the paper container onto a plate with the provided chopsticks and pulled up a stool, his plate and book in front of him. He slurped a frisky noodle into his mouth. "Credit card abuse, hmm?" He pointed his bare chopsticks at AquaLung. "Grissom's cases are never that simple." He plucked a piece of shrimp and dangling veggie from his plate. "You just watch!"

Charlie opened the cover of the novel and flipped past the table of contents and dedication to chapter one, "Give Me A Little Credit", before returning to his dinner, which had dropped to room temperature.

11 – Matt (Eureka, CA)

Assembling the portal – that's what his father's voice called it - had interrupted Matt's fieldwork, but there was still a week before that assignment was due. *Plenty of time. Finishing the portal comes first.*

As he trotted down the stairs, leaving the Applied Technology building after a Forestry class, Fred accosted him. "Hey, I got a date, but only if you'll come along for her roommate."

Every time Fred leveraged their friendship to get a date, Matt got progressively angrier. "Sheesh. Who asked you?"

"Well, I knew you wouldn't do it for yourself. What are friends for?" Fred put his fat hand on Matt's shoulder.

This isn't for me, and he knows it. "If I was going to make you responsible for my love life, you'd be the first to know. And I haven't. So just back off, okay?"

Fred shook his finger. "Just for that, I'm never going to set you up again." He raised an eyebrow and leaned close, preparing for a low volume exchange. "You've done it, haven't you?"

"Done what?"

"You found somebody, and you meet her in the woods. That's why you're always sneaking off." Fred hung his head. "And you won't ask her to find me a date because I embarrass you -"

"There's no 'her'. God, you're fixated. Do you think about anything besides girls?"

Fred scratched his head. "Guess not. I've got hormones."

"Everybody's got hormones. But most people aren't slaves to them. You'd better get your head around your classes or you'll flunk out. And there goes your access to coeds."

"I'm doing okay." Fred stuck out his chest but all that moved forward was his stomach. "I've got a solid C average."

"Celebrate your mediocrity if you want. But I'm not going to mess up at school again. If I flunk out, the default is working with my Dad." Even if he got terrific grades, Matt expected his folks would evaluate his career choice. What if they didn't approve? "Financial planning is not what I want to do for the rest of my life." His father had been extremely successful at it, but the thought of a life juggling spreadsheet cells turned his stomach.

"Okay, tree hugger. Enjoy yourself in the forest, see if I care. But you can't take some shrub to the spring fling."

I never considered attending. Matt crossed the parking lot, leaving Fred behind. *I've got to build that portal.*

Fred shouted, "And those girls were hot too."

Matt saw the surrounding students glare at Fred's outburst. *Serves him right.*

Matt jogged to the clearing where he'd begun construction. The first tier of the portal was still in place. The sticks he'd connected seemed fatter, and the connections between the sticks had grown together. The structure wouldn't shake, even with his hardest tug.

There are sure a lot of sticks. I hope I don't run out.

When he lifted a stick for the next layer up, it was somewhat heavier than the last one. Just as an experiment, he tried lifting it over his head and failed. *Above waist height, the sticks are too heavy for one person to lift.* Were they fighting gravity?

Matt realized he needed help, but who could he get that would be discreet but muscular? As he completed the lower levels of both towers, Matt considered his options for assistance. *Maybe one or two guys in the automotive program?* Most of them looked strong enough to lift a motor with their bare hands. *Someone from the wrestling team?* He didn't know any jocks, no matter the sport. He dare not ask Fred, or everyone on campus would know about the project. *Much less jeopardy if I keep it secret.* In desperation, he posted a note in the campus commons, "wanted: an able bodied student for heavy lifting."

12 – Kwashay (Brooklyn, NY)

Kwashay had to pass at least three high schools on the train ride home from BTHS. Any of them would have provided a good education, some even more modern than the uninspired brick fortress she attended. But Mother insisted she have the best education, even if the consequence was an hour commute each way.

When she got home, her mother was aloof. Just a brusque "Hello" from her favorite place on the sofa, the television blaring. No big outburst, as if her anger was bottled up. Kwashay dreaded the moment when all of her mother's emotion would escape in a huge explosion. *Maybe her show will keep her occupied.*

No such luck. It happened just like Kwashay expected, in the middle of eating reheated macaroni and cheese, into which her mother had mixed chopped broccoli.

Her mother marched into the kitchen, slammed both palms on the table, arms stiff. "How dare you!"

Kwashay's mouth was full, as she sat at the table with a general science book open, one she'd taken off the shelf in her room. She knew the house rules of no eating during homework, but the evening had been shortened by her stay over at school and a later-than-normal bus connection that threw off her transfer. She chewed fast and swallowed too big a lump. Her throat stretched. She took a quick sip of milk. "What did I do?"

"You know very well. Coming home late, after I went to the trouble of making a warm meal. And then burying your face in that book without so much as a kind word." Her mother crossed her arms.

"My special class ran late. And I had to take a detour. For my safety." Kwashay didn't mention the pile of rods and the vision. "Just avoiding those street kids-"

"Hoodlums!" Her mother marched from table to sink to refrigerator in an imprecise triangle. "Good, I'm glad you're concerned about your safety. And your school work." Her mother walked to the edge of the kitchen, peeked down the short hall and scanned the foyer floor by the front door. "Where's your backpack?"

"I – I – I finished all of my work at school." Kwashay lacked the courage to tell her mother about the vision and the portal, which even in her mind sounded ridiculous.

"Well, for your sake, I hope you didn't rush and make mistakes." Her mother stopped pacing and sat down at the table. "How many times do I have to tell you, you can't mess up. You're in a good school, Lord knows what I had to do to get you in."

She and her mother had filed for special dispensation to get her into BTHS because of where they lived. Their apartment on the third floor of a red brick building on Herzl Street was well outside the school's normal boundaries. But it was also half a block from her mother's job as laboratory manager at Brookdale University Hospital, a benefit her mother would not abandon.

Kwashay was expected to attend college, probably because her mother hadn't, and reach the pinnacle of her profession. Her mother had made it clear many times - too many - that becoming a doctor was the ultimate goal for her. Even if that wasn't what she wanted for herself.

"I'll leave earlier, Momma. So if the buses run off schedule-"

"As long as you have a good breakfast and have all your homework done. Now finish your food before it gets cold."

While Kwashay's mother disappeared into the living room, she wolfed down the remainder of her lukewarm dinner. She cleaned her plate and approached her mother, curled up in the corner of the sofa, the television tuned to a fashion reality show. *Given the styles, that's got to be a rerun.*

"You're prettier than any of those girls." Her mother padded the space next to her. "Come, sit with me."

Her experience with the rods was fresh in her mind, and she had numerous questions. "Can I have some time on the computer? Please? I have no homework." *It's in my backpack in the park!*

"I was hoping to have some quality time with you." Her mother's forehead wrinkled. "All right, but only thirty minutes. Then join me."

"Thanks." Kwashay was lucky to have a computer in their apartment at all, because her mother chose not to afford one. The alternative to a purchase was a hand-me-down from Uncle Lamar when his law office upgraded their machines. It was old and slow but it worked. Uncle Lamar even picked up the monthly cost for their high-speed Internet connection, which was the slowest available. He called the monthly bill "his investment in his niece's future."

Once the computer was in their possession, they had to decide where to put it. A computer system with the monitor and separate metal box would interfere with TV watching if it was in the living room, her mother refused to have it in her bedroom or Kwashay's, and there was no space in either their tiny dining room or cramped kitchen. The computer's final resting place was at the rear of their walk-in pantry. Mother reluctantly relocated the canned goods and boxes from that location to the side shelves. Uncle Lamar assisted with the installation, which included drilling holes in the wall between the kitchen and the pantry, so that an extension cord and a telephone cable could reach the device.

Kwashay dragged one of the vinyl-covered kitchen chairs into the pantry, closed the door for privacy, and then used the shelves on both sides to climb over the back of the chair and into the seat in front of the seventeen-inch screen. She toyed with her locket as she waited five minutes for the computer to boot up. When the login screen appeared, she chose her account, separate from her mother's unused one, and entered the password.

Thirty minutes? Kwashay had so many things to search for.

Her first word choice was portal. Her connection churned. The first result, portals as gates, doors, or ends of a tunnel, wasn't helpful. Neither was the second, a magical or technological doorway that connects two locations, dimensions, or points in time. She wasn't a believer in any of that stuff. The third result was familiar: web portal, a site that functions as a point of access to information on the Internet. *My portal will be physical.* The last result was completely unfamiliar: Portal, a 2007 video game by Valve Corporation. She had never played a video game in her life. *I agree with Mother about those. A big waste of time.*

Time? No help, and over eight minutes gone.

Next search: hexagon. Quick response: a geometric figure. Her request had been too generic. *Maybe hexagon structure.* That fetched the Wandsworth Common Windmill, the Greensville Correctional Center, and The New York Supreme Court at 60 Centre Street, all hexagonal in shape. *These are all solid buildings, not hollow frameworks.*

By the time she'd clicked through the results, fifteen minutes had passed.

Maybe the rods themselves. She searched for synthetic wood, yielding composite decking, wood-plastic composites, and engineered plastics. Plastic rods led her to an infinite list of suppliers eager to sell her solid and hollow pipes in all sizes. *I already have dozens.* Kwashay wondered precisely how many she had.

A quick check of the onscreen clock. Twenty-two minutes had elapsed.

What about my mother's disembodied voice? Disembodied voices delivered references to voices over an intercom on a train, ghosts and spirits. *Hooey!*

Twenty-five minutes.

Jungle gyms? She requested images and got hundreds of them, twelve per page, none of a hexagonal design. Looking at images made her think about PictureNet, where web users posted their photos for public consumption. She navigated to the web site, her fingers ready to type in her search criteria.

The glare of light behind her washed out the computer screen. Her mother had opened the pantry door. "Times up."

Kwashay checked the on-screen clock. "It's only been twenty-eight minutes."

"And by the time we finish arguing, it will be thirty or longer. Nothing can be that important."

Kwashay shut down the computer, which itself took another four minutes of rumbling and grinding. Her mother was back on the sofa, channel surfing, patting the area next to her.

Her mother's directive, to build the portal, echoed in her mind. "You weren't downtown today, near my school, were you?"

Her mother scowled and crossed her arms. "How can you ask such a thing? You know I was here making dinner after a hard day at work."

"Yes, of course." *I shouldn't have asked.* Kwashay stretched her arms and faked a yawn. "I'm going to bed."

"So early? We hardly ever see each other these days."

"I have a project to start. Before school's the only time I have to get it done."

"All right then, you'll need your rest. I'll turn down the volume." She pressed some buttons on the remote, but the sound didn't seem to change. "Sleep well, dear."

"Yes, Mama."

13 – Selton (Kearney, NE)

Kearney, Nebraska at latitude 40.694777 was as far north as Selton had dared to travel. Most cities on his itinerary had been in warmer climates, to accommodate his plant physiology. Only because this region was experiencing a spring season with atypical warmth had Selton dared to travel this far from the equator. That his former hobo consorts liked the rail line that ran straight through town didn't hurt.

The head librarian in Kearney – his hobo pals would have called her a Jane even though her name was Bernice – had arrived for work, locked her car and was approaching the front stairs. Names were another fascinating concept to Selton. Were other members of his species named uniquely? Although he'd never met another Serulian, he'd met many librarians with the same name. Numerous Bobs and Michaels. Many Bettys and Anns.

When Selton arrived in Kearney, on his first library visit, Bernice had asked if he wanted to sign up for a library card. Normally, that was not his procedure since he never removed books from the libraries, choosing to read them on premises. The way she asked, her tone, the tilt of her head and her expectant smile, enticed him to accept her offer.

He remembered distinctly the awkward and disconcerting moment when he was first asked his name. A librarian in Albuquerque, NM, latitude 35.113281, longitude -106.621216.had demanded it to use their facility. He expected to be an anonymous visitor who didn't need identification and so was unprepared. Neither Punkin nor Professor seemed proper answers. To satisfy her request, he adopted an adjusted version of his planet's name as his own. Planet Serulia in the Seltus galaxy became his name, Selton Serulia. It was a joke his hosts would never understand.

Bernice paused at the top of the stairs and waved to Selton. She often allowed him early entrée to the facility. It violated library rules, and Selton appreciated her hospitality. It had been very much the same at other libraries, smiling and helpful staff who accommodated his desire for the maximum time.

Bernice held the door so he could enter first. "Are you going to read every book in here?" She flicked the switches to turn on the overhead lights.

He'd heard the same question from many librarians as he spent weeks methodically pulling books off the shelf, one after the other, reading each cover to cover. Picking up the next day precisely where he'd left off.

"Only the ones I haven't read before." Selton's voice was deeper than when he was green.

Bernice's fingers skittered across the keyboard of a computer terminal. "You'll want to check out the new arrivals then."

Selton nodded and paused at the cabinets, examining the titles and topics.

"For someone who spends all day inside, you certainly have a nice tan," said Bernice. "And have I told you, you have very green eyes?"

Selton's veneer darkened as he slipped the current edition of the *Kearney Hub* newspaper off the shelf and settled in to get the latest local news, his daily ritual. He removed his trusty blue rubber glove from his pocket, a gift from a hobo acquaintance that had a spare, and thrust his stick-like fingers inside. The friction of rubber facilitated expedient page turning.

There were scant important facts, but reading the local newspaper bonded Selton to the community in which he resided. The photo essay about the migrating sandhill cranes that had just departed the state filled most of the front page of the tabloid. His blue photoreceptor-enabled eyes flicked to the left-side list of other stories. Nothing of consequence. The most interesting part was the classified ads, which always exposed the culture of the community. That day's edition sported a two-column ad under the heading RELIGION. It solicited reports of brown spots on lawns, in both private and public areas, especially near train routes. Citizens were asked to send details to the Dogood Campaign Against Satan.

Selton recognized the name Dogood. By accident two decades ago, he'd met the Reverend Billi Dogood, a traveling preacher who showed up while his hobo family was camped outside Huntsville, Alabama. She arrived alone in a rusted pickup truck with a camper body, and preached the gospel to their hobo village. She stood on the rear bumper wearing a long black skirt, black blouse and black sport coat hanging on her tall, thin frame, an outfit inappropriate for the warm weather. At least a ponytail kept her brunette hair off her neck. She held onto the camper body with one hand, the other displayed an open Bible in her outstretched arm.

Per Marathon's fatherly advice to be wary of interlopers, he'd kept his distance, staying far back from the crowd next to her vehicle. The hobos were polite to the stranger, as usual, but not overly enthusiastic to her message of redemption. When she finished her preaching, he thought she'd departed.

That night, as he slept in a private spot within a grove of trees, he felt the poke of a shoe in his side. He opened his eyes. Reverend Dogood stood over him, her hair unleashed, her blouse half unbuttoned, a canned beverage in one hand, a hand-rolled cigarette in the other. "Don't you want to be saved?" Her voice was slurred. Before he could grab a shirt to cover his torso or respond, she'd kicked him again, harder. He sat up, afraid of the damage the preacher could do with repeated pummeling. His backroots, pulled from a voracious feeding, thrashed around seeking fertile soil. A full moon cast squirming shadows on the ground all around him. She screamed, dropped the red-tipped shriveled cigarette and ran away begging for mercy on her soul. Even though it was in the middle of the night and he hadn't had a complete feeding, Selton had gotten dressed while standing on the brown turf, grabbed his bindle and caught the first train leaving the yard. His major disappointment was missing out on access to a specialty science library at the U. S. Space and Rocket Center later that week.

Over the years, Rev. Dogood had shown up in various hobo villages at which Selton stayed. On those occasions, he'd kept out of sight, nursing the uncorroborated feeling she was looking for him. He'd done his best to avoid a subsequent confrontation. For quite a few years, she disappeared. Now, it seemed, she was back in business.

14 – Charlie (Washington, DC)

Charlie had just returned from the sample room, verifying a late arrival, yet another can of insecticide, an unconfirmed feeling of ants running up and down his arms.

He had just plopped into his chair and taken a cleansing breath when Jane appeared from out of nowhere. "The Director! He asking to see you." Her grin showed perfect white teeth.

"Now? Right now?" He grabbed his suit jacket from the back of his chair. It was creased but clean. "Is it-" He didn't dare jinx the opportunity.

Jane nodded, almost bouncing out of her shoes. She led Charlie past her desk and stuck her head into Director Stanton's office. "Mr. Keyson is here."

"Thank you, Ms. Yong."

Jane stood aside.

Charlie took one step, just past the doorframe. "You wanted to see me?"

Director Stanton had his nose buried in the contents of a thin manila folder. "Yes, Charles. Come in. Have a seat."

He chose the only available chair across from the Director's desk. It felt like they were miles apart.

"Pesticide updates completed?"

Charlie nodded, rubbing his arms from shoulder to elbow.

"Anything wrong?"

"No sir." The feeling of creepy-crawlies faded.

"I expect they're accurate, if I'm any judge of your work quality."

"Thank you." *Is this just an in-person status report?* Charlie's shoulders slumped.

"And documentation updates in progress?"

Charlie nodded. "I'm right in the middle of them-"

Director Stanton cleared his throat. "Are you still interested in a field assignment?"

Charlie restored his posture. "Yes, sir."

The Director closed the folder. Rubber stamp marks and sticky labels in a variety of colors covered the front surface. "Well, it looks like I have one for you." He hefted the folder, which flapped like a pigeon. "It feels about right for your first. We want to set you up for success, right?"

He nodded.

"Well, here you go." Director Stanton held out the folder.

Charlie leaned out of his chair to take hold. Anxious to get underway, he tried not to rip it from the Director's grasp.

"This case has been like a football, kicked around all over Washington," Director Stanton went on, "But now it's yours." He stared at Charlie. "Ours."

The stamps, reroute tags and dates on the front indicated that the folder had passed through many government agencies quickly. Charlie wondered why it had finally landed at the Environmental Protection Agency, and now in his lap. *Is it difficult?* He swallowed hard.

"The Department of the Interior was the first agency notified. They passed it off to the Food and Drug Administration, probably because they misread it. The FDA wasn't the right place - Interior should have just handled it - but the FDA tossed it over here. And Interior won't take it back. At the moment, I'm short on field agents."

"Great!" Charlie didn't mean that being short on field agents was great. Layoffs mostly affected those with clerical duties, but field agents were not immune.

Director Stanton puffed and folded his arms. "We'll see what you think after you read the file. Should only take you a day at the most, maybe two including travel. Grass is dying in New York City."

What kind of assignment is that? "You want me to investigate dead grass?" Charlie remembered his failed garden. His neighbor had commented, "Boy, you couldn't even grow grass."

"This isn't somebody's back yard. A government-managed facility, Governors Island, between Manhattan and Brooklyn, reported the problem. They can't figure out why large sections of their lawn have gone brown. I'm sure they're exaggerating about the extent, but we have to take it seriously."

Maybe it was Charlie's uncertain expression. The Director added, "Aren't you the guy that wrote that paper about soil samples?" He spun around, pulled open a drawer in his credenza, and thumbed through the contents. His hand came forward with a copy of Charlie's document, including the handwritten comment on the front page about crap. "Yep, written and submitted by Charles Keyson."

He kept one?

"I thought I remembered. You're the perfect person for this assignment. You'll be up to your eyeballs in soil samples."

A successful field assignment would make his job more secure. Charlie was also pleased that, for the first time, he'd be taking soil samples instead of reading the results of someone else's. "Absolutely."

"Okay then, take your samples, do your interviews, and then come back here and we'll discuss next steps.". Director Stanton leaned back, hands on his head. "Run any questions by Bradley Lane. He'll mentor you through it."

So much for trust! And Lane is decent enough, with a conservative approach to his assignments and the most tenure in the bureau. He not only plays it by the book, he probably wrote the book. "Got it!"

Director Stanton's lips curled. "Ask Ms. Yong to make your travel arrangements. I've arranged for a local agent from our Region 2 office in New York to be your chauffeur and guide, for efficiency."

And to avoid the expense of a car rental. Charlie had never traveled for business before. In fact, he rarely traveled at all. His "Thanks" was tarnished with anxiety as he exited the Director's office.

Jane stood at her desk, almost leaping like a cheerleader, clapping her hands. "So, did you get it?" Her voice was half an octave higher than normal.

"Yeah." Charlie was pleased but stood contemplating the details. "It's in New York City." The thought of walking the streets of New York gave him goose bumps.

"Oooh. I hear so many things about Big Apple. Maybe you can take in show or visit Empire State Building."

Charlie lacked her enthusiasm. *Dead grass?* He looked at Jane with needy eyes as a major consequence of traveling popped to mind. "Who will take care of AquaLung?"

She tilted her head. "What is aqualung?"

"My goldfish."

"I'll do it." Jane seemed more than happy, even enthusiastic.

"You will? Thanks."

"My pleasure." Jane must have thought a hug was appropriate, her arms around him, pressing her body against his.

Charlie hugged back involuntarily. He was flattered by Jane's attention, but flustered when his arms dropped and she was still hugging. "Listen, Director Stanton said you could take care of the travel logistics-"

Jane let go, smoothed her clothes and sat down. "Of course." Her fingers flew across the keyboard, making selection after selection. "Special trip." Web pages appeared, selections were made, and then vanished. "There, all done." She reached below her desk and snagged the travel documents from her printer. "I want you to be happy, Mr. Keyson." She blushed and handed him the papers. "And successful. You deserve it."

Charlie noticed his increased heart rate. "It's all up to me now."

15 – Matt (Eureka, CA)

Matt's motivation for completing the portal was overwhelming. He decided to skip his engineering class the next morning and head straight for the woods and the knee-high structure. As expected, the higher he had to lift the sticks into place, the heavier they got. At knee height, they'd been heavy. At waist height, they felt massive, barely manageable. He decided he needed a ladder or some scaffolding to get the sticks high enough to assemble in addition to some additional muscle.

Matt headed back towards campus just as his engineering class was letting out. He tried to avoid Fred walking toward him, but it was too late.

"Hey, buddy boy," Fred said. "I didn't see you in class. For the quiz?"

Matt smacked the side of his head. Despite getting the schedule of quizzes and exams the first day of class, he'd forgotten. "I messed up." *Damn portal!*

There was no excuse, and no opportunity for a make-up. That had been shared on day one as well. Taking a zero on an exam wasn't going to put him in a good place to discuss a four-year college with his folks. *Maybe I can convince the teacher to accept the portal as a special project to help my grade.* Even while Matt considered his options for redemption, his attention was dominated by the unfinished structure.

Both young men were distracted by the arrival of an expensive foreign-made convertible, top down, piloted by a man in a dark gray suit who seemed only slightly older than them.

"Wow!" Fred was impressed. He nursed an old Toyota that barely ran.

The driver headed in the direction of the baseball field, next to the Emergency Response Training Center, which was adjacent to the woods that hid the portal!

Matt's adrenalin bubbled as he sidestepped away from his friend.

"What's up? You okay?"

"I – I – I've got to go." Matt moved off, keeping his distance. He wanted to observe, not confront. He ran along the southern path, keeping his eyes peeled for the convertible. The driver had parked in front of the Warehouse/Mailroom building, his suit jacket draped over the passenger seat and was walking into the woods.

At first, Matt hid behind the "Future Home of" sign. Next, behind a series of trees. He witnessed the stranger move deeper into the woods until he came to the clearing. *Damn, he found it.*

Matt watched the stranger circumnavigate the portal structure, his eyebrows compressed, bending to run his hands over the horizontal components, yanking at them. "Boy, that's really solid!"

Why doesn't he just go away?

The stranger pulled a cellphone from his pocket and touched the screen. He held the phone to his head but evidently the call didn't go through because he didn't say a word. He walked around the incomplete construction once more, taking photos with his phone. It dawned on Matt that he should have taken pictures of the portal, to document his progress. The possibility of a second portal nagged at his subconscious. Maybe if he posted a photo on the Internet someone on the Internet would recognize it and respond. *Maybe the other operator knows why it's so important.*

The stranger pocketed the phone and noticed the pile of not-yet-assembled sticks lying on the ground. He picked one up, just like Matt had done, most likely as a souvenir from his discovery. When the man got a couple of feet from the structure, his arm began to drag lower. Matt held his breath. The stranger grabbed the stick with both hands and held it at about stomach height. He took one step, his balance disrupted, his legs wobbling. On his next step, the stick yanked him towards the ground. With both hands occupied, the stranger made a hard face plant.

He struggled to get his hands free from the stick, tugging and swearing. Matt stifled a giggle. He remembered how startled he was when the same thing had happened to him. Eventually, the stranger extracted his hands from beneath the stick, pushed himself up, brushed off his shirt and pants, and wiped his face with a handkerchief.

The stranger looked back one more time and then strode out of the woods toward his car.

Matt finally exhaled. His portal had been discovered. *I hope I can finish and operate this thing before anyone interferes. Whatever operate means.*

16 – Kwashay (Brooklyn, NY)

Kwashay got up extra early. She needed to begin construction of the portal, and maybe even retrieve of her backpack. She cleaned up, got dressed and poured a bowl of cereal. When she opened the kitchen drawer for a spoon, she spied a box of drinking straws. *Hmm, just like the rods.* In a different drawer were a scissors and superglue. She multitasked over breakfast, eating and chewing while she assembled a miniature version of the portal structure thrust into her head the previous evening. *A little wobbly but it's good to see the completed thing.*

As she grabbed the front door handle, her mother ambled out of her bedroom, grunted "Good morning," turned on the television and headed for the kitchen. "What's this?"

Kwashay peeked around the corner at the drinking straw model and improvised an answer. "That's – uh – a sculpture for my art class." Her impromptu reply provided a justification she could use for constructing the full-sized portal in the park across from school.

The pile of sticks was still there in the park, as was the backpack, with one rod still inside. Her books and assignments were missing. While she knelt trying to figure out how she'd build the portal with the obstinate rods, what to tell her calculus teacher, and how she'd replace her books, a shadow appeared on the ground in front of her. She looked up.

It was the Boxer with the twisted baseball cap she'd named Sideways. Close up, he looked shorter, with a solid build. "Why you run off?"

Kwashay stood up and brushed dirt off her knees. Proximity to the Boxer gave her a chill despite the mild spring temperature. She didn't want a conversation with this young man, but he was there when the backpack was still full. *Maybe he knows something useful.* She made sure her locket was tucked inside her blouse. "I was late for home. Did you see who took my books and papers?"

He stuck out his scrawny chest. "I did."

His two accomplices leaned against a nearby tree, whispering to one another. "Well, can I have them back?" Reluctantly, she added, "Please?"

"Sure, sister. If you can make some time to hang with me."

A soft breeze teased her kinky hair. "I'm not your sister. And I don't hang with-" She glanced at the backpack. "I'll make you a deal. Carry my backpack with that rod inside to the door of the school, and I'll go out with you. A real date. But if you can't carry it just across the street, I don't have to go out with you, and you'll return my stuff."

"You got a deal!" His smile stretched as wide as his face as he grabbed the backpack by one shoulder strap and struggled to lift it. He grimaced but raised it to waist level, higher than his half-mast pants. "Okay, lead the way."

Kwashay took a few steps towards the sidewalk.

Sideways took one step and was thrown to the ground. "Damn!"

"What's the matter?" She stifled a snicker. His companions stared in disbelief.

"This is some kind of trick." He let go of the bag and stood up, everything but his ego intact.

"Now you know why I left it. With that rod inside, the bag is too heavy."

Sideways kicked the backpack, launching the rod just past the bag's zipper. The backpack lifted easily. "There, now I can carry it."

"That's nice, but our deal was carrying it with the rod inside." Sideways' two companions made eye contact. "And I have witnesses."

"Okay, you win." Sideways nodded his head towards his associates, one of whom skulked off. "But something that small shouldn't weigh so much."

"I agree, it isn't logical." Neither was the glowing vision. "I can't get it to school to examine it."

Sideways shifted his stance, one leg stiff, and the other bent at the knee. "Maybe you could, like, bring the school here?"

It wasn't an outrageous suggestion. Maybe some of the machines were portable. "I'll try that. Thanks."

One of Sideways' companions returned with a brown paper shopping bag. He handed the bag to Sideways, who handed it to Kwashay.

Inside were the missing contents of her backpack. "Thanks."

"I wasn't gonna keep your stuff anyhow."

She filled her empty backpack with the books and papers and left it on the ground. Then she approached the pile. She noticed for the first time both longer and shorter rods, mostly longer. She picked up one of each length and compared them.

Sideways scratched his head, further tipping his off-balance cap. "Whatcha doin?"

"I have to build a portal." She inspected the ground for a level area on which to build the prescribed hexagonal structures.

"What's a portal?"

"It looks like two hexagon frameworks, one inside the other."

"How come?"

All these questions! She looked up from her survey. "What do you mean?"

"How come you have to build it? Some kind of school project?"

The reason she gave her mother would suffice. "Yes, exactly. An art project. But first I need to count them." She knelt on the ground and grouped the rods into sets of ten.

"We can help." Sideways summoned his colleagues with a wave.

The two stood leaning against each other, concentrating on their cellphones. Sideways ignored them and grabbed as many rods as he could carry. Then he dropped to his knees and made his own collections, never taking his eyes off the young woman.

For a few minutes, they slid rods from the haphazard pile and created neat bundles. The grass beneath showed numerous straight brown lines, each one matching a rod's previous position.

"How many do you have?" she asked.

Sideways stood back, arms folded like he'd won some sort of contest. He'd collected up all of the short ones. "Three of ten shorties is thirty. Two of ten longies is twenty."

"All of mine are longies." She adopted his naming convention. "And I have fifty-eight." *It will be terrible if I don't have enough.*

She closed her eyes to accurately assess what the portal required. "Let's see, the outer part has five layers of long rod hexagons making thirty, plus four layers of long connectors is twenty-four more. The inner one has shorter sides, which needs-"

"Also five layers? 'Cause that would make thirty, what I got here."

"But the inner part is the same height, so-"

"Four times six is another twenty-four. Thirty plus twenty-four twice is seventy-eight." Sideways grinned. "I'm good at maths."

Impressive! "I've got exactly the right number." She was pleased but not surprised that the mysterious mother voice would provide her with the raw material to succeed. *Not when it insisted on the importance of the task. I wonder what she meant by making the world better?*

On a flat area near the collections, she reached out to lay the first long rod in position. It dipped and slid, like two same-poled magnets in proximity.

"What's up?" asked Sideways.

"It seems to have a preference about where it goes." She stopped fighting. The rod torqued its position to a north/south orientation, forcing Kwashay to face west toward the Upper Bay. With the first one in position, she laid out the remaining rods for the base, which snapped together at the ends. "The smaller, inner framework uses shorties as the sides. The larger, outer one uses longies." She fetched more rods. "You know what hexagons are?"

"I'm not stupid. Six sides. Pentagons has five, like the building in Washington. Octagons has eight, like a stop sign."

"Exactly." Kwashay grabbed some more rods and attached them vertically at each vertex. "These will hold the next level."

"You building it up? Like one of those playground climbing things?"

She remembered the model she'd made that morning using straws. "Yes, I guess that's what it will look like when it's finished."

"Looks wobbly to me. You sure about this?"

Kwashay had faith in the mental blueprint. "It'll be fine." She glanced at her watch. "Oh my! I've got to go. I can't be late again."

Sideways stroked the brim of his cap. "Can you have help? Or would that be cheating?"

If the portal had actually been an art project, she would have provided a swift affirmative reply. But this was no art project, and the mystery mother voice didn't say she couldn't have help. "I'll just have to disclose the fact that I got assistance. Why, are you volunteering?"

"Sound like a good cause, right guys?"

One of them looked up and asked, "Don't we got someplace else to be?" Neither budged.

"Like I said, we'll help." Sideways tugged at his pants, to no effect. "We don't got no pressing engagements."

Kwashay couldn't impart the blueprint vision or the urgency that had been communicated to her. She also didn't want to owe this Boxer a favor. "Are you sure-"

Sideways picked up a couple of rods and followed her lead, adding the verticals to both the inner and outer parts. "See, we can do this."

She was hesitant but couldn't exactly stop them from continuing. "Okay, keep adding tiers – levels – until the rods have all been used. The inner one uses the shorties. And we know there's exactly the correct number-"

"Don't worry. We got this." Sideways' smile returned.

"Okay. I'm trusting you. This is important."

Sideways trotted over to his friends "Then we'll do it proper." They pocketed their technology when he dragged them by the arms to the piles of rods. He called for shorties and longies as he repeated the assembly technique, glancing up after each rod was installed.

She kept checking over her shoulder as she crossed the street, startled by almost walking into the path of a honking car.

She fidgeted all day wondering what Sideways and his pals were doing with the rods. *At least they can't carry them away.*

Before she caught a bus home, Kwashay crossed the street to the park. Sideways and his associates had completed three levels of the structure. She breathed a sigh of relief that they had been helpful after all. Their head start meant she wouldn't have to arrive extra early or stay late as often to build the structure herself. She didn't know precisely when it would become operational, but the day was coming, that was certain, and she'd have to be ready. At least, she'd be sharing the responsibility. There was another builder operator out there somewhere.

She glanced around the park. Sideways and his friends weren't around to thank. *I'll bet anything he'll ask me to go out with him, as a reward. Mama will never allow it.*

Kwashay checked her watch. *Better get home and put up dinner.* She rode public transit in a good mood. Nothing her mother could say or do, or the double math homework as penance for being tardy, would spoil that.

17 – Selton (Kearney, NE)

Selton put the current edition of the *Kearney Hub* newspaper back on the shelf and shook off his trepidation from reading Dogood's classified ad by concentrating on his mission and his current surroundings. *I've got books to ingest.* He examined the layout of the library in the context of all of the previous libraries, public, private and specialty he'd patronized. Open space with good lighting, and plenty of padded chairs. His favorite, off on the side almost hidden behind precisely aligned rows of shelves, was particularly comfortable and private for book consumption.

Selton made his way to the new titles shelves. There were only fiction titles on display, so he chose one whose author he recognized. He was on his way to his comfy chair with the new Quincy Grissom mystery when one of Kearney's police officers sauntered in and stopped at Bernice's desk. The bull – that's what Marathon would have called him - kept his eyes on Selton, even as he conversed with the librarian. Bernice stood, said something with a shake of her body, and the officer departed. She threw Selton a smile and a nod. He took that as a form of assurance, that Bernice would do what she could to protect him from harm. *Hopefully, that will support my effective recall to Serulia.*

Selton settled in and put the Quincy Grissom novel on the table next to his chair. After decades, his cells fattened with information, he awarded himself the privilege of choosing books according to his interest, supplemented by new publications that occurred with regular frequency. He mixed a balance of non-fiction and fiction in his sampling, although under duress he would have admitted to spending more time with novels. Although his mission didn't include retaining non-fiction, Selton gained broad insight into what otherwise would have been flat descriptions of human emotion. The made-up stories brought bland descriptions of emotions to life, even if to pretend lives.

From "The Odyssey" and “Adventures of Huckleberry Finn”, he came to understand bravery and adventure. Through “To Kill a Mockingbird,” he experienced empathy and bravery in the face of danger. “The Karamazov Brothers” exposed life, death, and living a moral life so that people are sad that we’re gone and rejoice for having known us. “Charlotte's Web” showed Selton what it meant to be a good friend and inspired him with the book's messages about the power of love. “The Hunger Games” contained characters that exhibited self-sacrifice as well as skills in survival. “Cyrano de Bergerac” suffered unrequited love from afar. Besides the positive emotions, there were darker lessons delivered by the stories he consumed. Deception and manipulation were clear lessons from “1984.” *Too bad my mission is to collect only facts. There are lessons in those made-up stories that could be useful back on Serulia.*

As had been happening more frequently, Selton’s attention drifted. *How many libraries have there been?* Dozens at least, all documented in his Personal Information Journal. Retrieving that information would be slow, since the various entries were scattered across his body. *I used to be able to name every one, their latitude and longitude and the dates of his visits from recent memory.* He associated his gradual deterioration with Earth fruit and vegetable ripening, even though he had no facts to support his belief.

Other patrons arrived, some of them familiar residents, many stopping at Bernice’s desk. In modern facilities, checkout and check-in were automated processes. Scanners would read patron identification cards and book barcodes for checkout and return. Not so in Kearney. Checkout was still a manual process involving an interaction with Bernice and a rubber stamp. Check-in was a circular bin on wheels, to move the returned books to the back room for reintegration onto the shelves.

The Kearney library had advanced in some aspects. Computer terminals had replaced the physical card catalog. They'd done away with microfiche; instead DVDs stored newspaper and periodical back issues for random access. DVDs had likely taken the place of videotapes to support community entertainment. Selton had no TV set or player to enjoy them. Tiny's Bar and Grill down the street had one visible from the sidewalk, but Selton had never been a customer. Human food and drink were useless to him.

Occasionally, Selton would come across a small community library that had clung to a physical card catalog. Since his methodology was to read books in sequence off the shelves, the card catalog was of no particular use. Reading everything about philosophy or biology or space travel had the added benefit of simplifying his internal organization of the material. *I've developed my own implementation of the Dewey Decimal System, inside my body.*

Selton didn't need to read the same volume twice, although when newer editions of a book were released, he would indulge himself with a quick review, to absorb the changes or updates. Fortunately, the selections made by the various libraries across the country were diverse enough to make each stay a rich and rewarding visit.

Since rereading any book had no benefit, Selton's task at subsequent libraries was simpler, merely finding unique tomes and adding them to his collected memories.

Periodicals were another consistent source of new material, which kept those topics fresh.

When libraries began to put their information online, providing computer terminals for access, Selton's physiology failed him. The phototropins and phytochromes embedded in place of human eyeballs became strained by CRT radiation, resulting in excruciating phylum aches. His body was optimized for consuming the contents of written pages, black on white.

Besides, his twiggy fingers weren't designed to be used on keyboards. Selton opted for holding physical books with a bare hand, turning pages with his other hand embedded inside the blue rubber glove.

Selton glanced at Bernice, head down at her computer. Since facts took priority over fiction, he left the novel unopened, proceeded to section 612, human physiology and plucked a revised copy of *Gray's Anatomy* off the shelf.

18 – Charlie (Washington, DC)

Charlie stopped by the office the morning of his flight to New York City and the dead grass. Jane had arranged for a limo to take him from EPA headquarters to the airport. He dumped his bags at his desk and approached Bradley Lane's cubicle, expecting it to be empty. Instead, there Lane sat, the half-walls decorated with citations and photo ops with various government celebrities, most of whom Charlie didn't recognize. A pile of small boxes cowered in the far corner of Lane's desk.

Lane didn't look up from the crossword puzzle in his newspaper. His pen marks were precise, filling squares with the correct letters. There were no cross-outs.

Charlie tapped on the metal frame. "Hi. I thought you'd be at Dan River."

Lane didn't look up. "Nothing I can't do from here. Agents from Region 4 are on the scene. Besides, the whole agency was hit by Congressional budget cuts. What's up?"

"I thought I needed to check in with you, before I left."

Lane concentrated on the puzzle, groping for his open bag of crunchy cheese snacks. "Stanton showed me your case file." Lane said it loud enough for others in the vicinity to hear, maybe not intentionally. *He does have a commanding voice.* When chuckles shot over one of the cubicle partitions, Lane looked up and grimaced. "This is a simple assignment, right? A patch of dead grass on Governors Island."

Charlie focused on his mentor. "Any advice? This is my first-"

"I know. Listen, maybe Stanton didn't tell you in so many words, but this is a test, to see if you're ready for field work."

Charlie's heart beat a little faster. He couldn't hold back a smile.

"Keep it simple, the simpler the better." Lane popped a curly cheesy morsel into his mouth and bit down hard. "And watch your expenses." His chair bumped the desk as he repositioned himself. His eyes returned to the page as the stack of boxes wobbled.

Charlie wondered what the small boxes held and pointed. "What are those?"

"Awards." Lane pulled his face from the paper, took the blue velvet one from the pile, blew off the dust and opened it. "See? I was presented the EPA Gold Medal for Exceptional Service when I was in college."

The medal was a horizontal ribbon in blue, with vertical stripes in yellow and two shades of green, the style of award a general would wear on his chest.

Lane snapped the box closed. "At the time, it cemented my resolve to work for the agency after I graduated. Now it's just a relic." He placed the closed box back on top of the stack and returned to his puzzle. "Keep in touch."

Charlie took a few steps away from Lane's desk and then heard a comment from one of Lane's loudmouth colleagues. "If I were you, I'd just order some sod and call it a day." As Charlie turned to identify the speaker, a few chuckles escaped nearby desks.

Lane had stood up and bolted across the aisle. "Would you like me to remind you about <u>your</u> first field assignment?" Lane winked in Charlie's direction.

The nearby cubes filled with outright laughter.

Charlie was only half-pleased that Lane defended him. *Quincy Grissom takes care of himself. I need to be strong.*

Charlie retreated to his desk to fetch his black ballistic-nylon rolling carry-on and matching messenger bag. Price tags adorned the handles.

Director Stanton approached Charlie's cube. "By the way, I almost forgot to give you this." A brown fold-over leather case held a gold and blue EPA agent badge. Charlie stared at the authority token. "Don't abuse the privilege. Federal agents have a fragile reputation with locals."

Charlie slipped the case into his shirt pocket. "Yes sir."

The Director faded back into his private office.

Jane stood up in her cubicle and walked over. "The limo driver call. He downstairs."

Charlie handed her a spare apartment key dangling from a piece of oval leather. "For my place, so you can feed AquaLung." He tensed, hoping Jane didn't see this as cause for another prolonged hug. *She's attractive and smart, and anybody would be lucky to have her. I just don't date work colleagues.*

She held the fob to her chest as if it was a gold medal. As Charlie headed for the elevator, she waved. "Good luck!"

Investigating dead grass? I'll hardly need it. Charlie returned a half-hearted wave as the elevator doors closed.

The limo was downstairs as requested, a stretch that could have accommodated an entire aisle of agents. The ride was smooth and quick, and Charlie felt pampered. Jane had also arranged for an expedited airport pass, so with a flash of his driver's license and newly assigned badge, Charlie flew through security.

Despite that quick passage, Charlie still waited at the gate for his flight to New York. A local team would meet and escort him to the site of the dead grass, Governors Island, which had been closed to visitors. Thousands of tourists had been disappointed. Even worse, the news agencies found out about the unscheduled closing of the park and made it their headline story.

On overhead flat-screen TVs, Charlie watched major channel news anchors report and then speculate about the reasons for the closing. And of course, they did their best to portray the situation in the worst possible light. They even invoked the 'T' word - terrorism. Charlie wanted a field assignment, but he was EPA, not Homeland Security. *It's just dead grass.*

Passengers boarded single file like a chain gang. He found his seat on the aisle in an exit row, gaining a few inches of legroom. *Probably Jane's doing.*

The takeoff was less traumatic than Charlie expected. He waited until the plane leveled off before he buried his nose in the repeatedly redirected incident folder. The grounds maintenance staff of Governors Island had filed the initial report. On the northeast corner, a sizable area of grass had gone completely brown. No one on the grounds staff could figure out the cause. Because the island is a national monument, they contacted Washington.

Charlie decided to take his mind off the flight by reinserting himself into the intriguing new Quincy Grissom novel.

📖

> Grissom had taken the case of a wealthy importer named Harrison Bainbridge who'd been the victim of identity theft. Bainbridge showed Grissom the translucent Indulge Tanzanite card, which he could use with either the traditional magnetic stripe or the embedded security chip.
>
> The evidence made it seem like simple credit fraud, the criminal using the client's exclusive card for a brief series of transactions. Bainbridge had successfully resolved all of the known impacts on his Indulge Financial Services statement,

limited though they were in number and amount, but was annoyed by the hassle. He wanted to understand the cause and prevent a recurrence.

📖

A young female flight attendant, one of several on the plane, interrupted Charlie with a gentle shake of his shoulder. She offered him a pillow and a blanket, almost insisting he take advantage. When she stood her ground with a smile, he reluctantly lifted his tray table and its contents so she could spread the blanket across his lap. Charlie blushed.

As soon as she departed, Charlie dove back into the novel.

📖

Grissom planned his strategy. Instead of investigating the long list of transactions that may have exposed his client's information, Grissom went straight to the credit card company. Was his client's situation an isolated incident, or had other cardholders had similar breaches, forming a pattern? Grissom was all about patterns.

The transaction history shared by the client contained two patterns of note: a series of transactions with a company named Galileo's, and a singular transaction at Prestige Appraisers. Although they were anomalies by frequency, these establishments were no more or less likely candidates for his client's exposure. There was much legwork ahead for the venerable sleuth.

Charlie pulled his nose out of the book when a voice over the PA system called for "trays up." After a two-bounce, white-knuckle landing, the plane taxied to the arrival gate. Charlie grabbed his messenger bag from beneath the seat in front of him, stood and opened the overhead storage bin, but a flight attendant insisted on yanking down his rolling carry-on. He figured he'd be in New York one or two days and then head back home. *How long does it take to diagnose dead grass?*

Charlie walked down the jetway, wondering how he would recognize his contact, the local New York agent. It was simpler than he thought – she wore a distinctive blue nylon jacket with large yellow letters on the left side: EPA. She was just about Charlie's height, with short brown hair, parted on the left like his.

Before Charlie could introduce himself, she stuck out her hand and spoke. "Welcome to New York, Agent Keyson. Stephanie Potter, Region 2 EPA at your service."

Am I that obvious, a caricature of a Washington bureaucrat? "How did you know I was me?" The words came out badly.

"Your admin Jane sent me your photo and CV."

Does Jane have access to that stuff? Charlie's phone rang as he adjusted the strap of his messenger bag. "Excuse me." He pulled it from his pocket and answered with his name, the same way Grissom did. "Keyson."

Charlie heard a crunch followed by the words, "Have you hooked up with your New York City counterpart?"

Lane couldn't have meant what he said. *He doesn't even know if the local agent is female.* "I just got here."

"Just trying to be on top of things." Another crunch.

Hasn't Lane finished that bag yet? Charlie changed the subject. "How's Dan River?"

"Coming along just fine. A couple of field agents are documenting the situation."

I would have flown down there myself, if I'd been assigned that case. The budget can't be that tight. They flew me to New York as a test. Given Lane's style, Charlie's visit to New York City probably wasn't necessary. He imagined Lane saying, "Let the regionals handle it." "The plane just landed and I've met the local EPA contact. I'll call you as soon as I learn something new."

Charlie tapped on the recent button and stored Lane's name and number. *At least I'll know when he's calling.* He looked at Potter. "Sorry." Before he forgot, he wrote Potter's full name in his breast-pocket spiral notebook.

"No sweat. There's a boat waiting for us at Brooklyn Pier 1. Taking a public ferry didn't make sense for someone of your position."

At least someone takes me seriously. Charlie stood a bit straighter as they walked towards the exit. "So what do you think killed the grass?"

Potter wrestled the handle of the rolling bag from Charlie's grip. "It may only be dormant. I took the liberty of gathering plant and soil samples."

Darn, she beat me to it!

"I'm waiting for test results." Potter led them past the revolving door and held open a door marked NO EXIT.

A white hybrid sedan waited at the curb, unattended. A police officer nodded in Potter's direction as she hefted Charlie's suitcase into the back.

Ms. Potter seems to be doing a fine job without my help. Charlie expected that the local EPA lab would have test results before he checked into his hotel. *Lane could have easily managed this assignment remotely from his desk. I guess I should feel lucky, that Director Stanton is giving me this opportunity, but it doesn't feel like I'll have anything to do.*

After they both buckled in, Potter pulled away from the curb and merged onto Grand Central Parkway. "Ever been in New York City?"

"First time." The expressway looked like any other he'd ever seen, on the rare occasions he rented a car.

"Maybe we'll have time for some sightseeing."

Same thing Jane suggested. Charlie peered out the window. Trees, plants and other foliage lined the highway filled with vehicles belching pollution. *I wonder how they survive in such a hostile environment.* Perhaps plants acclimated to the car exhaust. His lungs, however, might not.

A while back, Charlie had considered requesting a transfer to a local EPA office, which by definition would place him in the field. This trip would be the perfect opportunity to collaborate with field officers and assess the nature of their work.

Charlie was happy with the silence, but evidently Potter wasn't. "It must be so exciting, working at EPA headquarters."

"It's okay." Charlie wasn't about to expose all of the mundane and clerical work he'd been saddled with.

"Work out in the field must be much more exciting. Closer to reality, I mean."

"I suppose, after you slash your way through the trivial situations. And the bureaucracy." Potter exited Grand Central Parkway for the Brooklyn Queens Expressway. "And the paperwork!"

The lawn of a cemetery on the passenger side reminded him of his task. "I guess the grass is always greener."

Agent Potter laughed. "You're really funny."

Charlie hadn't meant his comment as word play. He assessed her expression, delivered with a sideways glance. *Don't tell me she's attracted to me! Thanks, Dad.* He flushed with embarrassment and changed the subject. "You've seen the problem first-hand. What can you tell me, besides what's in the file?"

"The problem showed up on the east edge of Governors Island but it's spread west from there."

Charlie strained against his seatbelt. "It's spreading?" The report had been a snapshot in time, but the situation had changed. *Maybe this will a substantial test after all.* "How far?"

"Didn't you get my status update? I submitted it as soon as I got back from the soil sampling." Potter exited I-278 just before the Brooklyn Bridge, then made a quick right turn into a parking lot along the Hudson River.

Charlie imagined Potter's update, bouncing from agency in-box to agency in-box, the same path as the original report. *No wonder I didn't get it.* "Sorry."

She turned off the engine. "You'll see for yourself shortly."

The neighboring parks looked completely normal. Across the river, Charlie witnessed the New York City profile, a monstrous number of huge buildings that had no height shame.

19 – Matt (Eureka, CA)

Duke, a senior from the automotive repair school, responded to Matt's posting for assistance. He certainly qualified as strong and was immediately a big help. Sticks that weighed heavily on Matt were much easier for Duke. The hexagonal framework had grown to chest high. Yet, the architectural vision of the completed structure imparted into Matt's mind was twice its current height.

Duke complained of a strained back as he lifted sticks to form the next level. "These are just too heavy, man. I can't reach as high as you need."

Duke was right. Matt needed scaffolding to complete the portal. Maybe some of the students with welding skills could construct a metal frame. Or carpentry students could build one of wood. Fred studied construction, but would he cooperate and be discreet? *If someone in authority finds out, they could put a stop to the whole project. For Earth's sake, the portal needs to be completed.*

Matt evaluated the risk and decided to invite Fred's participation. He was easy to find, in the cafeteria circling a table full of female students with a large bag of potato chips in his hand. One by one, he offered to share, and each one refused in turn.

He pulled Fred aside and asked for his assistance.

"You want me to help you build a what?" asked Fred.

"A scaffold, out in the southeast woods past the ball fields. You're handy with wood. I've seen those bookcases you build."

"A scaffold is nothing like a bookcase. But why do you need one out there? Did you find some magic beans and there's a giant living at the top of a huge stalk?" Fred pulled a big chip from the bag and crunched.

"No. I'm making a, uh-" Matt remembered the wall of trellises along the path near the football field. "I'm building a trellis. You know, to support vines. It's a unique design, really tall. An extra credit project for my engineering class, to make up for my missed exam."

"A trellis for our engineering class?" Fred wiped his hand on his thigh. "Sounds weird."

"Please? I don't have anyone else to turn to." Matt put his hand on Fred's shoulder. "Buddy?"

Fred glanced at the table of females and then at Matt. "Okay, I'll make you a deal. I'll find a crew of guys to build you a scaffold. But in exchange, you have to go on a double date with me and those two hot girls I met."

Matt considered the offer. His fixation with dating and video games had been poison at Dartmouth. But the portal would never get built if he couldn't reach high enough. *Small price to pay given what's at stake Huge benefits for the entire planet.* "Just one date?"

"Yeah. How about we go to Eureka Bowling Emporium and then for pizza at Paul's Live From New York? Deal?" Fred's hand disappeared into the bag for another chip.

Matt exhaled hard. *I can do this.* "Okay. One double date in exchange for a scaffold. Gather up the team and stop by my room. I'll show you where to build it."

"Great." Potato chip crumbs fell from Fred's lips. He half patted, half wiped his hand on Matt's shoulder. "You'll love yours."

"My what?"

"Your date! Sheesh, did you forget already? She's got a great personality."

20 – Kwashay (Brooklyn, NY)

Kwashay grabbed a bag of rice cakes and filled a thermos with milk instead of eating breakfast at home. She was more than anxious to see how much of the portal Sideways and his friends had completed.

Her mother wandered out from her bedroom and stretched her arms above her head just as Kwashay was about to open the front door. "Good morning, sweetie. Why are you leaving so early?"

"Big project, and I need to get a head start."

"Good! I love that attitude. And I love you." She blew her daughter a kiss.

Kwashay ambled down the stairs. She had a couple of choices for her route to Brooklyn Technical High School. Given that either way included a several block walk on both ends, by habit her feet marched up Herzl to Lott Avenue, west on Lott past Lott Meat Market to E 98th St.

As she walked, Kwashay mulled the urgency of portal construction. Even if Sideways and his buddies had only done a little more than what she'd seen the previous afternoon when school let out, the project felt like it was ahead of schedule. *It's got to be finished on time.* She was unclear as to why, but believed in her heart that once operational, the portal was going to make things so much better on Earth, for everybody. *The other portal builder better be just as diligent.*

When Kwashay looked up, she'd reached Fine Fare Supermarket on the corner of Legion and Saratoga and dutifully waved to Ms. Schmidt, the owner. One more block, and she climbed the stairs to the Metro train station.

From the platform, Kwashay looked down at the wooden beams supporting the tracks for the Number 2 Seventh Avenue Express train. She and Sideways had counted the rods, to ensure there were enough for the structure's design in her mind. *We should have enough if we built it properly. But what if they damaged some during construction?*

The Express train pulled into the station precisely six minutes after Kwashay got there. No one got out. Saratoga station was an origination point, not a destination at that time of the morning. That far out, it was easy for Kwashay to get a seat to herself by the window.

She'd only just met Sideways the Boxer. He seemed nice enough, but he and his associates were still strangers. *Should I have trusted them to take this as seriously as me? Their day job seems to be hanging out, looking for trouble.*

The train route was lined with strip malls below, stores with brightly colored signs and awnings. One shop owner was outside with a sponge on a long stick, washing the windows of his store. She pictured the completed hexagon structures in her mind, one inside the other. *The completed portal will be eight feet tall. How can anyone reach that high? And won't the rods be too heavy?*

She was tall for her age, or maybe just tall. She'd turned down offers to play basketball or volleyball. Not because she wasn't interested, but because her mother didn't approve of anything that made demands and therefore distracted from her studies. Two students sitting across from her snickered as they shared private thoughts with whispers. *I bet I missed out on some valuable friendships.*

Below the elevated train tracks, shoppers were already out, carrying their purchases in all shapes and sizes. *What if Sideways figured out a way to remove rods from the site?* Kwashay was sure the rods were valuable beyond being components for the portal because of their unique weight property. Closing her eyes, she remembered how a single rod practically threw Sideways to the ground. *No way!*

As the train took the curve at Eastern Parkway, it descended into a subway tunnel. The loud rush of air and the amplified rumble of the wheels on the tracks, less noticeable when the train was elevated above the street, drowned out the ambient conversations. By the time they got to Utica station, her car was filled with men and women headed for work, standing room only. She gave up her seat for an older woman with two full shopping bags in hand. Kwashay held onto a strap, swaying with the train car, eyes closed. Her intention before school was to add another level to the structure. Lies of omission with her mother were accumulating. Her hand made the strap moist.

Kwashay wasn't the only student jostling for position as the train approached her exit. She wiggled her way through the crowd at Atlantic and Barclay

Center. The crowds swept her up Flatbush Avenue over to Lafayette and one last block to BTHS.

Except she didn't enter the school. Across DeKalb, the structure waited for completion. Kwashay couldn't assume that Sideways and his associates had finished the work for her. She stepped into the construction area, surrounded by mature trees and stopped dead in her tracks. *It's finished!*

The portal structures stood approximately eight feet tall, as designed. And, there were no rods left on the ground. *Perfect, they used them all!* Sideways and his friends, or someone else, had erected a tubular metal construction scaffold supporting a wooden platform around her structure, almost like a third hexagon. *So that's how they reached the top layers.*

She gave Sideways points for ingenuity as she circumnavigated the framed structure, examining the connections between the rods. Sideways and his friends had done an excellent job. She couldn't have done better herself, and certainly not as quickly.

She was overjoyed at seeing the complete structure. *Sideways must have worked really hard to get it done overnight.* She reached through the scaffold and stroked one of the rods. Her arm tingled. *It knows me!* Now, all she had to do was wait for the signal to operate it. She didn't know what the signal would be, or what operating meant. But she'd been chosen for this honor, that was certain, from the moment she picked up the first rod. She beamed at participating in something that would make Earth a better place. She and one other.

She leaned against the scaffold, examining the craftsmanship of the Boxers, when someone hollered, "Hey you, girl!" It was a construction worker in overalls, a patterned flannel shirt, and a hard hat. "What are you doing with our scaffold?"

Kwashay looked around. A police officer approached from the east side of the park, coming her way. The construction worker was closing from the west. She knew that if she fled, the situation would escalate. So she stood there, clutching her locket, waiting for the confrontation.

21 - Selton (Kearney, NE)

In the Kearney Public Library, Selton had only scanned a few dozen pages, accelerating up to his optimal pace when his body began to tilt towards the side. He lamented the loss of his torso's firmness. He hadn't become squishy – yet – but that was likely his fate. *They have to recall me soon, so I can deliver all of the accumulated information.* Selton couldn't accept the notion that decades of dutiful effort would come to naught. Seeking distraction from the possibility he'd be abandoned, he put down his current book and grabbed one from section 586, seedless plants, the logical analogy to the human physiology text in his hands.

Although he was obligated by his mission to obtain knowledge in an even, uniform manner, Selton afforded himself the small luxury of dawdling over books in section 580. Plants. He felt a kinship to the flora on Earth, and considered every blade of grass, every flower, every bush and tree a 'cousin.' Selton knew it didn't make sense, from a logical perspective. As product of a foreign seed, he had no common ancestry with Earth flora. And his biological processes didn't match Earth vegetation's photosynthesis.

Rather, his nutrition and gas generation were literally alien.

All of the information in the seedless book was comforting but had already been collected in his cells. He reluctantly put the volume back in place and wandered to section 940, World Wars.

The behavior of Earthlings was frequently not aligned with their documented objectives or best interests. Most countries had clearly stated laws promoting the welfare of their citizens, yet actively engaged in battles that put their citizens at risk. Over the decades, armed conflicts continuously raged all over the planet. Selton cringed at the level of violence Earthlings tolerated on both small and large scale. *Despite all of the wisdom collected in their books, Earthlings are a confused and self-destructive species. From their history, why haven't they understood the futility of intra-species hostility?* Selton hoped that these aspects of Earthling behavior weren't why Serulians were interested.

Selton couldn't rationalize how a species so steeped in fine arts, as documented by section 800 Literature and 700 Arts & Recreation, could be so cruel and violent to each other. Topics of disagreement such as land, politics, religion, revenge, ancient rivalries, were familiar to Selton, but only as concepts on a page, minor in comparison to honoring life in all its forms. That was the singular aspect of Earthling behavior he found most incomprehensible. *Perhaps there are limitations to knowledge gained from books.* Despite their tendency to violence, he'd developed an extreme fondness for certain categories of human beings, specifically librarians and hobos.

The temperatures in the north frequently became harmful. For his physical well-being, he'd stayed south of forty-one degrees north latitude. Especially in colder weather, Selton shifted his travels south, skimming the North American southern coastline. The temperament and demeanor of the southern Americans were quite distinct from those in the north. He never felt welcome, shunned as if the darker tone of his outer covering was abhorrent to the residents. Political and social attitudes were much more conservative, so different from the northern residents. Selton wondered how they'd managed as one country until he read section 973.7 about the United States Civil War, which gave him a better perspective on what he'd observed. Something down deep inside his memory, perhaps a core value embedded in his seed, convinced Selton that Serulians were peace-loving, allowing all species of flora to grow and live together in harmony.

Selton startled when Bernice tapped him on the shoulder. "You shouldn't sit for long periods without getting up and stretching. It's not good for your body or mind."

He thanked her for her concern, put down the book after memorizing the page number and strolled to the front window. Sitting outside was a patrol car and that same policeman leaning against the vehicle, staring into the library. *He's keeping track of me.* He felt a cold chill, like dew on a frosty morning against his body. Selton retreated to his chair and picked up his book but didn't open it.

Librarians are a special kind of people. Wherever Selton traveled, they were patient and kind, selfless in their interactions. Generous to a fault. After he'd left

Marathon and the other hobos, several librarians in different towns offered to provide food and shelter to what they thought was a homeless young man. Only once did he accept such an offer, from a young female whose tear-filled eyes he could not refuse.

Her husband was less than hospitable, asking about Selton's name and ethnic background. The husband even tried conversing with him in Spanish, perhaps because of his darker outer skin. Selton's stilted use of the language with vague references to "my home" and "far way" failed to satisfy the husband.

She became almost frantic when Selton wouldn't eat. He made excuses about his gastronomy and assured her he was getting ample nutrition. His growth and stable weight stood as proof. She became distraught when he refused to attend school. Instead, he traveled with her to her library, working his way through the shelves.

Over her objections, Selton insisted on camping out in their backyard instead of cozying up in a soft bed in their guest room. He professed his love of nature and the night sky as his preferred blanket. Selton accepted her offer of a small tent which had no floor to obstruct his nightly feedings. After a week, her husband commented about Selton relocating the tent each night, leaving behind a brown patch. Before he was invited to leave, Selton voluntarily departed their domicile. He thrived using public parks or grassy areas alongside railroad tracks for his nightly feedings.

Selton accepted his own mortality, which he joked to himself was akin to his shelf life. Based on the models of Earth's fruits and vegetables, he expected his inner pulp to age until he was ripe. Beyond that was overripe, when his body mass would lose coherence, his outer skin would no longer retain his human shape, and he would spoil. *Certainly the Serulians will fetch me before that happens, so I can deliver the results of my mission.* Communications from Serulia had been annual, occurring each spring. *There should be another one soon.* Every day he remained on alert for a message from his Serulian brethren, informing him about their plans for recall.

22 – Charlie (New York City, NY)

Charlie lurched forward when Potter slammed on the breaks. They'd arrived in the drop off/pick up lane at Brooklyn Bridge Park and Brooklyn Heights Promenade along the river's edge. The grassy areas, bright green, overflowed with tourists taking selfies with the New York skyline in the background. Adding to the melee were roving television reporters with camera crews, poised to pounce on any news about why Governors Island was closed. A half dozen television station vans filled the small parking lot.

Potter refrained from pulling into an empty space and shook her head. "Nope, we're not doing this. We'll get swarmed for sure." She hit a button on her steering wheel and selected a phone number from the touch screen in the dashboard.

A voice came through the speakers. "New York Port Authority. This is Captain Vance." Background noise made hearing him difficult.

"This is Potter, EPA. Change of plans. Meet us at Pier 2." She disconnected, looked over her shoulder and merged into traffic. "I requisitioned a boat from the city's

Port Authority so we wouldn't have to wait for one of the scheduled ferries."

"Good thinking." Their sudden departure from the promenade raised the question, "What just happened?"

"We don't need media exposure. Best to avoid the press.."

Charlie breathed a sigh of relief as he glanced back at the meandering reporters. *I wonder what Director Stanton and Lane would think if they saw me on the evening news.*

Pier 2 was just down the road from the promenade, with a bigger parking lot.

Potter parked and took a salesman's sample case, black with "EPA" in large yellow letters, from the trunk. "My tools," she explained.

Charlie had brought nothing, not even a tape measure. *Great investigator I am.*

She locked her arm through his. "Come on, the boat should be here by now." She led Charlie across the street and over a concrete path connecting the mainland to the pier, a huge cement square. The pier was covered, edge-to-edge, by a blue-roofed pavilion used for roller-skating. Open sides instead of glass windows meant unobstructed views of the city, suitable only in the warmer months. Per the sign, public skating didn't start until noon so the rink was empty.

Potter walked quickly, forcing Charlie to skitter along. On the north edge, a ramp led down to the water.

'Be careful, it's slippery." Potter hugged Charlie's arm even tighter.

His black dress oxfords were a poor match for the damp plastic incline. Only then did he observe Potter's rubber-soled shoes. Alongside the ramp, a motorboat with Port of New York markings waited with engines running.

Potter climbed aboard first, then extended a hand to help Charlie. "This run-about should get us there quick."

They sat side-by-side on the rear-padded bench. Charlie reached under the bench seat and found life vests. He pulled one out and clenched it between his feet. Once underway in open water, the boat bounced violently. Charlie grabbed the side rail and squeezed.

Potter leaned her head close to Charlie's ear. "It'll be a short ride, under twenty minutes. The island's administrators are waiting for us." Her breath tickled.

As they got closer to the island, he began to appreciate its size. Although smaller than Manhattan, Governors Island was plenty big. *I wonder how much the dead grass has expanded.*

As they got closer, Charlie read the Governors Island sign on a wide red arch at the ferryboat landing, designed for larger boats. The pilot steered their run-about further south. On shore, a sign on the end of their thin wooden dock read 'Pier 101.'

"This is where the kayaks usually land." Potter stood and threw a rope to a man on the pier.

Dressed in jeans and polo shirt with gardening gloves tucked into his belt, he caught the rope and tied up the front end of the boat.

"Sorry the administrators aren't here to greet you," he said. "I'm Marty, the grounds manager." His handshake was also an assist to disembark.

"Nice to meet you." It made more sense to speak with someone close to the situation rather than upper management. “I’m Charlie Keyson, EPA, from Washington.” He scribbled Marty’s name in his notepad.

“And I’m Stephanie Potter, EPA regional office.” She hopped out of the boat without assistance. “I was here before, taking soil samples.”

“I remember. Let me show you; the problem’s gotten worse.” Marty led the couple up past two chain-link fenced areas to an electric golf cart parked on the asphalt road. “Motor vehicles are prohibited. Most people bicycle but I got us one of these.”

Potter put her toolbag on the front passenger seat and joined Charlie in back. Marty drove south along a paved road through a cluster of old two-story brick houses.

Charlie hadn’t expected so many buildings, and old ones at that. *Grissom would have done his research before visiting.* “Who lives here?”

“Nobody at the moment. Sorry, Agent Potter, you’ve heard my spiel before. The U. S. Army and then the Coast Guard used these Mid-19th Century brick houses. Many others have been demolished south of here, to allow development of the island as open park space.”

Sticking out from both sides of the road on which they drove were wide brown grass areas. Charlie turned his head as they passed by. “I think you missed it.”

“The roads crisscross the stripe a number of times,” said Marty. “Seems like nothing – neither roads nor buildings – gets in its way. I’m taking you a bit further inland, to see the problem better.”

“It’s not far.” Potter patted Charlie’s hand. ”Be patient.”

Marty alternated looking forward and speaking to his two rear seat passengers. “Fortunately, the problem’s been confined to the National Monument on the north end. So far, at least. The off-limits and public park areas on the south end haven't been affected."

When they reached what looked like a church, the road split into a soft curve and a hard right.

Potter pointed at the building. "That's St. Cornelius Chapel, for servicemen who were stationed here as far back as World War I, right?"

"You were listening." Marty chose the sharp right option, which took them north.

Potter's body leaned against Charlie's through the turn and continued the tour monologue. "That's the Parade Grounds on the left, and Nolan Park on the right."

All of the grass seemed normal, at least as far as Charlie could tell.

Marty pulled the golf cart around a circular cul-de-sac. "We're here."

From the vantage point Marty had chosen, Charlie clearly witnessed the extent of the troubling devastation. Like a white stripe on a skunk's black back, a wide brown strip of dead grass extended both east and west as far as he could see. "Oh man!"

"It's longer." Potter pulled a camera from her jacket pocket and shot a few pictures. "Way longer!"

Charlie jogged from the cart. On sodded ground, he fell to one knee and felt the texture of the lawn. The brown blades were dry and brittle. He felt compelled to ask the obvious question. "Are these areas getting the appropriate feeding and watering?"

"That's part of my job." Marty pushed back his hat, exposing a tan forehead.

Did I accidentally insult our host? "Just checking."

In the large grassy area, lush expanses surrounded the brown. "Why is the dead grass confined to a strip?"

Marty put his hands on his hips. “Isn't that why you're here?”

Charlie's stomach tightened. Director Stanton had severely misjudged the problem's complexity. *This is not some patch of dead grass, and certainly not simple.* Charlie's only confidence came from the prospect of channeling Quincy Grissom to solve the mystery.

He leaned forward, closer to the ground, and examined the boundary between the green and brown areas. “It's sharp, as if someone had drawn a line using a ruler.” He laid on his stomach at the boundary of the healthy and damaged grass. "Can your camera take close-ups?"

"Do you mean macro?"

"I just want to document how sharp this boundary is."

Potter fiddled with the controls and handed him the camera. "Macro auto focus. Just point and shoot." She took her smartphone from her pocket and shot a couple more pictures of the stripe.

Charlie moved in so close that only a few shoots of grass filled the screen. He took a couple of shots to be sure, got to one knee and held out the camera. "See?"

Potter brought the device close to her face. "You're right. One blade is brown and dead immediately next to a healthy green one. This makes no sense."

Charlie ran his fingers through the sod, considering what might cause the stripe to be confined in width yet expanding in length. “This can't be caused by disease.” *Defoliants aren't precise enough. They'd spread out in all directions. Do they make lasers with beams this wide?* Nothing in Charlie's experience explained the distinct separation. He called back to Potter, "Where did you take samples?"

She came along side and pointed. "See, the spots marked with orange flags."

Charlie stood, overwhelmed at the breadth of the damage. "How about the green areas? Did you take samples of those?"

"I didn't think it was necessary." Her tone was apologetic.

"For comparison, we should take samples in the normal areas as well." By "we", Charlie meant himself.

"Great idea." Potter ran back to the golf cart, fetched her bag and pulled her tools from the sample case in an instant.

The first item she extracted was a hollow tube with a horizontal piece, which Potter stepped on to drive the tube into the soil. Charlie wanted a chance to take a sample but Potter was already bagging her first and on to her second. He would have looked like a rookie if he tried.

He approached Potter. "Take a few extra samples from the dead spots, will you?

Potter nodded, efficiently probing and bagging the thin dirt cylinders.

Charlie considered the pattern – the physical pattern – of green and brown grass. "You say it spread from east to west?"

"That's right." Marty's fingertip traced the path of a bouncing ball in the air. "A methodical advance, yard by yard, longer every day. Farther west than when Agent Potter was here last."

Daily? "And it goes all the way to the western edge of the island?"

Marty took a few steps in that direction and pointed. "Yes, all the way to the river."

Charlie focused on gathering information, just like Grissom did. He approached Potter. She was taking more photos of the brown stripe. "How wide is it? Did you measure?"

"No, but we should. I don't have a tape measure long enough. Maybe we can use trigonometry to figure it out." Potter took a handheld telescope from her case. "I can make a rough sextant."

"Excuse me." Marty drove off.

I wonder where he's going? Instead of speculating, which Grissom always avoided, Charlie observed Potter's imagination and ingenuity. She was still typing measurements into her cell phone, focusing on a tree on the other side of the brown stripe when Marty returned in the golf cart.

"Almost exactly fifty feet," he announced.

Charlie was startled. "How'd you figure it out so quick?"

"Length of my watering hose."

In the distance, Charlie saw a black hose stretched across the brown stripe. "Good thinking." He made a note of the stripe's width and put question marks next to the labels "length", "start" and "end."

He walked over to Potter and interrupted her geometry exercise. "It's fifty feet wide. Marty measured." *If we're going to track the spread of the stripe, we'd better know where it is, with some precision. Quincy Grissom once used global positioning to locate an adversary.* He asked Potter, "Do you have a GPS unit in your bag?"

"I don't need a GPS device. I've got my smartphone." She held it up. "There's an app for that."

"It looks like it runs almost exactly east and west. Will you take a measurement in the middle of the stripe?" *If I'm right, all I need is the latitude. The longitude will change along the east-west length.*

"Sure."

Instead of measuring from an approximate middle, Potter took a measurement on one side, then strode the fifty feet to the other side and remeasured. She approached Charlie, holding up her phone. "Here's the latitude. I took two measurements and computed the center."

"Great." Charlie noted latitude 40.690274 in his spiral notebook.

Potter stashed her phone and snapped her tool bag shut. "Is there anything else we should do?"

"I'd like to see the far west end of the stripe, if I could," said Charlie.

"Sure thing." Marty led them back to the cart. "It's not that far."

Potter put the soil samples in a bag and put them on the floor.

Marty drove them south, back the way they'd come, but turned right at the chapel. That put the Parade Grounds on their right. The brown stripe approached them at an angle.

On the left side, a sign read Liggett Hall, a long building containing a variety of food venues.

Potter pointed. "Stop. I have to buy something."

"We've got work to do." Charlie was anxious to see the far end of the island.

"You just have to try one of these. They're delicious." Potter ran inside.

While they waited, Charlie noticed that the brown stripe ran under the road just ahead and came out on the other side. *Marty was right. Nothing gets in its way.*

Potter came out a couple of minutes later with small cylinders in her hands. "They're push-up pops with cake, ice cream and a topping. Take your pick: Almond Vanilla or Harvest Berry." She held the Almond Vanilla treat closer to Charlie, who took the hint.

They consumed their frozen desserts while Marty completed the drive to the west coast of the island, then hung a left through a fenced off area. "This isn't open to the public yet, until development is complete." Their drive followed the coastline, water lapping on the shore.

"Here we are." Marty stayed in the golf cart while Charlie stood on the west bank of the island, where the brown stripe continued under the rocky shore and submerged.

"Should I take another GPS measurement?" asked Potter.

"Good idea."

Potter repeated her process and brought her phone over to show Charlie. "Almost exactly the same value, accounting for measurement error."

Not only is the stripe precise in damage, but also in direction. Charlie scratched his head. *How would Grissom deal with something like this?* He perspired from exposure to the sun. *If roads and buildings don't stop it, then water surely won't.* "Tell me, do you think plant life west of here been affected?"

Potter donned a blue hat with yellow EPA lettering. "You mean, in New Jersey?" Without being asked, Potter took her tool bag from the cart.

"Yes, if that's what's west." He hadn't asked, but Potter was taking additional soil samples.

Potter stopped with a tube still embedded in the ground. "I don't know." She aimed her handheld telescope in that direction. "It's too far to see from here."

"Here's what I think." Charlie gestured with his arm. "The stripe approached from the east, crossed the island and is continuing west." *Predicting its path will be easy, but we still need to figure out where it starts.* "But we need to be sure. What about there?" He pointed to Liberty Island, obvious by its statue, which was approximately west of their position. "Can we take the boat and check if the stripe reached them?" Charlie also wanted a higher vantage point, and the Statue of Liberty might give him that.

Potter looked like she'd just bitten into a dill pickle. "They're not expecting us."

"That isn't a problem, is it?" asked Charlie. "I have Federal jurisdiction."

"I guess not." Potter completed her sampling and packed up her tools.

Charlie's phone rang. It was Lane again. *Is this the way he shows interest, by pestering me? He's plenty to do with the Dan River disaster.*

"Have you learned anything?" Lane asked. *No crunch.*

Lane must have finished his cheesy snack. "Matter of fact, I have. The affected area isn't stagnant in size. It initially appeared on the east side of the island but has spread all the way across with daily progress. Oh, and it's approximately fifty feet wide."

Lane's voice fluttered. "I know this is your first field assignment, and it can get you all pumped up, but don't make this a bigger deal than it is."

Does Lane think I'm exaggerating? "I'm not doing any such thing. The brown stripe is getting longer on its own. Listen, I've got an investigation to run. I'll be in touch." Charlie pocketed his phone.

Marty stuck one leg out of the golf cart and stood up. "Are you folks about finished? I have some things to attend to."

"I think we're done here, at least for the moment." Charlie didn't want to foreclose the possibility of another visit.

Marty drove them back to Pier 101, using a different route. "On your right, that's the New York Harbor School." They approached a huge round brick structure. "And that's Castle Williams, an old coastal fortification."

"Oh, wow. We didn't go this way last time," said Potter.

Further down the coast stood a red metal archway. "That's Soissons Dock, where ferry boats land," said Marty.

"Isn't the view spectacular? Better than a carriage ride in Central Park." Potter hugged Charlie's arm.

Charlie didn't need distractions from their case. Potter's physical attention and the tour around the north coast weren't helping. Another round structure, much smaller, stuck out of the water just off the north coast. "Another fortification?" asked Charlie.

Marty chuckled. "Nope that's the Brooklyn-Battery Tunnel vent shaft. The tunnel runs under the East River very close to the island."

Charlie remembered the bouncy white-knuckled trip over. "Too bad we couldn't have driven here." The soil samples rumbled around on the floor. From his experience, twenty-four-hour turnaround on soil samples was the norm. He expected results from Potter's original soil samples soon, perhaps before he checked into his hotel. "How long will these additional samples take?"

Potter let go. "About two weeks. My original samples are still at the lab."

"Two weeks? It shouldn't take anywhere near that long."

Everybody leaned as Marty took a fast turn. Potter, plastered against Charlie, explained, "Our office outsourced the work to Cayuga Services, an independent lab about two hours away in Poughkeepsie." The passengers regained vertical positions on the straightaway. "Probably a sweetheart deal. They just aren't as responsive as our in-house folks used to be."

"The testing will be more accurate if they're tested quick-"

Potter gave Charlie's shoulder a gentle but firm shove. "I know. I do this for a living."

Charlie silently chastised himself. He had to treat Potter and others like professionals. Too much time as a desk jockey had dulled his skills with people. Assuming he ever had any.

She continued, "The best they've ever done for me was a week, and that's pushing aside some other customers."

"No way to escalate?" Charlie didn't have two weeks to resolve this project. The Director and Lane both thought this was trivial, to test his field skills.

Potter adjusted her cap. "Well, I suppose if it was a national emergency."

Marty turned his head a bit and slowed the cart. "Sorry for eavesdropping. Brooklyn College does soil analysis, and my oldest son goes there. Training to replace his old man some day." He pulled up to the thin wooden dock at Pier 101. The Port Authority boat bobbed in the water, awaiting their departure.

"Can I get his number?" Charlie offered a generic department business card and pen.

"Sure." Marty scribbled his son's name and phone number on the reverse side and handed it back.

"Thanks for all of your help." The boat driver helped Charlie and Potter board. "We're going to Liberty Island," Charlie directed.

The pilot checked his watch. "Not today. This runabout was requisitioned for this afternoon only. It has to go back."

Charlie was disappointed. *That's it, my first day?* He didn't have nearly enough information to solve his case. *I won't be judged successful if I bring back soil sample results but the stripe keeps spreading.*

On the trip back, Potter opened her case and extracted a sandwich in a sealed plastic bag. "Often when I'm in the field, time gets away from me, so I pack something just in case. Hungry?

"No thanks." Charlie had no appetite while the boat jerked and bounced.

Potter shrugged, unzipped the bag and tore into the sandwich. "Mmm, peanut butter and banana."

While she ate, Charlie considered how he could get a better view of the stripe. *How high would I have to be to see its progress, or an origin if there is one?* A tourist helicopter flew over their heads, in the direction of Governors Island.

They pulled into the pier at the Brooklyn Heights Promenade, not the roller-skating one. "Are we supposed to be here?" asked Charlie.

"We should have gone back to Pier 2." She scowled at the pilot.

He pulled a crumpled paper from his pocket. "The requisition says drop off and pick up at Pier 1. I made the detour as a favor."

Charlie handed Potter her tool bag after she climbed out. Then, she gave him a helping hand to disembark.

While they stood on the concrete dock, Charlie asked Potter, “Does your office have any helicopters?”

She shook her head.

Charlie waited for the noise from the boat’s engine to fade before pulling out his phone and calling Lane back at the office. The way Lane answered, it sounded like Charlie had woken him from a nap.

“Okay, here’s what I’ve learned. The affected area has spread east to west across Governors Island who knows how far.” Charlie was speculating, but without the perceived threat, he wouldn’t get what he wanted. “I need air support.”

“What, are you going to drop fertilizer bombs on it?” Lane laughed once at his quip.

“I need to survey from the air how far it extends. The damage isn’t natural, that’s for sure. No disease limits itself to a fifty-foot stripe.”

“I told you, keep it simple.” Lane’s voice had changed from teasing to deadly serious. “Air support is not simple. And helicopters aren't cheap. Why do you need air support for a patch of dead grass?"

"Haven't you been listening to me?" Charlie didn't want to accuse his handler, but needed to ask. "You didn't read the original report, did you?"

"This doesn't happen on any of my other projects." Lane didn't answer Charlie's question.

Charlie raised his voice. "It's an expanding fifty-foot wide swath of dead grass. Do I have to show it to you?" He leaned over to Potter. "Can you send my colleague one of your photos of the stripe? A panoramic shot if you've got one." Given Lane's attitude, Charlie didn't use the term "mentor."

She nodded, swiped and tapped at her smartphone screen. "Got one."

Charlie dictated Lane's email address. She touched SEND, followed by a nod to Charlie. "Check your inbox." He waited.

Lane shouted, "What the hell is that?"

"See? I can only keep it as simple as it is, and it isn't." *That sounded lame.* Charlie took a deep breath. "It's not some run-of-the-mill virus or blight."

"And it's still spreading?"

Finally, a reasonable question, at the heart of Charlie's request. "That's exactly what we need to find out. The most effective way to tell is by air." *And if it spread from east to west, maybe find a point of origin to the east?*

"I've never heard of anything like this. This isn't Photoshopped, is it?"

"Nope, straight from my colleague's phone to you. Just imagine if it keeps spreading west, through the agricultural heartland." Charlie wasn't confident in that prediction, but needed something to push back against Lane's reluctance. "So, about that helicopter?"

"Ignoring the cost for a moment, thing is, I've never done that."

"I'm sure there's a way. Heck, Jane probably knows how, off the top of her head. Do I have to go to Director Stanton?" The Director would take direct contact as a failure on Lane's part.

"No! He made me responsible for you. Okay, I'll figure out how to submit a requisition for a chopper. Maybe I can get some other department to pay for it."

Charlie knew how slow DC bureaucracy worked. "Thanks, and make it a priority request."

"This better not be some wild goose chase, or it's all on your doorstep!"

"This is real enough. You should have seen the definition between the live and dead grass. It's amazingly sharp."

"Okay, I get it. Where should I have the helicopter service contact you?"

"They can just call. I'll use the New York group's office as a temporary home base." Charlie looked at Potter, who nodded.

"I'll let Stanton know what's up. I hope he doesn't crap his pants when I tell him I ordered you a helicopter."

Finally, he's acting like a mentor. "He'll be okay if you show him the photo and advise him it's the best way to find out how far it's spread."

Charlie hung up, with Lane engaged in his assignment. *I hope he'll be helpful instead of just quoting standard procedure. On the other hand, if he takes over, that means I failed.*

A flight of cement steps led up from the dock to promenade level.

"I'll go get the car. Just watch my bag." Potter jogged away as if in a race.

Charlie carried the case to the drop-off/pick-up lane. The number of tourists hadn't dwindled but there was one lone TV truck in the lot. Perhaps there were events to be covered, more exciting than dead grass.

Charlie hugged himself and glanced around attempting to identify threats. *After all, this is New York.*

A tap on his shoulder startled him. "Hi," said the stranger. The "NY1" logo on his jacket and the microphone dangling from his fingers made both his identity and intention obvious.

"Hello." *And that's all he's going to get out of me.*

"Chandler Cummings, NY1 Cable News. I noticed the case." He gestured at the tool bag at Charlie's feet. "You with the EPA? I ask because I cover the environmental beat for my station, and I've never seen you before."

"Just visiting New York." Charlie's answer was intentionally vague.

"Have you heard about the closing of Governors Island? No one is saying anything. Isn't that strange?" The microphone came up slowly, from the reporter's waist to chest-high.

"Maybe there's nothing to tell." Charlie's comment carried more truth than the reporter knew. *I haven't figured anything out yet.*

The mike was now in front of Charlie's face. "There has to be something, otherwise why would the island be closed?"

Charlie wanted to run. *A reporter wouldn't scare off Quincy Grissom.* Cummings didn't deserve any more information. "Who knows?" Charlie punctuated the comment with a shrug.

The sound of squealing tires provided a welcome distraction from the tense conversation Cummings was provoking. Potter had completed a hairpin U-turn and sped towards them. After an abrupt stop, she bolted from the driver's seat and yanked Charlie back. He stumbled but stayed on his feet. She took Charlie's place, face to face with the reporter. "Leave him alone!"

"Hi, Stef. Long time, no see." Cummings raised his arms for a hug but Potter stood frozen. He let his arms drop. "I was just talking to your boyfriend -"

"Back off, or you'll never get insider information again, and I mean ever."

Cummings nodded. "Whatever you say. Nice running into you." He waved off his cameraman with a finger swipe across his throat and walked in the direction of his truck.

"Let's get out of here." Potter's face, redder during her confrontation, was fading back to normal.

She led Charlie to her car. They got in and buckled up.

Charlie didn't want to pry. Besides, he wasn't sure how to phrase the question. *How would Grissom probe for details?* "Why did he call me your boyfriend?"

Potter turned in her seat to face Charlie. "Chan and I were a couple for a while but it didn't work out. His idea of a date was hanging out at my place, eating my food, and watching college sports on my big screen TV."

He sounds like a leech. "I'm sorry."

She patted his knee. "Don't be. I'm glad I found out he was a cheapskate before we got serious. But since he's on the ecology beat, we run into each other. Too often. Sorry you got involved in our drama." Potter started the car. "So, what's next?" She glanced at her watch. "You're probably tired from the trip and all."

Charlie wasn't all that tired, but he did want some time to think about their case. "A little."

"How about if I take you to your hotel before I drop off the soil samples?"

Charlie fished the card with Marty's son's name and number from his pocket. "Here's your contact at Brooklyn College."

"Great, I'll call him before I stop by." She tucked the card in her visor. "Where are you staying?"

He pulled Jane's paperwork from his suit coat pocket. "The Ritz-Carlton New York, Battery Park."

Potter stiffened her arms and pushed herself back in her seat. "Whoa! Is that how Feds travel?"

"Why? Jane said it would be nice-"

"Nice? Probably the best hotel in south Manhattan. And the most expensive."

First a limo, and then an extravagant hotel room? With our departmental budget crisis, I hope Jane doesn't get into trouble.

"I'll take you the scenic route, via the Brooklyn Bridge. You've heard of it?" Potter made a left out of the parking lot, then a quick right onto Old Fulton Street. "Maybe you should take me out to dinner. Someplace upscale. After all, I bought breakfast and lunch."

Even though she's part of the local EPA organization, my dating rule still stands. Would dinner out be a date? Besides, Charlie had read the departmental travel guidelines before he left. "I'm on a limited per diem-"

"I was joking." She slapped his shoulder. "But we could go Dutch treat, if you'd like the company."

"I'm pretty tired. The flight and all. Besides, I could use some time to just think. Make a plan to figure this out." Charlie tucked the paperwork back into his jacket pocket.

"I understand. Maybe tomorrow night?"

Charlie didn't want to commit, one way or the other. "Sure, maybe."

23 – Matt (Eureka, CA)

The puzzle of the portal was bigger than Matt, and he knew it. There was at least one other pile of sticks someplace, and at least one other person was dealing with the same situation. Maybe they'd even figured out what the portal was for, or how to operate it! He took a few photos with his flip phone from different angles, and a photo of the remaining pile of sticks.

He heard the crunch of dry leaves and twigs. He grabbed his backpack from the ground, scurried a dozen feet back on all fours and threw himself behind a redwood.

The stranger Matt had seen before entered the portal construction site, brushing aside bushes and shrubs, this time with a hard-sided tool case. Evidently, photos hadn't been enough. The stranger removed a small box with wires and probes and took readings in the ground and on the portal rods themselves, both the assembled ones and the ones still piled up. The devices must have been retaining the measurements, because he took no notes. He moved deliberately, as if checking things off a list. Then he measured lengths using a laser tool all around the portal. Finally, he pulled out his cellphone and looked at the screen as he slow-stepped around, dawdling on the east edge of the hexagon structure.

The stranger pushed and shoved at the structure but the portal held firm. He pounded on one of the rods angrily and hurt his hand, which he cradled.

Matt's phone sounded a garbled ring in his pocket. The stranger looked around. Matt pulled out the phone, pressed TALK and immediately QUIT to terminate the call. Then he muted the phone to prevent a repeat and scurried out of the wooded area, back to campus.

When he got to his room, he hooked his phone up to his computer. While downloading the pictures, he was interrupted by another call. His folks.

"Just checking in." His mother sounded concerned and caring, as always.

"I'm fine, Mom. Really."

"Good. Your father and I are really pleased with the progress you've made this year."

How did they know?

"Up until this week." His father's voice joined the call and wasn't nearly as comforting. "Why did you get a zero grade on your last engineering quiz?"

Damn, my folks are logging in remotely to my class grade reports. That was one of the systems Bates had funded, implemented, and donated to the college.

Matt hated his parents' micromanagement. "It's complicated." No way could Matt describe the portal to his folks. Even he didn't fully understand, and he was sure they'd have questions. He remained positive. "I'll find a way to make it up." *Building the portal is even more important now.*

After his folks said goodbye, Matt heard a commotion outside. Through his window, he saw the stranger standing on the sidewalk in front of the Administration Building confronting one of the school officials – wasn't she the president of the college? – wagging a finger in her face as if scolding her. Then he jumped into his car, illegally parked and facing the wrong direction, and sped off.

I wonder what that was all about? Matt swallowed hard. *After all, he was just at my portal.*

Matt searched the Internet for a photo social media site and found PictureNet with billions of posted photographs. Perfect! He searched for 'hexagon' and found many matches on the word: photos of the geometric shape, the packaging for the original video game, album covers from a record publisher, and a brochure for an international learning conference. He decided to share a picture by uploading the best one using an old grammar school nickname for the new account: NeedleAndThready. When the form appeared on screen to provide keywords, Matt typed in 'hexagon' as the first entry. He typed 'portal' but deleted it. *No one on the planet would use the word 'portal.'* He typed in his false descriptor, 'trellis' and clicked submit.

24 – Kwashay (Brooklyn, NY)

Kwashay waited, just like the police officer had asked. Eventually, an older gentleman with gray hair around his temples in a dark suit approached from the path that led north. She made incidental eye contact. Per her mother's rules, she said nothing.

"What do you think it is?" asked the old man.

"I'm not supposed to talk to strangers." Kwashay realized that by disavowing a conversation, she'd broken the rule.

He reached into his suit jacket pocket and flashed open a badge holder. "That's okay. I'm Detective Henry Washington, Brooklyn division. What do you know about this?"

Except for the portal, they were alone in the clearing, shielded from the rest of the park by a grove of trees and bushes. Kwashay felt vulnerable – even guilty - but for no good reason. "I saw those rods yesterday on my way back from NYU Polytechnic."

"Oh, are you a college student?"

Kwashay explained her high school status with special dispensation for a college course.

"Well then, you must be pretty smart. Too smart to lie to a police officer."

Kwashay nodded. "I decided to use the rods to build a – a – an art project for school. I began construction yesterday morning."

"And you needed a scaffold to build the high parts?"

"Oh, no! I did like maybe the first layer – maybe two – but then I had to go to class."

"So it wasn't like this yesterday morning?"

"No, sir." Moisture accumulated in her armpits.

"So someone finished it. That's strange, isn't it?"

"Yes, I guess it is." Kwashay didn't volunteer anything about her interactions with Sideways. "I won't be able to claim it as my own work for school credit." She tried to show an ethical attitude.

"We're only interested in the scaffolding, which was stolen from a job site on Flatbush." 'We' became clear as other men wandered in from the walking path carrying satchels. They got to work immediately. Some took photographs, others dusted for fingerprints.

Kwashay glanced at her watch. "I really have to get to class." She stumbled a few steps towards the sidewalk.

"Before you go, I need to get some information from you. Name, phone number, address."

She reluctantly provided the information. If the police called and spoke to her mother, she'd never hear the end of it. Her mother might even die of a heart attack on the spot!

"You don't live in the neighborhood. That's quite a commute."

"Mother wanted me in the best possible school." Kwashay realized she should have included herself in the answer. *Too late.*

"Well, I hope your alternative art project works out."

She nodded, then ran to her school building, Sideways' involvement weighing heavily. *I never wanted him to get into trouble.*

25 – Selton (Kearney, NE)

Selton departed the Kearney Public Library in the late afternoon after reviewing much of section 910, Geography and Travel and an assortment of corresponding fiction titles, the rubber glove tucked into his pocket. He realized that combining both perspectives, fiction and non-fiction, yielded the richest understanding. *I've come to appreciate Earth so much more. I can't wait to share with my fellow Serulians.* However, it took intense concentration and cross-referencing to achieve such a result, much more demanding than merely absorbing and cataloging facts. *The benefit is, I'm distracted from thinking about Dissemination Oversight.* Exhausted, he could barely keep his eyes open as he wandered south toward the railroad yard underpass a few blocks away. Reading in this manner took more out of him than when he had begun his learning journey. *Loss of energy might be another symptom of ripening, or perhaps the grass I've selected isn't as nutrient-rich.*

As he sauntered past the shiny black window of Tiny's Bar and Grill, he remembered an interaction with the owner of the establishment. On that day, Selton had paused to examine his reflection with the two lumps. The owner commented "You need something to cover those," went inside and returned with a resizable white baseball cap yellowed with human sweat. "Somebody left it behind. Here, you need it more than them." The oversized cap had been an ineffective covering for the two lumps, yielding to the alternative of an old cloth head wrap.

As he walked, Selton felt his healed head under Marathon's fedora, remembering the lumps, spongy to the touch, before he squeezed them open. What had they been? Intentional growths programmed into his physiology or some kind of allergic reaction? And if they were intentional, to what purpose? The floating filaments that blew away in both eastbound and westbound clusters hadn't looked like anything he'd learned from science texts. They couldn't be seeds because the ability to germinate would be useless for a Serulian information gatherer. *I still have that captured filament to analyze.*

Perhaps Selton was having a reaction to the elements in the local soil? That never happened in any of the other cities he'd ever visited. His unique horticultural physiology had always been an effective filter against hazardous contaminants. *Perhaps those filters are failing.* He indexed his way through the long list of flora-related diseases but stopped abruptly at the red light. *No value in guessing.*

Selton stood on the corner, obeying the traffic signal. There were few pedestrians, and none heading his way. Cars passing by likely viewed him as a vagrant, a homeless person, a hobo making a stop before boarding a freight car out of town, and good riddance. He dressed the part in a threadbare shirt covered by a thigh- length military jacket with big pockets, elbow patches and insignias on the shoulders and chest, well-worn work pants, no socks, and sneakers with holes that exposed several of his stick toes.

Selton crossed with the light, allowing a left-turning vehicle to pass in front of him. He almost tipped his hat in response to the driver's wave of thanks. The sun was dropping quickly, darkening the underpass, Selton's current home. His bindle with his few possessions, including the captured filament, was still there, undisturbed. He prepared for his evening feeding, examining the grass for a green patch. He stepped past many brown areas, each in the shape of his upper body, previous nourishment sites. A train hauling produce sat in the rail yard. *I could consider sleeping in a refrigerator car to slow my ripening, but then I wouldn't get the necessary nutrition.*

As Selton opened his shirt, the ground vibrated under his feet, either an earthquake or more likely an incoming communication from Dissemination Oversight. A glance around at the budding trees and shrubs confirmed the arrival of spring, the time for their annual message. *Finally! Hurray! I'm going home!* The frequency of this familiar oscillation measured lower than the rumble of a train on its tracks. The first time he'd experienced a message from them as a teenager, he'd panicked, thinking he'd gone mad or contracted some form of disease. Nothing was shaking except him.

The rumble moved up his legs, torso and neck, like plucks of a bass eventually reverberating inside his head. Low frequency, deep and resonant. So many of these annual communications were empty good wishes for his continued health and success. *This time, they must be ready to provide instructions for my return to Serulia with all of my accumulated knowledge.*

As usual, the vibrations translated into sounds, delivered through his own mouth. This year's message struggled in delivery, gibberish with no meaning. Selton squatted, as if being closer to the ground would clear up the transmission. Waiting for the sounds to make sense, he noticed a silhouetted individual with an exaggerated swagger approach the underpass, backlit by the setting sun. Selton stood up and clamped his lips shut. *Railroad security? Police? I can't be interrupted now!* He smoothed his roots discretely against his back and buttoned his shirt.

The evening sun formed an aura around the middle-aged man. "Hello, Punkin. I mean, Professor. And not looking a day older. How you do that?"

The face and the voice of the individual were familiar. "Suh-suh-suhhh" escaped from Selton's mouth.

He blinked and fought the urge to babble. "Sprint?" The vibrations subsided. *Not now!*

Marathon's son plucked his suspenders. "One in the same. Call myself Magic Jack now." The young man had grown into middle age, and by his looks, was obviously Marathon's offspring.

With the communications opportunity lost, Selton greeted his adoptive brother with open arms. Sprint extended his arm for a handshake instead. "I haven't seen you or your father for a long time. How is he?"

"Pops caught the Westbound a few years ago."

Marathon Man was dead? "I'm so sorry. He was a good friend when we traveled together." Marathon had shown Selton the ways of the traveling hobo, how to catch trains without getting caught, how and where to mooch food and supplies. Since a green lawn was all he ever needed for sustenance, the food lessons were irrelevant but Selton always played the dutiful and attentive student. "Where is he buried?"

"Out in Arizona, one of his favorites." Sprint rubbed his palms on his wrinkled slacks, a gesture he'd inherited.

Selton would have normally considered traveling to pay his respects, but his ties to Kearney were unusually strong.

"And how have you been?" Selton remembered Sprint's lackluster habits before they'd parted ways.

"Beatin' my way coast to coast, mostly below Mason/Dixon. Workin' some, when I have to. Make use of what others don't need."

Scrounging trash or by theft?

Sprint pulled a red bandana from his pocket and mopped perspiration from his expanded forehead. "One trip to the Big Burg and I got sloughed." He'd been arrested in New York City. "How about you?"

"I settled in." Selton had stayed in Kearney longer than any other destination. Would he be able to get home to Serulia before rotting? The instances of physiological trauma were mounting up: first the bumps and then his softening.

"You don't look so bad for the wear, though. How do you keep so fit?"

"A consistent diet." Sprint looked older than his years, gray hair, a pot belly and clothes as shabby as Selton's. "Are you sure you're okay?"

"I'm getting by. Say, you wanna keep that hat?"

Selton adjusted the fedora. "Yes, it's a memento of your father." He tugged it tight.

"Just askin'." Sprint pushed his hands deep into his pockets, dragging his pants down despite the suspenders. "Speaking of which, how strong are you?" Sprint wanted to know how much money he had.

Is that what I've become, just another mark? Marathon would have wept – his son the tramp. *If I gave Sprint my fedora, he'd probably sell it.* "A weak pile." Selton reached into his pocket and pulled out a few frogskins, some of the bills Marathon had given him that he never spent. "Here."

"Thanks." Sprint jammed them into his pocket, as if he were afraid Selton would ask for them back. "Listen, me and some of my crew are catching the 564 U. P. Want to ride along, for old times sake?"

It was surprising that Sprint made the invitation. Their relationship had suffered in the years before Selton had broken it off. However, crisscrossing the country with someone who can provide answers to any question was a solid benefit. "I can't go with you."

"I know. You found yourself a library."

Sprint had been a teenager when Selton had split off from Marathon, somewhere out East if memory served. The names of the cities Selton had visited faded, as a byproduct of his travels. His memory of librarians was stronger but not perfect. What was of ultimate importance, what Selton needed to reinforce by repetition, was Earth's knowledge.

Selton was planning on reviewing one of his favorite sections in the library – the 930s, ancient Earthling history – the next day. "At least, not at this time, but thank you for asking."

Selton repeated his offer of a hug. Sprint hesitated before participating, his hands making an impression on Selton's sides. "You look healthy but you feel a little soft. Get some exercise and tone up."

Yet another unwelcome confirmation of Selton's ripening. "Too much time sitting in the library, perhaps." Past that phase, his body would deteriorate to pulp and all of the accumulated knowledge would go to waste. His superiors had just tried to contact him when Sprint showed up. *They have to try again, don't they?* "You stay clear of John Law, you hear?" Selton wanted no part of the police, for either himself or Sprint.

Sprint pointed his index finger. "You too!"

Selton desired to lecture Sprint about his behavior, but thought better of it. *Marks provide money, not advice. He'll do what he wants.* "Be safe." One thing puzzled. "Why do you now call yourself Magic Jack? Sprint was a fine name."

"Watch closely." He pulled a quarter from his pocket, held it between his thumb and index finger and grabbed at it with his other hand. "Where did it go?" He held up his hands, both empty.

Selton didn't confront Sprint about the shiny object held out of sight by two tightly-pressed fingers. "Very good."

Sprint took a couple of steps, stopped, and turned around. "One thing. Remember that creepy preacher lady? Billi something?"

Selton's vivid memory of Reverend Billi Dogood interrupting his nightly feeding flashed back, her extreme reaction when he pulled loose from the soil. "Yes, I do."

"Well, she tracked us down, Pop and the rest, a couple of times, looking for you. And she's not traveling alone. She's got herself a flock of followers."

"I'll be on the lookout.

Selton watched Sprint dash through a gap between cars of a parked train and out of sight. *Reverend Dogood is tracking families of hobos on the move. She won't find a rooted one in Nebraska.*

Selton stood motionless, waiting for the vibrations that would instruct him to return. Time crawled by, his shadow lengthening. He rocked back and forth, trying to instigate the vibrations. No message. He sank to the ground and hugged himself. *If Dissemination Oversight tried to communicate, they're not going to let me rot.*

The appearance of his step brother was less than satisfying. Preparing to lie down for rest and replenishment, he contemplated Sprint's lifestyle. Life on the rails had been only a means to an end for Selton, a way of traversing the country, providing him access to the broadest variety of community, university, public, and occasionally, private libraries. His backroots punctured the soil, his attitude optimistic that the vibrations would return so that he could get instructions for a trip home.

26 – Charlie (New York City, NY)

The next morning, Charlie woke to his alarm clock. The mystery novel lay on the bed beside him. *Must have fallen asleep reading.* He wandered into the bathroom and showered, thinking about Quincy Grissom's progress on the credit card caper.

> After confirming that other credit card holders had been impacted in the same manner as his client, the Customer Service Vice President at Indulge Financial was nominally more receptive, providing a list of the common companies from which all of those affected cardholders had made purchases. *Always patterns!* To assist with the legwork, Grissom enlisted a few of his college student helpers in various cities to do preliminary investigations. Grissom called them The Undergrads, students he'd identified through the Admissions departments at major universities across the country, brought into service when necessary. Grissom knew many university administrators, having been a well-published college professor of mathematics and logic before transitioning to private investigation. Each of the hand-picked students understood the privilege, as well as the requirement to

keep their grades high, despite this added responsibility. It didn't hurt that they were paid for their work.

A plate containing the remnants of Charlie's room service, a steak bone, baked potato skin and the hard stalks from steamed broccoli, sat on the end table next to the sofa. He took a moment to stare out the window. His room faced the river, including Governors Island with its brown stripe and Liberty Island, his destination.

The room phone rang. "Keyson."

"It's Potter. You wanted an early start. I'm downstairs."

"I'll be right there." He put the room service tray outside his door, threw on his suit jacket, slung his bag over one shoulder and took the elevator.

Potter was leaning against the wood-framed archway leading to the main entrance. "Nice digs?"

Charlie had no frame of reference. "I guess. I had a view of the river."

"Ooh, fancy. Come on, the police will cut me only so much slack for double-parking." Potter led him out to her car. They both got in. "So, what did you do for dinner last night?"

"Just room service."

"And your novel, right?"

"Uh-huh." Charlie buckled up. "So, how much time can you afford? I mean, to work on this case?"

"It's a case, is it?" She smiled. "All the time you need. After all, I'm your partner." The way she said it gave Charlie pause. *She can't be interested in me. We're working together, that's all.*

Charlie's stomach gurgled. At home, he would have gobbled down a bowl of cereal. He'd been so eager, he'd forgotten about eating. "Can you stop at a fast food drive-through? I haven't had any breakfast."

"So I heard." She patted his knee. "I know just the place. You must have a healthy diet, because you're in great shape."

Charlie thought about his daily commute. "I walk a lot."

"Maybe we should take a walk some night, for exercise and build our appetites for dinner." Potter pulled into the drive-thru lane of a QuickBites. Charlie leaned towards the driver's window and read the menu. "Order me an egg and sausage biscuit and a cup of black coffee." *Hardly healthy, but fast.* He reached for his wallet.

Potter pulled some bills from her shirt pocket. "This one's on me. You're on the hook for dinner." Another smile.

The food and her money were exchanged and they were on their way.

"I dropped off the soil samples last night with Dean-"

"Dean?" Charlie unwrapped the sandwich on his lap, leaving the coffee in a cup holder between their bucket seats.

"Marty, the caretaker's son?"

Charlie paused between bites and verified both names in his notepad. "Right," he mumbled.

Potter's route took them back over the Brooklyn Bridge. "So what's the plan for today? After breakfast, I mean."

Charlie quick-chewed a mouthful. "We'll examine the lawn at the Statue of Liberty, and use the statue's height to get a better vantage point."

"To see how far this disease has spread?" she asked.

Charlie took a quick sip of coffee and then wiped his mouth with a napkin. "Yeah, but I'm pretty sure it's not a disease. The boundaries between the healthy and dead areas are too sharp. Too crisp."

"Then what is it?" Potter checked her mirrors and changed lanes.

"That's what we're going to find out. If my contact Brad Lane back at the Bureau comes through with a helicopter, we'll get an aerial view."

"I have to tell you, I'm really impressed with how you've taken charge. The EPA in Washington is lucky to have you."

Charlie was a bit embarrassed. Taking charge hadn't been his style in the office, but field work required a different demeanor. *If I'm ever going to get a second field assignment, I'd better be successful with this first one.* He'd been making things up as he went along, logical steps in the face of absurdity. "Thanks."

There was more traffic entering Manhattan than leaving, so the drive to Pier One didn't take very long. Charlie finished his breakfast and chugged about half of the coffee.

The crowd of reporters had thinned out considerably. Only a couple of news teams had trucks parked and cameras aimed at Governors Island. *No sign of Chandler Cummings.*

One attempted an interview, but Potter deflected their approach. "We don't handle PR." She swung her tool case in a wide arc, keeping the reporter at a distance.

"Yeah, that's why we want to talk to you," complained the reporter from Channel 6. "To get the real scoop."

It looked like the same boat as the previous day, with the same pilot. Potter handed the pilot her tool bag, which had been essential the previous day. Charlie nodded an acknowledgment to the pilot, took a seat and held on.

This ride was longer and choppier, maybe because they were further out in the river.

Three-quarters of the way, Potter leaned over and shouted, "Welcome to New Jersey. My office covers both states."

"Great," Charlie hollered back. *And if there are any issues, I'm Federal.*

When they arrived at a small pier at Liberty Island, uniformed guards waved them off.

"Can't they read?" Charlie stood and pointed to the official markings on the side of the boat. They kept waving for the boat to depart. Charlie tried holding up his badge, as if the guards could see it from their distance. "Federal agent," he shouted.

Potter tugged his jacket. "There's a jurisdiction thing out here. The island is technically run by New York but the water surrounding it is New Jersey.

"I don't care about local squabbles. Take us in!" said Charlie.

The pilot obliged despite the armed guards' protests.

Because there was no way for the guards to effectively fend off the boat, the pilot successfully pulled alongside a small jetty.

One guard stood on the pier, waving his arms. "Private boats aren't allowed."

"This isn't a private boat. Property of Port Authority." He pointed to the logo on the hull and showed his badge. “We’re here on official government business. Same team, right?”

As soon as the two guards heard “Port Authority”, they backed off.

Charlie and Potter climbed off the boat, finally on site at Liberty Park. In the background stood the Lady herself, watching out across the harbor. Charlie was also a watcher, looking out for toxins and imbalances that threatened the population at large, keeping the huddled masses safe.

The pair walked toward the north edge of the island. Sure enough, there was a stripe, but not the same uniform color as on Governor’s Island. *Is the stripe fading? That would be a good thing.*

Charlie pointed to Potter’s pocket. “You got your phone?”

“Never without it. You want another GPS reading?”

Potter is smart. And, we’re working like partners. “I sure do.” Although Charlie couldn’t see Governors Island clearly, he was willing to bet that the stripes lined up perfectly.

Potter took two measurements and delivered the averaged latitude. Charlie checked the number against the one from Governors Island in his notebook. “Almost an exact match.”

But why the discoloration? It breaks the pattern.

“They can’t be from the same cause,” said Potter. “There’s water in between.“

“Maybe the cause is airborne. Or maybe-” He was distracted by a grounds maintenance man pushing a manual lawn feeder, walking up and back on the turf. Charlie approached him. “How’s it going?”

"Could be better. Keeping this lawn healthy is more than a full-time job."

"Really? What's the problem?"

"We got this brown patch, more like a runway, right along the northern tip of the island. I figure must be watering or nutrients, so I overfeeded when the grass went brown. And I over-fertilize it, just to be sure."

"And have you been successful?"

"Works every time, but then it goes brown again." He pushed his New York Yankees baseball cap back on his head. "It's taking heavier applications every time to bring the grass back, though. Doesn't make sense. Where's it all going?"

Charlie made a note of the question but had no answer. "How much watering has it received?"

The man glanced at Potter, who'd joined Charlie at his side. "You've got a lot of questions."

Charlie flashed the badge again. "Federal agent, EPA. We're investigating the issue."

The lawn man smiled. "Glad you folks finally took an interest. I've complained I don't know how many times. We water the grounds on a fixed schedule." He pointed at a maintenance building. "I can fetch the logbook-"

"That's not necessary. But my partner and I are going to take some soil samples." Charlie remembered their procedure from the previous day. "And some photographs."

"Fair enough. I got to keep going if I'm gonna keep this lawn healthy." The maintenance man grabbed the handles of his feeder and marched away in a straight line.

"Would you like to use my camera -- partner?" asked Potter.

"Yes, please." He took the camera from her and pointed at the striped grass. "Equally-spaced samples, just like yesterday. Green and brown locations."

Potter saluted. While she performed the sampling, Charlie took photos.

Potter returned with eight tubes of soil. "Four each, marked with flags."

"Great. We'll need to get them analyzed." He reached out to return the camera.

"You keep it. It'll give me an excuse to requisition a newer model. Better zoom. More pixels." Potter took a couple of shots with her phone. "Just in case you want to send Lane some more documentation."

"Thanks. All right, we'll use-" The card with Marty's son's name and number was missing from his wallet.

Potter removed the card from her pocket. "You mean Marty's son Dean at Brooklyn College?"

"Yeah, him." Charlie looked east toward Manhattan. "I wish I had a better view." He pointed to the crown on the Statue. "How about from there?"

They walked towards the statue. A line extended from the entrance around the base, people waiting for a climb to the top.

Charlie's phone rang. Caller ID said it was Lane. "Keyson."

"This is Brad Lane. I had to pull in a favor, but I got you the helicopter. It's scheduled for three days from now."

"Three days? The Director thinks I'll have this all wrapped up and be back in DC in a couple of days at worst." *Lane's been useless.*

"Listen, that's the best I can do. If you're so smart, get one yourself." The click was immediate.

So much for support.

27 – Matt (Eureka, CA)

A group of three students with tool belts on their waists met up with Matt at his room, just like Fred had promised. Fred himself was noticeably absent. Matt gave them directions and jogged along as they drove to the corner of campus. They parked their pick-up truck full of two-by-fours and plywood planks near the Warehouse/Mailroom building adjacent to the portal's wooded area. Matt escorted them to the clearing where the portal stood, barely half complete.

"I've never seen anything like that before," said one of the guys. "What is it?"

Matt reused his previous lie. "A trellis, for my engineering class."

"How high you gotta go?" asked the unofficial foreman.

Matt closed his eyes and pictured the final result. "Eight feet total. Another two levels, so about four feet higher."

The foreman looked at the portal, the sticks and his crew. "You want us to just finish building the trellis instead of a scaffold?"

Matt remembered the shop student who wrenched his back in an attempt to construct the portal. *These guys don't look nearly as strong.* "No thanks. I've gotta do it myself to get credit."

"Okay, but with four of us, we'd be done a lot quicker."

They don't know that the sticks get heavier the higher you lift them. "Thanks for the offer. Really."

The foreman shrugged. "No problem."

First, the crew fetched the lumber from their truck, a few pieces at a time. Then, using battery-powered nail guns and a circular saw, they assembled the raised platform that surrounded the portal, per Matt's direction. Matt sat on the ground, watching their progress. Quicker than Matt expected, they were done.

"That's terrific!" Matt pictured himself finishing the portal and then waiting for instruction on how to operate it. *I wonder how the other portal is coming.*

The foreman hung back as the others left. "If you need us to, we can raise it. That might have to be done, you know, if you're going eight feet high."

Matt was pleased with Fred's negotiation. "Gee, thanks. I'll let Fred know."

He waited until they departed, and then began stacking sticks onto the scaffold. At four feet, it took all of Matt's strength to lift each stick. Once a few were on the raised surface, he climbed up. Although he could position a stick at a junction point, the weight of a stick made it impossible to lift into vertical position. And if he couldn't do that, then putting horizontals in place above the verticals was a lost cause. The platform was a failure, a dud.

What now? Matt planted his head in his hands. *I've got to get the portal completed. The planet depends on it.* Matt laid down on the platform and curled up, clutching a stick, exhausted. *I just need a minute to rest.*

28 – Kwashay (Brooklyn, NY)

Kwashay left BTHS at the end of the school day, the weight of her encounter with the police that morning on her shoulders. One block up Flatbush towards NYU Polytechnic, a police car pulled up alongside.

"Ms. Williams-Jackson?" It was Detective Washington, being driven by a uniformed officer.

Had he waited all day outside school for her? "Yes, sir?"

"I'm afraid you're going to have to come with us. You're what we call a 'person of interest' in the theft of the scaffolding."

Despite the fact that Sideways used the scaffold to complete the portal, Kwashay wanted the whole issue to go away. "The construction company will get it back, right? And no one got hurt."

"Yes, but that doesn't erase the fact that a crime was committed."

She wasn't done pleading her case. "But I'll miss my class-"

"It's all right." Washington stepped from the passenger seat. "I'll give you a note for your teacher." He opened the back door. "Please, get in and watch your head."

The advice was valuable, because the roofline of the sedan was thicker and the door frame smaller than on a regular car. "Where are we going?"

"Not far. Just to the 84th Precinct."

Their destination was only a few blocks from school on Gold Street.

Kwashay couldn't ignore the wetness in her armpits. Hopefully, her mother would never know about this.

Detective Washington led Kwashay through a room full of desks, down the hall to a series of meeting rooms. The detective chose an empty one and, with a wave of his arm, invited her to enter.

Kwashay sat across the table from him, examining his face, the creases at the corners of his eyes and lips.

He spoke softly. "That structure in the park, that's an art project you said?"

"Yes." Kwashay was supposed to do a project for her art class. She'd decided to sculpt in clay but neither the detective nor her teacher knew that. "I probably should have asked for permission to build it in the park -"

"That's not why you're here. I'm only interested in the scaffold. You told the officers you didn't know where it came from?"

"That's right. It was there that morning. I'd never seen it before."

"And you told me that you didn't build the whole art thing. You just started on it. So you didn't personally finish it?" He pushed a glossy photo in front of her, the structure surrounded by the scaffold.

I'm glad it's done. "That's correct. I had to get to class, so I left." *I wonder how soon I'll be called on to operate it?*

"Well, it seems pretty clear to me that someone was trying to be nice to you. Do you a favor. Given the weight and the number of pieces for the scaffold, it probably wasn't an individual."

Sideways and his crew. But she couldn't tell, could she? "I don't know, I mean-"

The detective leaned on the table. "Do you have any idea who might have wanted to help you?"

Commotion outside the room meant only one thing. *Someone called my mother.*

The door opened a crack. A voice outside said, "You can't go in-"

"The heck I can't. You've got my little girl in there, and I want to see her." The door swung wide. Mother strode in, marched to the far side of the table and threw her arms around her daughter's neck. "Are you all right? What have they done to you?"

"We're just talking." Kwashay was both pleased and embarrassed.

Mother turned her attention to the detective, who'd stood up. "What gives you the right to haul my daughter down here and treat her like a criminal?"

"Mrs. Williams-Jackson?" He stood and buttoned his suit jacket. "I'm Detective Washington." He maintained his low-key demeanor. "A section of scaffolding was stolen from a construction site and the parts have been used to build a platform around your daughter's art project."

She glared at her daughter. "Well, I'm sure she didn't have anything to do with it. Tell them, dear, and we'll be on our way."

"I already told them I didn't take-"

Washington held up his open palm. "Please, let me be clear. We don't believe Kwashay dismantled the scaffold from the job site and reassembled it in the park. It would have been a big job, even for a crew of men."

"Well, then that's that." Mother took Kwashay by the upper arm and dragged her to standing.

Washington blocked their exit. "But we think she might know who did. We have witnesses who remember a group of local youth in the vicinity the night before, and a pick-up truck parked alongside the park."

"Tell them you don't socialize with any thieves or criminals."

Kwashay paused.

"Tell them, sweetheart. You don't know anything about this, right?"

"I don't know how it got there. Honest." She looked to her mother with moist eyes. She couldn't lie. "But there's this boy-"

Her mother grabbed her shoulders, forcing eye contact. "You're hanging out with some boy? Is that why you've been late? You're grounded now for sure. No more excuses about coming home late from school for you."

"What's his name?" asked the detective.

"I, I, I don't know his name."

"Come now. Can you really expect us to believe that you never exchanged names?"

Kwashay stood at attention, whipping her shoulders to free herself from her mother's grasp. "That's right. In my head, I call him Sideways because that's how he wears his cap."

"All of the young street kids in that neighborhood wear their hats that way. But you could probably recognize him from a photograph?"

"Yes, I guess I could." *But I won't.*

"Fine. I'll have someone bring in an album of young men from the area-"

Her mother shielded her daughter with an outstretched arm. "Oh no you don't. You're not putting my daughter in jeopardy. Fingering criminals. And then they find out and take revenge on us. You can't protect us, so don't even say you can. We're leaving."

Washington took one step forward. "I could force Kwashay to stay as a material witness-"

Mother glared at him.

He pulled at his suit lapels. "- but you can go for now. Here's my card, in case you remember something or want to talk."

Kwashay slid the detective's card into her pocket. She was glad to be leaving the police station but dreaded the lecture and punishments her mother would impose.

Her mother didn't even wait until they'd walked down the station steps. "How could you? I'm doing everything I can to save up for college, scrimping and saving, skipping things just so you can be the success I know you can be. And how do you thank me? You slap me in the face by hanging out with street thugs and lying about it."

Kwashay's head turned at the warble of a fire engine racing past the park.

"Pay attention to what I'm saying! I'm in hot water with my supervisor for taking time off at such short notice. A cab down here emptied my wallet! And you? You could have been thrown in jail as an accessory after the fact, you know that?"

"But I didn't ask him to-"

"You didn't need to ask. A pretty young lady like you, any young man would move heaven and earth to make a good impression. Before dragging you off, I mean, and doing unspeakable things. Lord have mercy!"

Kwashay stopped in her tracks. "Sideways isn't like that. He's a gentleman."

"And a thief and maybe even worse. You got to stay away from him, you hear me? He'll bring you nothing but bad news." Her mother led them to the train station.

Kwashay hung her head and strode to keep up. "Yes, Mama."

"Besides, what kind of art project needs a scaffold? Couldn't you make a vase or a coffee cup, or maybe crochet something?"

Mama would never understand her obligation to building the portal and the benefits it would bring to humanity. "You always taught me to think big."

29 – Selton (Kearney, NE)

Sprint's appearance the previous evening triggered Selton's visit the next morning to section 170, Ethics of Sex and Reproduction seeking new or updated information. He had always been fascinated by the social order of families within hobo communities, especially parental responsibilities. Marathon had done his best, which evidently hadn't been good enough. Selton was relieved that, as a non-seed bearing information gatherer, he'd face no such dilemma.

After a full day of reading and absorbing new and updated facts and figures about population, genetics and space travel, Selton returned to home base, the shaded arched space of the train underpass. The mixture of broken concrete and gravel, although a safe place for Selton to hide his limited personal belongings tucked along the wall, was useless for nutrition. Because he'd exhausted adjacent green spaces, he was forced to wander further out to grassy areas for his evening feeding and regeneration rituals.

That night, before he could take one step on his quest, a tink-tink-tink sound came from his bag. Upon examination, the captured filament was banging against the preserves jar, desperate for release. Despite memories about the bumps on his head from which the filaments escaped, Selton had not yet examined the lone captive. Fading sunlight provided less than optimum conditions. He decided to defer the analysis until the light was better and he was rested and replenished.

The City of Kearney Parks and Recreation headquarters on 1st Avenue and Railroad Street across from the train depot offered a lush, maintained lawn. Selton crossed the street, the filaments a nagging memory. He stumbled toward the grassy patch between the main building and the garage at the back of the property, avoiding previously used brown areas and direct visibility from the street. The weather had been unusually warm and the dirt was crumbly, not at all inviting. He removed his coat and shirt and placed them on the nearby sidewalk to prevent them from getting any dirtier. His backroots, pressed tight against his body all day, stretched out as he lay down. They dug deeper than normal and suckled the ground, seeking a filling comfort. Although Selton felt pinned down, almost as if he was being sucked below the surface, he was glad to feel earth against his body.

Shallow inhales alternated with expansive exhales pushing oxygen into the Nebraska sky. Selton crooned softly as he rested. To Selton's untrained ears, he sounded like a musical instrument searching for the proper pitch. In a library in Pottsville, PA, longitude 40.685646, latitude 76.195499, he'd listened to hours of classical music, from Claudio Monteverdi to Igor Stravinsky. Although it wasn't the kind of information he'd been tasked with accumulating, it soothed him. He'd thought briefly about acquiring a music-playing device.

But carting heavy or awkward-shaped possessions across the country in a bindle wasn't convenient.

Nightly regeneration remained easy, as long as Selton could find patches of ground that hadn't been covered by asphalt or concrete, and had not been depleted of nutrients, either by native biology or his nightly rituals. He would soon need to broaden his range of exploration as time passed, because the grassy areas both near the rail yard and the park district office were nearly depleted from his nightly visits.

Selton's curiosity wouldn't let go of the two lumps mystery. He had no expectation that Earthling resources, no matter how wide-ranging his exploration for information, would bring clarity or resolution to the issue. His speculation drifted to a common Earthling disorder: cancer. Could the bumps have been Selton's version? So many Earthling inhabitants suffered with such cellular conditions. As vegetable instead of animal, perhaps this was the way a cancer would expose itself. If so, what were the filaments, and why did they fly off in opposite directions?

And the vibrations that almost forced those unintelligible sounds out of his mouth? All of the previous communications with Dissemination Oversight had been clear. *Why was the last one so garbled?* Selton was waiting anxiously for recall instructions. If his body was ripening, then the timing and method for his return to Serulia had to be approaching. It was another mystery piled on top of the others. Hours passed before Selton could purge his mind enough to relax and reenergize.

30 – Charlie (Liberty Island, NY)

Charlie looked up at the New York skyline. "There are helicopters all over." One, performing a sightseeing tour by air, flew close enough for him to read the name on its fuselage: NY SIGHTS. "See, why can't we get one of those?"

"Brilliant!" Potter closed up her bag. "We'll rent a private chopper, and you can expense it."

Charlie didn't know how his Director would react to such a travel expense, but expectations for quick resolution were clear. And, obtaining one himself would rise to Lane's challenge. It was worth the risk. "Okay, find us one."

Potter tapped and swiped on her cellphone, waiting intermittently for results. "I've got one. Perfect name. Liberty Helicopters. They claim to have the biggest fleet." Without asking, Potter changed from searching to calling. Her conversation was brief. "They'll have one here in fifteen minutes."

"Great." He glanced at the growing tourist line for the statue. "Then we can skip the climb." He hadn't been looking forward to it, and a helicopter would be mobile and provide better visibility.

On time, a bright red helicopter with the name "Liberty" on the side flew overhead and landed at a distance from the statue and the pair.

The pilot got out and came over. "Are you the couple looking for a private tour? We can do that, but the best value is one of our standards. Brooklyn Bridge, Statue of Liberty of course, -"

The pilot talked in one continuous stream. Charlie chose not to interrupt.

"- Ellis Island, Chrysler Building, Empire State Building, Central Park, and a Manhattan scenic tour including Yankee Stadium, the George Washington Bridge, Uptown, midtown and downtown Manhattan, plus the Verrazano bridge, all for the low price of $295 plus a $30 heliport fee." He smiled at the completion of his memorized sales pitch.

"We're EPA agents." Once more, he flashed his badge. "We want a custom flight plan."

"Oh, I'm sorry. I thought you were a couple looking for a private excursion. I had no idea-"

This guy thinks we're a couple? "You'll take us where we want to go?"

The pilot almost saluted. "Yes. Of course. For government business, anywhere."

He'll probably charge inflated government rates. "Great. Then let's get going. I'll explain after we're airborne."

Charlie and Potter got into the back seat, both with window views. "You got headsets?"

"Sure do. We use them mostly for aerial engagements. You know, popping the question?"

"We're already partners." Potter grinned.

Charlie curled his lip. "We'll need them for in-flight communication."

The pilot fetched a pair from rear storage. "They're voice activated. I can hear everything you say, so keep it clean." He winked.

"Start out heading west, okay?" To Potter, Charlie said, "You know what we're looking for."

She nodded: the helmet slid forward on her head.

The chopper took off, hovering over Liberty Island.

Charlie hadn't expected the noise level. Even with heavily padded headphones, the sound of blades rotating above his head made him want to shout. Follow it west."

"Where should I head, specifically?" asked the pilot.

"See the brown stripe down there?"

It took a moment, but then the pilot nodded. "Got it. Boy, that's big!"

"Follow it straight west." Charlie wanted to know if the brown stripe had any limitations for expansion.

"I can't go much farther into New Jersey due to air traffic. Newark Airport airspace is strictly off limits. Our company has special approval for the islands only."

Charlie was frustrated but understood the safety concerns. "Okay. Take us as far as you can without getting into trouble, then double back and follow it east."

"What is it? Some kind of fungus?"

"That's what we're trying to find out. With your help."

They'd flown west for only a minute when the helicopter banked at a sharp angle. It was clear the pilot had gotten radio communication from some air authority, probably Newark Airport control or the FAA. "They're warning me off. I've got to change course."

"Fine. Due east, follow the trail."

As the helicopter made its turn, Charlie surveyed Jersey below. "Looks like they took some damage."

The brown stripe had continued west at a consistent width through the south end of what was obviously a golf course.

The helicopter, now headed east, made a pass over Liberty Island. As instructed, the pilot used the striped lawn at the north end of the island as a directional beacon. Less than a minute later, they approached Governors Island. "Boy, that place is in worse shape."

"We saw it up close." Charlie appreciated the extent of the problem better from the air.

The pilot maintained a straight course, headed over the Brooklyn Piers area. "Sorry, but I've lost it. It's all buildings."

"No, look, there's a small park, all brown." Charlie kept watch for other markers.

"I recognize it," said Potter. "Van Voorhees Park, near Pier 7."

"Keep going straight. Follow it.." Charlie put his face at the window, straining to maintain his view the brown stripe.

"That's what I'm doing. But I don't know what you expect to find-"

"There." Charlie pointed. He and Potter leaned against their windows. "The stripe ends right down there. We found the origin!" Charlie felt the blush of first success.

It was as if someone had painted a narrowing brown stripe across the grass and foliage, terminating at a small structure standing in an otherwise green expanse among a cluster of trees.

"Where is that?" asked Charlie. "And what's that thing?"

"Looks like something for climbing on in a playground." said the pilot.

"Swing around so we can take a better look." *The pot of gold at the end of a brown rainbow?*

The chopper pivoted and hovered, pointing the front window at the object so both passengers could see.

"It's the wrong shape for a playground climber," said Potter. "Those get smaller at the top, closed like a dome. This is a hexagon, open at the top. Wait, two hexagons, one inside the other."

"So then what is it?" The pilot had become fully engaged in the mystery.

"Surrounded by scaffolding," said Potter. "Should be easy to tell who built it from permits."

"Let's find out." Charlie pointed to the floor of the chopper. "Put her down."

"We can't. It's not an approved landing site. I don't want to lose my license."

"Then where's the closest spot?" Charlie was anxious to examine the origin of the mysterious brown stripe as soon as possible.

"I can take us to Pier 6." The pilot lifted the helicopter higher.

"Great. That's not far from where I parked."

The copter swung around but the pilot had them over the water again.

"You missed it," shouted Potter.

"No, it's right there." The pilot pointed. "See?" He was indicating the Manhattan side of the river.

"We're parked at Pier 1, Brooklyn."

"Oh, sorry. I thought you meant one of our piers in Manhattan."

"Now what?" Charlie's frustration grew. "Can you put it down near where we parked?"

Potter shook her head, the helmet covering her face. "Too public and too many reporters."

Charlie remembered the swarm of microphones thrust into his face. *Potter probably wants to avoid her old boyfriend.* "Is there a small airport nearby?"

The pilot chimed in. "We could use Floyd Bennett Field in southeast Brooklyn – "

"Too far," said Potter. "How about on the Baylander IX-514? You know where that is?"

"Pier 5, Brooklyn side!" said the pilot.

Potter nodded. "Perfect."

31 – Matt (Eureka, CA)

Matt rolled to his back and squinted. The sky was black, and it took a moment for his eyes to adjust. *Where am I?* Still in the woods, lying on the upper level of the wooden scaffold, a stick beside him. His body ached from sleeping on the hard surface. His mouth was pasty, his hands dirty. Looking around, the remaining sticks taunted him. *Why am I so motivated to build this stupid structure anyway?*

Matt jumped down, grabbed his book bag and slogged his way toward his dorm room. He'd just crossed the parking lot when Fred ran over, his fists waving. "You jerk!"

"What?" Matt was barely awake.

Fred's voice was several decibels too loud. "I got you that stupid scaffold, didn't I? And what did you do?"

"What? What's the matter?" Matt stifled a yawn.

"You didn't show up, that's what! The girls got pissed from waiting and blew me off."

The double date! Matt's preoccupation with the portal had blocked out everything else. "That was tonight?"

"Now he remembers!" Fred turned in a slow pirouette; arms open wide like a carnival barker. "Now, when its too late. You and your damn trellis!" He marched away.

Matt was thankful that his public humiliation was only to a few scattered students walking to their cars.

The show was over, and so was the project. If Matt couldn't lift the sticks, how could he assemble the structure? He closed his eyes, still sleepy despite his nap in the woods. The nagging image of the glowing hexagonal structures tormented him. *The portal needs to be built, for the good of humanity.* Matt would not be deterred, even though he had no clue about the portal's eventual purpose.

His stomach rumbled, so he headed for the student cafeteria. He paid the clerk for the last slice of cheese pizza, tanning under a heat lamp, and filled a cup with ice and soda. He didn't bother reheating the slice, nibbling at it and sucking the soda cup dry.

Matt poked at the ice in the bottom of his empty cup with a straw. If the sticks were too heavy to lift, then the scaffold was useless. And in the process, he'd lost Fred as a friend. Matt couldn't afford to lose one. He didn't have many.

A group of three adults – one short and thin, one overweight and one with fuzzy hair - came into the cafeteria, smiling, laughing, and poking at each other. Matt recognized them as students in the evening adult education program. *Aren't they taking accounting?* They'd acknowledged each other on previous occasions. In his mind, he had nicknamed them The Three Stooges due to their physical similarities with Moe, Larry and Curly.

At that moment, Matt was an obvious point of focus, being the only day student in the room. They went through the food line but only picked up mugs and poured coffee.

Larry came over. "You got the last slice, huh? I was really looking forward to some."

"Sorry." Matt considered offering him what was left, about half if he cut away the bite marks.

Larry nudged his shoulder. "Just kidding. So what's got you out so late? Not the cuisine."

Matt mumbled. "Nothing."

Curly laughed, came over to Matt's table and leaned on a nearby chair. "Must be girl trouble."

Moe didn't join the laughter but took a seat next to Matt. "Nah, it's not girls. It's something else." He leaned closer. "What's the matter, kid?"

"I haven't been getting much sleep, and I've been skipping classes."

"And you've got some nasty sunburn on your arms. Partying on the beach?" asked Larry.

Matt hadn't been paying much attention to anything but the portal. "I have to finish something, but I don't know how." Matt's head slumped toward the table.

"Well, seeing as how you've got a table full of experience sitting here, how's about letting us in on this problem." Moe smoothed his hair over his forehead. "Maybe we can help you solve it."

Matt had no confidence that these three guys had anything to offer. Then again, it wouldn't hurt. The worst they might do is laugh. "Come on, I'll show you."

Matt led them from the campus commons building north, skirting the fine arts building and across the parking lot. "Do any of you have a flashlight?"

"I've got a set of DayBeams in my truck," said Moe.

As he jogged off, Larry asked, "So where are we going?"

Matt picked his way around the trees and shrubs in the dark. "A clearing in these woods."

"You're not setting us up, are you?" asked Larry. "To mug us or something?"

"Come on, he's not that kind." Curly puffed as he tried to keep up. "We approached him, remember? And it's three against one."

Moe returned with two huge lantern-style flashlights shaped like headlights. The trampled path in front of them brightened with one of the units turned on. Matt led them to the incomplete structure.

"Is this it?" asked Curly. "It looks like you've got the problem well in hand. Nice scaffold."

"Useless, you mean." Matt pointed at the pile near the base. "Take one of those sticks and lift it up, over your head."

Curly bent at the waist, grabbed one of the two-foot long sticks and lifted his arm. Except his arm only got to waist high before it stopped. "Whoa, this is really heavy."

"Weakling. Let me try," said Larry. He followed suit, and only got it marginally higher. "What's this made of?"

"Something that defies the laws of physics, that's for sure," said Curly.

"So you see, the scaffold is useless if I can't raise the sticks high enough," Matt said.

"What is this thing supposed to be?" Moe turned on the second beam. The entire portal structure and surroundings basked in the light.

Matt wasn't going to let them in on his secret. *Besides, they won't believe it.* "An engineering assignment. I know what the completed thing looks like in my mind, and I have to build it. It's important." *Whatever it is.*

"For a class, right? And the sticks you're making this with, where did they come from?"

"Great question," said Matt. "I found them here while doing a class surveying exercise. Not that they're cooperating-"

"But why do they get heavier the higher you lift them?" Moe aimed one of the lights at the pile of sticks.

"Beats me." Matt invented an excuse. "But I don't have enough time to get different materials and still finish by the due date. I've got to use these."

Larry rubbed his head vigorously. "How do they fit together?"

Matt demonstrated by connecting three together on the ground, forming one half a hexagon. "See?"

Larry dragged three more over and added them to Matt's three, making a full hexagon, the next level for the inner trellis. He attempted to lift the completed geometric figure. "It doesn't feel any heavier than just one."

"That's nuts." Curly came closer to examine the result.

"Try it for yourself." Curly stood back. "Take the other side."

"Let me help." Larry took hold at one vertex.

Moe propped the DayBeams up with twigs and rocks and aimed the lights at the portal, Then he joined his friends and together they held the completed hexagon aloft. "This isn't so heavy."

"Lift it up to me." Matt climbed up on the scaffold to lend a hand until the three men could climb up.

The trio scaled the wood scaffold and put the complete hexagon into position on top of the verticals.

"Great!" Matt couldn't have wished for a better result. "Now all we need to do is lift the verticals into place and add the next level."

"Hey, give me a hand with these." Matt held one vertical support.

Two guys lifted the vertical into place. After five more on the inner trellis and six on the outer, the structure was ready for the next tier.

"We're making great progress." Larry wiped his hands on his pants.

It took all four of them to lift the larger hexagon.

"Yeah, we'll have it done in no time." Matt took a moment to inventory the sticks, and then counted on his fingers how many he'd need to match the blueprint in his mind. "We're missing one."

Moe raised his hands, palms open. "We didn't take any! Honest!"

"I didn't say you did." Matt hadn't seen any of the strangers steal a stick, or anyone else for that matter. *Could that guy have dragged one away?* "Maybe I missed one." Matt used one of the high-beam flashlights to search the ground around where he'd found the pile. *Nothing.*

"You'll never find it out here in the dark," said Curly.

Moe grabbed another stick from the pile but couldn't lift it alone. "Yeah, look for it tomorrow."

Matt removed one of the newly placed vertical rods from the outer hexagon, which promptly dragged him to his knees. "We'll leave this spot empty so we can finish the higher ones."

Larry dragged a couple of sticks into position, ready to be lifted into position with some assistance. "Good thinking, kid."

When the final tiers were in place, Matt stood back in awe of their construction. "Just like I pictured it."

Curly wiped his brow with a handkerchief. "I thought you said one piece was missing."

Matt's grin evaporated.

"Party pooper!" Moe put his hand on Matt's shoulder. "Aw, you'll find it."

The nearly complete portal was a hollow victory. *I don't know if it can even be operated in this condition.* Matt looked at the wooden structure. *I don't need that anymore.* "Before you go, can you help me take the scaffold apart?"

"Can we keep the wood?" asked Curly.

"Sure. I don't have any use for it."

The three men and Matt broke apart the scaffold, whose plywood surfaces weren't nailed onto the cross-members, and carted the pieces to the street.

"I'll get my SUV." Moe vanished into the darkness.

Larry and Curly each took one of the DayBeams to light their way out of the woods.

"Thanks a lot." Matt shook hands with the remaining men. "I never could have done it without your help."

"Glad to be of service." Curly patted Matt's back so hard, he stumbled forward. "I hope you get a good grade. And our lips are sealed."

Are they worried they helped me cheat?

As soon as Moe's truck pulled up, the men loaded the wood and lanterns in back. Larry and Curly chatted as they walked out to the parking lot together to find their cars.

Everything looked darker without the additional illumination. Instead of going back to his dorm, Matt felt his way past the trees to the portal. He could barely see, but a faint hum acted as an audible beacon. The sound led him to the portal. His hands found one of the horizontal supports. The sound sputtered, like a video game rocket almost out of fuel. *It's the missing stick, I know it. Boy, I really screwed up!*

Matt stumbled out of the woods, exhausted, his head shaking. *I guess I should consider this a success, even though there's a piece missing.* He hoped that he'd find it in the daylight, or that the portal would still operate with a piece missing. That night, he dreamed of chasing a misbehaving portal stick that bounced and spun, always out of reach.

32 - Kwashay (Brooklyn, NY)

The next morning before school, Kwashay strolled past her portal, surrounded by the stolen scaffold. Perhaps the police were retaining it as evidence, or the rightful owners just hadn't claimed their property. The police interrogation was nothing compared to the evening-long lecture by her mother about how Kwashay had disappointed her, the family, practically the whole country by her association with criminals. *There's no way Mama would understand how important the portal is. I'm not sure I do.*

Although Kwashay felt compelled to spend time in the portal's vicinity, she limited herself to one ritual visit per day, either in the morning, at lunch or after school. Despite the partially blocked view, it was evident the rods had swollen in diameter. *It's growing?* Kwashay didn't understand why the rods needed to grow, or much else about the portal except it's urgency. *When will I be called on to operate it? Maybe when it finishes growing?*

Sideways made an unexpected appearance from behind a tree. "Hey!" His crew were further back, at a distance.

"Are you crazy?" Kwashay tried not to look at the policeman standing guard. "Go away." She shuffled east, along the south edge of the park, putting space between her and the scene of the crime. "I shouldn't be seen speaking with you. For your own sake."

"I heard a jake picked you up."

She stopped walking. "Darn right. They thought I stole that scaffolding material."

"But you didn't rat me out. That was righteous."

Kwashay didn't tell him she had brought him up, but without his name, he was anonymous. "In any case, they might have me under surveillance. You're better off not being seen with me.

Sideways chuckled. "Usually, it's the other way."

Her mother agreed, warning her to stay away from Sideways and others like him. Kwashay kept walking away from the portal and her school. "I suppose I should thank you and your friends for finishing the assembly. It was my responsibility-"

"No problem, girly girl. Thing was, the scaffold didn't help much. We couldn't lift the bars high enough."

"Riiiiight!" *The gravity-defying nature of the rods.*

Sideways skipped a few quick steps, walking backwards in front of her.

Kwashay stopped and put her hands on her hips. "So, smart guy, then how were you able to complete it?"

"For a minute, we thought about adding levels to the bottom. You know, tilting it over? But the thing has roots! I mean, it's planted firm in the ground."

So that's how it's growing! It's a vegetable?

Sideways continued, "So then LeBron over there was sitting on the ground putting some of them together? He noticed that six of them weighed about the same as one, maybe a little lighter."

"Really?" Kwashay had never thought about constructing the hexagons a whole level at a time.

"That's the dealy. So we built the hexagons first and then lifted them up. The rods just got heavy alone. It's like homeboys and homegirls. They belong together." Sideways stood uncomfortably close.

"Well, that was very creative of you. And I am grateful."

Sideways' eyebrows danced. "Grateful enough to spend some time with your new smart guy?"

Kwashay glanced over her shoulder. They were out of range of the guard, but patrol cars rolled by occasionally. "I don't think that's a very good idea. The police are still looking for the thieves."

Sideways scraped the ground with his shoe. "You right. We'd better cool it until the case gets cold. So, did you get credit for it? As your art project?"

Kwashay had forgotten the excuse she'd given Sideways in the first place. "I couldn't lie to my teacher about it being my own work, so I'll submit something else." Sideways ripped his hat off his head and thrashed it against his leg. "You mean we did all that for nothing? Damn!"

I can't have him believe he committed a crime for no reason. "No, no, it's very important. I just can't explain why." Kwashay recalled the faint image of a second portal with another builder/operator. "Maybe if I locate the other one-" She slapped her hand in front of her mouth.

Sideways' demeanor flipped from dropped eyebrow anger to wide-eyed enthusiasm. "Who's putting that one together? 'Cause maybe I can share what we learned the hard way. Me and my crew, we'll keep a lookout. And when we find it, I'll let you know quick." He put his hand back on and rubbed the brim.

Kwashay didn't know where the second one was, but having them close together didn't seem correct. "Well, see you around, I guess."

"Yeah, we gonna bail." Sideways hopped and skipped north along the east edge of the park, his two companions running to catch up.

With a burst of speed, Kwashay ran past the portal towards her school, locket bouncing, determined not to be late for class. The burnt-out brown grass crunched under her feet. *They really should water this better.*

33 – Selton (Kearney, NE)

Selton basked in the morning sun, paying more attention to the shelves of books around him than to the mystery novel in his lap. His comfy chair next to a large picture window afforded his body maximum exposure to sunlight. Genres, books of similar nature, was another epiphany after discovering fiction versus non-fiction. Those themes explained why extremely similar events and resolutions played out over and over in multiple novels. Although his mission revolved around collection of non-fiction information, Selton reflected on the value of the stories, how they provided sample contexts and informed his understanding of how information was used in society. *I'm amazed at how dry facts come to life in novels.* History and science combined with speculation about the possibilities of life explained much about the human condition, which was also ripening, just at a slower pace.

Selton sighed, his body mass much heavier than when he'd begun his quest, and not because of his diet. *How much more can I absorb before my cells burst? I hope my Personal Information Journal isn't taking up too much valuable space.* As the sun rose higher in the sky, Selton shifted his position to achieve the greatest exposure without changing seats.

Bernice glanced up from her computer with her daylight smile. Selton smiled back, as well as he could with a rind face. He'd become fond of Earthlings through the relationships he'd built. Especially the librarians, who were the bulk of the native inhabitants Selton had come to know. In most towns, some shopkeepers and neighborhood folks freely offered helping hands and donations to Selton. Most treated him as someone to be avoided and ignored.

The previous evening, Sprint had commented, before moving on, about Selton's softening when giving him a hug. A confirmation occurred while Selton was assisting a shorter customer obtain a book from a high shelf. The customer had just thanked Selton, who backed out of the way and bumped into a mobile book cart. No harm from such a glancing encounter, but when he checked in the bathroom mirror, Selton witnessed his first physical indication of ripening - a dark and soft bruise on his lower rear torso. He stroked the point of impact gently. *I need to return to Serulia before my body turns to pulp.*

Bernice stood and covered her computer terminal with a handmade patchwork cloth, her indication that it was closing time. Selton was surprised at how quickly the day had passed. Had he been daydreaming so much?

The weather had turned a bit colder and wet. Selton raised his collar before he marched through the rain, his fedora providing nominal cover after a hard day absorbing ever more information. His clothes were soaked, clinging to his body. He hoped no one paid attention to the lumpy root system that must have been evident on his back.

Shielded by the underpass, Selton poked around in his pack. He took a moment before feeding to examine the filament he'd caught the night he'd squeezed the two lumps on his head. Its motion was sluggish, and it was darkening. *Is it dying? I wanted to examine it, not kill it.* It barely moved against the inside wall of the jar, only an occasional twitch. *Does it require nutrition? Sunlight*? He shook the jar. No response. He carefully opened the lid and plucked the dark strand from its captivity. Selton ran out from the underpass and stuck the filament into the wet soil, covering it with the glass bottle. *Maybe it's not too late.*

Exhausted, he wandered south to a human's backyard in which he'd previously fed. The decayed wooden fence shook when he opened the gate. Just beyond a rusted metal shed, out of sight, was a green area adjacent to his brown spotted feeding location. The grass was soft, wet and comforting after a long day. But before he could doze off, the ground below him shook. The reverberations had returned, delivering a clearer set of sounds. *These must be from Dissemination Oversight, letting me know how I'm going to return to Serulia.* He listened closely. "Local communication portals operational."

What were portals? Hadn't all previous communication been local? *Why won't they tell me how I'm to be recalled?* Selton suddenly understood the human feeling of frustration. *Am I an alien Gutman, searching for the Maltese Falcon?*

34 – Charlie (Brooklyn, NY)

The helicopter pilot brought the craft around another one-eighty, heading for the east bank of the river. Seven piers stuck out from the Brooklyn Heights shore like beckoning fingers. They'd crisscrossed the area so many times, Charlie was a bit disoriented.

"There it is!" shouted Potter.

The helicopter came down onto a large ship docked at one of the Brooklyn piers.

Charlie and Potter waited until the pilot completed landing procedures and signaled that it was okay to depart. Only then, they took off their helmets and climbed out.

"This ship was active during the Vietnam War and was later used to train helicopter pilots." Potter grabbed her tool bag from the luggage compartment at the back of the copter. "I'm glad I remembered it."

"That was the strangest private ride I've ever done." The pilot pulled off his helmet, a slip of paper waving in his hand.

Charlie scribbled his office address and Jane's name on a generic business card. "Send the bill here, attention Jane Yong."

"Good doing business with you." The pilot held out his hand for a shake. "And when you find out what that thing is, let me know, okay?"

With a little luck. Charlie accepted the handshake, then walked the gangplank off the ship to catch up with Potter.

"I'll jog over and get the car. Be right back. Watch my bag, okay?" Potter didn't wait for an answer.

Charlie wasn't in good enough shape to keep up at the pace she was running. *Too much desk work. Maybe I should join a health club.* While he waited, he glanced around. Pier Five and Pier Six both had grassy areas, bright green and in great condition. The brown blight was astoundingly limited, precise in a way no disease would allow. *And directional – straight west.*

His phone rang. Caller ID showed it was Lane. "What's up?"

"I got a call from Liberty National Golf Club in New Jersey. They wanted to know if we knew anything about a brown stripe running through the middle of holes eight, twelve and thirteen."

"I saw it with my own eyes a little while ago, at a distance. From the helicopter I rented."

"Oh." Lane paused. "I guess I should cancel the requisition?"

"Good idea. Maybe now you'll believe me when I tell you it's spreading. Tell Director Stanton this is bigger than we thought. I'll talk to you later." Charlie hung up.

Potter pulled up in her EPA-labeled car. Charlie put her tool bag in the trunk, which Potter had popped open, then got into the passenger seat. "Let's go."

"The structure seems to be in Fort Greene Park, or close by." She checked her mirror and pulled out into traffic. "We'll have to go around the block, because DeKalb Avenue is one way westbound."

"So is the brown stripe. Westbound from the spot we saw." Five blocks from the pier, Charlie examined the parks they drove past. Cadman Plaza Park, Walt Whitman Park, and an unnamed space at Tillary and Flatbush were all lush, green spaces. *Why is the brown so limited?*

"While I was getting the car, I got a call from Dean. He'll have the soil sample analysis tonight." Potter headed south on Navy Street. "I have plans, so I told him to come by your hotel room. I hope that's okay."

"Sure. Twenty-four hours is way better than two weeks." Charlie wiggled in his seat, anxious to see the brown stripe's origin. The color of the grass at the north end of Fort Greene Park matched its name. "This case is just like a Quincy Grissom novel."

"I've never read one. How so?"

"Oh, you should." They sat idle in congestion at another stoplight. "His stories always start with something simple and through his investigation become much bigger and complicated."

"And you like the fact that our case is weird and not easily solved?"

"I wanted a field assignment I could sink my teeth into."

"Maybe next time, you should be careful what you wish for."

The parking spaces along DeKalb Avenue on the south boundary of Fort Greene Park were clogged with a bus labeled 'Reverend Billi Dogood's Mobile Morality Mission' and half a dozen police cars, lights flashing.

"Looks like somebody got here ahead of us." Charlie wrote the bus legend in his notepad.

Potter pulled the car over the curb onto the wide stone sidewalk and turned on her flashers. "This should buy us some time."

They got out and walked along the stone wall and up the path to a rise among a set of trees. A tall woman with long white hair in an ankle-length white robe argued with policemen as they gently escorted her in the direction of her bus. "I'm doing God's work," she pleaded. Her followers shuffled along, staying close, but not interfering.

"Even God's work requires a permit." One police officer held his arms out to provide a clear path in front of her. "You and your friends have to disperse until you get an approved Parks Special Event Request."

Charlie caught a momentary glimpse of her eyes, steel-blue and intensely focused. *I wonder why she picked this spot for a rally?*

"That's perfectly fine. We don't need Brooklyn." She jerked her head, sending her white hair flying. "We'll just follow the trail!" She waved one arm like a drum major as she marched towards her bus. Her throng followed close behind.

After they loaded up, Potter said, "I've never seen anything like that."

"Me neither." *Trail? Did she mean the brown stripe?* As the crowd dissipated and their police entourage departed, Charlie got his first clear view of the structure, two hexagon-shaped frameworks about eight feet high sitting in a brown patch that continued off to the west. "Well, there it is, the origin!"

Surrounding the structure was a partially disassembled scaffold, half the height of the hexagon structures. The whole area was surrounded by yellow police tape. One police officer stood guard, as if the structure or the scaffolds were precious. Two construction workers were casually disassembling the scaffold, piece by piece, and carrying the pieces under the tape to a waiting truck parked on the lawn away from the brown stripe. They didn't seem to be in any hurry.

Charlie recalled numerous scenes when Grissom interacted with police as he flashed his badge at the cop. "Keyson, EPA. What's going on here?"

The officer maintained a stoic expression as he adjusted his hat. "You'll have to talk to the detective in charge."

No one in the vicinity looked like a detective. *What would Grissom do? He'd get the information he needed.* "Get in touch with him." He glanced at Potter. "Or her. This structure is an object of interest in our investigation." Charlie left out the phrase 'of dead grass.'

"Okay, but he's got a lot more pressing cases than this one." The officer talked into his shoulder-mounted radio. All Charlie heard was static. "Give me a minute." The officer ducked under the tape and walked halfway down the block. Evidently his communication problems cleared, because he came back with news. "He'll be here, but it'll be a while."

"We'll wait."

Charlie and Potter made their way to a park bench, within eyesight of the structure.

Potter sat down and crossed her legs. "It's so tall, no wonder somebody needed a scaffold."

"And did you look at the ground? The rest of the park is perfect, except for the area that starts at the structure and heads due west." Charlie formulated the central question in his mind: why did the brown stripe start at the structure?

"Is the structure causing the dead grass?" asked Potter.

Potter's mind works like mine. She's a good partner. "We'll find out more when Dean delivers the results." Charlie couldn't just sit there. He walked around, staying outside the yellow tape, attempting to get a good look at the hexagonal tower. *This distance and that scaffold don't help.* He snapped a few low quality pictures, which mostly showed the scaffold bars and planks.

Potter joined him and took a couple of steps toward her car. "Too bad, the policeman probably won't let me take soil samples."

"I could force the issue, but let's stay on law enforcement's good side. At least, until we learn what they know." Charlie looked at his watch. "You hungry?"

She considered the question for a moment, returned to the bench and sat down. "I could use a bite."

Charlie went back to the yellow tape and the officer. "Where can we get something to eat nearby?"

The police officer pointed at the blacktop walking path. "There's Cyber Cafe, inside Long Island University just up that way." Then he aimed at the street. "And there's a pizza joint a half block down."

"Got it." Charlie returned to the bench and offered to buy lunch for both of them. "It's not dinner, but it's my turn." *She's going to insist on a evening meal on me, I just know it.*

"I trust you. Pick something."

Charlie walked up the path and returned in twenty minutes with a white paper bag and two cups in a cardboard carrier. Potter had retrieved her tool case from the car in the interim. *She's optimistic.* "Any sign of the detective?"

"Nope. What'd you get us?" She brushed off the bench with her hand.

"Subs. One Italian. One chicken."

Potter grimaced. "Chicken is fine."

I should have guessed she's a vegetarian. "I can go back-"

Potter patted the bench. "Sit down and eat."

"I got a couple of sodas." Charlie handed her the sandwich labeled 'chick.'

She glared at the word before unwrapping the bundle. "Do you think the police know who constructed that thing?" Potter nibbled at the edges of her chicken sub.

"Don't know." As Charlie chewed, he noticed two females walk up to the police tape and stop, and not for just a glance. One was a young woman, tall, thin, African-American, the other a middle-aged Caucasian with her hair in a bun. They stood there for several minutes by Charlie's watch, staring at the structures and taking photos. He nudged Potter and pointed.

"What are they doing?" She wiped her lips with a napkin.

Charlie chewed quick and swallowed. "Studying and documenting our object of interest. With great interest." He stood to approach them but they left as quickly as they appeared, crossing DeKalb and disappearing into a large cube-shaped brick building. "What's that?"

"Brooklyn Technology High School. The younger one is probably a student."

Accompanied by a teacher? "We should find out who she is."

35 – Matt (Eureka, CA)

With the portal complete minus one stick, Matt told himself he could devote time and effort to his Biology, Intro to Surveying, English and Math classes. However, that didn't mean he had to ignore the structure. One stick was still missing, plus he carried an obligation to be the portal's operator. He was confident he'd be a good one, whatever that meant. Despite his Internet posting of a photo, no one came forth as his teammate, counterpart, co-operator, whatever.

On his next visit to the clearing, he did yet another search for the missing stick. He'd expanded his search pattern with no luck. He was far enough away that he could see the whole thing. To Matt's eye, it looked like the portal had grown. *The sticks are fatter.* Was it a plant? He had always considered the sticks as dead twigs - straight and uniform - not living. *This whole thing is like out of a sci-fi movie.* Yet there it was, sturdier and bigger. Matt came close and got down on his hands and knees near the base. The bottom sticks, which originally had been loose, now were planted in the soil. Matt tried to rock the structure. It didn't budge.

Three students, one with a clipboard, another with a tape measure, and the third with a drawing pad, accompanied a teacher with a shoulder bag into the clearing. *What are they doing here?* The teacher and student with the tape ignored Matt, taking measurements, sticking probes into the soil, measuring the heights of various bushes and plants.

The student with the drawing pad began sketching the area. The female student with the clipboard walked around the portal and almost bumped into Matt. "Sorry." She looked Matt up and down over her glasses. "Don't I know you from Biology? You're not part of the special study group."

Her name is Valerie or Victoria, something with a V. "What group is that?"

"Professor Shockley picked a few of us to check out this area. A stand of trees fell over just east of here, and there were reports of plants and trees dying. See?" She pointed at yellowed shrubs and brown grass that led straight east, a fifty-foot path.

"I hadn't noticed." In fact, Matt had noticed the growing brown area, but that wasn't his problem. *The portal deserves all of my attention.*

"We're supposed to figure out what's killing the plant life." She repositioned her glasses further up her nose.

The student with the tape measure walked over. "Do you have that list of candidate diseases?"

"Yep." She read through the list, one disease at a time. "Cankers? Botrytis Blight? Collar, Foot, Root and Crown Rots?"

The student with the tape measure scurried among the trees and bushes, looking for signs of the disease. "No sunken areas of dead tissue, or layers of lumpy, disfigured bark. No fungus or gray-brown spore masses on twigs, or dieback. The leaves aren't discolored or stunted. No stains or vertical streaks on the trunks. And, no lethal cankers present."

The student looked up from her clipboard. "Last one. What about Sudden Oak Death?"

Her colleague replied, "These are redwoods."

Matt was impressed. *They must be sophomores.*

The third team member who'd been doing the drawing approached Matt. "Aren't you taking Introduction to Surveying? Matt, right? What are you doing here?"

Matt wasn't pleased that he'd been identified. "That's me. I was doing my field assignment out here because I couldn't get a ride to the Headwaters Forest Reserve."

"Well, there's going to be a lot of activity here. You'd probably be better off someplace else." The sketchpad hung from his hand.

Matt tried to look at the drawing without being obvious. "I also come here for peace and quiet."

"When there's no games or practices, the stadium can be pretty isolated." The student tapped his pencil one of the thick cross-members of the portal. "Do you know what this is?"

"I thought it was a trellis, you know, to hold vines." Matt noticed that his portal was part of the sketch. *So much for secrecy!* "Why?"

"Just that it'll have to come down for the new building. Professor Shockley will have to check with grounds management to see who it belongs to."

It's mine. "I saw the sign, but I didn't think construction was starting for a while, maybe even next year."

"Well, Bates Corporation accelerated the schedule. Rumor is it's a tax dodge."

Matt's blood throbbed. "Can they do that?"

"Based on the money Bates Foundation pours into this school, they can do anything they want."

The team member with the tape measure scuffed his foot in the dirt. "The grass is dead here and east, just as reported." He extended the metal ribbon and pointed. "And see, the bushes are all dying, like they're being starved. The trees might have been affected, but they're pretty sturdy."

The teacher, one of the few Matt had ever seen wearing a sport coat and tie, approached and took a head count. He strode up to Matt. "You're not on my team. I knew I should have put up a barrier. You're going to have to leave."

"Why? It's part of campus, and I'm a student." *I'll need access when I install the last stick and when it's time to operate the portal.* Matt reached for his wallet. "I can show you my ID-"

"We can't have distractions. We're doing a survey of the property and we have to be efficient and accurate."

"Won't the contractors do a survey before they start construction?" *That might provide enough delay.*

"We're going to dig up the viable plants before construction and relocate them. Isn't that wonderful!" The teacher threw his hands up as if to gesture "Hallelujah." "But first we need to complete our inventory and survey, draw up the plans and submit them before the grant date runs out. So please, let us get on with our work."

The portal was in jeopardy. "So you're going to remove everything?"

"Yes. Everything." The teacher leaned against the portal, grasping one of the vertical sticks. "Including this thing, whatever it is."

"He says it a trellis," said the student with the clipboard.

"Out here?" The teacher shook his head. "Too tall, too wide, completely the wrong shape. Maybe the frame of a gazebo." He pulled a notepad from his sport coat pocket. "Give me your name."

Two of his helpers recognized me from classes. Matt had no option and complied. "Can't the trellis stay up until construction starts?"

"Trellis? Ha! As soon as we relocate the plants, construction begins." The teacher tucked the notepad into an inner pocket. "Bates Foundation has made this project a high priority."

His heart sunk. They couldn't tear down the trellis. It was necessary. *And I just completed it.* Matt slogged back to his dorm, violated and helpless.

36 – Kwashay (Brooklyn, NY)

Despite her confession to the police that she'd had help building the portal, Kwashay escorted her art teacher out to the completed structure, to get a photo of the portal. "See, here it is."

The teacher tapped her fingers on the camera in her hand. "And what is it supposed to be?"

"The skeleton of a modern high rise building." Kwashay had concocted her story during lunch, scribbling a diagram while she ate. "When it's finished, it'll look kind of like this." She handed the teacher her sketch.

"Ambitious. And so how can I help? It looks like you've got things under control."

"I've got concerns from an architectural perspective. I don't know if a building designed like this will be structurally stable. So I thought I'd post a picture to some architectural web sites and get some professional assistance. That's why I asked you to bring your camera."

"Good idea. Although, I understand this wasn't your work alone."

Did the detective tell her that? "That's correct." *Thanks to Sideways and his crew, it got done quickly.*

"You'll need another project, that you do by yourself." The teacher smiled. "Still, we should document the work." The teacher raised her camera. "Okay, stand back and I'll take a few shots."

The teacher moved in an arc, taking a series of digital pictures. "The light is terrible out here, with the tree and building shadows. And the scaffold you used isn't helping either." She snapped off a couple more. "You should be in one. A newspaper might want to do an article."

Kwashay sidled up to the yellow police tape. "Nobody will be interested in this." She smoothed her hair. "Do I look all right?"

"You look fine." The teacher took a couple more pictures.

Two adults, a man and a woman, were sitting on a nearby bench eating sandwiches. They seemed focused on the portal and her, staring at everyone and everything near the yellow tape.

"Give me your email address and I'll send these to you as soon I get back to my classroom. I'm also going to share them with your math teacher." Her art teacher winked. "Maybe he'll give you extra credit."

"Thanks." *Anything to help my math grade.*

"No matter what kind of assistance you received, I'm impressed. This must have taken a lot of effort." She leaned against the tape, stretching it, reaching for the structure but falling short. "The rods look like an unusual material. Metal?"

"No." Kwashay invented an answer. "A synthetic, sanded and polished." The rods were too warm for metal, too precise and shiny for wood.

The man on the bench stood and took a step in their direction.

"I should get back. My last class isn't over yet," Kwashay said.

The art teacher checked her watch. "It's almost end of the day. Why don't you gather your books and go home a bit early?"

Kwashay had planned on going home immediately after school to post the photos to social networking sites before her mother got home from work. Maybe the other operator would recognize the structure and get in touch. *An early departure will give me more time.* An added benefit, her mother would be happy that she prepared dinner.

37 - Selton (Kearney, NE)

Selton batted his eyes, adjusting to the rising sun. Because he'd chosen a private backyard in which to feed overnight, he needed to depart before he was discovered. As he leaned forward on his elbows, he saw a flower with rainbow colored petals, all hues across the visible light spectrum, laying on his bare lower stomach. He brushed at it with a whisk of his hand, except the flower swayed in place.

Selton tipped the flower to the side. *It's not on my body, it's growing out of my body.* Sure enough, the flower stem was embedded into his torso, about an inch tall. He jumped to his feet. *There must be a mistake. As an information gatherer, there would be no need for me to have germination capability. It would only be a physiological complication.* But there it was, a clear sign that Selton was able to blossom. Selton knew that if he somehow germinated, the result would be another version of him, a humanoid-shaped Serulian. *Serulia doesn't need more than one of me to accomplish my mission. Others would be redundant. This is a serious mistake. I'm sure I was supposed to be seedless!*

Train whistles indicated that raw materials and goods were on the move. Selton had to be on the move as well before families awoke and looked out into their yards.

But Selton couldn't walk around with a flower growing out of his stomach. *I'm not exactly inconspicuous as it is.*

He hiked back to the train yard, washed, and dressed. The filament under the glass bottle dome had regained its translucency and flickered against its captivity with renewed vigor. It was even a bit thicker, as if it had been nurtured by the soil, just like him. Selton was pleased he'd nursed the filament back to health, but decided to keep it hostage. *I still don't know what these filaments are for, or why they formed within me.* He capped the bottle and stored it in his ruck sack, promising to give the filament sufficient sun, water and nutrition.

Before he could depart for the library, his footing was rocked by another set of vibrations. At a higher frequency than the last time, they shook Selton's body. He listened closely, picking out only a few intelligible words.

Knowledge. Spread. Thrive.

Selton invented a complete sentence in his mind. *With the knowledge you'll spread, Serulians will thrive.*

Finally, my efforts have been validated! Selton was disappointed that the message didn't contain details about how he'd return to his home planet. *It's good to know that my work will have positive consequences, as soon as I get back.*

On the way to the library, Selton stopped at Tiny's Bar. The owner was sweeping up the sidewalk from the previous night's revelers. One of his employees was washing the dark, reflective window.

"Good morning." Selton tipped his fedora. The flower tickled his tummy under his shirt. "By any chance, do you have a knife I can borrow?"

"I've got just the thing, pal." Tiny went into his store and came out with a box of small pocket knives, each with the name of the bar printed in gold on a black enclosure. "They're promos – giveaways. You want a couple, maybe for your friends?"

Is it smart to be providing weapons to inebriated humans? Selton didn't know if Bernice would want or appreciate the gift of a knife. Just in case, he replied, "Two, please." He accepted the gifts and thrust them into his pocket.

The employee was struggling to wash the higher portion of the window so Tiny lent a hand, spraying and using a squeegee on the top area. "I know it's early, but how about a drink? On the house."

Selton shook his head. An alcoholic beverage might damage his internals. was just about to cross the street when a police car pulled up. Tiny retreated inside his establishment while the employee finished the lower part of the window.

"Good day, officer." Selton had learned from his fellow hobo travelers to always be nice to bulls. This one wore his name – Clayton – on his chest.

"You still here?" He hooked his thumbs in his belt.

"Yes, officer." With knives in his pocket, Selton wanted to avoid a shakedown.

The officer tipped his cap up, exposing a crew-cut. "I figured you'd be tired of us by now. Moved on, know what I mean?" He closed the distance between them.

Selton understood the concept of personal space. *He's trying to intimidate me.* "I'm having a excellent time, enjoying your public library."

"Yeah, well, that's for citizens. Taxpayers. Which you aren't." Clayton tapped Selton's chest.

His shirt rubbed the flower petals, which tickled his exodermis. Selton couldn't help but scratch at his belly.

"What's going on? What you got in there?"

"Nothing." Selton dropped his arms to his sides.

It was too late. He'd drawn attention. "Open your shirt so I can see." The bull unlatched the safety strap on his sidearm.

Selton pulled his coat open and unbuttoned his shirt, exposing his stomach, including the flower.

The officer stared at Selton's stomach. "What are you, some kind of hippy? Aren't you supposed to wear that in your hair? Go on, button up."

Selton did as asked.

"Some time real soon, there's a train coming through Kearney with your name on it."

Selton had never seen Selton or Serulia emblazoned on the side of a train car. "If you say so, sir."

"I do say. Finish up your business and then get out of town. Got it?"

Selton internally hoped that his recall was imminent. "Yes, officer. Have a nice day."

Officer Clayton got back into his vehicle and drove off.

Bernice, who had arrived for work a moment prior, marched over from across the street. "Is anything wrong?"

Selton glanced at the police car, now at the next intersection. "I don't think he likes me very much."

"Maybe you should know, Chief Rogers was asking about you." Bernice looked both ways and escorted Selton across to the library in the middle of the block.

Selton felt like an abscess was growing within his pulp core. *Repeated scrutiny by law enforcement isn't a good thing.* It had happened before, in other towns, hastening his departure from them. But Selton felt obligated to stay in Kearney. He wasn't sure he could leave if he wanted to, or was ordered to.

"We shouldn't be jaywalking." Selton looked to see if the officer was in sight.

Bernice smiled momentarily, but the smile evaporated. "The Chief wanted to know if you were reading anything in particular, doing anything unusual or maybe dangerous."

"What did you tell him?"

"Besides the fact that I've never had a homeless person patronize the library for such a long period of time, and that you read from every possible category and discipline, and that you're my favorite customer?" Her smile was deep and genuine. "I told him you were harmless and he shouldn't worry."

"Thank you so much." Selton resolved to keep himself out of trouble, to give Chief Rogers no excuse for more intimate involvement. *Not this close to my recall.*

Once inside the library, Selton took out one of the pocket knives. "I got this for you from Mr. Tiny."

Bernice took it from him. "Thank you. I'll use it for opening letters and such." She opened a desk drawer and placed it inside.

Selton excused himself and entered the men's washroom. In a stall with a door, Selton opened his shirt and carefully dug the root of the growing blossom from his stomach using the penknife, leaving a cone-shaped indentation. *It looks like I have a human belly button.* The idea of mimicking a human body in this detail almost broke his wooden expression.

On the way to his chair, he left the flower on the shelf in front of Bernice's desk. *She deserves pretty things.*

38 - Charlie (Brooklyn, NY)

"This waiting is awful." Charlie uncrossed and recrossed his legs on the park bench overlooking the hexagonal stick structure in Fort Greene Park. He reached for the latest Grissom novel in his bag to pass the time but stopped. It wouldn't be polite with Potter sitting next to him.

She didn't look up, dragging multicolored dots around her phone's screen. "Sometimes private detectives are stuck doing stakeouts, right? But I think we've been stood up."

Time to take charge, like Grissom does. Charlie folded the empty paper food bag, tucked it into his back pocket and advanced on the young policeman who was guarding the hexagonal object. "Any word from your detective?"

"No."

"Well, we can't wait here forever. I hope we'll have your cooperation." Potter joined him at his side, tool case in hand. "We're going to take some soil samples-"

The policeman, whose shirt showed creases from its packaging, held out his arm, as if that would be a sufficient deterrent. "This is an active crime scene. It's not to be disturbed."

I need details. Charlie pulled out his notepad. "What precisely is the crime being investigated?"

"Grand theft. The scaffold." He pointed at the partial structure. The men disassembling it had vanished.

Charlie made a brief entry. "We won't touch the scaffold or that thing, if that's what you're worried about."

"We're only going to take a few dirt samples." Potter held up a hollow cylinder to demonstrate the tool of choice. "Maybe five or six. Then we'll out of here."

The officer's posture stiffened. "You can't do that."

"Has your forensics team been here yet?" Potter asked.

"Yes, ma'am."

"Good. Then our footprints, yours included, won't disrupt any of the evidence that's already been gathered."

Charlie lifted the yellow tape so Potter could enter. "So, we'll just get on with our work."

The policeman stuttered an ill-formed complaint but Charlie and Potter were already within the cordoned-off area.

Charlie moved counter-clockwise, taking photos of the hexagonal structure from various angles. Made of cylindrical rods, it looked about eight feet tall, four sections of two-feet each. *Completely symmetrical.* The remaining scaffold obstructed completely clear views. He also took a perspective photo of the brown streak from the side where the discoloration originated. It ran directly west, past the walkway, all the way to Governors Island. Potter diligently took samples from both brown and green areas and pushed colored flags into the turf.

Behind the policeman's back, Charlie stuck his arm through the scaffold supports and ran his hand along one of the hexagon's horizontal bars. *Smooth. Warm. Not wood or metal, something else.* He lamented that he couldn't get away with taking a sample. One of the bars in his hand would be completely obvious.

Potter interrupted his examination of the bars. "I'm finished, and I took a few pictures too." The soil sample tubes lay on the ground near her case.

Charlie approached the police officer and pointed to the flags stuck in the ground. "We've placed markers where we took our soil samples." Then he scribbled his cell phone number and hotel name on the back of his business card and handed it to the policeman. "When your detective shows up, give him this and ask him to call me. Any time."

Three young black men were hanging around in between the trees just east of the taped-off area. Charlie nudged Potter's shoulder as she knelt at her bag. "Seems like our structure has drawn some interest." *Besides the Reverend and her followers.*

She looked up from packing away the soil samples. "They're probably harmless. After all, a police crime scene in the middle of a park is hardly unusual in Brooklyn."

Charlie wasn't so sure. Lots of people walked the path nearby without taking a second look. "The only ones who've shown interest were the two women and now these young men." *Maybe they'd seen something.* As Charlie took a step in their direction, they scattered.

When they got to Potter's car, a ticket under a wiper blade flapped in the breeze. Potter pulled it loose. "Damn!"

"You don't have to pay that, do you?"

"No, but there's a bunch of paperwork I have to file to make it go away." She grabbed the ticket and tossed it into the back seat. "So what now?"

Charlie noticed that the back seat was littered with close to a dozen tickets. "I guess we'll have to wait for Dean. When he shows up with the results from the first batch, I can give him the new ones."

"Good idea." Potter put the samples in the trunk while Charlie got in. "He's supposed to show up at your hotel. I guess that's our next stop."

Charlie glanced out his car window for a last look. The hexagon was pretty well hidden by surrounding trees. "I wish I could have examined the structure more closely. Maybe sent a sample to your lab."

"And piss off the police? You'll get a chance, after they remove the scaffold and open the crime scene. Assuming someone doesn't take it down." Potter checked her mirrors before pulling into traffic.

Charlie hadn't considered that possibility. "Then we'd better make sure they don't." The hexagonal structures were his first physical clues tied to the brown stripe.

"Mind if I wait with you?" asked Potter. "At the hotel?"

He looked at his watch. "No. Too early for dinner, though." *I expect that's the next thing she'll say.*

"Maybe just a cup of coffee?"

"Sure."

Potter headed in the direction of the Ritz-Carlton New York, Battery Park. "So, that hexagon thing is the origin of the brown streak?" She giggled. "Sounds like the name of an Amtrak train."

Charlie thought the name sounded gross, not funny. "Seems pretty clear, but we don't have any confirming evidence of cause and effect."

At the hotel garage, they avoided paying a parking fee when Charlie flashed his key card. She parked her car and they both got out.

"Give me the samples you just took at the park." He pulled the paper bag from his back pocket. "I'll give them to Dean when he shows up."

"Fine." Potter transferred the park soil samples from her case into the bag.

They entered the hotel from the garage. The most convenient restaurant, just off the lobby, was 2West. Charlie surveyed the place. Padded chairs. Goblets that served as a vases for fresh cut yellow flowers. Cloth tablecloths. "Too ritzy for coffee." The place was almost deserted.

"They'll appreciate our business. By the time we leave, the place will be packed, you just watch." Potter tugged his sleeve. "Come on."

A hostess greeted them. Charlie requested a table off in the corner for privacy, far from the few patrons.

"Good afternoon." The waitress who showed up offered them menus. She looked disappointed when he ordered coffee and Potter ordered hot tea.

Potter rearranged her silverware, perched her chin on one bent arm and smiled. "So, what's your story?"

"I don't have a story." He wanted to keep their relationship strictly business. Personal details were irrelevant.

The waitress delivered two steaming hot cups. Charlie watched Potter pour cream and a packet of sugar into hers.

He took a sip. "I'm just me, Charlie Keyson, EPA analyst."

"Okay Charlie Keyson, EPA analyst. What do you do for fun? Any hobbies?" She stared at him and licked her lower lip.

Charlie squirmed in his chair. His work at the EPA consumed all of his thoughts and energy, even when he wasn't at work. "I love reading mystery novels, especially Quincy Grissom." The book in his bag called to him, begging to be read.

"So that's why you call this a case. You think about it like it's a mystery." Potter slurped from her cup. "That's really cool."

Charlie's phone rang. He held up his hand to signal timeout. "Keyson." He paused and listened. "Let me put you on speakerphone." The waitress was two tables away, rolling silverware in cloth napkins. He put the phone on the table between them and leaned close. "I'm here with my partner Stephanie Potter from New York's EPA bureau."

A baritone voice emerged from the flip phone, louder than Charlie expected. "This is Detective Henry Washington, 84th Precinct. One of my patrolmen told me you have some interest in our scaffold theft case?"

Charlie turned the volume down. Potter got closer, her head inches from his. *Is she wearing perfume?* "Not the scaffold. The structure in the center."

"Oh, that? It's a school project. Something about math and art. We questioned the artist, a Brooklyn Technology High School student from across the street."

"Is she tall and thin, African-American?" Charlie asked.

"Why yes. How did you know?"

"She was there today, staring at it for quite a while. With a teacher, I presume." Charlie leaned back and stole another sip.

"She's anxious, because she's supposed to get it graded, and we learned that she had help building it. I let her teacher know. Anyway, we'll be out of her hair pretty soon."

"The scaffold has been partially removed." Charlie raised his head to see if anyone was seated near them. *Not so far*. "Did you know about that?"

"We gave the construction company the go-ahead after we gathered forensics, but I'm surprised any of it is still there. Must be low priority."

Potter chimed in. "This is Agent Potter. We'd like to speak with that student, if you don't mind."

The waitress's head was turned towards them. *She's listening in, or maybe checking if I need a refill.* Charlie reduced the volume one more time and put his hand over his cup as a signal.

The detective's voice was faint. "No problem. I'm on my way home, and my notes are all in the office. I'll text you her name first thing tomorrow, if that's okay."

Charlie hesitated. He never used his company flip phone for texting. Too many buttons to press for each letter. "Send it to my partner's phone." Charlie nodded to Potter, who gave Washington her phone number.

"Will do. And if she tells you anything about the scaffold, let me know. She claims she didn't steal it, and I believe her. But I think she knows more than she's saying."

"We'll pass along anything that might help. Any problem if we examine her art project?" Charlie winked at his partner.

"I don't see why not. But she's protective, so don't mess with it, okay?"

"Oh, we won't. Are there plans to take it down?" Charlie was prepared to contact the appropriate parties to leave it in place.

"That's between the park district and the school. By the way, beware of her mother! She is one piece of work."

"Got it!" Charlie made a few more notes.

Washington paused before continuing the conversation. "EPA, huh? Is there a problem I should know about?"

"Nope. No problem at all." *Just a fifty-foot stripe of dead grass heading west for who knows how long.* "Thanks for calling us back." Charlie snapped his phone shut. "It sounds like we have full permission to examine the structure as early as tomorrow."

"Great."

Charlie's phone rang. *Lane again.* "Keyson. What now?" The waitress approached with a pot and freshened his cup. He forced a smile.

"I've gotten more calls about your brown stripe." He sounded excited or worried.

"Mine?" With the waitress hovering, Charlie didn't put Lane on speaker.

"Sorry, but my phone's been ringing off the hook."

Disturbing his crossword puzzles? "From who?"

"The first one was the Watchung Reservation. Seems their grounds and golf course now have a disturbing brown stripe."

Charlie nodded at his partner. "See, I told you-"

Lane talked faster than normal. "Then there's the Ken Lockwood Gorge Wildlife Management Area. They called their owner - the NJ Department of Environmental Protection – and they called me. Hunters reported a brown stripe crossing their trout stream, on both banks. And, their hikers on the Columbia Trail confirmed it."

"You're proving my point." As long as the waitress had gone to the to the trouble, Charlie took a drink.

Lane had more to share. "The last call was from the US Army Corps of Engineers."

"What did they want?"

"Seems they're the managing partner for Crooked Creek Lake Park."

"In New Jersey?" asked Charlie.

"Pennsylvania. "

Charlie's hand shook as he put his cup on the saucer. He took a deep breath. "Pennsylvania."

Potter's jaw dropped. "It's heading west a lot faster than I ever imagined."

"Their historic property with the country's first water-powered sawmill and one-room schoolhouses dating back to 1867 has a brown stripe running through the center of it. Their historic tour trail is ruined. Charlie, what's happening out there?"

"The brown stripe isn't stopping for state borders, that's for sure. It may go cross-country." Charlie kept his voice low.

"Are you saying this is out of control? That's unacceptable!" Lane's voice became a whisper. "Listen, so far, I've managed to keep these reports from Stanton, but I don't know how much longer I can cover for you."

The restaurant was staring to fill up. Their waitress had gone off to serve other customers.

"You're supposed to keep our Director in the loop." *What was Lane thinking? When he finds out, he'll be really angry.* "Listen, you've done field work forever. Give me some guidance." Lane was silent for a long time. Charlie checked their connection. "Shouldn't you be mentoring me or something?"

Lane's voice was soft, unsure. "Sorry, kid. Nothing like this has ever happened before. This was supposed to be a simple assignment, so you could get your feet wet with field work. It wasn't supposed to get complicated."

"But it has." Charlie waited for a reply but got more dead air. "Thanks anyway." As he disconnected, it was clear to Charlie he was on his own. "Lane's been getting calls. The stripe is continuing west."

"I heard. Pennsylvania." Potter held her cup near her lips. "You got your wish, partner. Our case is a whole lot bigger than even I expected."

Charlie nodded. *Maybe too big? Can I really handle something this complicated, even with Potter's help?*

Potter checked her watch. "Sorry, I'd love to stay and think this through with you over dinner, but it's getting late." Potter took one last gulp and stood up from the table. "I promised to see my folks tonight. You going to be okay?" She put her hand on Charlie's shoulder and squeezed.

It's impossible to brainstorm on my own. "No problem. Before you go, could you please email my associate Lane a picture of the hexagon structures? You still have his cell number?"

Potter scrolled through texts on her phone. "Yeah." A few more taps. "Any message?"

"Tell him, 'This is where the brown stripe begins. Who knows where it will end?'"

More taps. "Done." Potter looked up from her device. "I wish I could stay. Should I call my folks and beg off?"

"No, go on. Family is important." Charlie made an educated guess, since he didn't have any.

"Okay, see you tomorrow." She meandered through the occupied tables, leaving Charlie alone.

He surrounded his cup with both hands, staring into the liquid.

The waitress came by with a pot and his bill. "Freshen your cup?"

"No thanks." He checked his watch, still too early for dinner. He put the charges on his hotel bill by signing and providing his room number.

In the elevator, he considered the path of the brown stripe, starting at that hexagon thing and spreading progressively west, all the way into Pennsylvania with no sign of stopping. With a clear pattern of expansion, the obvious question, the one Quincy Grissom would ask, was 'Why?'

39 – Matt (Eureka, California)

Matt was summoned to the President's office by means of a formal invitation on the President's letterhead, slid under his door during the night.

With a bony chill and goosebumps, he walked to the Administration building. A secretary escorted him in. Half-paneled walls with formal oak wainscoting below, white walls above, and matching oak crown molding at the ceiling decorated the President's office. She came around from behind her desk, her grey hair tucked neatly into a bun. She greeted Matt with an extended arm and open hand. "Mr. Thready, nice to meet you. I would have preferred better circumstances. Please, have a seat."

Two low-backed leather chairs faced the large oak desk.

"I'll stand, if you don't mind." Matt stood behind one chair and assumed the traditional at ease position with his hands behind his back.

"All right." The President sat on the edge of her desk, facing him. "I understand you were out in the east area of campus, interfering with a survey commissioned by my office."

"I wasn't in the way, and I didn't prevent them from doing their job." *Snotty sophomores didn't have to tattle.*

"Your mere presence was a distraction, and time is of the essence. As of now, that area is off limits to everyone except that team,"

I still need to find the missing stick. "But-"

She picked up a pen and absentmindedly clicked it. "Is there some reason for you to be loitering in that vicinity?"

The sound distracted Matt. "I – I – " *I can't tell the President I'm the operator of a portal.*

"I mentioned this in passing to Mr. Dixon, the Bates Foundation representative, who is coordinating the construction of our newly funded nanotechnology facility.

He volunteered to investigate, so I gave him your name. And do you know what he found?" The President reached for a manila folder, opened it, and slid out a color photograph of the portal.

The picture I posted! "He had no right-"

"I approved giving him the technical information he needed to access our servers. Needle And Thready, that's you, isn't it?"

Matt nodded in slow motion.

"You seem to have a significant interest in that structure. It wasn't authorized, and I don't know who built it." The President paused, perhaps to allow Matt the opportunity to confess. When that didn't happen, she continued. "Given its size and weight, I can't believe it's the result of a single individual's efforts. Do you have anything to say for yourself?"

"No ma'am. Except, I think you should leave it alone."

She scratched her head with the pen. "Really? Despite its location in a construction zone?"

"You're in charge, not the guy from Bates. Construction can wait. At least for a while." *Until I operate it.*

"How do you justify this delay? For what reason?" She stood and folded her arms. Sunlight through the blinds painted diagonal stripes on her dark blue dress.

Matt shook his head. "You wouldn't understand."

"You are correct, Mr. Thready. I don't. The Bates Foundation established a schedule, but now they've accelerated it. From my perspective, the sooner they start, the sooner students will be able to take advantage." She took a deep breath. "Let me be blunt. Did you build that thing?"

"I'm not taking credit, ma'am." *The same kind of non-answer I use with my parents.*

"All right, but given your posting and your presence in the vicinity, you seem to be very interested in it. Mr. Dixon is preparing to demolish it, but if it's related to one of your classes, you might be happier if it was disassembled. Possibly relocated to another area on campus?"

Matt remembered how firmly the portal was rooted. *I can't let it be damaged.* "It has to stay where it is. Besides, your survey team can tell you, the sticks that form the structures have grown together. It can't be disassembled."

A rumbling outside interrupted their conversation. The President walked to her window and peeked through the blinds. Matt chose an adjacent one. Dozens of students lined the street as a convoy of vehicles, led by Dixon in his convertible followed by a huge motor home, a semitrailer and several smaller trucks, drove through campus towards the football field. The crowd followed the entourage as the vehicles continued out of sight.

The President stood, releasing the blinds. "It seems Mr. Dixon has returned, in force."

Preparing his attack on my portal. "Dixon will confirm there are no seams, and the whole thing seems to have taken root."

"No one shared those details with me. Thank you." She touched her forehead with her index finger, as if trying to remember the question. "Well then, what do you suggest as an alternative?"

Aside from kicking Dixon off campus? "Leave the trellises alone, at least for a little while." Matt didn't know how soon he'd operate the portal. "If you're patient, they'll help all of us more than some science building." He imagined new inventions, unlimited cheap power, all kinds of Earth-shattering improvements. "After that, they'll simply disappear." Matt wondered how he knew that, but he did.

"It sounds like a fairy tale. Vanishing trellises, hmm? Not a credible solution, I'm afraid. Mr. Dixon is on a deadline. He won't be pleased with waiting for the situation to fix itself."

"Why not? It won't be too much longer, and it'll be easier and cheaper than paying for removal." *Assuming he can dig it out.*

The second rumble was louder than the first. They both sprinted to their respective windows.

Heavy machinery – bulldozers, backhoes and dump trucks – formed the second wave, heading in the same direction.

"The Bates Foundation is being very generous. I'd hate for any delay to cause them to change their minds. As you'll learn eventually, corporations are driven by financial deadlines with large consequences. Demolition of your trellis is pocket change." She turned from the window.

"And you're okay with him digging up campus? Perhaps if you talked to him-"

"He's not digging up campus. He's starting construction of a state-of-the-art nanotechnology center. As a gift!" The President walked around her desk and plopped down in her leather chair. "It isn't only him you're dealing with. There is also the matter of defacing campus property."

Matt hadn't considered building the portal as harmful. Just the opposite. "It's hidden in the woods." He strode to the desk and leaned on it with stiff arms. "Everything will be resolved, I promise. Just be patient."

"That doesn't excuse the fact that, today, there is an unauthorized structure in the far southeast corner of college property. Someone must be held responsible." The President stood, and placed her hand on Matt's shoulder. "Your status as advocate, if not architect and builder, puts the spotlight on you."

Matt pulled back, fell into one of the chairs and gripped the padded leather arms. "Are you expelling me?" *I'll never hear the end of this from Dad. Financial management apprenticeship, here I come!*

"Nothing quite so drastic. A probationary period, during which student affairs will monitor your behavior. Any deviations from acceptable practices, and I will take more drastic measures."

The President didn't have to be more explicit. One more incident, and Matt was out on his ear. He stood. "Thank you, ma'am. I appreciate your consideration."

"Let's hope these trellises of yours finish their business quickly. Or, that Mr. Dixon is successful. In the meantime, stay away from them. Understood?"

Until I need to operate them. "Absolutely!"

40 – Kwashay (Brooklyn, New York)

One of the ways Kwashay maintained excellent grades was thorough copious note taking. She accumulated volumes of notes from her classes, which she used to review her course material.

Lately, her notebooks were nearly void of anything relevant to her classes, instead filled with sketches of the dual hexagonal structures and their roots. On a double page, she'd drawn a detailed root system, twelve major root stems, six from each structure, growing together into a massive root trunk. The images were clear in her head, as opposed to her classroom material, which was vague and imprecise. *I wonder how I'm supposed to operate a bunch of rods?*

Her answers to pop quizzes from her biology and history teachers were riddled with mistakes, atypical for Kwashay.

"What's wrong?" both teachers had asked.

"It's- it's my mother," Kwashay had answered. She let them assume the worst.

The only positive result was in her art class. Her teacher had already rejected the portal across the street in the park because, according to the police detective, it wasn't solely her work.

As the teacher walked the aisles, she saw Kwashay's sketches in her math notebook. "This is beautiful! What is it?"

"The portal's root system, heading directly west." The words flowed without thinking.

"Well, I don't care what it is. The detail is amazing! How about if we use this as your project assignment?"

The portal had secrets, even though it stood in public view. Kwashay reluctantly held her notebook up. The teacher tore two pages from it and posted them to the classroom wall.

As she drew another sketch, this one including a brown stripe starting at the base, Kwashay wondered the cause of the delay. *I'm ready to operate it. Maybe the other one isn't built yet.* Her anxiety was fueled by the promised benefits. *I hope it cures illnesses or puts an end to starvation. That would be awesome.*

Later, during Kwashay's study hall period, she asked to use the computer lab, where she examined her PictureNet account for messages about the photo of the portal she'd posted, one without her. Nothing. *It was a long shot.*

41 - Selton (Kearney, Nebraska)

Selton put down a selection from 383.49, Mail Service, a new edition of a book he'd previously read. It had become much more difficult to store new information in his bloated cells, often forcing a reorganization of existing material, which in turn gave Selton more time to daydream and speculate.

The amount of information Selton had gathered was staggering. Even he was impressed with his success. Under the weight of all of that information, he constantly battled the urge to share it. After all, that's what his genetics had programmed him to do, with fellow Serulians.

Selton had decided he was full, unable to ingest even one more magazine, not the richest of resources. He struggled to get out of his chair but finally got to his feet. He was about to depart early from the library when a book on the Specials table caught his eye: Moonwalking with Einstein: The Art and Science of Remembering Everything by Joshua Foer. The title contained the name of one of Selton's Earthling heroes, in his view the smartest human who ever lived. And the subject, remembering everything, so directly relevant to his circumstance.

He considered the possibility of deleting his Personal Information Journal. *Removing that information could risk everything else.* "One more book" he said out loud.

Selton landed heavy in his preferred chair. He turned the pages more slowly than normal, to allow his physiology to keep up with his reading. When he'd completed the tome, he slumped back. He couldn't move, like a boulder was on his chest.

When a fellow library patron, an older gentleman with white hair walking with the aid of a cane, asked if he knew where the books on transportation were filed, Selton couldn't hold back.

Selton pointed to a specific row of shelves. "The main section is 380, which also includes commerce and communications. Section 385 covers railroad transportation, 386 deals with inland waterway and ferry transportation, and 387 describes water, air and space exploration. There's also 388 for city transit."

The gentleman nodded in thanks, but Selton wasn't finished. He sat up and kept talking. "The international standard rail gauge of 1,435 mm (4 feet 8 1□2 inch) width, still used by about 60% of the world's railways, was adopted based on the early wagon-ways." He prattled on about railway gauges in the U.S. and Europe.

Other patrons began to stare. Selton attempted to silence himself but failed. The urge to share was too strong. "The years between 1850 and 1890 saw phenomenal growth in the US railroad system, which at its peak constituted one third of the world's total mileage. Although the American Civil War placed a temporary halt to major new developments, the conflict did demonstrate the enormous strategic importance of railways at times of war." He described innovations in the 19th and 20th centuries regarding train car and rail construction materials, and heating, cooling and lighting improvements.

People in the vicinity shooshed. The man waved his hand furiously, attempting to stop the outpouring, but Selton had lost control. The best he could do was to switch subjects. "A ferry or ferryboat is a boat or ship, a merchant vessel, used to carry primarily passengers, and sometimes vehicles and cargo as well, across a body of water. Ferries form a part of the public transport systems of many waterside cities and islands, allowing direct transit between points at a capital cost much lower than bridges or tunnels."

"That's quite enough." The gentleman's face was bright red. Selton worried that he'd cause the man a stroke. Still, the information flowed. "Washington State Ferries operate the most extensive ferry system in the United States, with ten routes on Puget Sound and the Strait of Juan de Fuca serving terminals in Washington and Vancouver Island." Selton continued with details about the Staten Island Ferry and others that shuttle commuters along the Hudson River from locations in New Jersey and Northern Manhattan down to the midtown, downtown and Wall Street business centers.

"Can you just shut up?" shouted someone behind the table of consumer reference materials.

Bernice, who had been standing on a ladder observing Selton's unusual behavior, scurried over to his chair and put her hand on his shoulder. "What's wrong?"

Selton slowly shook his head. He'd completely lost control.

The elder patron leaned into Bernice's face. "Can you do something? All I asked was where the transportation books are filed."

Selton looked at Bernice with pleading eyes as he continued his information dump about modern aviation for another five minutes that felt like eternity. He decided to depart lest he be precluded from further visits due to disturbing library rules.

Bernice had to assist him to his feet when he struggled to stand on his own. "Selton?"

As he exited the building and walked towards the rail yard, his monologue continued, passersby the audience. They jaywalked to get away from the stranger who instructed everyone in sight. "The first rocket to reach space, an altitude of 189 km, was the German V-2 rocket, on a test flight in June 1944. The first human spaceflight was Vostok 1 on April 12, 1961, aboard which Soviet cosmonaut Yuri Gagarin made one orbit around the Earth."

As Selton waited for the stoplight to change, he lectured passing vehicles. "NASA considered launching Apollo missions directly into lunar trajectories but adopted the strategy of first entering a temporary parking orbit and then performing a separate burn several orbits later onto a lunar trajectory."

The light changed, but not Selton's urge to continue sharing. "The parking orbit was a stable 'mission plateau' that gave the crew and controllers several hours to thoroughly check out the spacecraft after the stresses of launch before committing it to a long lunar flight." Selton thought about Dissemination Oversight and wondered if they would use a similar technique when they came for him.

Sheltered by the underpass, Selton plopped down against the concrete wall exhausted and gathered his breath. His mission was to gather information, not become the center of attention. Although there were hours to go before the library closed, he viewed a return as certainly embarrassing and potentially disruptive.

All of the knowledge and insights Selton had accumulated must be valuable to Serulia. *Otherwise, why go to all the effort and expense to send me here?* His previous skepticism about the potential use of Earth information was heightened by his recent episode. *How will I share the Earth information when I return to Serulia? There won't be enough time for me to pass along everything I've gathered.* His mission made less and less sense the more he considered the details and implications.

Selton's physiology was still searching for the proper place to store his recent ingestion about remembering. Regurgitating information about space travel stoked his curiosity about how the project leaders would execute his recall. After all, he had arrived as a seed implanted within a nutritive-laded meteorite, so small it wasn't detected by any of the sophisticated scanning and radar systems employed for national security. But now, as large as most Earthling males, how could Selton escape undetected? He invented scenarios, all of which were problematic. Buying a seat on a Russian launch to the International Space Station, where a Serulian ship would arrive to take him back? Replicate a stunt by a man who ascended to the outer reaches of the atmosphere by balloon, to again be greeted by a Serulian ship? All of these required technology and resources unavailable to him.

He had absorbed vast amounts of knowledge but almost nothing in the way of material wealth, only the funds Marathon Man had provided, and much of that had been donated to American gypsies whose needs were greater than his own. His half-sibling Sprint also took a share.

Perhaps the return mechanism was delivered along with Selton, and it would be triggered at the proper moment? *But where was it, and how would it work?*

Selton inventoried the unanswered questions. How would he be recalled? How would he communicate the gathered information once back on Serulia? For the first time, Selton considered how Dissemination Oversight would use the information he'd absorbed. *I'm clueless about Serulian intentions.* From books, he'd learned how Earthlings had taken beneficial technology and used it for dangerous and fatal purposes. Could delivering the accumulated knowledge be harmful to Earthlings? Who knows what unscrupulous Serulians would do with this information? To protect Earthlings, when he returned to Serulia, Selton decided he would err on the side of caution.

42 – Charlie (New York, NY)

Charlie waited for Dean in his hotel room at a small round table, absentmindedly taking bites of New York-style cheese, sausage and mushroom pizza while reading his Quincy Grissom novel.

> Grissom's Undergrads visited the companies that were common to the defrauded cardholders but without luck. No

employees remembered the transactions or had any instinct they were fraudulent. Grissom was at a dead end until he got a call from Indulge Financial. Seems there were more instances of fraud, and they wanted Grissom's help before their reputation as a secure provider of financial services was ruined. As a show of good faith, they provided unredacted lists of transactions from all of the affected clients, previous and new.

From these more complete documents, Grissom found some interesting details. Every defrauded cardholder's account included a legitimate transaction at an appraisal service or pawnshop, followed by fraudulent purchase of a one-way airline ticket and rental of a full-sized car. *Finally, some patterns!*

With this additional information, Grissom again dispatched his Undergrads, this time to visit the appraisers and pawn shops in the corresponding cities. He advised them to browse the merchandise and ask how the shop would appraise a hypothetical family heirloom. He was going to do something similar at the local shop used by his client, Harrison Bainbridge, but needed to obtain a special prop first.

Grissom also scanned through the list of fraudulently purchased airline tickets, all obtained through a website named www.flyzone.com: Los Angeles to

Sacramento, New York City to Albany, Chicago to Springfield, Houston to Austin and Miami to Tallahassee. The coordination of overlapping travel dates was just too precise for a group to pull off without a coordinator. A master planner was Grissom's target.

A knock at his door startled Charlie. "Who's there?"

The voice through the door said, "Dean Matthews. I have the results from the soil tests."

Charlie placed a bookmark and checked his watch. It was nearly eight o'clock. He yanked open the door.

"Nice to meet you." Dean offered his hand and Charlie shook it. "Sorry it took so long, but I had to rerun some of the tests twice." He handed Charlie a manila envelope with a butterfly clasp.

Did Dean mean rerun the tests, or rerun them twice? "How come?"

Dean's eyes returned to Charlie after checking out the room. "Because the first time, we found a whole lot of nothing."

Wasn't this case difficult enough? Why did this young man have to speak in riddles? "Nothing?"

"Exactly! Open it." Dean pointed to the envelope. As Charlie pressed the clasp, Dean kept talking. "We found no traces of any known pathogens. None."

"So that's a good thing, right?" One possible cause of dead grass was eliminated.

"If only. We also found no traces of physical harm at the microscopic level, so we ruled out insects."

Charlie finally got the drift. "So you came up empty?"

"You don't understand." Dean was agitated, almost shaking. "There were also no nutrients in the soil. None. And no microorganisms. Not even a single mycelium."

Charlie slid the papers from the envelope. "That's impossible."

"What you brought us was completely dead dirt. It's no wonder the grass died."

Charlie didn't have to brainstorm regarding the root cause. *The hexagonal structure is sucking everything out of the soil. No nutrients, no microorganisms, nothing to support life.* He fetched the white food bag from the flat counter that held the TV set. "I have a few more samples from a park in Brooklyn. Can you do the same analysis?"

Dean grinned. "Sure. Do you want them tonight?"

"Not necessary." Charlie expected identical results, based on what Dean had learned from Governors Island and Liberty Island samples. "Within the next day or two-"

"I'll do them first thing tomorrow." Dean grasped the bag, cradling it.

Charlie expected Dean to leave, but he hung around with questions about the soil analysis. "My first guess was high levels of radiation. But the soil samples had no signs of radioactivity."

"Uh huh." Charlie couldn't share the details of an incomplete investigation. *Grissom never does that.*

"Besides, this was a big area, right?" Dean rocked back and forth.

Charlie nodded. "Anything generating radiation over all of those square miles would have been noticed." *Why won't he just leave?*

"So then what?" Dean glanced at the pizza box. "Some kind of botanical virus?" He wiggled his fingers. "Or aliens?"

Soil sucking creatures from outer space? Is that what the hexagonal structure is? "Not likely." Charlie shifted the topic. "What about the samples of live grass?"

"Picture perfect, just like you'd expect. The report documents all of my measurements in detail. Would you like me to run through the numbers?" Dean reached for the papers in Charlie's hand.

Charlie pulled the first real facts for his case close. "No, no need. What do I owe you?" He reached for a business card, so Dean could submit an invoice.

Dean waved him off. "No, sir. It was a privilege. I've never seen anything like this. Would it be okay if I wrote it up, kind of like a case study?"

Charlie didn't want any of this made public, at least not in the middle of his investigation. "After this is all sorted out and resolved, the agency will make that decision."

For the first time since he arrived, Dean's smile faded. "All right, if you say so." He half-saluted, then stared at the flat box. "You going to eat all that? I was working on the analysis and skipped dinner-"

Charlie lifted the cardboard lid. "Go on, take a slice."

Dean pulled one from the box and folded it over. "Thanks."

"No, thank you for your good work." Charlie grabbed a napkin from the table and handed it to the young man.

Dean left, pizza in his mouth, cradling the samples with one hand and shutting the door behind him with the other. Charlie plopped down in his chair. The pizza was stone cold. He put down the papers and fondled the closed novel. “No nutrients. No microorganisms. Grass won’t grow in dead dirt.” He made a note to send a copy of the report to Lane.

Dean had identified the dead grass’s cause, but Charlie and Potter were no closer to the bigger questions, let alone answers. *Why would that structure drain everything from the soil?* Frustrated, Charlie returned to his bookmarked place in the novel.

> Grissom didn’t believe in coincidences, only patterns. The authorities, however, would demand proof in the form of facts and evidence before engaging.
>
> Visits to appraisers and pawnshops were hot clues, but Grissom had even more insights from the details. From his experience, he knew that people rent the least expensive and therefore smallest car possible, so these folks needed to carry either people or cargo. Grissom also noticed that the bad transactions always began on the first day of a new billing period, giving them the longest possible time before they’d be detected. *Smart.* There had to be more than one perpetrator, since some flights were on the same dates. He searched his tall mahogany credenza for maps, among the travel guides, foreign dictionaries, and previous case files, and came up empty. He decided fresh air would help him think better

so he left his office for a stroll, concentrating on the airline flights.

At the corner, Grissom took a diagonal shortcut across a gas station. Through the filthy window, he saw a yellowed continental US map pinned to a corkboard on the office wall. He wandered in and bought it for a crisp dollar bill from a puzzled proprietor.

Back in his office, Grissom used a highlighter to mark the origin cities in blue and the destinations in red. After just three pairs of markings, the pattern was obvious: the destinations were all state capitals.

Charlie doubted there was a master planner behind the brown stripe. The hexagon tower was messing with Mother Nature. And just like Grissom, he had a list of cities, each new one further west, but none of them were state capitals. *Maybe I should get a map.* He glanced at the clock: ten fifteen. He marked his place and went to bed.

43 - Matt (Eureka, CA)

Matt left the President's office, grabbed his books from his room and headed for History class. He'd taken one step off the sidewalk when somebody grabbed his arm from behind, spinning him around.

Fred? His former best friend had been ignoring him ever since Matt failed to show up for their double date. "You gotta come with me."

Matt pulled his arm free, surprised Fred would have anything to say to him. "I can't. My History teacher is going to cover what's on the final."

"Copy somebody's notes. If anybody should be interested in seeing that trellis thing of yours bulldozed, it's you."

Matt's stomach felt empty, and not because he'd skipped breakfast for the meeting with the President. "Today?" He'd heard and seen the heavy equipment, but had no idea that Dixon would move that fast. *The portal needs to remain standing long enough for me to operate it. I wish they'd give me the go ahead already. What's it waiting for?*

"I've got a piece of the action, too. I found the guys who built the scaffold for you, remember?" Groups of students passed by, all going in the direction of the portal. "You'll need a friend to lean on, when they smash it to pieces."

"That's what I'll need all right." *Why couldn't Fred just let me go to class? Why do I have to see it?* Operating the portal would have been Matt's chance to succeed at something really important. *Not just some first place video game trophy. And after Dixon knocks it down, there'll only be one portal and some other operator, and that's not enough.*

Fred took a couple of bouncy sidesteps. "Come on, before all of the good spots are taken."

Matt remembered the President's order to stay away. *After demolition, there'll be nothing to stay away from.* Maybe as operator, he had an obligation to be there. "Okay, let's go."

Matt's pace left Fred behind, huffing, puffing and churning his arms. "Save me a spot."

Matt ran past other students, bobbing and weaving. When he reached the football field, he slowed. The motor home and trucks had parked on the grass, destroying the playing surface. Several people were moving from the motorhome to the semitrailer, whose open rear doors exposed a mobile laboratory filled with scientific instruments Matt couldn't identify. Most of the people were dressed uniformly: blue polo shirts, khaki slacks and thigh-length white lab coats. A few of them were setting up tents.

Fred still hadn't caught up. Matt accelerated to a taped-off area at the street, well away from the portal. A thick red streamer reading BATES every three feet surrounded the entire wooded area. He tested the material. Flexible and strong. It held not only his weight but also the others in the crowd who leaned on it for support, straining to witness the destruction. The heavy machinery was still being positioned. Diesel fumes blew in their direction.

Students milled about, anxious for something to happen, even if they were kept a distance. A bulldozer and a backhoe were moving back and forth, threading a path into the wooded area. The waiting was too much for Matt. It reminded him of the months his family stood by before his grandmother passed away. *When they knock it down, they'll mess up the planet's chance for a better future and kill my dream at the same time.*

Matt made his way through the crowd and wandered back toward the student center. Fred was just arriving. "Where are you going?"

"They've blocked it off. I can't see anything anyway. Let me know when it's done." Matt's backpack hung from one shoulder as he trudged to the student union. His stomach insisted that he grab an early lunch before his History class.

The atmosphere in the cafeteria was electric, students buzzing about the invasion of campus and the impending construction of a state-of-the-art nanotechnology center. Because protected redwood forests surrounded the school, new buildings didn't happen very often, even if the college could afford them. This one was a gift from Bates.

Evidently the few students buying food and eating didn't feel they needed to witness the groundbreaking. *Dixon's justification for the demolition.* Short lines for the grill allowed Matt to order a burger and fries without much wait except cooking time.

Even inside the cafeteria, Matt heard the remote growl of engines. He decided that after the portal was demolished, he didn't want to stay any longer than necessary. *How will I be able to concentrate with that memory pounding in my head? If I pass all of my finals with good grades, maybe I can convince my folks to put me back in a four-year school.*

Matt reviewed his History notes as he toyed with his fries. The final was supposed to be an essay. He sucked at essays, forced to drone on and on with some analysis of meaningless events that happened a long time ago.

Clusters of students came though the doors, a steady stream. Soon, the place was packed. *The show must be over.*

Fred lurched into the cafeteria, his jeans and cotton jacket streaked with dirt, winded. He looked around, smiled at a couple of female students, and finally approached Matt's table. "You won't believe it." He bent over, using the table for support.

"Where have you been?"

Fred's body heaved as he caught his breath. "I walked all the way around, to get a decent view." His breathing was slowing to normal. "And guess what?"

Why is Fred being so cruel? "The trellis is a pile of rubble?" Matt picked up his tasteless sandwich and took another bite.

The room got noisier as more students arrived after Fred, all chattering.

Fred leaned closer. "Nope. It's still standing." He swiped a French fry from Matt's plate.

Matt almost choked. "What?"

"After you left, I walked around to the other side, and I had a clear shot. Maybe they didn't bother roping that off because that's where the College property ends." Fred brushed at his dirty pants, then wolfed down the thin piece of potato, almost without chewing. "All I know is, they pushed at it with a bulldozer and it didn't budge. Then that guy we saw in the convertible – he's from Bates – forced his way into the driver seat and rammed the trellis a couple of times. All he did was dent the front scoop."

"He did?" Matt knew the portal was gaining mass, but he had no idea it was so impervious to damage. "I can't believe it!"

Fred stood, hands on his thighs for support, still breathing deep. "Then they tried digging it out with a backhoe, but it has really thick roots, so they gave up."

Matt had examined those himself. "That's amazing!"

"I saw the Bates guy storm toward the motor home." Fred finally stood up straight and pulled his pants to his waist. "He was really pissed."

"I bet." Matt relaxed in his chair, as the possibility of portal damage shrunk. *If it's that strong, maybe it's ready to be operated. I just wish they'd tell me how. What's taking so long?*

"So what is that thing, anyway, huh?", asked Fred. "You can't tell your best friend?"

Matt stood up, emptied his tray into a trash bin, and put his arm around Fred. "Let's find someplace more private and I'll tell you a story." He felt the burden of secrecy begin to drain even before he shared the tale.

44 – Kwashay (Brooklyn, NY)

Kwashay nestled into the corner of the couch in her living room, turning pages in her English composition textbook without looking at them, ignoring the TV show her mother was watching. When the phone rang, Kwashay swung her feet from beneath her, preparing to answer it.

Instead, her mother waved her off and picked up the cordless receiver, an atypical luxury she'd purchased at the local flea market. "Williams-Jackson residence."

She listened for a moment and then said, "Kwashay lost her telephone privileges because of some recent bad behavior choices. You can see her at school-"

More listening, then an explosion. "You? Are you the punk she was seeing?"

Sideways was calling? Kwashay muted the TV, got up and moved closer to the phone. Her mother made a "zip your lip" gesture and pressed the speakerphone button.

Sideways' voice blasted out of the speaker in mid-sentence. "- sculpture thing in the park. Hardly seein'. Just hung out. Listen, the cops picked me up. I told them I did the deed. You know, the scaffold? That was me and my crew."

"I knew it." Mother stared daggers. "I told her not to have anything to do with people like you-"

"You're right. I messed up real bad. But this is serious. Grand theft they're sayin."

"How did you get our number?" Her mother's eyes were focused like lasers. "Did my daughter give it to you?"

"No, ma'am. It was on her papers. In her backpack. I copied it down."

Kwashay pressed the mute button on the phone base. "Sideways returned my backpack after I lost it."

Through the speaker, Sideways' voice said, "They're telling me only three minutes."

"His name is Vondell. You can tell me about losing your backpack later." Her mother unmuted the call. "So why are you calling my daughter?"

"I didn't know who else to call. She's wicked smart. Plus, I did her a favor, building that thing."

Her mother rocked back and forth, hands behind her back. "How about your own family?"

"Ain't got none to speak of. Folks passed. Brother hangs with some kind of gang. He's the kind I try to protect Girly-girl from."

Her mother silently mouthed 'Girly-girl' with one raised eyebrow. "Are you telling me you hang around in the park, watching out for my daughter?"

"You got it. Listen, can she talk already, cause they're telling me to hang up?"

Kwashay watched her mother's expression melt from angled-eyebrow anger to droopy-eyed concern. She leaned forward so far, she almost fell on her face. Waiting for her mother to respond was torture.

This time, her mother pressed mute. "Vondell thinks he's your protector, a self-appointed body guard. Has he ever done anything to make you think he's dangerous?"

Vondell's voice blared from the speaker. "You still there? Hello?"

"In our few face-to-face conversations, he's been a gentleman. And no one else has ever accosted me, so maybe he-"

Her mother motioned a finger to her lips and unmuted the call. "I'm here. I'll bring Kwashay down to see you personally."

"You don't has to do that. Just maybe find somebody who can-"

"It's no bother. I want to meet you anyway. Where are they holding you?"

"They're keepin' me in lock up. 84th Precinct down on Gold Street."

"We know the place. We'll see you –" The line went dead. "Did he hang up on me?'

"The officer probably did." *What is she planning?* "Mama-" said Kwashay.

"Get your jacket-" Her voice became nasal. "Girly-girl." Back to normal. "That young man is all on his own, and that's not proper, no matter what he did. And on the way, you'll tell me all about losing your backpack and books, and what he built for you." She took one long last look at the TV before turning it off and escorting her daughter out of their apartment.

Kwashay knew the route, the same train she took to school every day.

"This is the train I took to rescue from Detective Washington." Her mother sat with her purse firmly planted in her lap, covered by both hands. "Now, why don't you tell me how Vondell found your backpack?"

After explaining the circumstances of her backpack loss and return, omitting the part about portal rods too heavy to lift, they remained silent on the train ride, and during the walk towards the police station. Kwashay took them on a detour only slightly out of their way so she could show her mother the portal.

"That's what Vondell built?" her mother asked. "I didn't expect it to be so big."

"Shhh. About eight feet tall." Two people wearing blue nylon jackets worked within the yellow taped-off area. One used a red beam laser to measure its height, diameter and the length of each of the six sides. The other took close-up photos and ran his hand along the surface of the horizontal and vertical rods. *The rods look thicker. It's growing!*

Yellow lettering on their jackets said EPA. *Even worse than the police!* She found herself wandering closer, right up to the tape, to be sure they weren't hurting it by taking samples. *Is it ready to be operated? The longer we wait, the more likely someone will interfere.* They seemed just as interested in the browned-out grass and dead bushes as the structure.

Her mother came up from behind. "What are they doing?"

"Whatever it is, I wish they'd just go away." *I'm the operator, the one who'll make the planet better.* The portals depended on her and her partner. *Anyone else will just mess things up.*

Kwashay's mother took her by the arm. "Come on now, Vondell is waiting for us."

After they left the vicinity of the portal and continued on the sidewalk, she saw cars parked nearby marked with emblems for the Environmental Protection Agency. *A Federal agency has more authority than the police. They'll probably want to remove it.*

Kwashay and her mother entered the police station and were escorted to the visitor area. They requested Vondell but neither could answer the officer's question, "First or last name?" He scowled and commanded them to take a seat in the first open position.

Kwashay had to pull up a second chair, since each visitor position had one phone and one chair. A few minutes later, Sideways -- Vondell -- was escorted out in an orange prisoner uniform, without his hat. He swung the chair backwards, plopped down and picked up the receiver. Kwashay did the same, holding it between their heads. "Hi." She introduced her mother.

Sideways nodded his head. "Pleasure to meet you."

"So, what happened?" asked Kwashay's mother. "The truth!"

"We couldn't finish building Girly-girl's sculpture 'cause it was too tall to reach, so we borrowed the scaffold. We would have put it back, honest, but the cops showed up just when we were finishin'. Me and my crew, we ran like hell. They traced the heist back to us. Video from the construction site, somethin' like that. Anyway, I didn't make a fuss. We did it, just like they said. Now they gotta' figure out what to do to me."

Sideways became a thief just to get the portal built. As a favor for me. "I'll vouch for you." Kwashay put her open hand on the glass.

Her mother pulled it down. "You'll do no such thing. You put my daughter in jeopardy."

"You got it backwards." Vondell squirmed in his chair. "There's bad folks, really bad, stalk the area by the school. They pick off young ones like Girly-girl, don't think nothin' of it. Me and my crew, we hang out, keep them away. We protecting her."

Like my grandma's spirit, watching out for me. Kwashay rubbed her locket between her thumb and index finger.

"I find that hard to believe. I've heard stories about – about young men like you." Her mother threw Kwashay a stern glance.

I believe Sideways' motives were pure. And I still can't tell him how important his efforts were.

Kwashay allowed her mother to lead the conversation. "Why did you choose Kwashay? There are lots of girls at her school."

"I dunno. Maybe 'cause she looked like the stray sheep what gets eaten by the wolf. Maybe 'cause she were messing with those sticks, and I like puzzles. Maybe instinct. Not sure for sure."

"Sideways has never done anything to hurt me. Just the opposite." She kept her hands flat on the table and glanced at her mother. *Is that why my mother came down here? To accuse Sideways?* "What happens next?"

"They got me a public defender. He can plead me out."

A guard approached. "Time's up."

Kwashay tugged her mother's arm. "Sideways will end up in prison, and it's my fault. Please, can't you do something?"

"His name is Vondell, and you didn't force him to steal that scaffold."

The guard helped Vondell to his feet. He clutched the phone in his outstretched arm.

Kwashay felt a tear run down her cheek.

"Give us a minute!" Kwashay's mother waved a hand at the guard and grabbed the phone from her daughter.

The guard checked his watch and let go of Vondell's arm. He plopped down hard in his chair and brought the receiver to his ear.

"It seems my daughter was a motivating factor in what you did. And if you've been watching out for her like you claim, then I owe you."

Kwashay startled at her mother's change of attitude. *Did Sideways convince her?*

"My brother, Kwashay's uncle, is a lawyer," said her mother. "He doesn't do criminal cases, but his firm does. I'll have him find someone to take your case, pro bono."

Kwashay leaned in and said, "That means free."

"I know what it means. I may work the street instead of a classroom, but that don't mean I'm stupid."

The guard tugged at Vondell's chair, so he stood up and followed him out of the room, glancing back at Kwashay and her mother.

"If there's a way to spin this to Vondell's advantage, your uncle can do it." Mother patted Kwashay's hand. "You just watch!"

On the walk back to the train station, Kwashay decided to share the entire story with her mother, visions, portal and all. *I can't go on, keeping this from her. If I keep her in the dark, how will I ever explain my obligation when it comes time to operate the portal?*

45 - Selton (Kearney, NE)

Selton watched a hobo jump from a slowing train, glance around at the trains in motion, select one and run alongside, grasping a handrail and pulling himself aboard before it picked up speed and chugged out of the yard. His internals were throbbing, remembering the days of his own travels. Back then, it was easier to find new green spaces in the places they stopped and made camp. Not so now.

Thoughts of nutrition led him to seek fertile soil earlier than usual. Since he'd had success south of the train yard in private backyards, that was the direction he headed.

Selton had many questions that weren't answered by the books he'd read. In section 640 of the library, he had read all about home economics and family living. Selton lacked the experience and imagination to fully understand the nature of families or households, despite his years of travel with hobos. Novels about family life made concepts more real, but even great stories were no substitute for personal experience. If Marathon and his son Sprint had been his real father and brother, Selton expected his relationships with them would have been much richer and more complicated.

That same section contained books about cooking, preparing foods for consumption. Selton felt lucky, that he could just absorb the nutrients he required from the land in his unique way. Earth's soil was a gift that sustained him.

Every one of the tomes in that section left him wondering what the results of heating and chopping and blending and seasoning would taste like. Without taste buds, he would never experience those Earthling sensations. Nightly, his body processed chemicals from the soil, the closest simulation.

As he crossed three sets of rails, he stopped to examine the haphazard vegetation along the railroad tracks. Sumac trees with thin trunks spread unencumbered. Red sumac bushes had lined the track beds down in Florida. Stands of green St. John's wort with bright black-speckled yellow flowers decorated the areas along the steel trails. Beds of shiny green tri-leaf poison ivy covered the ground, pretty from a distance.

A few office buildings sat just south of the rail yard, a buffer to the nearby neighborhood. Both the Buffalo County Justice Center and a single-story lawyer's office across the street had lush green front lawns but were too exposed.

Further south, most private residences had well-manicured and well-fed lawns. The outdoor spaces were much larger than human families required, wasteful allocations. Selton examined the formerly green landscape of a yard he'd used for many previous feedings. At random locations on the lawn, his backroots inflicted puncture wounds in the soil surrounded by brown circles, dark in the center and feathered out to light brown near the edges. Splotchy patterns from dozens of visits created a canvas that made additional feedings unviable.

A couple of houses down, the backyard was unmowed with no obvious fecal droppings and no fence, which predicted no family pets. The sun was just disappearing on the horizon, making this an early feeding. He doffed his jacket and shirt, examined the excavation site in his belly to be certain the blossom had not regrown, and settled in. His body almost disappeared in the tall grass.

It wasn't too long after his roots had planted themselves when floodlights illuminated his feeding ground and a young voice shouted, "Look, mommy, a naked man!"

Selton ripped himself from the soil, grabbed his shirt and coat. Two humans were silhouetted behind a large sliding glass door. Through the opening, he heard a female scream. Out from the back of the house leaped a bone polisher, growling and panting. Selton didn't take the time to determine the breed. He ran through several open yards, busted through a couple of gates and out to the sidewalk. Barking continued until he heard the animal's owner call its name – Pluto? Selton didn't stop running until he reached an open green space. The sign read Centennial Park. He leaned against a tree, hoping the animal had given up the chase. Would those homeowners come looking for him?

When it was clear that no one was in pursuit, he took up his normal prone position shielded from street view by scattered trees. Before he could doze off, the ground beneath him shook, announcing another communication.

"It is almost time. You will receive specific instructions."

Selton almost jumped for joy but his backroots held him fast. *I'm going home!*

Despite his pleasure at the news, Selton lamented the fact that he wouldn't be able to say good-byes to all of the humans who'd nurtured him, extended kindnesses to him, had become friends with him. Good-byes to the hobos with whom he traveled. Good-bye to Sprint. Good-bye to the librarians.

All of Selton's remaining attention and energy would be directed at planning for and executing his departure, as soon as he received the details. Even with the end in sight, his worries multiplied. *I wonder how they're going to get me home? I hope they don't make me wait too long for the details. Can I trust them to follow through? Every message feels incomplete, as if they're holding back.* Selton stared at the black sky, his mental gymnastics an obstacle to a restful slumber.

46 – Charlie (New York City, NY)

Charlie spent a restless night tossing and turning. He'd dreamt about microscopic organisms dumped into the agricultural heartland by foreign terrorists, spreading across the country via rain and wind, turning grass brown.

He woke in a cold sweat, shivering with an ache in his stomach. He dragged himself into the shower, but the hot water didn't wash away the nightmare. After drying, shaving and dressing, he took advantage of the breakfast buffet in his hotel. While he gobbled up eggs, bacon and hash browns washed down with a cup of coffee, he picked up where he'd left off in the novel.

Grissom had identified a number of useful patterns from the new data, most recently that the perpetrators all took one-way flights that terminated in state capitals. Identifying patterns in pursuit of the solution warmed Grissom's heart, chilled after many dead ends from the original limited documents. Obviously, government was of interest to the thieves.

The fraudulent restaurant purchases were random with little overlap, mostly independent ethnic eateries. Grissom acknowledged the pattern but stopped short of profiling. The car rentals used a variety of agencies.

Grissom's attention lurched back to his client's credit card statement. Like the other Indulge Financial clients, the bad transactions appeared a day after the billing period ended, and just a couple of days after Bainbridge's visit to Prestige Appraisals. His client was in the import business, after all, but a clarifying phone call was in order.

Grissom was surprised when Bainbridge answered on the first ring. "Please, tell me why you visited Prestige Appraisals."

"I inherited an antique pocket watch a couple of months ago. Since I didn't have any emotional attachment to the piece, I decided to part with it. I checked the catalogs and online to get a general idea of its value before visiting Prestige."

Grissom had already done a background check on the small, privately-owned shop. "How did you find them?"

"A recommendation from a friend who found their service and pricing superb."

"How did it work out?"

"I asked for ten percent over the highest valuation I'd found and they agreed, just like that. The broker obviously wasn't very sophisticated about negotiating. While I was there, I used the money to purchase an unusual ring from North Africa at a bargain price. The watch value didn't quite cover, so I put the small balance on my card. Perhaps to encourage future business, they gave me an unexpected discount."

A charge of $1749.32 on the Indulge statement was hardly small by Grissom's standards. Of significant interest was the limited negotiation expertise of the employee in the pawnshop and their pricing.

"Do you think the pawnshop is involved in the theft of my credit card information?" asked Bainbridge.

"Much too soon to tell." Grissom ran his finger down the printed statement and tallied the transactions with one oddly-named business. "Tell me sir, what is Galileo's?"

There was an awkward silence before his client answered. "It's a gentleman's club."

Interesting euphemism. Bainbridge had been a frequent customer. Who better to make illicit use of a credit card than a gentleman's club?

"They promise the upmost in client confidentiality." Bainbridge's voice cracked. "They wouldn't do something illegal, would they?"

Charlie's head spun. *Travel to state capitals? Pawn shops? A gentleman's club? Grissom's case is on a completely different trajectory than mine.* He glanced at his watch. Potter! He marked his place, grabbed his messenger bag and scurried through the lobby.

Sure enough, Potter waited by her car outside the entrance, blocking the horseshoe shaped driveway, giving the bellman at the curb the evil eye. At the sight of Charlie, she opened her eyes wide and smiled. Then she pulled a tissue from her pocket and wiped the corners of Charlie's mouth. "Guess we won't need a stop at QuickBites this morning"

Charlie rubbed his mouth on his sleeve. "Nope, ate before you got here. Let's take a closer look at that art project thing in the park."

Potter pulled away from the hotel entrance. "I asked a couple of my colleagues to take measurements and such. They worked yesterday afternoon and should be back today."

"Great!" Charlie hoped to get a better look at the rods that formed the structure, and get closer to figuring out how it was extracting nutrients from the soil, leaving a cross-country brown stripe.

It was a quick ride, and this time there was an available parking space. The police had left their yellow tape up surrounding the stick structure, intact but a bit tattered and sagging. *Will it keep folks away or draw their attention?* The scaffolding had been removed, allowing complete access to the hexagonal structure, and no police officer was on guard.

Two people in blue nylon EPA jackets like Potter's were at the scene with laser measuring devices, compasses, levels, assaying the structure.

Charlie lifted the yellow tape to get closer to the structure.

Potter grabbed his hand. "We should let them finish. We'll just be in their way."

Charlie wanted to examine the structure himself. "All right." He dropped the tape barrier. The EPA team seemed to be focused on gathering statistics rather than examining the structure itself. "Can you requisition a few specialists to examine the material in close detail?" Charlie didn't want to accidentally disparage his partner's skills. "Or maybe you can."

Potter waved the idea off. "My major in college was psychology. I'll ask one of our biologists and one of our chemists to come by and take a look, if they haven't already."

In DC, getting resources was a lot more formal, with a lot more paperwork. "Great."

"What was your major?" asked Potter.

Charlie smiled broadly. "Natural Resources and Environmental Science at Purdue University."

"Good school."

Charlie was relieved that she didn't ask about his grade point average. He thought for a moment about the policeman who'd been standing guard on their previous visit. "Can you also ask an electronics technician to come on-site? The policeman had trouble with his radio when he was close to the sculpture, but it worked fine at a distance. I'm wondering if this structure is the cause."

Potter scratched her head. Her short hair fell back into place. "They're just sticks. How could they generate electrical interference?"

"We'll never know for sure unless we check it out."

"I'll ask, but finding someone in my office with that expertise will be a stretch. We might have to call in a specialist and that'll cost."

Charlie stared across DeKalb Blvd. at the square brick high school building. Students filled the sidewalk arriving for classes. A familiar tall, thin African-American young woman stood out from the crowd, glancing in the direction of the park. Charlie put his hand on Potter's and hung his head. "Don't look now, but our female student is back, across the street."

Potter turned her head a bit. "You still want to interview that girl?"

"Yes." Charlie reached for the notebook in his pocket. "Do you still have Detective Washington's details about her?"

"The female student he interviewed? Sure thing." Potter grabbed her phone from her back pocket and tapped her way to the information. "Here." She held the phone so he could read the screen. "Do you still want interview her?"

Charlie copied the name Kwashay Williams-Jackson, into his notepad. "I sure do. I'll arrange a meeting while you direct the assessment."

As the girl paused and looked in their direction, Charlie thought he made eye contact because she jerked her head away. *I'd bet anything she has a story to tell.*

His phone rang, showing Lane as the caller.

Lane's voice crackled so Charlie wandered over to a nearby bench, putting some distance between himself and the structure.

Charlie didn't answer with his name. "More parks and golf courses complaining?".

"Very funny. While you're out there, I'm back here playing secretary. Most of the recent calls were from government agencies."

"Like who?" Several had turned down the opportunity to work on the dead grass case.

"For one, the Department of Agriculture. Their Plant Health group wants in. Oh yeah, and the acting director of their Agricultural Research Center down in Beltsville thinks they should be involved."

"I don't need their help. "The vegetation isn't diseased. The hexagonal tower is sucking the nutrients from the soil." *I understand why Lane might be reluctant to deliver that information.* "I've overnighted you a copy of the soil evaluation report."

"Which brings me to the Agricultural Research Service. Their senior director reminded me that they're one of the world's premier scientific organizations."

"Finally, something that could be useful. Text Potter his name and number. And feel free to share the report with them. Maybe they can make sense out of it."

"Okay." Lane paused. "Are you sure you're in control?"

"Absolutely" he told Lane, thinking; *No agency, not even ours, has the means of controlling the brown stripe. And none of those folks would approach the problem with an open mind. Maybe that's my most valuable asset. For them, everything looks like a nail because the only tool they have is a hammer.*

"Charlie, be straight with me, are there any public health issues here? I mean, will people start getting sick?"

Lane sounded sincerely worried.

"There's no disease. No infestations. Why do you ask?"

"I got a call from the Agency for Toxic Substances and Disease Registry down in Atlanta."

Part of the U.S. Department of Health and Human Services. "Tell them there's no disease or microbes. Heck, send them the soil analysis too, and anybody else who asks."

"All right, I'll pass along your expert opinion. But you've really stirred things up."

Dead dirt was a fact, not an opinion. "It's not me, it's the stripe! I'm just trying to respond to a unique situation. Is there something else you think I should be doing?" Lane had offered only one suggestion: "Keep it simple."

"I know you're doing your best. I'll try to contain things back here."

Still no mentoring. Charlie considered the long list Lane had shared. "Strange, that all of these agencies are coming out of the woodwork after dumping the problem on us."

"Speaking of strange-" It sounded like Lane was shuffling papers. "Some woman called, asking who was investigating the brown stripe in Brooklyn. Jane forwarded the call to me. Give me a second and I'll read you her message." Another short pause. "Here it is. 'Quote, tell Mr. Keyson I'm pleased he's joined me in our search for The Devil. May the Lord bless and protect us.' Said her name was the Reverend Billi Dogood. Do you know her or what she meant?"

The woman I saw here at Fort Greene Park! Charlie remembered her stark white look from head to toe. "Nope. I just hope she doesn't interfere with an official government investigation." Lane's current case popped into Charlie's mind. ". Speaking of investigations, what kind of progress have you made on Dan River?"

"Oh, that case is almost closed. Just a few loose ends to work out. Why do you ask?"

Isn't that what colleagues do, share with each other? "Professional curiosity. Who are you negotiating with on the power company side?"

"Edgar Phillips, Government Relations at Bates Corporation. Do you know him?"

"Nope. Never heard of him. Talk to you later." Charlie hung up, wrote another name into his notepad for future reference, stood, and rejoined Potter at the structure inside the yellow tape. "I'm going to see if I can find our student." He ran hand along one of the horizontal struts. *Did this get thicker since than the last time we were here?* "When you have a chance, meet me in the principal's office."

"After I get briefed by the forensics team. Just don't end up in detention." Potter walked away to join her EPA colleagues as Charlie ducked under the tape and headed across the street.

47 – Matt (Eureka, CA)

After class, Matt sat at the miniature desk in his room, thumbing through a history textbook, trying to review class material. Concern over operating the portal surged forward and demolished his concentration. A knock on the door killed any consideration of Pearl Harbor. Standing in the door was Dixon, the dapper guy who'd discovered the portal. The guy who'd found the posting of the portal photo online. The guy whose heavy equipment couldn't demolish it. "What's up?"

He stepped over the threshold. "Are you Matt Thready?"

"Junior. Matt Thready Junior."

"Sorry. My name is Trevor Dixon, from the Bates Foundation. Didn't I see you out by those hexagonal structures?"

"I had a surveying project to do, and the woods was convenient." *Best to give him as much.*

"But not every student takes a photo and posts it, looking for others who'd be interested." Dixon leaned against the doorframe.

"I thought it looked interesting, so I shared." The President of the college had told Matt she'd given Dixon permission to investigate. "It's a trellis. You know, for holding up vines?"

"Oh really? And just how do you know that?"

"Another student told me." Matt swallowed hard. "Besides, it's pretty obvious."

"Not to me. I thought it was a model for some modern high-rise."

Matt nodded. "Actually, I heard another student call them that."

"Seems like lots of students are talking about those towers." Dixon's tone changed, from friend to interrogator, as he stood tall. "Well, I think you built the portal, maybe with some help."

Dixon's use of the term shocked Matt. *He shouldn't know that.* Matt maintained a denial. "Says who?" *The President of the college had only circumstantial evidence.*

"I asked around. A muscular kid from the school auto body shop told me that he assisted, and some others who built a scaffold to reach the higher sections said they did it for you. Are they all lying?" Before Matt could respond, Dixon added, " Oh yeah, and your good friend Fred confirmed he was the middleman."

Fred swore he wouldn't say a word to anyone. "And you believe him? He's got one wild and crazy imagination." *Why couldn't he keep his big mouth shut?* Matt slumped in his chair. *I wonder what else Fred told him?* "So what if I built the trellises, not that I'm admitting it?"

"Well, there's the issue of violating college property with an unauthorized structure. Unless you got permission first."

"Old news. I've already spoken to President Stanley. I'm on probation and have to stay away from that part of campus. Besides, the college wasn't using that area for anything before the sticks showed up."

Dixon raised one eyebrow. "Showed up as in imported, or did they just fall out of the sky?" asked Dixon.

Matt mentally kicked himself for giving Dixon took one more insight. *I need to keep my mouth shut.*

Dixon made one step into the room. "They're really unique, but you know that. No matter. That portal of yours is trespassing on land Bates Foundation will be using shortly to construct another science building."

"I saw the sign."

"Ah, but you didn't understand its meaning. Instead of holding up vines, that portal of yours is holding up construction. We're letting the school relocate any of the viable plants from the area, but that hexagonal eyesore has to go before we can excavate. So, I'll make you a deal. If you're willing to help me disassemble the monstrosity so Bates can move it down to our headquarters in Houston, at our expense, the college and Bates Foundation will see it in our hearts to forgive and forget. Why, you could come down this summer as a paid intern and teach us all about it. I'm sure your portal has some amazing capabilities."

I'll have more leverage as the builder and owner. "Okay!" Matt hadn't intended on shouting. He sat up straight, prepared to leap out of the chair if necessary. "Okay, I admit it. I built the portal." *No point in using the word trellis now.* "But out of curiosity, what did it cost you to get Fred to rat me out?"

Dixon flashed a crooked smile. "Cheaper than I expected. One extra large meat-lovers pizza, which I can expense."

“Figures. It was either food or a date.” Matt slammed his history book shut. “So now what? You going to tell the President and get me expelled?”

Dixon stroked his chin. “That doesn’t help either of us.” His face told the story of failure.

Matt remembered Fred’s ranting that had interrupted his lunch with good news, that the portal had survived a bulldozer. “You can’t do it, can you? You can’t knock it down, and you don’t know how to take it apart.”

Color bloomed in Dixon’s face with rising blood pressure. “Don’t you believe it. With enough horsepower and manpower, I can get rid of it. But I’ll admit, it intrigues me. Portals are doorways to wondrous places. We can both come out of this as winners, but time is of the essence.”

Matt recalled how the sticks fought to be positioned in a particular orientation and location. *Anyplace else would be the wrong spot.* “That’s a nice offer, but it can’t be moved.” *It just needs more time. Maybe I can stall.* “Just not yet.”

“What’s so special about that location? What kind of portal is it, anyway?” Dixon was leaning forward, as if he expected Matt to spill the portal’s secrets.”

All I know is, the portal needs to stay put until I operate it. “The portal is very important. You don’t need to know why. If you can just wait until – well, until it’s not needed any more, it’s all yours.”

Dixon’s assertive behavior softened, just a little. “And when will that be?”

“I – I – I don’t exactly know. But pretty soon.”

“That’s not good enough. The construction date for the school’s new building has already been established, and there are expectations. I won't fall behind schedule. Pretty soon doesn't cut it."

Matt decided to motivate a different behavior by appealing to Dixon's moral sense. However, that required sharing what he'd been told by the bodyless voice when he first found the sticks. "The portal is going to make everything better for the whole planet. Isn't that worth waiting for?"

"Yeah, right." Dixon's eyes scanned the room. "You're not going to give me a straight answer are you? Will you help me or not?"

A cold chill ran through Matt's body. "Sorry, not yet."

Dixon waved his finger. "Something strange is going on. I'll figure it out, with or without you, just watch." He was out the door and out of sight for only a few seconds when he stuck his head past the doorframe. "Come with me to your portal. I want to show you a few things maybe even you don't know."

Matt stayed in his chair. "You're just trying to get me in trouble. I promised the President I'd stay away."

"She won't object, because I invited you. You'll be safe as my guest. She does what I tell her."

Matt didn't believe that the college President was Dixon's puppet. *I don't need to be invited. It's my portal. I'm the operator.* "Okay I'll go with you, but I'm not going to help disassemble it." *Assuming I knew how.*

Matt trailed along, following in Dixon's footsteps.

48 – Kwashay (Brooklyn, NY)

Kwashay sat in English class, Ms. Guthrie handing out a poem for them to explicate. Her teacher liked to surprise students with these pop quizzes, although she never graded them. Instead, she told her students to use these "assignments" to figure out their own "strengths and opportunities." God, Kwashay was tired of hearing that phrase.

Ms. Guthrie handed Kwashay her copy. "I think you'll enjoy this one."

Kwashay held the paper in front of her face and read:

"here is the deepest secret nobody knows
(here is the root of the root and the bud of the bud
and the sky of the sky of a tree called life; which grows-"

Kwashay stopped in the middle of the third stanza, lowered the paper and took a deep breath. Analyzing poetry was usually one of Kwashay's "opportunities" but this poem by e e cummings spoke directly to her. *Is Ms. Guthrie a mind reader? This sounds like me and the portal.*

The part about "the deepest secret nobody knows" was no longer correct. She had shared with her mother all of the details about the rods, the vision, the portal and the advancement of humanity it would facilitate after she operated it. Her mother had listened attentively without interrupting. Only after her mother suggested a free consultation with a psychologist on staff at her hospital did Kwashay disavow the whole tale as a story she'd made up and was writing for Ms. Guthrie's class.

Before she could begin writing her analysis, her teacher stood over her. "You're wanted in the principal's office."

"Me?" Her underarms perspired, her typical response to stress. On bad days with her mother, Kwashay sometimes had to change her around-the-house t-shirt two or three times.

"Yes. Here's a hall pass." Ms. Guthrie handed her a paperback-sized hunk of wood painted glossy blue with a cutout handle. "Take your books, just in case you're still there when class ends."

All eyes were on Kwashay as she gathered her things. Her teacher's remark was loud enough that the reason for her departure buzzed through the room before she reached the door.

Her teacher patted her shoulder before she stepped out into the hallway. "You'll be fine."

Kwashay wasn't so sure. She walked down the hall, books hugged to her chest, the blue pass dangling from her fingertips. As she passed an exit, an alternative came to mind. *Maybe I should leave and catch a bus home.* She'd have time alone until her mother came home from work to plan for being the portal operator, even though she didn't know what that meant. No, that would just postpone the inevitable.

She pushed through a set of swinging doors that separated one wing of the school from the core area and flashed the pass at hallway guards, who enforced only authorized travel during class periods. If she wasn't carrying a pass, she'd be escorted to the principal's office anyway. That irony brought a smile to her face, which dissolved as soon as she entered the main office. She walked up to the long wood counter and slid the pass to the clerk on the other side. "Hi, I'm Kwashay Williams-Jackson. Someone wanted to see me."

The clerk took the pass, nodded, stuck her head into the principal's office, and returned. "Give them a moment."

Them? Kwashay snuck a glance. The man she'd locked eyes with near the portal, possibly one of the EPA guys, was talking with the principal. *Now what?*

He turned his head in her direction, made eye contact and gave a tentative smile. She tried to maintain a flat expression, except he looked so out of place in a high school that she just had to turn up her lips a bit.

A voice from the office instructed the clerk to bring Kwashay over.

The principal met her at the door to his office. "Kwashay, I don't believe we've ever met. Which is probably a good thing." He held out his hand. "I'm Principal Unger."

Kwashay shook it.

"And this is, well, why don't you introduce yourself?"

He stood. "Charlie Keyson, from the Environmental Protection Agency."

Kwashay's suspicions were confirmed. *I need to learn why they're investigating my portal.* She smiled, expecting to extract more information than she would share.

49 - Selton (Kearney, NE)

Selton woke later than usual from a fitful recuperation after being contacted that he was finally going home. *I seem to need heavier doses of nutrition these days. Perhaps in proportion to my cell density?*

Before he sat up, he ran his hands over his body, from chest to waist. The depression in his stomach was still empty. *Good, the flower hasn't grown back.* His texture had changed, or perhaps he hadn't noticed before. Thousands of small nubs – humans would have characterized them as goose bumps or acne – textured his endodermis. *My cells must be bulging with information.*

Selton pulled his backroots from the soil, dressed and used the sidewalks instead of private backyards to reach the train yard. After his usual morning shower in the train yard and a check on the captured filament which was still lively, he was ready to start his day, fresh.

In the Kearney Public Library, Selton was nervous about continuing his review of books. How many patrons had been there during his uncontrollable outburst the previous day? Would that happen again? He was already overloaded with information. The urge to assimilate even more overwhelmed his sensibility. *Perhaps my nubby texture has expanded my capacity. I should try.*

He was poised to open a low numbered book dealing with Earthling Psychology. Understanding the inner motivations of these creatures in stark comparison to their actions was one of the primary reasons Selton had concluded that the whole collection of knowledge he had absorbed was internally inconsistent.

History, a section of the library he'd ingested before, had proven it time and time again. Earthlings say they yearn for peace and yet take up arms against their own species for trivial excuses like land, revenge or differing beliefs in the supernatural. Selton hoped that there was some new book, some advanced thinking by the best of the species, that would explain, and by exposing, prevent such horrible and fatal results. He went over to the proper shelf and reached for the first book, numbered 150.0. Bernice the librarian, silent on the telephone, looked in his direction. She seemed upset about what she was hearing. He nodded, bypassing his favorite padded seat near a window for a chair at an empty table further away.

Selton's fingers had gotten weaker. Instead of holding a book in his hands, he lay the book on a flat surface. That forced him to bend over instead of his healthier straight back posture. How predictable was the ripening? And what followed? Selton was frightened of not knowing how his Earthling-shaped physiology would change. And of course none of the Earth books he'd read provided answers.

Selton thought ahead to what he'd review next. *If I'm going home soon, I want to reinforce my favorite subject matter.* He promised himself to jump to reading about childcare when this section was complete.

Selton enjoyed the library more than ever in light of his forthcoming recall. He swooned at the opportunity to embrace Class 700 - Arts & Recreation. The first tomes would be about architecture, an area of study irrelevant on Serulia. On his home planet, there were no structures, no buildings to hide from the natural climate. As flora, Serulians were one with their environment. Then, drawings and paintings. Collections of photographs of famous works executed in such diverse styles awaited Selton's visits. Photography, capturing still images that represent an instant of time. And then the strangest and yet most beautiful of all - music. Serulians were serenaded by the sounds of nature. Wind rushing past, rustling of leaves. Air claps that sent sharp sounds for miles. Last of all, performance art and games, played on separate individual stages. Serulians were entertained by passing cloud formations.

Bernice walked up and cleared her throat. "Selton?"

"Yes, ma'am?"

"Have you heard about a prowler, sneaking through people's backyards in the middle of the night?" She stood alongside, arms folded.

He shook his head. "No." *I'm no prowler. I'm just hungry.*

"You wouldn't do something like that, would you?" She shook her head as a prompt.

"No, ma'am."

Although it would reduce his choices, Selton promised himself to avoid the residential neighborhood. *Now that I have Centennial Park.*

"Good. By the way, you forgot to take The Hub." She handed him the town's daily newspaper and walked back to her desk.

On the front page, the lead story described planned upgrades to the power station. A small box on the bottom corner, promising a story a few pages in about a traveling preacher, caught Selton's attention and thickened his sap. He flipped to the corresponding page for the full article. A photo showed the Reverend Billi Dogood, white hair and flowing white robe like a gaunt angel, standing in the middle of a fifty-foot wide brown stripe outside Elderton, Pennsylvania surrounded by about a hundred followers. *She's changed her hair and clothes, but I'd recognize that face anywhere.* The memory of her standing over him in the hobo camp would remain with him forever. Her bus with the words 'Reverend Billi Dogood's Mobile Morality Mission' stood as the backdrop.

The newspaper article referenced a local radio show appearances, where she'd urged listeners to call in about brown spots on their lawns. *Just like her classified ad. She's looking for patterns. She's looking for me.* She'd also announced a forthcoming book, and a series of rallies, starting in Brooklyn and heading west. *If she's coming this way, I have yet another reason for an expedient recall.*

Selton put down the newspaper and flipped the page of a textbook specializing on the topic of Behavioral and Cognitive Psychology. The wooden floor beneath him shook. The book jumped on the table. *Another communication from Dissemination Oversight?* He leapt from his chair and ran out the front door, clothes flapping, the book in his hand.

"Selton, you have to check that out!" called Bernice.

He ran around the corner of the building toward the back where the dumpster sat. The gravel shifted beneath his feet. In his head, another message, this one clear.

"Prepare for the megafeeding."

The vibrations disappeared as quickly as they'd arrived. *Megafeeding? I need to know how I'm going to get back to Serulia. What's a megafeeding anyway?*

Selton strolled back into the library, holding up the book for Bernice to see. She smiled and nodded. He returned to his chair, contemplating the new message. *The prefix mega- in metric systems denotes a factor of one million, but in common use it means large or big. Large feeding?* Maybe Dissemination Oversight anticipated that it would become increasingly difficult as he matured, to draw nutrition from the ground, and they planned to boost his regenerative sleep with a blast of high-energy nutrients. *How prescient they are! Too bad they left out the part about how they're bringing me home.*

50 - Charlie (Brooklyn, NY)

Charlie stood in the principal's office and extended his hand. Kwashay barely touched it. "We've seen each other before, right?"

Principal Unger waved his arm. "Have a seat." He took his place behind the desk.

"Maybe, I, I don't remember." The young woman squirmed in her chair.

Charlie sat down and shared some details to jog her memory. "My partner and I were on a bench near that climbing apparatus, across the street-"

"It's not for climbing!" Kwashay straightened her posture. "It's my art project."

"So I understand, from the detective who interviewed you. A model of a futuristic high rise, isn't that what you told your art teacher?" *She remembers. I can see it in her eyes.*

"I guess." Kwashay tugged at her hair, which snapped back into its original position.

"And she took some photos of it." He pulled her art teacher's camera from his jacket pocket and put it on the principal's desk, like evidence in a courtroom. "She told us you were planning on posting at least one photo to the Internet. We found it on PictureNet under an alias." Potter's technical folks had performed a miracle and tracked the account to Kwashay's home computer.

"My mother taught me to be safe so I didn't use my real name or email address. I didn't want to make myself a target for bad people."

Charlie nodded. "Smart. And have you gotten any replies?"

"No." Kwashay's eyes wandered, to the framed certificates on the wall behind the principal, to the bookcase under the window, anywhere but Charlie's face.

It was obvious the young woman was either nervous or getting bored. Charlie had never been trained in the art of interviewing, but he plodded on. "You're probably wondering why I wanted to talk with you."

"Uh huh. So far, you've been asking questions to which you already know the answers."

Bored. The young lady was quite bright. She could handle a more direct approach. "Okay, you deserve the facts. There's a pattern of botanical devastation, and your sculpture is the origin."

"Devastation? You've got to be kidding." She snapped her attention back and forth between the EPA agent and her principal." What are you talking about?"

Good, she's engaging. "Didn't you notice the fifty-foot brown stripe? Grass, plants, bushes, trees, flowers, anything that grows has died off in an area that starts with your sculpture and continues west. Liberty Park and Governor's Island are affected, and we're investigating just how far the blight reaches."

Kwashay stiffened her arms and came out of her chair. "That can't be true!"

"There have been reports of impact as far away as Pennsylvania. And if it keeps going, who knows how severe the consequences will be? I could show you by helicopter that it's already affected New Jersey." Charlie wasn't really going to hire a helicopter to prove his claims, but he wanted to demonstrate confidence. He leaned forward. "And I assure you, we don't have those answers."

The young woman dropped down and thought for a moment before answering. "The portal is here to help us. There must be some mistake. Something else is the cause."

Portal? That's what she calls it? "The cause is dead soil. Void of nutrients, microbes, anything." He pulled a copy of the soil analysis reports from his bag and waved them. "Nothing can grow in such a sterile environment. So, how does it work? And, most important, how can we shut it down?"

Kwashay's eyes went wide. "You can't shut it off!" She took a deep breath and relaxed. "I mean, there's no off switch."

"Okay, we can't turn it off, but we've got to get it under control." Charlie had interlaced his fingers. "What is it really?"

Kwashay lowered her head. "I don't understand it very well at all."

"Then tell me what you know. Please?" He pulled out his pocket notepad, ready to be educated.

Kwashay was sitting silently when Potter stepped into the room. "Sorry to be late. I'm Stephanie Potter, from New York City Department of Environmental Protection."

Charlie introduced Principal Unger and Kwashay and then gestured over his shoulder. "Agent Potter is working with me on this case. The structure across the street is called a portal."

"Really? To where?" asked Potter.

Kwashay didn't reply.

Charlie turned to a fresh page in his notepad. "Kwashay was about to tell us what she knows."

"Great! I'm all ears." Potter remained standing, leaning against the open door.

"Start at the beginning," said Charlie.

Kwashay took a cleansing breath and made eye contact. "I found a pile of rods laying in the park on my way home one night."

"Do you always go through the park?" asked Potter.

"No, I was trying to avoid a group of Boxers who were hanging around."

"Boxers?" asked Charlie.

"I call them that because their sagging pants expose their boxers."

"I've never heard them called that." Potter chuckled. "Go on."

"I cut across the park to get to the bus, and that's where I found the rods. I'd never seen anything like them before, and I was curious. Based on the shape of the ends, I knew they were sculpted to be connected. When I picked two of them up and put them together, I got shocked."

"An electric shock?" Charlie wrote the word portal in his notebook and continued documenting Kwashay's story.

"More like a tingle, followed by a vision in my mind, of how the structure was supposed to look – two concentric hexagonal towers."

"Really? Like a blueprint?" asked Potter.

"Exactly, the completed sculpture like a picture in my mind. So I assembled them, just like the mental instructions required."

Potter continued while Charlie kept writing. "That same night?"

"No, over the next day. And I had some help."

Charlie looked up from his notepad. "From who?"

"Those same Boxers. It turned out, they really aren't dangerous, just pesky." A half-smile formed on her face.

"You should be careful who you associate with," said Principal Unger.

"But helpful, right? I'd like to interview them, too. Can I get their names?" Charlie's pen was poised.

"I don't know their names. We just talked about the rods and when I went to class, they kept assembling."

"Did they see the vision?" asked Potter.

"No, I demonstrated how to do it, and they picked up on it really quick."

Charlie closed his notebook. He knew what happened next. "And they borrowed some scaffolding to build the upper portion?"

Kwashay hugged herself. "I didn't ask them to do anything illegal. That was their own bad idea."

Principal Unger cleared his throat. "See what I mean?"

"Detective Washington believes you. But now, the sculpture – what you call a portal – has put down roots and is sucking everything from the soil. And if I'm not mistaken, the rods increased in diameter over the last two days."

"I hadn't noticed." Kwashay's knee bounced.

She's not telling the truth.

“If it’s growing, it needs nutrition, which might explain why plants in the vicinity are affected,” said Potter. “But as far away as New Jersey? That’s on the other side of the river.”

“And all the way to Pennsylvania, at last report,” added Charlie.

Kwashay folded her fingers, her eyebrows sagging. “I didn’t mean for anything bad to happen. Honest. You have to believe me.”

“I do. Honest.” Charlie leaned forward, elbows on his knees. “But you’re the one who put it together. So you’re our best chance of taking it apart.”

Kwashay stood up. “I told you, you can’t do that!”

“Why not? It’s causing damage that has to be stopped.”

“Because, well, because the portal has something important to do, something that will make the whole world better, and we should let it.” She sat down hard, examining her hands.

Charlie let her vague reason stand. He noticed damp patches under her armpits. “It’s not doing anything good at the moment. If we let this thing spread further west, it could affect farms, our agricultural heartland and grazing land for cattle.” Charlie tried not to make it a lecture. “Would food shortages make you happy? We might not only lose exports, maybe we’d be forced to import food from other countries. Think of the financial and economic disruption.”

Kwashay lifted her eyes to make contact with Charlie’s. “Is it doing that?”

“You’ve only seen the tip of the iceberg, in the park.”

Kwashay's eyes took on a mournful look, as if she'd learned her best friend lied to her. "But the portal isn't supposed to harm us. Just the opposite."

She honestly believes the portal is benign at worst, maybe even beneficial. "Really? How do you know? Whispers in your ear? Some unsubstantiated mission you can't explain?" Charlie considered threatening to remove the portal by force but hoped it wouldn't come to that.

Kwashay slid down into her chair. "I guess I don't have much choice." She took a deep breath. "I'll help." She got up and led the two government agents out of the building, her principal close behind.

Charlie jogged to close the distance as she crossed the street. "So let's start with the simple stuff first. Show us where you found them?"

The group walked up a path and then through the trees to the clearing where the portal stood. They ducked under the deteriorating yellow police tape.

Kwashay walked over to a specific tree in the park and pointed. "Right here, in a pile. You're right, the grass is dead."

Brown lines showed where the rods had been stacked. "Not just here." He pointed at the brown stripe that began at the west side of the structure. "And what is it constructed of?"

"My first guess was wood. Smooth with a high gloss coating. But now I think it's a biological synthetic of some kind."

Charlie had never heard of biological synthetics, just varieties of man-made materials that had to pass EPA scrutiny.

"The rods fit together, like a child's construction toy."

"Weren't you worried that someone might take them, or the sculpture?" asked Potter.

"The rods have this property - they got heavier the further you took them from the area. No one could carry one more than a few feet before the rod got impossibly heavy."

Potter pushed her hair off her forehead. "Too bad we don't have a sample to try out your hypothesis."

"It's not a hypothesis. Sideways tried and it nearly broke his hand."

"Who's Sideways?" asked Charlie.

"One of the Boxers, a guy who helped me with the assembly." Kwashay didn't offer his real name.

Out came Charlie's notepad. "Where can I get in touch with him?"

"He isn't anybody. He has nothing to do with this."

Charlie wrote down the nickname. "You just admitted he did."

"Are you're certain he wasn't faking the whole heaviness thing?" asked the principal. "Street kids often pull cons."

"I tried to take one with me, so my biology teacher could examine and test it, but I couldn't carry it either."

Charlie tried a different approach. "And Sideways didn't make these rods?"

"He isn't technically sophisticated enough to engineer these. Besides, he couldn't put the blueprints in my head."

"Okay, so then what happened, after you found them?" asked Potter.

"The pile of rods had precisely the number of pieces for the structures. I put some together the next morning but I had class, so Sideways and his friends volunteered to do the rest."

"We really should talk to your friend Sideways," said Charlie. "It would help if we knew his real name."

"I'll help you, but you have to leave Sideways out of this. He's out on parole for stealing the scaffolding. He's probably being watched. If the judge thinks he's involved in anything whatsoever, they'll throw him back in jail. If you need to know something, I'll find out for you."

Charlie made a note to get Sideways' real name from Detective Washington, and permission to speak with him. *At a minimum, he can corroborate Kwashay's story.*

"Do you two have a relationship?" asked Potter.

"Us? No. My mother would never allow it."

"Okay, Sideways and his friends built the portal," said Charlie. "When did you see it next?"

"Before school the next morning it was finished. Ever since, I come by once a day to check on it. The rods have grown thicker and the whole structure has planted itself into the ground."

She did notice! "You keep using words like 'grown' and 'planted.' Do you think this is some botanical abnormality?" asked the principal.

"I think it's vegetable, as opposed to animal or mineral, yes. The rods always seemed to be, at their core, plants or something like it. And you said it has a root system that's expanding, so you're making similar references."

"So I did." Charlie was satisfied that he was getting the truth, as well as the young woman understood it. "You're pretty smart, you know that?

So how do you think your art project would react to plant killer?"

Kwashay's jaw dropped. "You wouldn't!"

Charlie's phone rang. The number indicated it was Lane, probably calling to harass him. Again. "I need to take this. I'll be right back." He retreated to a distance from the portal and answered. "If you don't have anything that'll help, why must you keep bothering me?"

"I didn't know calling one of my subordinates for some status was bothering them." It was Director Stanton, not Lane.

He must be standing at the Lane desk using his phone. I wonder how that conversation went? "I didn't know it was you, sir."

"Obviously not. Even Lane deserves some respect. But I didn't call to teach you manners. Or discuss how you've blown through my budget, even though staffers from the Congressional Committee on Energy and Commerce want to know why one my agents took a helicopter joyride in New York City to the tune of a thousand dollars."

That pilot ripped us off good!

The Director cleared his throat and continued, "We have a situation out in California. A community college reported damaged foliage in and around a redwood forest near Eureka, California. Wouldn't you know it, they found another one of those paired hexagon things."

At least Lane had shared some of my findings. Multiple cities, just like Grissom's case! "Really? Don't tell me. It's the origin of a strip of dead grass and plants heading directly east, right?"

Potter wandered closer to Charlie.

"I can't confirm that. When one of our field agents went to investigate, he was turned away," said the Director. "Basically, they said they'd care for it privately."

Patterns, finally. One on the east coast aiming west implies the west one pointing east. "They're coming at it from both sides."

"Coming at what? And who are they?"

"Those are fair questions, and I'll figure them out." Charlie was excited about the expanding nature of his assignment. "Things here are in good hands with the local EPA agent-"

"Partner," interjected Potter.

Charlie continued, "So I'll finish up any loose ends and then leave for California. Let them know I'm coming out to lead the investigation-"

"The hell you will! The west coast hexagon thing is on private property. Why would you be any more successful than our local agent? Besides, you haven't proven any cause and effect relationship between these structures and the damage."

It was obvious to Charlie, and with Potter's photos in Lane's hands- "Did Lane show you the photos? Plus, I've got analysis reports that show the soil within the brown stripe is absolutely dead." Charlie lost confidence in his mentor. "Have you seen them?"

The Director ignored his question. "Got a pen and paper? Jot down the name and phone number of the Region 9 EPA agent who is working the case so you can provide relevant details from your New York experience. Then finish up and get back here."

Maybe he'll listen to logic. "It's no coincidence that there's a second portal. I'm already familiar with the details. I should be handling the California situation."

"I have no idea what a portal is." There was silence on the Director's end of the call for a few seconds that felt longer. "You sound different, Charles, and I don't like it. I'll expect a complete report."

Charlie didn't relent. "But I'm better equipped-"

"No means no," barked the Director. "Got it?"

"Yes sir." Charlie thought about a way to circumvent his orders. "Listen, I've really appreciated getting this field assignment. But this is a whole lot more strenuous than deskwork. Mind if I take a couple of days off?"

"You investigate dead grass for a couple of days and you need a few days off to recuperate? Maybe field work isn't appropriate for you after all. Okay, you've got enough accumulated vacation. Three days and then I want you back here. There's some important work waiting."

Like alphabetizing global temperature reports. "Thanks."

The Director's tone reminded Charlie of his father. "You're not thinking about taking a trip to California, are you?"

Charlie winked at Potter. "Hadn't crossed my mind. I do have some family on the West Coast. Why, is it nice this time of year?"

"Beautiful but off limits. To be blunt, the situation is highly political and therefore complicated. After our California agent tried to get access, I received a call from a Congressmen who advised me the situation was being cared for, and I should have my agent withdraw."

If their portal is like ours, no one is caring for it. "I understand. See you in a few days." Charlie snapped his phone closed.

Charlie turned to Potter and whispered. "There's a second structure – portal - out in California. Eureka."

"As in, I found it?" asked Potter.

"No, as in Eureka the city. I have to go out and see it."

"Sounds like you were warned off." Potter leaned on Charlie's shoulder. "Can I come with? Partner?"

"I've been advised to stay away despite my federal jurisdiction. As a New York agent, how could you justify flying out to California? Way outside your jurisdiction. Besides I need someone highly capable to hold down the fort while I'm away. Partner."

"Hold down the Fort Greene Park? You're just full of quips, aren't you?"

Charlie hadn't made the comment intentionally.

When the pair rejoined Kwashay at the portal, Charlie wondered whether or not he should disclose the existence of a second portal.

51 – Matt (Eureka, CA)

Dixon slowed his pace so Matt could keep up. "I'll show you what we're doing, and what we've learned." Dixon half-chuckled. "I know a few things that even you don't."

Dixon might know some techy stuff, but he has no clue I'm the operator. "Fine by me."

Dixon muttered as he passed the "Coming Soon" sign, "Damn right." He left the sidewalk for the grass turf, stepping over two extra-long heavy-duty orange extension cords that connected the motor home and semi-trailer to power outlets on the sidelines.

"So, what are you majoring in?" Dixon asked.

"Forestry, if my folks let me."

Dixon stopped at the ten-yard line. "It's your life, kid. Do what makes you happy."

"Do you enjoy working for Bates Corporation?" Matt asked.

"I'm ecstatic." Dixon's tone didn't match the words.

Various members of his staff approached, all wearing the same outfit: white lab coats with a stylized letter "B" embroidered in black on the shoulders and chest, worn over blue polo shirts and khaki slacks. Dixon was clearly in charge, giving directions with arm motions and terse orders, glancing at tablets thrust into his line of sight by his staff. "Come on, let's see our baby."

Matt followed Dixon straight toward the clearing. Dixon's military-style security folks had erected a barrier around the portal, a thick red plastic version of police tape, with the word BATES repeated every three feet. Four guards stood at attention, wearing black shirts with white "B" embroidering, black pants and black berets. All wore wireless earpieces.

Matt and Dixon strode past a gathering of a few students and ducked under the red tape. Some students complained that Matt was allowed past the barrier but they weren't. "What makes him so special?" one shouted.

I'm the operator!

Folks in lab coats milled around the portal's two concentric hexagon structures, examining it inch by inch, using hand-held microscopes and other instruments Matt didn't recognize.

If a bulldozer bounced off, it's got to be safe from these devices.

The gathered students must have gotten bored watching scientists take precise measurements of length, width, height, thickness, density and color because all of them eventually left.

Dixon stood beside Matt, his arm around his shoulder. "Want some free career advice? Don't grow up to be one of them." He pointed at the folks doing the work. "Grow up to be like me, their boss."

A couple of the scientists glanced up from their work, mild sneers on their faces.

Dixon continued, "Success – whatever that means to you - comes from a combination of power and money." He removed his arm and backed up until he was at the portal, stroking one of the vertical sticks. "Did you know this portal of yours is a radio station?"

Matt shook his head.

"See, you've learned something. It's broadcasting at a very high data rate, precisely east. What's there, do you suppose?" He did his single laugh thing.

"I don't know."

One of Dixon's aids ran up with a plain brown box about the size of a loaf of bread. "This just came for you, Mr. Dixon."

"Good." Dixon opened the box with a penknife from his pocket. "You see, Matt, we tried taking a reading of the material with a portable molecular scanner. Didn't work worth a crap. Then we tried shaving off just a few particles to process in our mobile lab." He kicked a clear plastic bin that rattled with the impact. “Nothing, not even a speck, came off, even with professional-grade files, rasps, rotary grinders.” He popped the box open. “Until now.”

University President Stanley jogged up and attempted to cross the barrier. One of the guards intercepted her and held her at bay until Dixon nodded approval.

The red ribbon barrier rubbed her top bun as she ducked under. “Mr. Thready, we agreed that as a condition of your probation, you'd stay away. I'm afraid I have no choice-”

Dixon squeezed himself in between. “He's here at my invitation. That needs to be all right with you. Matt, give us a minute.”

Matt sauntered away, but still close enough to hear parts of the conversation.

Dixon was talking in a low volume, but not a whisper. “He's the key to this anomaly, I'm sure of it. I thought if I brought him here, he might share the secrets.”

“Mr. Dixon, just because Bates is funding a new building, you can't just show up and take over. Your employer is certainly a major benefactor and we all appreciate-”

“I can and I am. Remember who pays your bills. Keeps this place running. You have no idea what you've got here, do you?” Dixon laughed once and turned to one of the guards. “Would you please escort the President back to her office.”

President Stanley and the guard slipped under the red barrier. When they were a few yards away, President Stanley turned her head and caught Matt's eyes.

Is she scared, or just really unhappy?

"Where was I?" Dixon looked down at the open box near the portal. "Ah, yes, my new toy!" Dixon lifted a miniature circular saw from the box, a small diameter blade and no safety shield. "Diamond-tipped, hardest material on the planet. This planet, at least." One more signature single laugh. "Dobbs, would you please do the honor?"

"It's Doctor Dobbs, if you please. I worked hard for my advanced degrees."

"Whatever." He guided Matt so his back was at the red tape. "Give him room."

Dobbs attached a sample catcher tray to the saw. When he approached the portal with the tool, Matt panicked. He stepped forward, preparing to grab the scientist's arm. Dixon's grip stopped him. One of the guards stepped over to assist.

Matt shivered. "What is he going to do?"

"Take a sample." Dixon lowered his voice. "Unless you tell us all about this portal of yours."

The diamond-tipped saw looked menacing, and it wasn't even spinning. "I don't - you can't-

Dixon's scowl chilled Matt's blood. "Nobody tells me what I can and can't do, especially some punk student." Dixon nodded to Dobbs, who turned on the saw. It whined to life. He raised it, just above one of the horizontal sticks, and paused.

"Go ahead," Dixon commanded.

When the blade touched the stick, sparks flew. Matt grabbed his side and fell to the ground. His scream was loud enough to be heard across campus. The scientist pulled the saw away from its target, the sample tray empty.

Matt, wincing and still holding his side, looked up.

One of Dixon's eyebrows was almost at his hairline. "Again."

"But the boy-" Dobbs stood his ground.

Dixon rushed the scientist, grabbed the saw from his hands and brought it down - hard - on the target stick. Bits of dust fell into a tray attached to the saw. "Got it!"

Matt curled up into fetal position. *The pain!* "Stop! You're killing it."

Dixon withdrew the blade, stopped the saw and removed the sample tray. He turned to the closest guard. "We have a special young man here. Make him our guest in my quarters."

Dobbs approached Dixon. "He's hurt. I'm taking him to the infirmary. His well-being is on you!" Matt felt himself being lifted off the ground, and draped his arm over his benefactor's shoulder.

"You might be smart but you're a wuss." Dixon waved them off, flecks of portal dust in his possession. "Do what you'd like." The saw thudded as it fell into the box.

52 – Kwashay (Brooklyn, NY)

Agents Keyson and Potter returned from his phone call.

"I need a straight answer: did you know there was a second one of these portals?" he asked.

"There is!"

"So you knew! Why didn't you mention that?" Keyson's face was red.

"I didn't know, for a fact. No proof, just a, what do you call it, a gut instinct? Something inside told me that I had a partner."

The two adults exchanged a smiling glance.

"And you're happy there's another one, doing similar damage?" asked Potter.

"Of course not." Kwashay struggled to erase her smile. "But it means there's someone one out there who had the same vision as I did, and assembled the hexagons, and is waiting, just like I am." She slid the clasp of her locket chain to the back of her neck.

"For what? A bigger biological disaster?" asked Principal Ungar.

"No, no, it isn't like that at all. Like I told you, the portals, they're here to do good. To help us be better."

"Where did the rods come from?" asked Charlie.

"And how will killing vegetation do us good?" asked Potter.

Kwashay had never questioned her mission. She'd accepted as fact that the portals, when operated, would improve things on Earth. She shook her head. "I'd answer your questions if I could. I really would, but I don't know."

The two EPA agents looked at each other, as if performing mental telepathy.

"I have one last question: why does it need to grow?" Agent Keyson stood waiting.

Kwashay gave a generic answer. "All plants grow. To get bigger and stronger." She looked away.

"This is different, isn't it?" asked Keyson. "The portal has some purpose, right, unlike normal plants."

"You know something. Tell us, please." The female agent's eyes were pleading.

Kwashay closed her eyes and tried to recall the vision and the message she got from joining two rods.

"It has to get stronger. It can't reach - something - until it can generate more - it doesn't make sense."

"What doesn't?" asked Keyson.

Kwashay took a deep breath, her armpits damp. "Ever since I touched the first two rods, it's been talking to me. In my head. Whispers, kind of. That's how I knew what the structure needed to look like and how to put it together."

"Can you talk back to it?" asked Principal Ungar.

"No, not like a conversation. But if I think about something, about the portal, then sometimes I get impressions. They're not answers. Maybe hints, a sense of the answer. I can't really explain it."

Agent Keyson touched her shoulder. "Don't be upset and don't be scared." He was trying to be nice, but his interest in the portal worried her. "We're done here, for now. If necessary, we'll explain things to your parents."

"There's just my mother."

"I'm sorry. We'll make sure she knows you aren't in any trouble, and that you're a valued advisor in our investigation."

"I'd prefer if you didn't. Contact her, that is." Given how her mother reacted to her interactions with Sideways, and to the true story of the portal, Kwashay knew less information was better.

"Here's my card." Agent Keyson held it out. His name was hand-written. "When you're willing to talk, give me a call."

The female agent slipped Kwashay her card as well. "We're here to help. Really." Agent Potter's name was printed.

Kwashay nodded. "Okay." She followed the principal a few steps, and then turned around. "You're not going to hurt it or try to move it, are you?"

"Seems like it can take good care of itself. No, it isn't going anywhere, and it seems too sturdy to come down easily. So you don't have to worry."

"Good. Because it hasn't done its job yet." *With me as the operator.*

Kwashay walked into school accompanied by her principal, feeling relieved. *I thought for a moment they were going to arrest me. I can't operate the portal if I'm in jail.*

53 – Selton (Kearney, NE)

Selton, bloated with information, risked flipping through Thinking Fast and Slow by Daniel Kahneman, attempting to not only ingest it but understand it. The next thing he knew, Bernice was standing over him, holding his ungloved hand, crooning his name.

"What happened?" he asked.

"I thought you'd fallen asleep, but you didn't wake up when I tapped you on the shoulder. I think you passed out. You poor man, have you have enough to eat?"

Selton was not going to risk his mission by ingesting human food. "I ate. Really."

"I'm going to call the paramedics, just to be sure you're all right."

"No, really, I'm fine." Selton stood, wobbled and plopped back into his chair. "I just need a minute."

"I'm going to make the call." Bernice shuffled toward her desk.

Selton had to avoid a physical examination at all costs. He struggled to his feet and stumbled from the library to Bernice's shouts of his name.

The police officer outside responded to Bernice's shouts by entering the library. She must have put him at ease, because he didn't follow.

At the underpass, he stopped to catch his breath. *I think that megafeeding is going to be too late.*

Selton used the sidewalk to meander to Centennial Park. Along the way, he used trees and lamp poles to stay on his feet. It was a long commute for which he didn't really have the energy. *I hope the megafeeding comes soon, because I'm in need of an energy boost. Or to be recalled, which would be even better. I'm more than ready.*

54 – Charlie (Brooklyn, NY)

Charlie retreated to the bench he and Potter previously shared in Fort Greene Park in Brooklyn. He flipped open his phone, sat down and dialed Jane's number. He hadn't spoken to her in a few days. Potter took a seat next to him even thought, at that moment, he would have preferred privacy.

"EPA, Director Stanton's office."

"Hi Jane. It's Charlie."

"Oooh, Jane," whispered Potter.

Charlie scowled at her.

"Mr. Keyson! How is your field assignment? Did you go sightseeing?"

Jane was so formal. It didn't seem right, calling her Jane while she called him mister. "The assignment is everything I expected and more. And yes. I got to see Governors Island and the Statue of Liberty and Fort Greene Park. And the hotel room you booked was perfect."

"It should be, at that price," muttered Potter.

"I so happy for you. When will you be back? I want to hear all about it. Maybe over dinner?"

What is it with women and dinner? "Pretty soon. How is AquaLung?"

Potter nudged Charlie's arm. "AquaLung?"

Charlie moved his phone away from his face. "My goldfish."

"Doing very fine. I taught him a trick. He comes to the surface for food."

Charlie didn't have the heart to tell Jane his fish had done that from day one. "Maybe he'll do it for me too."

"Director Stanton say you finishing up and coming back. Do you need flight reservation?" Jane asked.

"Yes, but I'm taking a few days off. You know, rest and recuperation. I was wondering if you could make flight and hotel reservations for me? On my personal credit card of course."

"Oh yes. Where you going?"

"Eureka, California. A direct flight if you can. And this is just between us, right? Director Stanton doesn't have to know where I'm going on my free time."

"Of course. I try to get you a non-stop flight. When are you leaving New York?"

Charlie whispered to Potter, "Okay if I fly out tomorrow?"

"Do I have a choice?" She nodded as agreement.

"Tomorrow." Charlie couldn't wait to see the portal's mate.

"Good! Do you have budget for hotel?"

Charlie remembered Potter's comment about his current hotel. "Nothing as fancy as here. Just a room."

"I make arrangements and send you email with you itinerary. Is that all right?"

"Perfect. I can get email at the New York EPA office. Thanks. And don't mention this to the Director."

"But he know you going to be away?"

"He knows. I just don't want him interrupting me during my time off." *Stanton will blow his stack if he learns I disobeyed a direct order, but I'm solving the dead grass case he assigned me.* "You understand?"

"Oh yes. I say nothing. Then I see you soon, in a few days. Bye."

Charlie pocketed his phone.

"So, what's new with Jane?" asked Potter.

"She's watching my fish while I'm away."

"That's very nice of her. Are you going to bring her something as a souvenir?"

Charlie hadn't thought about that possibility. "Maybe I'll just take her to dinner." She'd suggested it.

Potter sat up straight and threw her head back. "Oh sure, you'll go to dinner with her but not me!"

Charlie would have taken Potter's comment seriously if not for the wide smile that followed.

Potter stood up. "Come on, we'll go to my office."

"In Manhattan?"

"Nope, just south of here in Brooklyn. We can't afford the cost of office space over there."

They drove to Potter's office and parked in a flat asphalt lot next door to the building.

It was an open concept office layout, no partitions or privacy. At one of those desks, Charlie's procedure of using paper documents would be out in the open.

"You can use any of these for email. No restrictions, but all the porn sites are blocked." She raised an eyebrow but Charlie didn't react.

Charlie checked his email. There was one message from Jane. "Whoa. 6:00 am departure from JFK, one stop in San Francisco." He looked over at Potter, who was settling into her chair. "I didn't realize it was a nine hour flight."

"Don't get out much, huh? At least you gain three hours."

"Great. So when I get to California at 12:32 pm, it'll feel like 9:30 am. And then there's the second leg. God, I'll be exhausted."

"Just think of it as quality time with Quincy. That flight should give you enough time to finish the novel."

"If I can keep my eyes open."

Potter spun to face him. "Where will you be staying, if I can be so nosy?"

Charlie scrolled down the screen. "She got me a reservation at the Comfort Inn on Humboldt Bay."

"Well, that's no Ritz-Carlton, for sure."

"Come on, that was a fluke. But there must be some festival or convention, because her note says she got me the last available room." Why did Charlie feel the need to defend Jane's choice?

"Actually, it sounds quaint. Maybe even cozy."

Somehow, it seemed appropriate to share his itinerary details with his partner, despite her innuendo. Charlie kept reading. "And she's got me returning to Washington four days later."

"She really wants you back."

"I told her a few days. She took me literally, I guess. That's everything." Charlie checked his watch. "I'd better get back to the hotel and pack. I've got an early day tomorrow."

"Let me print that for you." Potter scooted to his side, almost leaning over his lap, and pushed a few keys. His itinerary rolled out of a nearby printer. "Give you a ride back to hotel?"

They're lucky to have workgroup printers. "That would be great."

Charlie had enjoyed working with Potter. She'd been a true partner, and an asset to the investigation. His experience as a desk jockey never gave him that kind of opportunity.

They pulled up to the Ritz in short order, ahead of rush hour traffic. "I'd offer to chauffeur you tomorrow morning, but if you have to be at the airport at 4 am-"

"It's okay. I'll catch a cab." Charlie got out.

Surprisingly, Potter turned off the car and left it blocking the hotel drive-up lane. "I'll let you know what my technicians find out. Promise you'll keep in touch."

"Oh for sure. This isn't anywhere close to finished. Keep an eye on Kwashay. She has a role to play before this is done."

"And you know this how?"

"Patterns. The vision. The fact that she expected a second structure. Her use of the words portal and operate a couple of times."

"Yeah that bothered me too. It's just a stick structure with no moving parts. It doesn't need to be operated."

"I'm not going to stop until I have all the answers." *I should have said "we."* He extended one arm. A handshake seemed inadequate but a hug would have sent the wrong message. "You're an asset to the New York EPA. And you've been a real partner – no kidding – during my stay."

"Sure thing, Holmes." She gripped his hand and tugged, but he resisted.

It took a second for him to get the reference. "We'll figure it out, Watson. The two of us." Charlie realized that his favorite private investigator had no sidekick.

"You and me and that PI Grissom you're so fond of." Potter retained the handshake. "You're not so bad yourself. I never would have known this was your first field assignment. Besides, you have to come back to New York." Potter added a second hand to her grip. "You owe me a dinner."

55 – Matt (Eureka, CA)

Matt rolled side-to-side, moans echoing in his head. Was he making the sounds, or was it the portal? The portal was damaged and he was the portal operator. But he couldn't operate an incomplete or damaged portal. A thought was pushed into his mind: What happened to the stamen seed? *What's a stamen seed? Is that missing too?*

Matt's mind couldn't successfully block the moaning sounds from the portal, but they seemed to be getting fainter. The portal was struggling to repair itself, despite being incomplete. Matt's bond with the portal grew stronger as they both healed. As the portal repaired itself, so would Matt. *I should go look for the last stick or stamen seed or whatever.* He threw one leg over the edge of the bed.

The portal urged him to remain in a prone position. *I guess we're not ready yet.*

President Stanley walked in, followed by his parents.

Great! This will only complicate things.

His mother took his hand. "Matty, are you all right?"

Matt nodded. "I'm fine." He was embarrassed that he hadn't protected himself better from Dixon, and that he'd failed to complete construction of the portal. *If only I could explain.*

"You don't look fine. And you haven't cut your hair since you left for school!" She smoothed stray strands off his face.

"Not now." His father stood, glaring at both of them.

President Stanley put her arm around Matt's mother and gently directed her away from the bed. "Let's move out into the hallway, to give Matt some peace and quiet."

Matt listened closely to the conversation just outside his room.

President Stanley's voice was soothing. "I heard you were on campus. I'm so sorry about Matt's condition –"

"We drove up as soon as we heard." His mother was agitated. "You're supposed to care for your students. Yet, you allowed that man –"

"Dixon!" His father blurted.

"- to hurt our son. Sorry isn't nearly good enough."

Matt could hear President Stanley's voice change to one of logical disposition. "Mr. Dixon did nothing to directly harm your son. According to him, one of his scientists – Dobbs – was trying to take a sample of the trellis when Matt collapsed. We've run every test we know of. Physiologically, there's nothing wrong."

"There are so many plants here," said his mother. "And Matty told me he likes spending time in the garden. Could he have an allergy or accidentally ingested something toxic?"

"To the best of our knowledge, there are no hazardous plants or flowers in the area."

"God, I hope he's been eating all right."

Mom always worries I'll have too much junk food.

"We've had a long drive," said his father. "We're tired, hungry and concerned about our son's health."

"Please, visit our cafeteria," said President Stanley. "Your meal is complementary."

"We can afford our own food." His father's tone was snippy. *She'd insulted him.* "On the drive up, we talked about pulling Matt from your school."

Matt wanted to jump from bed and argue. *I have to stay, to operate the portal!* He couldn't muster the strength.

Clicking heels on linoleum replaced the conversation in the hall. *They're leaving.*

Just as Matt closed his eyes to rest, the infirmary bed shook. He held on tight, his prone body vibrating at the same frequency. Something was thrashing through his mind, resuscitating past experiences. *They're doing it again!* They stopped at memories of playing video games, the kind where you pilot a ship to avoid collisions with asteroids, planets and other ships.

Matt mouthed a reinforced command. "You must prepare to be a portal operator," said his father's voice. He checked, but his father hadn't reentered the room.

Video games? You've got to be kidding! The shaking stopped. Matt bolted upright just as a nurse practitioner entered the room. "I have to go!" *I've got to get my skills back to tournament level.*

"Are you sure?" She approached, stethoscope at the ready. "I know you've been getting better but-"

"Feel great. Nope, I've got to go." He'd remained in street clothes, so all he had to do was put on his shoes and leave.

Now, where am I going to find a video game console and software?

56 – Kwashay (Brooklyn, NY)

Kwashay made her end-of-school day stop at the portal before walking to the Atlantic and Barclay Center Metro station. A white hybrid car with a big EPA decal blocked the sidewalk. Within the fluttering yellow police tape, the female EPA agent she'd previously met and two others in matching blue jackets with yellow EPA letters roamed around the portal carrying electronic devices.

The female agent – Potter? -- recognized her and came over. "What a coincidence, meeting you here." The agent's friendly smile made the greeting feel genuine.

"Nice to see you too." Kwashay examined the activities of the other agents. "What are they doing?"

"Taking more measurements. Some more pictures." Potter held up a pocket camera that looked brand new with the stickers still attached. "Taking a few more soil samples. Checking for radioactivity." She made a horror movie scowl and raised her hands like claws.

"But you're not hurting it, are you?"

"Nope. Wouldn't want to do that, would we? You've got big plans for this – portal."

Kwashay was pleased the agent used the proper name. It was her turn to smile. "Exactly!"

One of the others interrupted. "Agent Potter, the needle on the Geiger counter is bouncing all over. Maybe I should get a different machine from the office."

"It's not the device. There's some sort of electromagnetic interference. Step back as far as you need to until the machine begins working, then take a reading."

"But I won't be anywhere close-"

"I know. Just do it so we have that task checked off for Keyson."

Potter and Kwashay watched the agent walk in an expanding circle around the portal. He stopped about ten feet directly east of the structure. "It works here." He noted the reading. Then he continued around until he was at about the same distance directly west. "The interference is stronger here." He backed up until he was past the walking path, then came back to them. "For what it's worth, the interference isn't uniform. It's milder to the east, but much stronger to the west. Even ten yards out, I still couldn't take a reading."

Potter scratched her head. "You have any clues?" she asked Kwashay.

Kwashay shook her head.

"Makes some sense, since the dying grass heads west," said Potter. "Put that in your report."

"Where is your partner?" asked Kwashay.

"He's gone off to California without me." Potter tilted her head. "Did you see us as partners?"

"I guess. You seemed to work so well together. I just assumed."

"I thought so too." Potter sighed so hard her shoulders shook.

Kwashay hefted her backpack to reposition it. "Well. I've got to get going. Momma expects dinner on the table when she gets home."

"Call me if you need anything."

"I will." Kwashay was certain that operating her portal would be a one-person activity.

57 – Selton (Kearney, NE)

Selton was shaken awake even while his backroots were still planted. The vibrations were accompanied by the sound an Earth insect makes, a constant hum with rapidly changing harmonics. Then, it took an intelligible audio form. *This isn't like the previous messages.* The sounds were clearer than ever. However, the voice addressed him by an unfamiliar name.

Greetings, Sys2713-3.0.

Given everything he'd read about Earthling astronomy, he made educated guesses about the structure of the name. *Sys2713 must refer to Earth's solar system. Earth is the third planet from the sun, so that's the meaning of the number three. But why is there a sub-designation?* Selton listened carefully in the silence of the park:

Portals are preparing to deliver your megafeeding. Soon, you will achieve your function as host. Your seeds with full planetary knowledge will be distributed across the planet.

I'm a host? He ran his twiggy fingers up and down his arm, confirming the texture. *I expected to be seedless. There must be some mistake.* Selton had dutifully ingested most of Earth's information, to disseminate it with other Serulians. *Dissemination Oversight? Did that mean seed dissemination?*

Selton's mind could barely process the staggering implications. *If those bumps are seeds, then each of them will grow into an Earthling body with my same mission - intelligence gathering – but starting with what I've already accumulated. And given genetics, those Serulians would also go to seed.* He considered the time he'd spent on Earth. *Given my germination rate, soon Earth will become inundated with Serulians, overflowing freight trains, crowding libraries and sucking nutrients from the soil.*

The unacceptable truth blossomed in Selton's mind. *This is an invasion, and I'm the advanced guard.* Selton's pulp soured at the thought.

He sat up quick, clumps of soil and grass hanging from his backroots. Selton cradled his head in his twig fingers. *Serulians are conquerors?*

The transmission continued, advising Selton that a one-time megafeeding would soon be provided to bring his seeds through germination. He was told not to worry, because the megafeeding would come to him, no matter where he put down roots. Selton covered his ears but the transmission didn't need Earthling auditory organs. His whole body, acting like a receiver, detected the signal. Involuntarily, Selton's body emitted a burst reply - "Instructions received." As suddenly as the transmissions started, they stopped.

As hard as he tried to deny it, the signs had been there all along. *There was never a plan for recall. I can be left to rot because hundreds, maybe thousands of new Seltons will replace me.* Try as he might, he couldn't shake off the reality that he was the leader of an invasion by his species. That made the sub-designation perfectly logical. There would be Sys2713-3.1, Sys2713-3.2, et cetera, for as many seeds as Selton was carrying.

None of the previous messages had been as long. How could his home planet send a message from such a great distance? That was clearly impossible, which meant that the signals were coming from someone or something on Earth. *They mentioned portals that would provide the megafeeding.* Somehow, his travel planners had included communication capability in the portals for the last phase of his mission.

My mission? Selton shouted out loud. "That's not what I was sent here to do. I'm no invader!" No Earthlings were within the range of his voice.

Selton glanced at his manufactured navel. *The flower! I should have known!*

He was determined to sabotage Dissemination Oversight's plans. *How can a portal find me, to direct the megafeeding to my location?* The answer was obvious when he reconsidered the filaments that burst from his head. *There must be two portals, constructed from the filaments that grew within me and floated away. Because their genetic material is identical to mine, somehow they'll biangulate my position. That's why they blew away in opposite directions – for location detection.*

Selton shifted from self-pity to planning mode. One way to avoid the megafeeding was departing Earth, so that even if the seeds germinated, they would be no harm. But this was the same problem he had contemplated when he thought he would have to be responsible for his own recall, and that had dead-ended as not viable.

Since he was stuck on Earth, the next best option was evading detection by the portals. Since he'd assimilated nearly all of Earth's knowledge, he was confident he could create an avoidance strategy. *After the megafeeding fails, the seeds will remain dormant in my body until I rot away, and the threat to Earth will be eliminated.*

If the portals contained his genetic material and Serulian technology to pinpoint his location, Selton needed to make himself undetectable. Physical changes would be useless. He would have to make some change to his body chemistry, to make himself undetectable, as well as unable to answer or respond to future messages.

58 - Charlie (New York City, NY)

Charlie placed a call to Gregorio Nachas, the Region 9 EPA agent from his hotel room.

"Greg Nachas."

Okay, at least his answer included his last name. "This is Charlie Keyson, Washington EPA. I'm calling to share information I've learned from a similar situation here-"

"Don't bother. I've been pulled off the case."

Charlie had wanted Nachas to make the same kind of soil tests they'd did in New York. And with advanced notice, the confirming analysis would be done before he got there.

"What do you mean? There's a structure, right?" Charlie decided not to call it a portal. "And biological devastation?"

"I don't know anything about a structure. I can't get close enough to investigate the damaged trees and foliage. Somebody's got the College locked up tight."

A second portal was a vital clue. That reinforced Charlie's decision. "I'm coming out."

"I was told that Washington wasn't sending anyone, given the circumstances."

Director Stanton had mentioned politics, but Charlie's investigation had nothing to do with elections. "They're not. I'm coming out on my own time. After investigating one of these structures in Brooklyn-"

"There are two of those things?"

"Yes, which is why I'm coming out. I believe they're related – a matched set." *One of the only patterns to pursue.*

"Well, if you're willing to spend your own time and money, I'll do what I can to help."

"Great! Speaking of money, I haven't rented a car, and I don't know the area."

"Driving you around is a cheap price to pay for your expertise. I'd like a job in DC some day. Maybe you can give me some tips."

Charlie didn't feel like an expert, but absorbed the compliment silently. "My flight from San Francisco arrives about noon."

"Those United Express flights usually run late, but I'll be there."

Charlie wanted some soil samples taken and analyzed in advance of his arrival, but if Nachas didn't have access to the site, those tests would have to wait.

Why would anyone blockade a Federal investigation of dead grass?

Charlie settled into his seat onboard the six-hour flight from New York's JFK to San Francisco, California on his way to Eureka. It lacked the doting flight attendant from his last flight, for which he was relieved. Most passengers turned off their overhead lights and dozed off. As soon as they approached cruising altitude, Charlie fingered the novel open at the place marked by his old airline boarding pass.

🕮

> Besides the one-way flights to state capitals, Grissom's hottest clue was the series of appraisal and pawn shop visits by Indulge Financial cardholders who had subsequent fraudulent transactions. None of Grissom's Undergrads had been impressed with the knowledge or expertise of the folks they'd met at the various establishments. Of particular note was the report by the Undergrad in New York City. He'd met a clerk with an unusual tattoo on his forearm: an American flag overlaid with a red "not symbol" circle and slash. The Undergrad showed him his tattoo, the Statue of Liberty on his upper arm. The clerk seemed willing to talk until another employee showed up. Grissom was disappointed at the lost opportunity.
>
> The shops all had unique names: Standing Appraisals, Stature Pawn, Reputation Appraisal Service, Renown

Resale and Pawn, Honor Valuations, Esteemed Pawn Shop, Celebrity Appraisals, Prominent Pawn and, locally, Prestige Appraisals. It sounded like the names were picked out of a thesaurus.

From his research, Grissom learned that all of them were privately owned and claimed that their employees were certified. It sounded strange that small storefronts could afford certified appraisers, especially given the variety of disciplines they served - pottery, gems, artifacts, and mechanisms like watches.

To be certified, the appraisers needed accreditation through the Appraisers Association of America. Grissom contacted the association and discovered that each of the stores had filed for certification of employees at addresses other than the stores. They also, uncharacteristically, chose not to be listed in the association's directory. Based on the unpublished status, the association chose not to provide any more information. Grissom asked if the association had images of the checks for membership dues. "Why would we retain those? We got paid in full."

Grissom groped for something to tie the appraisal and pawnshops together. Running out of options, he called his friend at the FBI, Agent Clay, and summarized the investigation.

"I'd like you to subpoena some check images. I know only the issuer and the recipient."

"Nothing like making it easy on me. It can be done after some research, but I'll need approval for a request like this. I don't run the place, you know."

"Ah, but you should."

Clay laughed. "This sounds more complicated than check fraud, or whatever you're working."

"In geography, yes. Perhaps in scope as well." Grissom shared what he knew as fact, and what he believed based on patterns. "So, is that sufficient cause?"

"The dollar amounts would normally put this under the radar, but in total, they're sufficient, just barely, for me to request authority to investigate. But now you're obligated to keep me in the loop.

Grissom gave a verbal salute. "Yes sir."

The FBI can't help. This is on me. Charlie marked his place and tucked the book into the seatback pouch. The logic of the twin portals eluded him. And unavailability of the second portal for examination and soil samples made progress even less likely. He closed his eyes, hoping to dream up a plan for success.

A flight attendant shook his shoulder, asking him to raise his seatback to full upright for the landing. *Here already?* Inside the airport, he grabbed a snack in a convenient food venue, a cup of black coffee and a banana muffin, as he made his way to the proper concourse during his one and one-half hour layover.

The second leg of his journey was aboard a smaller plane with a turbulent ride. Charlie couldn't read let alone think about anything but his safety, barely hanging on.

After an unsteady flight and landing at Arcata/Eureka Airport, Charlie wobbled down a staircase that had been rolled over to the exit door. He spied a white sedan with a California state logo on the side and an electric vehicle sticker on the trunk. The olive-skinned driver leaned against the side of his vehicle.

"Are you Nachas?" asked Charlie.

"Call me Greg. I assume you're Charlie Keyson. Welcome to California." He came around the car and offered a handshake. "You want to stop at your hotel and freshen up?"

Charlie delivered his half of a firm two-handed grip. "Let's go straight to the scene. You can fill me in during the drive."

"Okay, you're the Fed. But my boss is going to be mucho pissed. He called me off this case so abruptly."

"Same here. I'm not going to say a word. And if it gets out, tell him or her I insisted. So, how bad is the situation?"

"I wouldn't be concerned if it was just shrubs and grass, but the Redwoods are threatened. The first call was from our destination, College of the Redwoods."

Charlie opened the door and slid into the passenger seat, but not before glancing at a bush in the rear area. "And they're a big deal out here?"

“Redwoods are a big deal, period. They only grow in specific places on the planet.” Nachas checked his mirrors and started the engine. No sound.

Charlie pointed to the back with a rear-facing thumb. “What’s that? A casualty?”

“The school brought it to the lab for an autopsy before they closed up.”

“Can you do that? Take an autopsy of a plant?”

“Coroners do it with people every day. Why not a plant?

Charlie realized that he’d essentially done the same thing by analyzing soil samples in the dead grass patches. “Okay, so what did you find?

“It didn’t make sense - it shouldn’t have died so quickly if it lost nutrition over time. It was a double punch. It died of starvation and thirst.”

“Sounds familiar to what we saw in New York. Dead soil, completely void of nutrients.”

“Wow! I’ve never heard of such a thing.” Nachas turned left on Airport Road and merged onto 101 south. “We reacted immediately when we learned a stand of redwoods fell over without warning.”

“Big trees like that must have massive root systems.”

Nachas shook his head as he changed lanes. “Common misconception. Their roots are pretty shallow. They’ve been known to topple when the soil gets wet, but it’s been dry. And in that area, very dry.”

“You said first call?”

“Yeah, many areas east of the University have been calling in since. Like I told you earlier, there was an initial report of fallen redwoods. Then they called back and expanded the report to include other vegetation – trees, bushes, and grass – in the same area. Southeast corner of the property. That's when we learned there was some geometric framework near the scene."

The second portal! "I have one of those, in Brooklyn."

"When my supervisor moved the case to the top of my list, I drove down to see for myself. But when I got to the college, I was turned away. It was like the campus was closed to visitors, with no explanation."

"Someone is hiding something." Charlie had a firm suspicion it was the portal.

"So, two of them couldn't be a coincidence, right?"

Seems like a pattern to me. Charlie looked out the window at the California coastline streaming past as they headed south on 101. "I can't be certain until I see for myself."

"And what do you expect me to do if the entrance is still barricaded?" asked Nachas. "Smash through?"

"If necessary." *And give the Director a heart attack.*

"You're kidding, right?" Nachas took the Tompkins Road exit and pulled up to the entrance. "Here we are. College of the Redwoods. Private junior college with a live-in option and an attached high school."

A makeshift barrier of sawhorses constructed from two-by-fours blocked their path. A guard, in black shirt and pants, a black beret and the letter B embroidered in white on the chest and shoulders approached the driver's side. He wore a wireless earpiece. "What's your business, please?"

Charlie pulled out his badge. "Keyson, Federal EPA. I'm here to see the principal." *Is that what they called the head of a college?*

The guard walked far enough away so Charlie couldn't hear the conversation he was having through his earpiece. The guard glanced back at Nachas' car a couple of times while conversing, then returned. "Administrative Building." He pulled a map from his back pocket, circled a building and handed it to Nachas. "Park in the visitor spaces near the front entrance." The guard swung a sawhorse out of their path. As Nachas pulled through the gap, Charlie saw the guard moving his lips. They were being announced.

Nachas drove to the parking lot as instructed and pulled his car into one of many available visitor spots. As Charlie walked into the specified building, he took a moment to absorb the scenery. *How devastating it would be if the same blight in New York occurred here. The damage would be so much worse for these ancient pristine forests.*

They walked up the steps and were greeted by a female administrator who escorted them directly to a room with an embossed redwood sign, "PRESIDENT'S OFFICE."

A woman stood at her desk in a conservative blue dress, grey hair immaculately coiffed. "I'm President Stanley. Please, don't bother sitting. This meeting will be brief."

I wouldn't have sat down until she did anyway. "All right, let's get to it. I'm Charlie Keyson, Federal EPA and this is Greg Nachas, California branch. Your school filed an EPA complaint about some biological trauma. Fallen redwoods and dead foliage-"

"Mr. Dixon from the Bates Foundation has promised to handle the situation. Your presence on campus is at his discretion."

"I don't know anything about Mr. Dixon's credentials to effectively handle this situation, for which the EPA has jurisdiction. The Redwoods are a national treasure. We can't just walk away." Nachas nodded in agreement.

"He expected you'd want to be briefed on the situation. He's willing to see you."

Willing? As if he gets to decide? "Where would we find him? To understand his plans for remediation?"

"He works out of a mobile home parked on the football field. Just follow the road east. Good bye."

Charlie and Nachas left the building, established their orientation, and drove east on the main campus road.

"Sounds to me like Mr. Dixon thinks a lot of himself," said Nachas.

"And President Stanley seems to concur." Charlie wondered what leverage Dixon and the Bates Foundation had over the school.

Sure enough, a motor home sat in the end zone. Expansion sections had been pulled out, almost doubling the width of the portable building. Tents had been erected along the twenty yard line and an extra-wide semitrailer truck was parked mid-field.

Nachas parked along the curb near the field. Before they could go any further, Charlie's phone rang. "A call from my colleague, Lane." He got out of the car and stepped to the side. Nachas gave him some space. "Keyson."

"The Director said you're taking a couple of days off, right?"

"That's right. Why?"

"I'm sorry to bother you, but farmers in downstate Indiana and Illinois have reported crop damage."

"Let me guess – a brown stripe running through their fields?"

"Precisely. The same one?"

"I told you it was expanding west." *Why won't they listen?*

"Damn!"

Maybe now Lane understands the severity of the situation. "Listen, I'm on vacation. I'll talk to you later." He flipped his phone shut.

"Anything new?" asked Nachas.

"Nope, just more of the same." Charlie, followed by Nachas, approached the motor home and knocked.

"Come in," blasted a voice from inside.

Charlie opened the door and ascended two steps.

A young man, late twenties or early thirties posed next to the oversized steering wheel wearing a blue polo shirt, the name Bates embroidered in white above a chest pocket. "Welcome. Mr. Keyson and Mr. Nachas. I'm Trevor Dixon from the Bates Foundation. How can I help you gentlemen?"

Charlie was impressed that Dixon knew his name but wanted to assert a level of authority. "I'm here in support of Agent Nachas of the California EPA office, who was alerted by the Principal of the school about serious problems with trees and other foliage-"

Dixon flicked his wrist. "All cared for. The Bates Foundation will make everything right. You got that message from your Director and still made the trip all the way out here?" Dixon took a step forward, like a sheep dog guiding its flock. "What a waste! So if that's all-"

How does he know Director Stanton called me off? Does Bates have spies inside the EPA? Charlie stood his ground, which put Dixon within breath-smelling range. *Spearmint.* "No, there's more."

Dixon slapped his hand on the dashboard, effectively blocking a path deeper into the vehicle. "I'd love to give you the grand tour of my mobile home – had it trucked in special - or maybe even offer you gentlemen a drink. But I know both of you are busy, and I just flew in from North Carolina."

North Carolina? Interesting, that's where the Bates' coal ash spill happened. Charlie heard Nachas open the door behind them but Charlie didn't move. *No point in wasting time, asking about remediation.* "I'm here to see the structure."

Dixon stumbled back a couple of feet, losing his grip on the dash and reestablishing a suitable buffer. "What structure?"

"The one that's hexagonal in shape, about eight feet tall, with roots holding it tight to the ground. That structure."

Dixon tilted his head. "How could you know about that?"

"You're clearly all business, so I have a proposal. The College is under your control, that's clear. So let's sit down and chat about a topic of mutual interest. You're going to want me as your friend, not your adversary."

Dixon seemed to consider the offer for a moment, his eyes examining the headliner. After about thirty seconds, he motioned them deeper into the vehicle.

Expanded sides allowed for a full-sized desk nicer than the Principal's and a couple of visitor chairs. They all sat. "How do you want to do this?"

"Why don't we share?" asked Charlie. "Tell me what you know, and I'll tell you what I know. We'll both be smarter for it."

Dixon stroked his chin. "Sounds like a plan. The Bates Corporation has close ties with many facets of government, and always cooperative. How about-"

Charlie interrupted. "Since we're on your turf, you go first."

Dixon hesitated. "Okay. Some background. I'm here as a representative of Bates Corporation, specifically the Bates Foundation. Mr. Bates is very fond of the College, and donates heavily to it."

Dixon was stalling. Charlie waited patiently.

Dixon continued, "In fact, we were planning to break ground next year on a new nanotechnology facility. Classrooms, laboratories, all state-of-the-art. Based on some windfall profits the Corporation achieved last quarter, we've moved up the schedule. I was dispatched to perform preliminary reconnaissance and pre-construction planning."

Charlie needed to move their conversation along. "And that's when you found the structure."

Dixon put his palms flat on his wooden desk. "I'd never seen anything like it before. Unique material, striking design-"

Charlie and Kwashay had speculated about the rods in Brooklyn but had come to no conclusion. "What have you learned about the material?"

Dixon seemed genuinely excited. "We've got a pocket-sized molecular sensor that scans physical objects and obtains information about the chemical makeup. Then, the chemical makeup is compared against items in a cloud-based database, and the information about the item is sent back."

Charlie was bored with the glossy brochure monologue. "Can you just tell me-"

Dixon prattled on. "The device is capable of scanning food for nutritional information, medicines, plants, oils, plastics, wood, and more."

"Terrific. So what are the rods-"

Dixon was not to be deterred. "The device works by shining a light on an object and using a spectrometer to analyze the properties of the light reflected back." He took a breath.

Charlie's patience had lapsed. "What are the rods made of?"

Dixon took a breath before answering. "The structure is giving off so much electromagnetic radiation, the device wouldn't work. But I managed to shave off a few particles for which we've performed the analysis in our state-of-the-art portable laboratory, in the semi-trailer."

Charlie was tired of asking, but Dixon was daring him. "The results, please?"

"The sticks aren't made of any known material on Earth. Which says a lot." Dixon folded his arms on his chest.

I guess he's done sharing. "One last item before we go to the structure. I'd like the precise latitude and longitude, if you have if. If not, maybe one of your scientists-"

"I've got that right here. It's the first measurement we made."

Charlie took out his spiral-bound notepad, flipped back to the first page for this case and recorded the numbers: 40.692841, -124.193224. The Eureka construction was nearly at the same latitude as the Brooklyn one. "Could you measure directly?"

"No, just like the molecular sensor, we had to move away. Couldn't get any closer than about twenty-five feet. We chose to approximate from due south. The coordinates I gave you include the measurement compensation."

Twenty-five feet was precisely half the width of the brown stripe. "Thanks." Charlie slapped his notepad shut. "Now I have the locations for both structures."

Dixon's eyes bugged out. "There's another one?"

"I guess it's my turn to share. Yes, there's another one. Mine's on public property. Sounds identical to yours, and I'll confirm as soon as I see it. The root system extends straight west, towards its twin. I haven't tried digging to be sure."

"Why don't you use underground radar?" Dixon leaned back in his chair.

"There is such a thing?"

"Bates has used it successfully in searching for land integrity, underground streams, even fracking sites."

Charlie winced at the mention of hydraulic fracturing. The agency was up to its neck in claims regarding underground water pollution and seismic events due to the process. "Can you refer me to a reputable outfit?

"Sure." Dixon handed Charlie a business card from his desk drawer. "This company works out east, if you want to trace the roots of your trellis. They use state-of-the-art equipment. I should know. Bates manufacturers it. Mention my name, and maybe they'll offer you a discount."

Trellis? In this environment, the hexagonal structure might look like a trellis. "Have you done that out here?"

"Nope. Hadn't thought about the length or direction of the root system." Dixon pulled out a second card. "Here, these folks are local."

"Great. I'll share what I find out. Now, can we see your structure?" Charlie stood to get them moving.

"All right." Dixon came around his desk.

The three men exited the mobile home. Dixon grabbed a briefcase and dawdled outside, holding the door.

Charlie didn't know which way to proceed, although the woods to the east was a likely spot. "Have you done soil analysis?"

Dixon pointed to the semi-trailer. "The scientists are working on those as we speak."

"Don't waste their time. They'll find the soil completely dead, stripped of nutrients, microorganisms, everything."

Dixon slapped his thigh with a flat hand. "So that's where it's getting its energy. From the ground!"

Charlie didn't understand Dixon's use of the word energy. *As far as I know, the nutrients are being used for expanding the portal's root system.* He went along. "Exactly."

"I was wondering how it could generate those signals."

Charlie remembered police officers having trouble with their radios when in proximity, and confirmed Dixon's issues using electronics in the structure's vicinity. He wondered how successful Potter's people had been. She hadn't called.

Dixon spoke as if Charlie looked surprised. "You didn't know the trellises were broadcasting like antennas?"

"Interference, yes. Broadcasting, no. To whom are they broadcasting?"

"Maybe to each other, if there are two." Dixon walked in the direction of a wooded area past the field. "Not us, if they expect us to understand. Complete gibberish. Believe me, we've tried every possible decoding and translation algorithm-"

"Wait a second." Charlie scratched his head. "Who is 'they'?"

Dixon pointed straight up. "The aliens, of course."

Nachas laughed.

Charlie stifled a similar response. "You think these are, what, extraterrestrial antennas?"

Dixon scowled and put fists on his hips. "Think about it. It's made out of unidentifiable stuff that's stronger than almost everything on Earth. It grows and puts down roots. It sucks nutrients from the soil, so it eats. And it communicates with an out-of-this world signal. You have a better explanation?"

Charlie stood stoic. He wasn't going to give Dixon the satisfaction of a negative response. "I'm working on one."

Potter hadn't been in touch with the results of the New York team's analysis. That would have come in handy.

Dixon kept walking, at a snail's pace. "These emissions are at higher frequencies than even ultrahigh energy gamma waves. Way past anything on the planet."

"You mean - aliens are trying to communicate with us?" asked Nachas.

"I sure hope so!" Dixon put his hand on Nachas' shoulder, as if he'd found a believer. "If this is beyond our scientific capabilities, then it must be from somewhere else."

"No." Charlie wasn't falling for Dixon's line of reasoning. "There has to be some other explanation."

"Think what you want, but my team believes that this trellis is an extraterrestrial organism, a living alien. Not the kind you'd expect from science fiction, hey? No 'Take me to your leader.' Just a growing erector set that's put down roots. And it looks like it's here to stay."

Charlie fell behind and whispered to Nachas, "I can't report this." *Director Stanton would laugh in my face. Probably fire me. My reputation would be permanently tarnished.*

Nachas nodded.

They eased through the woods until they reached a clearing, cordoned off by thick red streamers, Dixon's equivalent of yellow police tape, with the name 'BATES' repeating every three feet. Two guards in identical black garb stood watch.

A large patch of the wooded area looked like it had been defoliated by a strong chemical agent, the industrial kind. But just like in Fort Greene Park in Brooklyn, the effect was directional, as if a devil's wind had blown in from the west.

An identical portal stood as the origin point for the botanical devastation, except the rods had grown fatter. "Looks the same."

"Wow!" Nachas took out his phone. "That's some hexagonal prism. Two of them, one inside the other!" He raised his phone to eye level.

"No photos!" ordered Dixon.

"We need to get closer." Charlie intentionally didn't ask and stepped towards the portal.

Dixon nodded to the guards. The two EPA folks ducked under the tape and touched the structure. Nearby, a Bates employee in a white lab coat with the name Dobbs on the chest ran a probe along the portal's horizontal struts. Charlie walked to the east edge of the portal. As expected, a brown stripe extended directly east. *I wonder how far this one has spread?* He returned to the portal and confirmed the texture of the rods with his fingertips. "Feels the same." Along one horizontal rod, the surface was rough, as if filed or scoured. In the same vicinity, one vertical rod was missing. "It's incomplete."

"I know. I've had teams scouring the area. Nothing."

Kwashay's portal was complete. Would this have an effect? "Tell me, did you happen to notice anyone, perhaps a student, who was particularly interested in the structure?"

"Not that I can recall."

There had to be a Kwashay counterpart. "Someone who may have spent too much time hanging around it?"

"I don't think so." Dixon's eyes were flashing around.

Dobbs in the lab coat muttered, "There may have been a young man –"

"Thanks. I'd like to meet him. I have some questions."

Dixon flushed and pushed the scientist aside. "Why, does your trellis have someone similar?"

Charlie withheld the term portal. *That would only fuel Dixon's absurd notion about aliens.* "Fair question. A young woman. High school senior, who feels almost bonded to her version."

"Bonded!" Dixon clasped his hands. "Perfect word!"

"Why?"

Dobbs spoke over Dixon's shoulder. "He took a sample off one of the rods with a diamond blade saw-"

Charlie imagined how Kwashay would have reacted to physical damage to her portal. "You didn't! Is he all right?"

Dixon folded his arms. "No big deal."

"The young man is in the school infirmary," said Dobbs. "I took him there myself,"

"That's enough out of you." Dixon put his hand on Dobb's shoulder. "Go run some analysis in the lab."

Dobbs ducked under the red barrier and meandered toward the semi-trailer.

"Matt suffered no physical damage, thank goodness, but seeing a sample being taken must have been a severe emotional shock. His parents are coming to see him, and the Bates Foundation has offered to pay for all of his medical and educational expenses."

"How nice of you." *After causing him the trauma in the first place.* "My young woman seemed to know there was another structure with an operator." Charlie hadn't intended on using that word, but it was too late.

"Operator? The trellises need an operator? To do what?"

“I haven’t a clue. There doesn’t seem to be anything to operate.”

Dixon threw his arms in the air. “I knew it! It’s an invasion!”

Charlie shook his head. “You’ve read too many science fiction novels.”

“No, listen.” Dixon grabbed Charlie’s arm. “The aliens are planning to use these antennas to open a rift or portal so they can come through and take over the planet. Matt and your young woman were recruited to be the operators. Don’t you see?”

Charlie winced at the word portal. *Portals usually are doorways.* He waited a moment before responding. “You seem to be a rational man. Do you really believe this is part of an alien invasion?” Do aliens need to kill grass for their plan to succeed? Because they’re allergic?”

“I’m struggling for answers here.” Dixon opened the case and took out an unbranded black metal box with both analog and digital displays. A wand with concentric circles connected to the box with a curly cord. “This scanner is a device of our own design. It is over 1,000 times more sensitive than commercial equipment. And it can detect a broader range of signals. The ones being generated by this trellis is both - faint and off the scale. Watch.”

Dixon walked about twenty feet east of the portal, standing on brown grass. Charlie and Nachas followed, standing behind their host. When Dixon held up the wand, the needle on the analog scale barely moved. The digital display’s numbers accelerated and didn’t stop. “See, there’s your signal. Fainter than a whisper and approaching the speed of light. Imagine if our networks sent data this fast.”

Dixon's motives were clear. *If this technology could be harnessed, the Bates Foundation could fund start-ups for data transmission equipment that would bury the competition and create an instant monopoly.* "I'm impressed. The electromagnetic field being generated could be interpreted as transmitting. But maybe it's just a really strong localized field. I enjoyed your demonstration, really, but I'd prefer to speak with Matt, if he's recovered enough."

Dixon tucked his equipment back into the briefcase. "When Matt is strong enough for visitors-"

"We'll all visit him," said Charlie.

Dixon nodded. "Agreed."

"We've seen all we need for now, but we'll need to come back." Charlie wanted to make sure he wouldn't be turned away on a subsequent visit. "Let's check in on Matt, just in case."

"The school infirmary is just across the football field. We can cut through." Dixon led Charlie and Nachas across the grass, between his motor home and the semi-trailer, to the school's Student Health Services in the Physical Education building. A woman dressed in white sat at a reception desk. "How can I help you?"

Dixon spoke up. "We're here to see Matt Thready."

She flipped through a multipage stapled document with her index finger. "Junior," she replied. "Matt Thready Jr. Please sign in."

Each of them dutifully signed the log page on the clipboard she handed them.

"Follow me. Matt's room is just down the hall on the right." When they got to the correct doorway, she motioned them to enter.

It looked and smelled like a typical hospital room, except the adjustable-height bed was empty.

59 – Matt (Eureka, CA)

Matt left his game console at home, an agreement his folks had forced on him. Even he admitted that not having the distraction was probably good for him,. *I wish I'd known I'd need it.* He knew where to find Fred, in the Union building, probably begging female students for attention. Matt jogged to the Union. Fred was there, as expected, sitting at a table of women, all of whom were ignoring him.

"Excuse me," said Matt.

The women looked up, smiled, and delivered an unsynchronized chorus of "Hi's and "Hello's.

"I need a conversation with my friend here." He tugged on Fred's arm until Fred got up from his chair and followed Matt off to the side.

"They were just warming up to me." Fred glanced over at the table. The female students were giggling. "I heard you got sick but now you're better? Great! Now maybe I can reask those two girls-"

Matt cut him off. "For the moment, I'll forget that you ratted me out to Dixon."

"Who's that?" Fred glanced back at the girls and smiled.

"The guy from Bates who bought you a pizza?"

"Oh yeah. Him." Fred hung his head. "I just told him the truth, that I got some guys to build a scaffold."

"For me!" Matt grabbed the front of Fred's shirt with both hands. "You've got a game console right?"

"Yeah, last year's Y-Box. Piece of crap compared to the new model but my folks refuse to buy me-"

"Give it to me."

Fred rocked up on his toes. "Whoa, do my ears deceive me? Study-all-the-time guy wants to buy my Y-Box?"

"Let's go get it." Matt tugged Fred in the direction of his dorm. Fred glanced back at the table of young women but didn't struggle, babbling about how the Y-Box wasn't such a loser, and that developers were still making games for it, and it was upgradable.

When they got to the concrete walkway in front of his dorm, Fred pulled up short. "I'll let you have it for a bargain price, if this time you'll actually show up for our double date."

Matt took Fred by the shoulders and stared into his eyes. "I said-", each word a sentence, "I. Need. It."

Fred thrashed his arms, breaking free. "Okay, okay, we'll settle on a price later."

An entourage of three men approached just before Matt and Fred entered the building.

"Hey, Matt, how are you doing?" Dixon's glad-handing style was unwelcome besides being phony. "And his sidekick Fred. How was the pizza, big guy?"

Fred remained silent.

"What do you care?" Matt glared. "Just stay the hell away from me! You're the guy who hurt the portal."

Fred averted his eyes, refusing to even look at Dixon.

Matt examined the two other men, both in suits. "Who are these guys? Bates executives with cattle prods?"

"We're with the Environmental Protection Agency. My name is Charlie Keyson. This is Agent Greg Nachas. I've come a long way to meet you."

Dixon smacked Charlie's shoulder. "See, it is a portal!" He faced Matt. "I was just trying to take a sample. We came here to find out-"

"Why would you damage something that's here to help us? That doesn't make sense." Matt shoved Fred through the entrance into the lobby of the dorm but didn't let go. The three men followed.

"I believe you, Matt," said Keyson. "The portal is here to help us. Just like the other one."

Charlie's comment got Matt's attention. His eyes widened. "Yes, the other one. They're both vital." He relaxed his grip on Fred.

Charlie kept talking. "I've met the other operator. She is very dedicated to her portal. Looks identical to yours."

Matt shook his head. "Not identical. One of my sticks is missing."

"What is the portal really?" Dixon raised his voice. "How is it going to help us?"

Keyson stepped between Dixon and Matt. "Calm down!" He faced Dixon. "Intimidation won't get the answers we want. The other builder didn't know either."

"The portal needs to be protected from people who want to hurt it. People like you!" Matt pointed an accusing finger.

Charlie looked deep into Matt's eyes. "You're the operator, right?"

"Yes. I'm the operator. But the portal won't work. There is a stick missing. Have you found the missing stick?"

Dixon stepped closer. "No, and we've looked everywhere."

"You must look harder. When the time comes, the portal must be complete."

Dixon interrupted Charlie's dialogue. "Who are the aliens?"

"What aliens?" said Matt. "Just leave me alone!"

"Be quiet! You're just confusing things," said Charlie. "Let me handle this."

"I didn't tell him anything about the portal. Honest!" said Fred. "But aliens? Why didn't you tell me you were into something really cool?"

The two EPA agents moved Fred away.

Dixon used that moment to grab Matt by the shoulders and shake him. "How does it work, damn it?"

"I don't know. You hurt the portal and you're hurting me!" His parents came trotting through the entrance. "Mom! Dad!"

Matt's father rushed forward. "Get your hands off my son!" With one smooth motion, he grasped Dixon and flung him away. Dixon stumbled backwards, collided with a lounge chair and fell to the floor.

"Are you okay?" asked Thready Senior.

Matt nodded.

Dixon slowly wobbled his way upright, holding his shoulder. "I only wanted – oh, never mind." He left the remainder unsaid and tottered out the door.

Matt's father rubbed his hands together. "Jerk! Who was that guy?"

"Trev Dixon, a representative of the Bates Foundation," said one of the EPA guys. *Charlie?*

“That’s Dixon?” Mr. Thready stared out the window at Trev standing on the sidewalk. “Did you say Bates? Bates Corporation?”

“Yes, the same.” Charlie and then Nachas performed their introductions to the Threadys.

Charlie gave Matt’s parents a synopsis. “Evidently, your son innocently used some sticks to build a – “ He considered his word choice. “- a trellis in the southeast corner of school property, precisely where Bates is planning to build a new science building.”

Mr. Thready shrugged. “So what? If the alternative to harassing my son is tearing the thing down, bulldoze it.”

“They tried, and it isn’t moving. And when Dixon tried using a high-tech diamond saw, your son was -.”

“Oh my God!” Mrs. Thready nearly collapsed, leaning heavily on her husband. “That man used a saw on my son?”

“No, not on him, on the trellis.” Charlie patted her arm. “No physical harm came to Matt, or Dixon would be in police custody, I assure you. But the sticks Matt used aren’t normal. In fact, we don’t know what they are or how they got here. Matt and the trellis he built need each other.”

“For what?” asked Matt’s father. “What are you saying?”

“This is crazy talk,” added his mother.

Matt leaned against the wall, whimpering. Dixon’s attack had only made things worse.

“My degree is in psychology. Matt has classic symptoms of post-traumatic stress,” said Nachas.

"It was school work, and pressure about grades, and the fact that we were out of the country. He missed us." Mrs. Thready looked at Nachas. "Being homesick can cause depression, can't it?"

Nachas didn't respond.

"I can't operate the portal if it's incomplete!" Matt whispered.

His mother's eyes flashed from her son to Charlie. "How could this have happened?"

"None of us know. There is another person, a young high school senior in Brooklyn, who has her own structure identical to Matt's. We used the terms 'bonded' and 'joined' to describe the phenomenon in her case."

"And is she okay?" asked Mrs. Thready.

"Yes. I have a partner in New York who's ensuring her safety. Agent Nachas and I are dedicated to the same thing with your son."

Matt's mother grasped Charlie's hand. "Thank you."

"Bates, hmm?" Matt's father added a pat on Nachas' back. "We'll see how long Mr. Dixon stays in charge."

Charlie continued, "Both portals seem to have extensive root systems that seem to be killing grass and other plants."

"And dead grass requires the EPA?" Mr. Thready jingled coins in his pocket. "My tax dollars at work."

"It's no joke. There's been extensive damage from the east, including disruptions of farm land in Illinois and Indiana." Charlie looked over at Nachas.

"And we've got reports of similar environmental impacts heading east from here," added Nachas. "We're doing our best to figure it out."

"Go ahead, do your research, just leave our son out of it," said Thready Senior.

"And leave the portal alone. It's suffered enough." Matt pulled himself away from the wall. "Come on, Fred."

"Bates," muttered Thready Senior.

Charlie and Nachas both gave Mrs. Thready their business cards. "We'll check in later."

60 – Kwashay (Brooklyn, NY)

Kwashay stirred the beef and vegetables brewing in the crock-pot as her mother came through the front door. "Hi, Mama. How was work?"

"Like every other day. They all melt together. Smells good. Have a good day at school?"

"Pretty good." Her conversation with the EPA agent was not a highlight to share.

Her mother's voice wafted in from the front hall, where she was likely taking off her coat and shoes, a daily ritual Kwashay had seen numerous times. "I heard from your Uncle Lamar today. I knew if anyone could work a miracle, he could." She turned on the television in the living room, then entered the kitchen and hugged her daughter.

"For Sideways? What did he do?"

"The young man's name is Vondell, and you should use it. Maybe then he'll stop calling you Girly-girl." She lifted the crock-pot lid and wafted the steam towards her face, taking a deep inhale. "Mmmm."

"Mama, aren't you going to tell me?"

"Oh yes. Lamar made the argument to the construction company that they'd be better served by hiring Vondell and garnishing his paycheck for their costs rather than pressing charges and having him spend unproductive time in jail."

"Really?" She threw her arms around her mother, almost knocking her to the floor. "That's terrific!"

"You like that young man?"

"I don't know. He's nice and kind of funny. Maybe, some day when I'm ready, I might want to go out with him."

"Let's see how he works out with his new job and then we'll see." Her mother took a turn stirring the stew. "Almost ready." She pulled out a chair and motioned for her daughter to sit down. "How's school?"

"Fine. I'm keeping up with all of my classes."

"Don't think I haven't noticed." She waved the stirring spoon in the air. "Your study habits have gone to hell in a hand basket, God forgive me, ever since you and Vondell built that art project thing. And then making up wild stories about it!"

"I'll do better, Mama. I promise." *And I'll do whatever it takes to be the best portal operator I can be.*

61 – Selton (Kearney, NE)

After a quick shower in the train yard, Selton rushed to the library. *The best starting point for me would be examples of when Earth resisted alien invasions.* That led him to Bernice's counter.

"Good morning, Selton! Are you all right?"

"Yes, fine. I just needed a good night's rest." Selton stifled the urge to share his newly discovered role with her. *She'd never understand.* "Please help me. What fiction novels would you recommend on the topic of alien invasions of Earth?" Selton would have examined his stored information, except fiction details were never retained.

Bernice's eyes widened. "I don't know off-hand. I'm not much of a science fiction reader, but let me check." Her fingers adeptly tapped at her keyboard and waited for a response. "I've found a list of the top ten novels on that topic. Let me see what I have in stock."

More taps. "I have three from the list, and another one is available through an interlibrary sharing agreement. Do you want the three I have?" She smiled. "As a voracious reader, of course you do. And I'll order the fourth one."

Selton followed Bernice as she came around her work area and strutted to the Science Fiction section. She scanned and plucked three books from various areas of the shelves.

"Here." She handed him the tomes. "Will you read them here or take them out?" She didn't bother waiting for a response. Selton had never checked out a book in all the time he'd been in Kearney. "Good reading!" She placed the *Kearney Hub* on top.

Selton had forgotten to pick up the local paper on his way in, but felt the urge to check it, now that Reverend Dogood was making local news. Sure enough, on page two, he found a relevant article. She'd held a rally in Lima, Ohio and made a local cable appearance on Channel 51's Farm Show in Peoria, Illinois. Next on her schedule was an outdoor tent event, to be erected directly on the brown stripe, in Benton, Iowa. The accompanying photo showed the

Reverend standing with her foot on a pitchfork stuck into the dead grass, surrounded by a couple of hundred people, two buses in the distance. *That brown stripe is leading her straight toward me.*

Selton dropped the open newspaper on the floor, anxious to avoid both the Reverend and his fate as invader. He inspected the covers of the science fiction novels: *Starship Troopers, Childhood's End,* and *The War of the Worlds.*

He could read the novels at high speed with no risk to his bloated capacity because he wasn't storing the facts, merely letting the prose scan past his eyes.

Selton plowed through Starship Troopers easily. *This is more a soap opera and love story than alien invasion. And the attack force is arachnids, not flora. Useless!*

Next, Selton turned his attention and rubber-gloved hand to *The War of the Worlds.* After he turned the last page, he slumped back. *Another blatant attack, aliens coming to Earth in cylinders. Hasn't anyone conceived of a stealth attack, or does Earthling propensity for violence make that seem inconceivable?*

Bernice came over. "How are those books working out for you?"

"Not well. I'm not learning anything useful."

"About alien invasions? I hope not!"

Finally, Selton picked up *Childhood's End.* He found the book unusual if not informative. *At least, this story is about alien colonizers with their own agenda. Although they start out benevolent, they are agents of fatal change. Is that what my fellow Serulians are planning, or merely expansion leading to domination?* Selton didn't know, and didn't want to. *My fellow Serulians have no idea what havoc hundreds of thousands of my species will do to existing flora here on Earth. Why, there won't be a square inch of green grass anywhere. Comparatively, Serulians are hardly Overlords.*

It had taken most of the day to consume and analyze the three novels. *Wasted time. I'm no closer to a solution. Not even an enjoyable diversion from the crisis at hand.*

62 - Charlie (Eureka, CA)

Charlie and Nachas left the building, meeting up with Dixon on the sidewalk, who was rubbing his upper arm. "You got what you came for. You saw my portal and you met my operator. Besides, you've got your own. If you leave now, I won't send a complaint up the line that will ruin your careers forever."

Charlie was tired of Dixon's threats and posturing. He fumbled for the notebook in his suit coat pocket. "I need to speak with you about next steps. A joint plan-"

"Get off campus before I have you thrown off!" Dixon limped away, unresponsive to Charlie's plea.

Charlie and Nachas stood for a moment, then walked to their car.

"My head is spinning." Nachas unlocked the vehicle and they both got in and buckled up.

"I feel like I got at least as much information as I shared," said Charlie.

"We didn't exactly leave on good terms. What you got is maybe all that you're going to get. The lack of a handshake says a lot." Nachas pulled up to the makeshift barrier at the college entrance and waited for the guard to remove the two-by-four saw horse. "What now?"

Charlie fingered the business cards in his pocket. *Underground radar scanning is probably very expensive.* He remembered the costly helicopter ride in Brooklyn. "I want to see things from the air."

"Private planes with pilots are rentable at a nearby air strip."

"Good. Let's get an aerial view of the situation." Charlie wanted to confirm a corresponding eastbound brown stripe, and how far it went.

A quick ride up 101 and a sharp left onto a peninsula brought them to a private field. The Pacific Ocean on one side, a thin inlet on the other, almost an island. Charlie noticed a small fleet of private planes and some older gentlemen standing around chatting.

One pilot with thinning grey hair was cleaning the fuselage of his two-seater.

Charlie approached the plane. A decal of an old fashioned pin-up girl, busty with shapely legs and blonde hair blowing, adorned the plane's side, with the letters D.O.M. on the pilot's door. "Do you hire out for private parties?"

"Sure." He patted the plane. "This here's my Cessna 162 Skycatcher. She's a beauty." The pilot looked at the two agents. "Only got one passenger seat."

Charlie could barely tolerate the commuter jet. He was not going up in a prop plane. Besides, he wanted Nachas with him as a witness. "Tell you what-"

"Name's Smitty."

"Hi, Smitty, I'm Charlie and this is Greg. How about I hire you to take a photographer up and take pictures of something very specific?"

The pilot stroked his stubble chin. “I reckon I can do that. Cost more, ‘cause I’ll have to pay the picture-taker.”

“That’s fine. I want you to fly over the College of the Redwoods. You know where that is?”

He nodded.

“On the southeast corner of the property, there’s a structure about eight feet tall. Looks like it’s made out of sticks.”

Another nod. “Yup.”

“I want photos of a fifty-foot wide brown stripe that starts there and goes directly east. Got it?”

“Clear as seltzer.” Smitty scratched his head. “Considerin’ airport fees, fuel, overhead, et cetera, I’ll charge ya’ $250 for an hour, takeoff to landing.”

“Seems a little high.” *This will have to come out of my own pocket.* “Will you do it for $150?”

Smitty picked at something on his chin. “$200 even and you got yourself a set of photos from upstairs. How many pictures you want?”

“As many as $200 buys.” Charlie smiled and shook Smitty’s hand. “And I need the pictures ready tomorrow morning at the latest.”

“Gotcha!” The pilot pulled a cell phone from his back pocket. “Know just who I’ll hire.” He grinned like he’d won the lottery and strutted away, pressing buttons on his phone.

“What a character!” Charlie made a note of the $200 personal expense.

Nachas stood by, a scowl on his face. “You paid too much.”

“Aerial photos that show a brown streak heading east from Matt’s portal would be priceless.”

"Brown streak?" asked Nachas. "Sounds like a second rate Amtrak line."

Charlie had heard that before. *Potter?* "There's one headed this way from the east. Didn't you see the one at the portal?"

"Maybe. I didn't know I was supposed to look for one. Do you expect them to meet up, like railroad tracks?" asked Nachas.

"Yes, I do. Exactly like what happened someplace in Utah, with the golden spike." Charlie needed to know where the brown stripes would meet. But first, he needed the results from Potter's team, so he had something to trade with Dixon.

Nachas sat in the driver's seat while Charlie stood alongside the car, door open, and dialed his Brooklyn partner.

"Stephanie Potter speaking."

"Hi, it's Charlie. I hadn't heard from you." *Not too subtle.*

"You still out in California? I'm jealous."

"Yep. On vacation." *She knows I'm still working.* "What's up with our case?"

"Well, as soon as you left, my escort and collaboration assignment evaporated. But not before my forensics team checked out Kwashay's portal. Not much to report, however."

Charlie had his notepad out, pen at the ready. "I'll take what you've got."

"Okay. You probably already expected this – I know I did – the portal is generating a pretty intense electromagnetic field that disrupted all of our equipment. The rod material is extremely hard, and it was impossible to get a sample for analysis with normal tools."

"Don't bother. A guy out here shaved off a few flakes. Seems the material can't be classified." Charlie didn't suggest it was from some other planet. "The one out here is also acting like an antenna and broadcasting, but we don't know what to whom."

"We? Did you pick up another partner? I'm jealous."

"I'm working with a local EPA agent, but he's not expecting dinner. A guy named Trev Dixon, from the Bates Foundation, is making things difficult for us." *An understatement.*

"Bates, as in Armand "Big Bucks" Bates, a politician's best friend?"

Charlie pictured Potter's sneer and smiled. "Must be. This Dixon character seems to wield a lot of clout. He locked down the whole college and seems to have at least one Congressman in his pocket. Says the portals were sent by aliens, and they're going to open a rift to allow an invasion."

Potter didn't laugh. "Do you think he's right?"

"No, of course not! But the answer to what 'operate' means is still open."

"So, you've seen the second portal?"

"Yes, identical to Kwashay's except for one missing rod. And we met Kwashay's counterpart, the second operator, a nice young man named Matt who seems a bit rattled about his role. He used exactly the same language Kwashay did, that the portals are vital and only here for our good. Is she doing okay?"

"I haven't talked to her since our interview, but she has our cards. She's a smart kid. If something happens, she'll call one of us."

"Don't do anything extreme with the portal, like try to get a sample. We know how closely bonded they are with these two young adults." Charlie left out the part about Dixon's actions affecting Matt. "By the way, Matt claims he can't operate it if it's not complete."

"Stranger and stranger. The rods in my portal keep getting fatter, and the roots have gotten so thick, it's essentially cemented in place."

"Ditto for this one. I'm having some aerial photography done, to confirm a brown stripe headed your way."

"It'll only have to go half way, because mine will meet it someplace."

Another reference to the midpoint. I have to figure out where that is. "And how are you?"

"Thanks for asking. Bored silly. Things were much more exciting when you were here. When are you coming back to buy me that dinner you owe me?"

"As soon as I can."

"Yeah, sure. Keep in touch, okay? Calls from you are the most exciting part of my week."

"Will do. Bye." Charlie slid into the passenger seat. "We didn't really complete our conversation with Dixon. Let's go back to the College."

"You really think he'll talk to us, after he rushed our collective asses from campus?" Nachas stiffened his arms against the steering wheel.

"I need to find out what he'd planning on doing with Matt's portal."

"Hexagonal prisms," said Nachas.

"Whatever."

Nachas did what Charlie asked, and drove them off the peninsula and back to the college entrance. They encountered the same guard, but this time their request to see either Dixon or the President was denied. Matt was also off limits because they weren't family.

As hard as Charlie pressed, the harder the guard's determination.

"Told you." Nachas drove away, headed north. "Okay, so we've been removed from Dixon's friend list. Now what?"

Charlie checked his watch. "I say we call it a day. Would you mind dropping me off at the Comfort Inn?"

"On Humboldt Bay? No problem. Nice place."

"So I've heard. We'll try Dixon again tomorrow."

"You sure are stubborn."

Just heavily motivated. "That portal and Matt are necessary players to solving this case. And right now, Dixon is control of both. We have to try."

Shortly, they arrived at the motel. Charlie got out, his shoulder bag in place and suitcase in hand. Before Nachas pulled away, Charlie leaned in through the open passenger window. "Pick me up at 9:30."

63 - Matt (Eureka, CA)

Matt stood by in Fred's dormitory lobby while his mother and father had a private conversation off to the side. *I've got things to do.* He put his hand on Fred's shoulder and aimed him at the staircase.

Matt's father marched out of the building leaving his mother behind. Before Matt could walk upstairs to Fred's room, she came up from behind and gave her son a hug. "Fred, can I have Matty for a while?"

Fred checked Matt's face before answering. "Sure. I'll be in my room, packing up my Y-Box."

"Come with me, dear." She took his hand in hers.

Matt hesitated, considering following his friend up to the game console so he could begin practice.

"Please? Take me to your room."

Matt couldn't refuse. "It's next door." He led his mother to the neighboring dorm building and up stairs.

In the room, over a dozen packing boxes folded flat leaned against the wall. "What's going on?" Matt glanced out into the hall. "Where's Dad?"

"Your father will meet us here in a little while." She wiped her finger along the edge of his dresser. "Fred was worried about you, so he called us. And then President Stanley called about the accident, so we drove up. After seeing the jeopardy you're in, as your parents we have to take action. Your father and I have agreed you're coming home."

Matt plopped down on his bed. "You can't! I'm the operator. The portal needs me."

She hugged herself and shivered. "You scare me with that kind of talk."

Matt's dad entered the room. "Come on, pack your things." He expanded a box and tucked in the bottom flaps. "I've worked things out with the College. They'll mark your current courses as incomplete as opposed to failed."

"I'm not going anywhere. You can take my stuff if you want but I'm staying."

"You can't. They're calculating the prorated refunds for this semester's tuition, room and board as we speak." Dad handed the empty box to his wife. "You have to pack up, and that's final."

"I'm not going anywhere." Matt folded his arms on his chest.

"You realize you've got no place to stay? This room is no longer yours, as of tonight. I've spoken with the President and told her we're removing you from this substandard institution." Dad moved to the door. "I'm going down to the Bursar's office to negotiate the details of the refund." His heavy footsteps echoed up the stairwell.

"Come on, I'll help you pack up your stuff." Mom opened the top drawer of Matt's dresser and grabbed an armful of socks and underwear and dumped them into the box.

Why do they insist on tearing me away from the chance to make a difference? "You can stop paying for my room, but I'm not leaving campus."

"Don't be silly. Come home with us and we'll figure things out together, like a family." She built a second box and opened the next drawer containing t-shirts.

"You can take all my stuff but I'm staying." *I can't leave the portal. I'm the operator.* Matt grabbed his pillow from the bed and his sleeping bag from the tiny closet floor. "Don't come after me. I don't want this to get ugly."

Mom stopped packing. "Your father expects you in the car."

"He also expects me to take responsibility for my life. Well, finally I am." He took a couple of steps toward the door. "This is what it looks like."

"Wait a second." His mother fumbled for an empty pillowcase and stuffed it with underwear, socks, random t-shirts and shorts. "You'll need something to wear." She glanced around the room, eyes darting. With a smooth swipe, she grasped his toothbrush, toothpaste comb and brush from his dresser top, threw those into the pillowcase and extended her arm. "Here."

Matt accepted her offering, slung the pillowcase over his shoulder, and with his pillow under one arm and sleeping bag under the other, marched out of his former room.

From the staircase, he heard his mother crying.

64 – Kwashay (Brooklyn, NY)

After dinner and her homework, Kwashay asked for and got permission to use their avuncular computer at the rear of their walk-in pantry. She pulled one of the kitchen chairs into the pantry, closed the door, and climbed over the back to sit in front of the screen. She tried to be patient, reading can and box labels and considering future dinner recipes while waiting for the computer to boot up.

After logging in, she aimed her web browser at PictureNet, the site she'd previously wanted to search. Many odd illustrations and photos were displayed in thumbnail when she searched for 'portal': the front cover of that old video game box, multiple pictures of various doorways and arches, hallways and covered paths, several artist renditions of imagined interstellar vortices, and a few blurred black and white photographs of females in motion.

Then she tried "hexagon.". There, in the midst of the geometric figures and oddly shaped buildings, was a photo of a partially constructed portal, just like hers. She almost shouted out loud, but contained her enthusiasm lest she attract her mother's attention. A dense forest of big trees in some anonymous location surrounded it. Finally, she had the name of the other operator, at least his PictureNet handle: NeedleAndThready.

Light from the open pantry door made the screen unreadable. Kwashay flicked off the switch on the monitor but left the computer powered up. "What's up?"

"I found business cards on your dresser. One from a Washington DC EPA agent and one from a local. Are you in trouble with the government?"

"No, Mama. They just had some questions about my art project, that's all."

"You make it sound like being interrogated by EPA agents is a normal thing." Her mother's voice got louder. "I'll have you know, it's not!"

Kwashay turned in the chair, but there wasn't enough room to swing her legs to the side. Instead, she scooted the chair back enough to stand up. Her mother was a silhouette. "They're pursuing an investigation, but they seemed to be more worried about what might happen to me than anything else."

"Well, if that's true, they sound like fine folks. Maybe some day, you'll introduce me."

Kwashay expected that the female agent would be hanging around the portal on a regular basis. "I'd be happy to, if the opportunity arises."

"So, what are you doing on the computer?"

"Extra credit for my biology class." *The portal was growing, the rods getting thicker and the root system expanding. Wasn't that biology?*

"Well then, I'll leave you to your work." Her mother closed the door.

In the dark, Kwashay fumbled for the power switch on the monitor. The screen bloomed to full brightness after about thirty seconds. She hastily typed a message to her partner, the other portal operator.

"Have you completed construction? Write back and share what you know so we can be successful together." She signed it with a pseudonym, PortalPal, and sent it.

65 – Selton (Kearney, NE)

After the science fiction novels failed to provide any relevant tactics, Selton needed to devise his own to prevent seed germination. *The message said that my seeds need nutrition to germinate, which is why they are sending a megafeeding.* One way to deprive them would be to prevent the megafeeding from reaching him. *I mistakenly assumed the megafeeding was for me, but it's not. It's for the seeds inside me.*

Selton understood that, to avoid the megafeeding, he might have to avoid his own nutrition as well.

He considered the function of the portals and the filaments of which they had been constructed. *The filaments grew inside me. They are part of my genetic makeup. That must be how they'll provide a compatible megafeeding.* Selton decided that, if the mechanisms were tuned to Selton's body chemistry, the appropriate action to take was to modify his chemical balance. But how? The nutritives Selton absorbed from the soil hadn't been different enough to prevent communication.

Selton considered other ways to disable the seeds. Radiation? *Humans use doses to kill cancer. Perhaps I can irradiate them and make them infertile.* He accessed a technical experiment manual from his storage and computed the amount of radiation necessary to ruin his seeds. *I don't have access to radiology machines, especially ones with sufficient power.* Poison? *Anything that would poison the seeds would also kill me. I'd like to avoid that if possible.*

From Selton's vast information storage, he recalled one aspect of physiology humans shared with flora: pH, the measurement of acidity. In addition, pH affected whether fertilizer and other nutrients in the soil are available. If the pH is wrong, some of the nutrients in the fertilizer get tied up in the soil chemistry so they are mostly useless. On the standard pH measurement scale, a score of seven is average, not acid and not alkaline.

Selton couldn't change the pH of Earth's soil. Even if he could, it would destroy all plant life on the planet. But he could change his own pH to the same result.

Then it came to him. Selton had avoided Earthling nutritives ever since he sprouted from his seed. Maybe that needed to change. *With a modified pH, I'll achieve two helpful results. I'll be undetectable by the portals, and my system will be more resistant if any of the megafeeding shows up in my vicinity.*

66 – Charlie (Eureka, CA)

Charlie slept well, with the sound of the ocean and nautical breezes soothing his rattled brain. He showered, shaved, and got dressed. During his complementary hot breakfast, he had second thoughts about the day's strategy.

Nachas arrived on time and parked near the main entrance. "Good morning. Back to campus?"

Charlie slid into the passenger seat. "Don't bother. You were right."

"I was?"

"It'd be a waste of time. The portals are on their own schedule, and there's nothing Dixon can do to change that. Besides, I'd hate to waste a half-day in a verbal boxing match with him. Let's explore what's east of here, to confirm the brown stripe."

"Okay. How about Shasta-Trinity National Forest?" Nachas pulled a California state map from his driver door pocket and opened a section. "We can take the south route on 36 through Heyfork – no, wait, the north route on 299 will be quicker, about two hours."

"As long as we can get to a spot that's directly east of the portal. Do you have GPS?" asked Charlie.

"I don't go anywhere without it. And, my car is fully charged."

From the hotel, Nachas headed north on 101 and forked east on 299. The wavy two-lane road was carved into the hills, a manmade channel with rises on both sides.

Charlie surveyed the increasing greenery: varieties of fir, pine, and cyprus. Snow-capped mountains loomed in the distance. He'd never experienced a landscape like this in DC. And certainly not in Brooklyn. "It's beautiful out here."

"Sure is. Folks with fresh eyes help us remember not to take it for granted."

Maintaining the viability of landscapes like this was at the heart of Charlie's reason to join the EPA in the first place. He was more motivated than ever to solve this mystery.

After about half an hour, Nachas announced, "This is Shasta-Trinity for the rest of the trip."

The woods were denser than before; trees, bushes, grass, all in great condition.

"How big is this place?" asked Charlie.

"Huge. Two million acres of forest and mountain trails, campgrounds and recreational lakes."

At the one hour point, the woods thinned and buildings appeared along the road. "Welcome to Junction City."

Tree trunks stacked and ready for local processing or transport filled the grounds of a lumber yard. *Did those escape the wrath of the brown streak?* Highway 299 became Main Street, running through a downtown lined with single-story shops. Not a franchise or national chain to be seen.

No sign of the brown stripe. "What are our coordinates?"

Nachas pulled over, parked and activated the GPS unit. He read Charlie the numbers.

Charlie checked the longitude and latitudes in his notepad. "We're still too far north."

Nachas retrieved his map. "We can drive through Weaverville and cut south on 3, but we'll be leaving the Park."

"I don't care." He repeated the mantra of a real estate agent who'd shown him possible condos in DC. "Location, location, location."

Nachas drove them down Main Street past the town golf course and back onto bare highway, a hill on their right side, a drop off on their left.

Highway 3 merged with 299 in Weaverville, a clone of Junction City. They headed almost directly south, according to the compass on the rear view mirror.

A few miles from town, before highway 299 split off to the east, Charlie shouted, “Stop the car.”

Nachas pulled over onto the shoulder. Running perpendicular to the highway, the brown streak ran down the hill directly across their path, continuing on the other side of the highway, down the embankment and out of sight.

“My goodness! Is that it?” asked Nachas. “A continuation from the portal?”

“Yes, just like in Brooklyn, heading west through New Jersey. Bodies of water don’t constrain it, so why would hills and valleys?”

“But we’re over a hundred miles away.”

“It has a reach, doesn’t it? Check your GPS near the center.”

Charlie got out of the car, pulled Potter’s camera from his bag and took shots from a number of different angles. Nachas paced the width, walked twenty-five feet to the middle and took a measurement. He brought the result back to Charlie.

Charlie compared the latitude with that of the portals. “Right in line, within measurement error. If I only had a soil sample kit-”

“You mean like the one I have in the trunk?” Nachas pointed with a closed fist and an outstretched thumb aimed at his car. “After all, I am EPA.”

“Great! I know the results already, but more data is always better than less.”

“And those results are?” asked Nachas.

Charlie explained what he and Potter had discovered about the soil in Brooklyn and on Governors Island. He extended an open palm. “May I?”

Nachas handed him the tool, almost exactly like the one Potter had used. He was almost giddy, taking soil samples for the first time: four on each side of the road, two in a green area and two in brown. Charlie dutifully put each sample in a bag, labeled it, and stored them in a collection box in Nachas' trunk.

He couldn't help smiling as they got back into the car. "Come on, lunch is my treat."

Nachas found a place to turn around safely. Just inside Weaverville city limits, Charlie saw a sign on the left side of the road. "How about Sawmill Grill and Bar?"

"Buyer's preference." Nachas pulled into the parking lot.

They went in, chose their own booth and reviewed the menus that were already at the table in a vertical holder.

A waiter walked up and began rattling off specials of the day that sounded like they belonged on a five-star dinner menu. Who ever heard of prime rib, planked salmon or skillet chicken marsala for lunch?

"Do you have a big house burger?" asked Charlie.

"Of course." The waiter looked surprised at the question.

Charlie looked over at Nachas, who nodded.

"Okay, two house burgers, fries on the side. I'll have a root beer on tap." He wanted to see the waiter's reaction.

"Would a can be okay?"

"I'll settle. What do you want to drink?"

"Hot tea, please," said Nachas.

The waiter departed.

"So, what brought you to the EPA?" asked Charlie.

"I graduated with a degree in psychology but didn't like either clinical or experimental. My uncle advised me that government service was a good way to make a living and give back to the community. He'd been with the postal service for years. So I took a few courses online and applied. That was four years ago, and I love it."

"That's great!" Charlie was about to ask Nachas about his career plans when the meals arrived.

They chowed down, occasionally pulling gristle from their mouths. Charlie left half of his burger uneaten. Somehow, Nachas was able to consume the whole thing.

They were just finishing their meals when Charlie's phone rang, showing a DC phone number in his office. He dreaded the likely identity of the caller. "Keyson."

"How's your vacation?" *Director Stanton.* "Never mind, I withdraw the question. We both know why you're out in California. And after explicit directions-"

Charlie took a calming breath. "If you'll let me explain-"

"You've pissed off a very influential person, specifically a California Congressman whose committee has the authority to decide our agency's funding levels. We'll talk about your insubordination when you get back."

"But I've confirmed that the two incidents, Governors Island and Eureka, are related. We just finished taking photos of the brown streak -"

"I don't care what you have pictures of. Your actions have been way out of bounds. Come back now."

Charlie experienced instant indigestion. "It'll take me several hours to get back to Eureka."

"Ms. Yong will send you an itinerary."

"I don't have a smart phone." He glanced across the table. Nachas was trying not to listen, rearranging the condiments. "Have her send it to Agent Nachas." He gave the Director Nachas' number, reading it off the agent's phone.

"No more side trips, no more vacation days. I expect to see you in the office tomorrow." The call ended abruptly.

As Charlie paid the bill, Nachas' phone buzzed. He checked the screen. "I've got your flight numbers." When they got into the car, Charlie wrote them down in his notebook. "Damn, after flying all night, I'll need to go straight into the office."

On the drive back to Eureka, Charlie mulled his next move. He was being forced to return to Washington, but the Director didn't say anything about not pursuing his assignment. Charlie absentmindedly reached into his pocket and rediscovered the two underground radar company business cards Dixon had provided. *The Director won't be able to dispute proof like this.* He flipped open his phone and read the phone number for the West Coast company. *Maybe they'll inform Dixon I've hired them, but I don't care.*

"Who are you calling?" asked Nachas.

"A west coast firm that does aerial underground radar scans."

"Really? After that conversation with your Director?"

"If the results show that the two portals are going to join up, then he'll have to view this as one expanded assignment." *And that all my expenses are justified.*

Charlie gave the company his specifications: an aerial radar scan starting at the College portal heading straight east, every fifty miles.

"How far?" they asked.

Charlie thought about it for a second. "Up to the next state."

"Nevada," they confirmed.

Charlie arranged for them to send their report, in the form of pictures and accompanying metrics, to Jane in his office.

"Well, that's one." He prepared to dial another number.

"Now what?" asked Nachas.

"I need one starting on the east coast, too." He keyed in his Brooklyn partner's number.

Nachas shook his head. "I've got to hand it to you, you've got guts."

From Charlie's perspective, he was just completing his assignment, like any field agent would do.

"Stephanie Potter speaking."

"Hey, it's Charlie."

"Another call, so soon? Not that I'm complaining."

"Listen, I have a favor to ask."

"Anything. What is it?"

Charlie appreciated her cooperation and confidence. "I've contracted a west coast company to perform an aerial underground radar scan of the root system, starting out here."

"Underground radar? Is that a thing?

"Evidently. I have the name of an east coast firm that provides the same service. I thought maybe-"

"Tackle the monster from both ends. Smart. I'll call them ASAP. I know the obvious starting point, but how far west should they scan? All the way to California? Half way?"

The concept of half way kept coming up. *How can I figure that out with precision? Maps would only approximate.* "I know it's already reached Illinois. Have them start there, every one hundred miles, into the next state. Iowa, I guess. Maybe a little further. Use your judgment.""

"If it hasn't stopped, maybe Nebraska should be far enough."

"Great. Bill it to my office, care of Jane."

"Good old Jane. I bet she's anxious to see you."

Charlie didn't understand the remark but let it pass. "I'm headed back to DC tonight." Charlie didn't describe the circumstances. "I'm not looking forward to those flights. All day!"

"At least that'll put you on my coast. Travel safe."

"Thanks. I'll keep you in the loop."

"You'd better, partner."

Charlie snapped his phone shut. "That should prove-"

"Prove what? That the portals are growing roots toward one another? But that doesn't help us understand what the portals are, or where they came from."

"You're right. We need to keep close tabs on Matt and Kwashay. They're our best chance." *The fewer answers, the less likely I'll get the Director's buy-in that the case still needs attention.*

"If we wait too long, it might be too late. Aliens, filling the skies!" Nachas laughed, waving his arms in the air before putting them back on the steering wheel.

Charlie laughed along. "Just drop me off at the hotel."

"Are you sure? There are things we could do. Analyze the samples? Take another shot at Dixon?"

"And have him get us both fired? Send the samples in for analysis, and if you find anything but dead dirt, let me know. I could use some time to just think. You're right, of course. We need better proof."

"Some proof." Nachas pulled up to the Comfort Inn. They both got out of the car.

"Thanks, Charlie. I learned a lot from you, believe it or not."

"It was good working with you." Charlie thought about Matt on campus and the threat of Dixon's presence. "If Matt needs help, can I call on you?"

"Of course. I can't believe how callous Dixon was about Matt's physical and emotional condition."

"Hopefully, you won't need to hear from me, but it's good to know you're close by." Charlie retreated to his room, threw his messenger bag and jacket on the bed and settled into a padded chair with his novel.

📖

With FBI agent Clay pursuing the possible linkage among the stores, Grissom planned his own first-hand evaluation. He contacted an old friend with an extensive collection of valuable artifacts and borrowed a special watch that looked normal but was in fact worth over three million dollars. Grissom carried the Patek Philippe 1895/1927 Yellow-Gold Minute Repeating watch into Prestige Appraisals. The young man behind the counter, no older than a college student, greeted him a broad smile. The tattoo of an American flag overlaid with a "do not" circle and slash was too unique to be a coincidence.

When Grissom produced the watch, the greeter asked permission to take it in back for the appraisal. When Grissom objected to having the watch out of his sight, the greeter explained that his shop was electronically connected via audio and high definition video to a team of certified appraisers. *That explains the addresses!* Grissom agreed, but only if he could accompany the item. The young man reluctantly accepted Grissom's terms.

Grissom witnessed their behind-the-curtain procedure, something his Undergrads probably didn't. The greeter had no clue, but the appraiser, who was never on camera, recognized the watch immediately and asked in a British accent how the customer had obtained the piece. Grissom answered, making up a story about considering a purchase but wary of the item's authenticity. The British voice seemed startled that he was talking directly to the customer, not the store's greeter, but proceeded anyway. The greeter zoomed in on the watch for the appraiser's benefit. The British-voiced appraiser, confirming himself as a horologist, gave Grissom his official opinion that the watch was the genuine article, last sold at a Sotheby's auction fetching exactly $2.994 million.

Grissom returned to the front of the store with the watch while the greeter remained in back for a few minutes. Grissom wondered if the young man was getting reprimanded for breaking protocol and letting him backstage. In fact, the greeter came out smiling, offering huge discounts on anything in the store as long as Grissom was an Indulge Financial Tanzanite cardholder. His client Bainbridge had experienced the same thing. The proprietor desperately wanted Grissom to transact, probably to then use Grissom's credit illegally. Grissom declined the overly generous offer.

Before departing, Grissom attempted to engage the clerk about his employment. "Are you new here?," implying Grissom was an ongoing customer.

"Yeah, just transferred in." The comment had no joy.

"You don't seem too happy about it."

"I'm not. I had to transfer schools, come to a new city where I don't know anyone and people talk funny. No offense. And I had to break off a relationship."

"I'm so sorry. Why did you relocate?"

The clerk pulled out a cloth and wiped fingerprints and smudges from the glass case. "Ever hear of golden handcuffs? I couldn't afford private university without the salary I get here. And when they told me to move, I had no choice."

"Who is they?"

The clerk stopped wiping. "My boss, Mukhtar Aziz."

Finally, a name! "You get paid well?"

"Oh yeah! More than I could get at any other place. But the checks always show up late. Forces me to budget, which I guess isn't a terrible thing."

Grissom examined the items in the glass showcase. "Just so my trip wasn't wasted, I'll take that antique peppermill."

"This one?" He pulled the mechanism, wood body with metal handle, from the display case. "You have good taste." He examined the attached tag. "It's French, ochre color with brass detailing, and dates back to the 1920's."

He pulled out his business credit card. "Sorry it isn't an Indulge Tanzanite card."

"Doesn't matter. It's still good. And I'll give you a small discount anyway."

Grissom walked away with an antique peppermill, the name Mukhtar Aziz, the fact that Mr. Aziz owned at least two of the shops in question, and an understanding how all of Indulge Financial's clients had been lured into vulnerability with exclusive bargains at the various appraisers and pawnshops.

Not bad for $81.

Funny, that's what this room costs per night. Charlie slid the boarding pass in as a bookmark, then grabbed his coat and a bite in the cafeteria next door before taking a cab to the local air strip. He had pictures to retrieve.

Smitty was working on his plane, the engine compartment open. A young woman with shoulder-length blonde hair, t-shirt with denim vest, jeans and sneakers stood in his general vicinity holding a yellow envelope. When Smitty saw Charlie exit the cab, he shooed her in his direction.

She intercepted him before he reached the tarmac. "Are you Mr. Keyson."

"That's me. And you are-"

"Missy. I'm the photographer. You know, the one you hired to take pictures of the brown thing?"

Technically, it was Smitty who'd hired her. "Yes. Are those the pictures?" He reached for the envelope.

She pulled it out of reach. "It'll cost you for overnight processing. $128.68."

Charlie was shocked. "Why so much?"

"Thirty eight-by-tens at $3.99 each plus tax."

Charlie reached for his wallet. He didn't have nearly enough cash for both her and the pilot. His face warmed. "Do you take plastic?"

"Sure." She pulled a smart phone from her back pocket and a magnetic swipe accessory from her vest. He handed her his card. With a smooth slide, her phone accepted payment. "You want to add a tip?"

"Let me see the pictures and I'll tell you."

She handed over the envelope from under her arm.

Charlie removed the stack of pictures. They showed the brown stripe, in all its glory.

"I overlapped the shots, so you could make a mural, end to end. So, what do you think?"

"Add twenty percent." He rechecked his wallet. "Can you collect for him too?" Charlie pointed at Smitty.

"I'll have to ask him." The young woman approached the pilot, Charlie following at a distance.

The pair chatted, out of range for Charlie to hear. He was shaking his head, she was responding. It looked like a negotiation. Finally, she motioned Charlie over.

Smitty wiped his dirty hands on a dirtier rag. "I shoulda said cash money. Go on, pay the lady."

Charlie gave her his credit card. "Two hundred dollars, as negotiated."

She swiped his card and looked at the pilot. "I'll transfer one hundred and eighty to your account." She looked at Charlie. "Ten percent transaction fee."

After looking closely, Charlie noticed pilot Smitty had a black eye. "Thanks, both of you."

The pilot grunted and returned to his engine. The young woman strutted away, whistling.

Charlie called after Missy. "Say, any chance you can give me a ride to the airport?"

She stopped and turned around. "Me? You mean the real airport? Arcata Field?

"That's the one.

She checked her watch. "Sure, I've got time. It's only half an hour away, across the bridge and up the coast."

That was the route Nachas had driven. Charlie followed her to her Jeep Cherokee, put his bag in her trunk, got in and buckled up.

Missy pulled out of her parking space. "So what is that brown thing? It looks like it goes on forever."

"A ribbon of dead grass. That's what I'm investigating. There's one that starts in New York headed this way, and the one you shot headed east."

"You make it sound like they're going to collide or something."

Charlie hadn't thought of their meeting as an explosive event. "I probably won't know until it happens. But I mean to find out."

She shot him a glance before returning her eyes to the road. "You do this for a hobby or what?"

"I work for the Environmental Protection Agency in Washington." It was none of her business that his trip wasn't authorized, and at his own expense.

"You need a photographer to document the event? I mean, the collision? I give discounts to repeat customers." She flashed Charlie an inviting smile.

"It's not in the budget, but I'll take your card if you have one."

She pulled a business card from her pocket. "Here. Something to remember me by." The card featured a breathtaking landscape of the California mountains with lush forests in the foreground.

"Thanks." There was one puzzle Charlie thought she might be able to solve. "Do you know what D.O.M. stands for?"

Missy giggled. "I sure do. You saw the decal on Smitty's plane, right?"

"Yes, the pin-up and the three letters."

"Well, D.O.M. stands for Dirty Old Man."

Charlie nodded. "Makes sense." He decided to ask one more nosey question. "Any chance you gave him that black eye?"

"Sure did. He tried to grope me while I was taking your photos, so I punched him. He's a real piece of work."

Missy pulled up at departures and threw the shift into park. "Here you go."

Charlie pulled his bag from the trunk.

Missy opened her door and stood on the doorframe, leaning on the roof. "You coming back?"

"I might need to, depending on how the case goes."

"Well then, I might get to see you again." She flipped her hair with a twirl of her fingers.

Charlie was a bit embarrassed. *Relationships with huge age differences seldom work out.* "What do I owe you?"

"Nothing. I got twenty bucks for Smitty's transaction fee. That'll cover." She smiled and slid into the driver's seat. Before he was inside the building, she'd driven away.

At Arcata/Eureka Airport, he checked in for his flight to San Francisco and took a seat in the waiting room. There was plenty of time to review the case.

Patterns filled his mind. *The structures are identical, the two kids talk about them the same way, like they're a salvation. So far, they've only caused destruction of plant life. The brown stripes are headed directly toward each other. What's the most important question Grissom would ask: What'll happen when they meet?*

The flight from Eureka to San Francisco was another white-knuckle experience. He almost kissed the ground upon arrival. The plane was thirty minutes late – a usual occurrence – so he grabbed a bite from a fast food counter on his run to the terminal and gate for his red eye to Washington.

While other passengers slept, Charlie turned on the overhead spotlight and opened his novel.

📖

Grissom called his friend, FBI agent Clay and gave him Mukhtar Aziz's name.

"We know of him. Works out of London. He's a person of interest for a lot of reasons, but we don't have anything nearly substantive enough to arrest him let alone request extradition."

A day later, Grissom got an unexpected call from one of his Undergrads in Lansing, Michigan. Seems the student freelanced and visited a car rental agency where one of the Indulge Financial Tanzanite cards was used. No employees remembered the customer. But less than a week later, one of the employees came back from vacation, heard about the Undergrad's visit and contacted him.

"Sure, I remember that guy," said the employee.

"Really, out of all your customers? How come?"

"I'm friends with a family in Detroit named McFefferson. Not a very common name, as you might expect. But my friend is African-American, and this guy wasn't."

"Did you ask for other ID?"

"Our agency has a strict policy against racial profiling, and I didn't want to lose my job. But, I set aside the security tape, just in case."

It was circumstantial, but Grissom was starving for clues. He gave Clay another call with the name of the employee at the car rental agency in Lansing who was prepared to hand over the security video.

Grissom thought hard about one of the patterns: all of the fraudulent transactions happened just after the billing closing date and stopped within about three weeks, well before the billing period ended.

Grissom made another call to his contact at Indulge Financial and explained the pattern.

"You think one of my employees bought airline tickets and hotel rooms?"

Grissom had to clarify. "Not the misuse, but I believe you have an insider who is providing billing period information for the compromised Tanzanite cards."

“That’s not possible. We do background checks and thoroughly screen candidates before job offers are made.”

“Then explain to me why the perpetrators’ transactions never – ever – span billing period boundaries? By the time a cardholder realizes their account has been compromised it’s too late and, by policy, you write off the bad charges. Indulge Financial is almost an accessory after the fact!”

“Fine. I’ll have HR reexamine employee backgrounds.”

67 – Matt (Eureka, CA)

After a short walk to the neighboring dorm building, Matt plodded up to the second floor and down the hall to Fred’s room. Fred laid on his bed with a book open, the Y-Box and accessories on his desk. “What did your folks want?”

“Like you don’t know? Thanks a lot. My folks are packing up my stuff and housekeeping is ready to clean out my room.”

“What are they doing that for?” He shut the book without inserting a bookmark. “I called them because I was worried about you. I thought you’d get expelled.”

“So instead, they pulled the plug and me from school. Same difference.” Matt landed hard in Fred’s desk chair.

“I didn’t think they’d do that. Really.”

Matt pointed a finger at Fred. “There are consequences! You’re going to have to put me up until this portal thing finishes.”

Fred glanced at the second empty bed. “I don’t think my roommates going to like that.”

“Who cares? You got me into this situation. The least you can do is let me bunk here until my job is done.”

Fred sighed. “There’s not much space, but you’re welcome to use the floor.”

“Oh and your gaming console.” Matt snuck a peek at the electronics. *Looks complete.*

“Your folks are leaving without you and you’re still thinking about video games?”

“Yep. What flight simulators do you have?”

Fred got up and bent over, searching his closet beyond a pile of clothes on the floor. He came up with a handful of plastic cartridges. “Let’s see: Drone Command, Luftwaffe, Space Fox-”

“And I’ll be using your TV set.” He pointed at the flat screen on Fred’s desk. “I need to practice.”

“If you say so.” Fred untangled the console power cable from the controller cables. “But why didn’t you go home with your folks?”

“I’m not leaving until my job is done. Need some help?” Matt’s fingers twitched, muscle memory from hundred of hours of video game play.

“I’ve got it.” Fred plugged the Y-Box console into a power strip and into the back of his TV set. “What job is that?”

Fred can’t keep a secret to save his life. “I’ve entered a video game contest and I need a place to practice.”

"What about your schoolwork? You used to be so studious."

"Priorities change. Let's finish so I can start." Matt pulled the controllers from Fred's hands and plugged them in. With a push of the power button, a harmonious chime played and the Y-Box booted to life, the logo spinning in 3D on screen.

"See, I told you it's in great condition."

Matt turned the TV a little and plugged in the Drone Command cart.

"So, how long you think you'll be staying?" asked Fred.

Matt's attention was already in the game, trying to revive his dormant muscle memory from years of previous game play. "Huh? Oh, I don't know. Not long. Just until-" He was about to say, 'until the portal calls me to operate it.' He was not going to disclose anything else to blabbermouth Fred. "Until the contest starts." He left the time period intentionally vague.

"Oh. Well, I guess I should leave you alone." Fred grabbed his textbook from the bed. "This'll give me an excuse to study in the library. Or maybe some girl will invite me to study in her room." Fred's eyes were wide, his eyebrows raised.

"Whatever." Matt made himself comfortable in Fred's guest chair, reset the game and dove headlong into a Drone Command adventure.

From the hallway, he heard Fred call out, "You could have said thanks."

Thanks for nothing.

68 – Kwashay (Brooklyn, NY)

Kwashay sat in the hallway outside the Dean of Students office at the NYU Polytechnic School of Engineering. She'd received special permission to skip an early calculus class. All of her admission and request for financial aid paperwork had been submitted. As expected, she'd been accepted. The face-to-face interview was a formality except for the impact on scholarships, grants and loans. She tugged once on her locket and hoped it brought her good luck.

A woman stuck her head out. "Please, come in." She pointed to a high-backed leather chair.

The Dean had one as well, but hers was on wheels.

The wall behind was plastered with diplomas and graduation photos, commencement address photos, and couple of posed pictures with Clinton and Reagan.

"We're looking forward to having you with us when classes begin this fall. I wanted the opportunity to get to know you better. Not every applicant comes to us with such strong credentials and recommendations-"

Kwashay's chair vibrated. *Oh no!*

The Dean stopped in mid-thought, or maybe Kwashay's mind had closed off all outside stimuli. Her memories were being searched. One after the other, random images appeared in her mind. This time, the probing was painful. She grimaced but stifled any sounds. Then, one memory came forward, riding with her mother on a roller coaster, on one of the few getaways they afforded themselves. Kwashay had been traumatized at the experience, vowing never to ride a roller coaster again.

Except the memory had been modified. Instead of blue sky, the roller coaster was traveling underground, through a complex of multiple tunnels, and Kwashay had to navigate the coaster to avoid constrictions and dead-ends.

"You must prepare to be a portal operator." The words coming out of her mouth in her mother's voice startled both Kwashay and the Dean.

The Dean leaned forward, her head tilted to put one ear closer to the candidate. "I must what?"

The obligation previously planted was reinforced. Kwashay blinked. The chair was stable. Her armpits were damp, and she wondered if it showed through her blouse. She stared at the Dean in embarrassed silence.

"Are you all right?" The Dean stood up.

"No. I mean, I don't know. I - I'm sorry." Kwashay ran out of the office, down the hall and out of the building, tears running down her cheeks. As she jogged past a construction site on Flatbush Avenue, someone from the second level of a scaffold called out "Hey girly-girl!" She looked up. Sideways waved and held up a gloved hand.

Kwashay waited, gripping her knees as she caught her breath, while he did an Olympic gymnast dismount of the metal frame. He wore a hardhat in place of his cockeyed baseball cap. "What's wrong?" He used his fingertip to wipe away the moisture on her cheek.

"They contacted me again. I need to learn-". She stuck her arms straight out in front, palms pressed together, leaning side to side. "-something."

"To swim?" he guessed.

She shook her head.

"To fly?"

She nodded but kept moving. "Yes, and avoid obstacles."

"That'd be smart. You gonna take lessons?"

The instruction had been for flying underground. "No, that won't help."

"I've got some video games that are kind of like flying."

"You do?"

"Yeah, they're cool. The point is to avoid smashing into things and getting the highest score."

"Perfect." She grabbed the front of his shirt. "Can I use it?"

Sideways adjusted his hardhat. "Sure, come on over to my place. We'll play around."

A self-protection alarm went off in Kwashay's head. She let go. "I've never done this before. I'll need a lot of practice."

"So you can come over every night." He shrugged. "Stay as late as you want." He winked.

As nice as Sideways had been, flashing red lights and alarm horns went off in her head. "It'd be better if I borrowed the game."

A voice from the third level of the scaffold shouted, "Vondell! Get back to work or I'll dock your ass."

"Right, boss." Sideways brushed off his overalls. "I'll get it on my lunch hour. Meet you after school?"

"Great. Thanks." Impulsively, she kissed him on the cheek, and then immediately regretted it.

On her way back to school, she detoured past the portal. Military vehicles, soldiers in uniform surrounded the structure. They stared at her as she sauntered by. She felt guilty and relieved simultaneously. *At least I know the portal won't be vandalized with soldiers protecting it. But operating it will be much more difficult.*

69 – Selton (Kearney, NE)

Selton went back to the section he'd previously read about Earthling body chemistry, specifically the attribute of pH, which measures the chemical property of acidic and basic. *The portals have the same pH as me, since the filaments grew inside my body. If I can modify my body chemistry, like an Earthling can do by altering their pH, then perhaps I can evade the detection mechanism and avoid the megafeeding.*

Selton decided to make his body more acidic, easily done by ingesting any number of consumable Earthling foods. Selton researched a list of Earth food that could perform the transformation and chose one normally taken in a liquid, eminently digestible even through Selton's oral cavity. But where would he obtain such a concoction? Certainly not in the library.

Selton still had some of the money provided by Marathon Man, but not very much, especially since Sprint hit him up for some. He crinkled the nickel note in his pants pocket. Selton had never begged or panhandled, especially from the benevolent keepers of Earth's knowledge. If the concoction was more expensive than what he had, he would have to find another way.

He left the library and walked down the block, examining each store that he passed. Halfway to Railroad Street, he came upon the answer: Tiny's Bar.

He stuck his head through the front door. Tiny was chatting with a few mid-day patrons while wiping off glasses.

Selton was afraid to enter the establishment and so hung out in the alley near the back door. He waited anxiously. Given his increased need for nutrition, he should have already found a nice fertile patch of grass and laid down for recuperation, at the risk of encountering the megafeeding. His roots were impatient for the opportunity to pierce the soil. They wiggled and squirmed under his shirt. *Not until my pH is modified.*

After a long period of waiting, the rear door opened. Out came the owner Tiny, a kind gentleman who Selton had interacted with before. Often, he'd seen him preparing his establishment for the after-work crowd at approximately the same time Bernice was closing the library.

"Hey, I didn't expect you. What's up? Run out of books?"

Selton swatted at his misbehaving roots. "I'd like to buy a drink."

"Well, come on in around front. I'll show you my specials for tonight. You got anything particular in mind?"

"I cannot visit your place of business, I'm afraid. Too many people pushing and shoving."

"Oh, claustrophobic, huh? My ex-wife suffered from the same thing. Said our house was too crowded for the two of us. Next thing you know, I'm out on the street."

Selton withheld a response, something he'd practiced for years with many Earthlings.

"Oh well, so what's your poison?"

"I don't want poison. I want lemonade. It is acidic, correct?"

"Your first time here, and you want a lemonade? Come on, Bumble. You have to have something with more of a kick. Wait here, and I'll mix you up something phenomenal."

"All I want is-" Selton's words fell on no ears. Tiny had already disappeared inside.

A few minutes later, he reappeared with a Styrofoam cup with a lid and straw. "Your lemonade." He winked. "Just in case the cops come by. Know what I mean?" He winked again.

Selton took the white cup from the owner's hand. "Thank you very much. How much do I owe?" Selton displayed a crumpled five-dollar bill.

"Hey, you been in this neighborhood for years, right? About time I bought you a drink. On the house, my friend. But the next one is twice the normal price." Tiny laughed and slipped back inside.

Selton put the cup behind him. His backroots, hungry for nutrition, absorbed nearly half the beverage. The effects of the acidic beverage were instantaneous. He could almost feel the raised acidity level. *If the Serulians attempt to locate me now, they'll fail. And I'll be able to stay here and enjoy learning.*

Tiny came out to dump a bag of garbage.

The ground felt unsteady. *Another communications?* There was no message, no sound except for Tiny's question. "How is it?"

Selton could no longer stand upright without holding on to something stable. He chose the side wall of Tiny's establishment. The world spun mercilessly. The chemical effects inside his body were drastic, much more intense than Selton had predicted.

"You're not much of a drinker, are you?" asked Tiny.

"No, this was my first."

"Oh my God. You've never had any alcohol?"

Selton knew what alcohol was, chemically, socially, in commerce. "I did not ask for alcohol. I asked for lemonade."

"Listen, pal, this is a bar. We don't serve that kind of stuff. I have a reputation. Besides, it was on the house."

"This is a bad thing. Do you have something to counteract the effects?"

"For one stinking drink? Hell yeah. A good night's sleep." He laughed.

Tiny shook his head as Selton stumbled from light pole to light pole. Crossing Railroad Street, he almost got hit by passing vehicles. It was taking much longer to traverse the street, and he had trouble timing the cross-traffic.

Selton wasn't sure he could make it all the way to the park. *I'll have to risk a feeding. Only a resuscitation period will rebalance me.*

Selton staggered down Central Street two blocks and came upon Kimball's Hardware. He'd seen it before, when he visited the Salvation Army building across the street. Stacked along the outside wall at Kimball's were wooden skids piled with topsoil, sand and fertilizer.

Selton experienced an epiphany. *I can feed off nutritives directly instead of extracting them from the ground.* The gate to the materials area was slid shut but not locked. He snuck onto the premises, took out his Tiny's Bar pen knife, slashed through the top bag of fertilizer with several vertical swipes and faced away from them. Selton's backroots wiggled frenetically from under his shirt and dove into the bag, forcing him to fall backward, overabsorbing the raw nutrients, bypassing their normal soil ingestion process. It was as if they couldn't get enough. The seeds inside Selton's body vibrated with their first opportunity for large-scale feeding. Selton panicked. *Will this have the same effect as a megafeeding?* He tried to stand but his backroots had punctured the next bag in the stack. *Have I done precisely what I wanted to avoid?* Rather than slipping into a restful recuperative state, Selton felt his body dropping into an overdose coma.

70 – Charlie (Washington, DC)

Charlie emerged from his cab, weary from the long, complicated flight home that took him from Eureka through San Francisco to Washington. It had taken almost nine hours, including a run through San Francisco Airport with sandwich in hand to catch the red eye to DC.

Being her usual efficient self, Jane had arranged for a limo to bring him home, prepaid. He trudged through the lobby of his apartment building in the wee hours of the morning and impatiently waited for the elevator, the only thing between him and sleep in his own bed.

He unlocked the door, dropped his bag and went to check on his pal AquaLung. Something smelled different but delicious, like someone had been cooking. He was startled to see Jane in the doorframe of his bedroom, wearing his long striped robe. "What are you doing here?"

"I sleeping here. I hope you not mind. You have nice place. Also shorter commute. Staying over easier because my apartment in opposite direction and I promise to feed AquaLung. He have quite an appetite."

She's been sleeping in my bed? I hadn't changed the sheets or anything. Who knew she'd move in? Charlie glanced at the fish tank. AquaLung had bulked up to over twice his normal size. "What happened?"

"You train him real good. When he hungry, he come to the surface and make bubbly noises. He does that a lot. I had to stop at pet store and buy more food."

Charlie mentally kicked himself for not giving Jane more instruction. "He gets fed only once a day, not on demand."

She hung her head. "So sorry. I hurt him?"

"No, I might just need to buy a bigger tank." He walked over. Her head was still down. "Jane?"

"You gave me responsibility and I mess up bad."

Charlie lifted her face with two fingers under her chin. "I should have told you." He sniffed the air. "What's that smell?"

"I cook dinner for you last night, but I forget the time zone difference. All put away in refrigerator now."

Charlie's stomach gurgled. "I didn't have much to eat since I left California, just some airline snacks. Most of the shops were closed by the time I got there."

"I get dressed and make you something. Be right back." Jane shuffled into Charlie's bedroom and closed the door.

Charlie sorted through individual stacks of mail. *Jane must have sorted these.* Her classification scheme included one stack for advertisements, one for what she thought were bills, one for personal communications, and one that evidently was miscellaneous. She'd gotten almost everything correct, which made examining the high-priority letters quicker. This verified just how organized she was.

Jane came out in a black long-sleeve pullover and matching slacks. "You want egg? Pancake?"

"Actually, this might sound silly, but can we have what you made last night? It smells wonderful. What is it?"

Jane led him into the kitchen, opened the fridge and took out a sealed container. "Bulgogi. Thin slices of sirloin, marinated to enhance flavor and tenderness." She removed the lid.

Charlie saw scallions, onions, mushrooms and chopped green peppers had been mixed in. "What's in the sauce?"

"Mixture of soy sauce, sugar, sesame oil, garlic, pepper. *T*raditionally grilled, but I pan cook."

"It's probably a little heavy for breakfast, but what the heck?"

"I prepare. You relax from long trip."

Charlie returned to the living room. An older Quincy Grissom novel lay on the coffee table with a red leather bookmark about at the halfway point. He called into the kitchen, "You're reading one of my detective novels?"

Jane stuck her head in the doorway. "I hope you not mind. I hear you talk about him You read him on your breaks in coffee room. I want to try."

"It's fine. Glad to share."

Jane returned to the kitchen while Charlie set out plates and utensils.

After a few minutes, Jane brought a tray to the table: reheated meat, large leaves of fresh lettuce and a bowl of red sauce. "I show you." She put a lettuce leaf in her hand, spooned some of the reheated bite-sized meat and vegetables into it, and spooned a dollop of sauce on top. Then she folded the lettuce around the filling. "See?"

Charlie followed her instructions. "What's the sauce called?"

"Ssamjang. Traditional Korean sauce for wrapped food."

Charlie mimicked her behavior and brought the folded bundle to his mouth. He took one bite. "This is delicious."

"I glad you like." Jane smiled, perky white teeth shining and a bit of color in her cheeks.

The heat snuck up on him. He scurried to the kitchen and poured himself a glass of ice water.

"Sauce have a kick," she said.

"So I noticed." Charlie took another large gulp of water. He was on his third bite when he noticed Jane wasn't eating. "Is something wrong?"

"No, I just be sure you have enough."

He chewed a while before attempting to speak. "You made plenty. Come on, dig in."

Jane brought her folded leaf stuffed with meat to her mouth and took a mouse-sized bite.

"That's better." He glanced at the coffee table. "How do you like that Quincy Grissom mystery?"

"Oh, he very smart." She took another nibble. "Almost as smart as you."

Charlie's cheeks flushed, from her comment and the sauce. "I meant about the story." He wasn't fishing for complements, just testing her grasp of the character and the plot.

"He uses patterns. Always talks patterns." She paused. "Do you find pattern in dead grass assignment?"

Jane evidently wanted to talk about the case. "I don't think it's just one pattern, but I'm not sure."

"What parts you know?" Her eyes were wide open, engaged in his work.

Charlie was delighted to be talking through the case. He'd appreciated both Potter and Nachas as partners. In their absence, Jane was a welcome substitute sounding board. "Well, there are two portals, one in California, the other in Brooklyn. They're pointing at each other, and they're identical, so that's one thing. And there's a brown stripe that starts at each of them, one running west, the other running east. They have that in common as well."

Jane pointed to one of Charlie's bookshelves. "Like bookends?"

"Yes, exactly! They're just like bookends for the stripe. What a great analogy!"

It was Jane's turn to blush. "So, what in the middle? Not books."

Charlie paused to think. "Besides an expanding brown stripe?"

Jane put her hands up a couple of feet apart, index fingers pointing at each other. She moved her hands closer together until the tips touched. "That middle?"

Charlie had heard and made references to a meeting point for the brown stripes but hadn't yet investigated it further. "I don't know. I have the longitude and latitude of both portals. How would I do the math?"

Jane smiled and stood up. "We can figure out."

Charlie pointed at their plates. "We should really finish-"

"No, we do this now. Important for your job." Jane got up from the table and brought her laptop out from the bedroom. "I use to watch movies, do email. I don't touch your things."

Except sleep in my bed. "I'll get the coordinates." He fetched the spiral notepad from his inner jacket pocket. "Let me know when you're ready." While he stood looking over her shoulder, he popped a breath mint.

Jane's fingers knew what keys to press, first doing a web search, then bringing up a geographic location site. "Okay, I ready."

"The New York portal is located at-" He paused as he examined the numbers. "Both portals have almost the exact same latitude."

"See, a pattern!" Her teeth glistened.

"You're right. That's no coincidence."

"That make it easy. We just compute distance and divide by two. That give us middle."

Charlie read her the longitudes.

"I compute." She typed them into her calculator. "Difference is 50.216234. Half is 25.108117. Add to west longitude gives -99.084547!" She flashed a blinding victory smile.

"So, where is that?"

Jane typed in the common latitude, the calculated longitude and pressed the LOCATE function on the web page. "Kearney, Nebraska. You know this place?"

Charlie wrote the name of the town in his notepad. "Not yet, but I will."

Jane pulled up a map corresponding to the coordinates and zoomed in. "It say grassy area east of underpass on Railroad Avenue, one block east of 1st Avenue."

"Can't get much more precise than that." Charlie made that notation. "What you just did is really important. Thank you so much."

Jane stood, faced Charlie and bowed her head.

"We'd better get back. Dinner is getting cold."

"I reheat." Jane picked up the platter of meat.

"No, you did all the hard work. I'll zap it in the microwave." Charlie took the platter from her and carried it into the kitchen.

Jane stood in the doorway, hands folded in front of her. "You make someone good partner some day."

"Thanks." Potter had used the word "partner" almost to the extreme. *I wonder what she meant.* Jane's context clearly meant "husband." *Jane can't be interested in me. She's so smart and attractive; she can have anyone she wants.*

Charlie had heard through office gossip about Jane's run-in with the national security types when she applied for government service. She'd been challenged at every turn because of her Korean heritage. Not that the accusations were explicit. But they were there, beneath the interview questions and the attitudes of the screeners. Jane had gotten the job through sheer determination and massive smarts. In any outside industry, she'd be at least a manager. At the EPA, a secretary. Charlie never understood why she hadn't left for more responsibility and more pay.

After Charlie zapped the meat, they finished eating in silence, casting furtive glances at each other as they emptied the platter. In the process, he'd refilled his glass of ice water three times.

Charlie put his hands on his stomach. "I'm full."

"You no want dessert?" Jane pointed at the kitchen.

Had she made that too? "You went to too much trouble. Why don't you take the dessert home?"

"It for you. Ginger cookies. You keep, eat later."

Charlie yawned and stretched. "I'm sorry, it's not the company. I'm a bit jet lagged."

"I understand. You sit, I clean up." She washed the dishes and put them away as if there hadn't been a meal. "I go now. I have work today." Jane put on her coat. "You want I come back, cook for you again? We talk about your assignment, Grissom book-"

Charlie was flummoxed. *I can't presume on her that way. Besides, she might misinterpret it.* "You've already done too much." Charlie felt as fat as AquaLung looked, stuffed to the gills. *Potter would have laughed at that quip.* "You've already done more than necessary. I'll be okay once I get over my jetlag." He burped, reliving the spicy sauce.

"Then I take my things." Jane disappeared into his bedroom. A few minutes later, she came out pulling an rolling suitcase small enough to be carry-on. "Thank you so much."

Charlie wondered "For what?" but didn't ask. He saw the half-read book on the table. "Oh, and take the Grissom novel. Let me know what you think when you're done."

Jane accepted the book and slid it into the front pocket of her bag.

"Should I call you a cab?" *This is role reversal.*

"I enjoy the walk. And I have plenty of time to get to office. I see you tomorrow?" She took the apartment key from her pocket and handed it to Charlie.

Charlie put the duplicate in his pocket. "Director Stanton expects to see me today."

She shook her head in disagreement with the Director's order. "I tell him you be in later. Plane delayed. You need sleep to be able to work."

"Thanks." Charlie didn't know if he should shake her hand or wave.

Jane made the decision for him, throwing her arms around him in a long-lasting tight hug. She whispered in his ear, "I so glad you back, Mr. Keyson."

He whispered back, "Call me Charlie." He was disappointed when she chose to break their clench first. "See you later."

Charlie locked the door after her and plopped down onto a counter stool to have a conversation with AquaLung. "I can't have a relationship with Jane. We work together. Every day we'd be on display. I'm not even sure if she has those kinds of feelings for me. And I can't ask. How embarrassed she'd be if I misread the situation."

Charlie set an alarm, climbed under the covers, breathed in Jane's scent and fell asleep thinking about Matt, Kwashay and a thick brown stripe running from coast to coast.

71 – Matt (Eureka, CA)

It took all night but Matt reached the expert level of Drone Command. *I guess a true gamer never loses his skills.* He stood up, stretched, twiddled his fingers and reached for the Space Fox cartridge. For the second time, he heard the distinct rumble of large vehicles passing by the dorm building. *Dixon is bringing reinforcements?*

Matt stumbled to the window. A convoy of National Guard troops rolled through campus in the direction of the football field. *Oh no, now the state government is involved too?*

Matt ran from the room, down the stairs and along the sidewalk, chasing the trucks. His fear of violating the President's ban on being near the portal had vanished. *She can't expel me now.*

The ball field was empty except for Dixon's motorhome. All of his trucks including the semitrailer, private guards and scientists were gone, leaving behind damaged sod and deep ruts on the playing field.

Matt jogged to the clearing. In place of Dixon's personal security force were National Guard personnel, six soldiers in patterned grey camouflage that didn't blend well with the surrounding vegetation.

Dixon stood on the outside of the red tape boundary. He marched over to Matt. "This is all your fault."

"Mine? You almost killed me with that saw of yours."

"I didn't cut you, I cut that – that - that thing."

"So, you should be happy now. My parents pulled me from school. I'm trespassing as we speak."

"You think I want soldiers here? The previous security guards were on my payroll. Now, I'm just another onlooker. On top of that, the construction schedule is shot to hell."

"Where's the rest of your team?

"They were reassigned or returned to the corporate office. When Mr. Bates heard that the National Guard was being deployed, he pulled my funding. See, he's too well connected to mess with the government. There are contracts at stake, bills being written in Congress – even I don't know the half of it. But I told him I was staying, to see it through."

"How come?" Matt understood his responsibility as operator required him to remain, but Dixon was free to leave.

"There's something funky about that - that portal. You lied when you told me it was a trellis. Trellises don't broadcast undecipherable messages, and they don't grow, and they certainly don't need operators."

"Looks like neither of us is getting what we want." *Now, instead of evading Dixon's guards, I'll need to slip past U. S. soldiers.* "How does it feel to lose control?"

"Just wait. I'll figure out its secrets and then I'll tear it down. A double win for me. And you? You've already lost, dropout. Beat it, before I call campus security."

"You're in no position of authority here. Bates backed off, and so should you. I bet President Stanley would be delighted to kick your ass off school property." Matt didn't believe Dixon would rat him out, but just to be sure, he walked back to Fred's room. His evasive flying tactics of dodging and weaving needed improvement.

72 – Kwashay (Brooklyn, NY)

Sideways had told Kwashay what wires from the game console to connect to her television set, but not how to operate the game controller. She brought one of the kitchen chairs into the living room right in front of the set, struggling by trial and error to figure out the functions of the buttons on the wired device.

She figured out basic movement, acceleration and firing by the time her mother walked through the front door. She dare not take her eyes off the screen lest she lose yet another game, and she was very tired of losing.

Her mother's voice came from close behind. "What is that doing in this house?"

"I need to practice." Kwashay flew a rocket ship through the blackness of space, meteors and asteroids littering the screen. She leaned and tilted along with the controller, but her body language had no affect.

"Stop that! I'll have no such thing under my roof."

Kwashay glanced at her mother, and her rocket ship collided with a small planet that came out of nowhere. "See what you made me do!"

"Video games are a waste of time and energy. Where did you get that thing anyway?"

"Sideways - Vondell- loaned it to me." Her fingertips traced the surfaces of the buttons.

"Disconnect it from my television and give it back to him."

"I can't. I need to practice." Kwashay pressed the reset button.

"At least connect it to the computer monitor in the pantry so I can watch my shows."

"I tried. They're not compatible. I have to use the TV." The intro music, tinny and buzzy, announced that a new game was about to begin. *Please, if I can just win once.*

"You can't keep it. It'll distract you from what's important." Her mother's voice faded as she moved into her bedroom.

"You should be pleased. If he hadn't loaned me his, I would have bought one."

Her mother returned to the living room in sweatpants and shirt. "Money doesn't grow on trees, young lady. What's wrong with you? Why do you keep taking your eye off the ball?"

Despite the trill of an emergency vehicle approaching the hospital down the block, Kwashay focused on her ship. The obstacles were randomly generated, so their appearance wasn't predictable from game to game. *Better to improve my skills.* She deftly piloted through a meteor storm, and scooted through an asteroid belt. "See how much better I'm getting?" A quick swerve avoided a ringed planet. She hadn't gotten this far before. Blip noises signaled something she hadn't experienced - incoming enemy ships.

"Kwashay! Are you listening to me?"

"Mother, please, I have to concentrate-" Her ship exploded from an inbound missile she hadn't noticed. "Shoot!" She leaned back in her chair and let the controller dangle from her hand. She couldn't tell her mother that the inanimate portal instructed her to practice. *Even I can't believe it.* "I have an obligation to my - my art project."

"Of course, it's important to you, but you completed it, and it was graded. What does that have to do with this nonsense? Stop right now-"

"Not yet." Kwashay felt obligated to explain. "I need to be a skilled operator."

"What in God's creation does that mean?"

"I don't know, not yet anyway. But that doesn't make my obligation any less real. And you taught me never to shirk my obligations." Kwashay gripped her locket. *Grandma would have understood.*

"You're not making any sense." Her mother plodded into the kitchen and rattled some pans.

"It doesn't make perfect sense to me either. All I'm asking is for you to trust me. Please."

Her mother came back in. "All right. Play your games after you finish your homework. And keep the volume down. It's irritating. Bad enough I'm going to miss some of my favorite shows."

Kwashay stood momentarily to give her mother a kiss. "Thanks." Then she returned to her seat, lowered the volume, and initiated a new game.

"And don't think I didn't notice that you shirked your dinner responsibility. Good thing we have some leftovers in the fridge."

Kwashay didn't think it was the best time to report about the interrupted funding interview.

The next morning, Kwashay rolled out of bed, muted the TV and resumed practicing her video game while still wearing her pajamas.

In the background, she heard her mother's bedroom door squeak open. "Well, for a change, I didn't have to wake you. Put that thing down and get ready for school."

"Can I stay home? Please? I have to get better-"

Her mother knelt down in between Kwashay and the TV, eye to eye with her daughter. "What is with you and video games? You've been at it without a break since you brought it home. An obsession it is!"

Kwashay had never lied to her mother, but the pattern had been established. She'd lied to her teacher about the portal. She'd lied to Sideways about wanting to go out with him. The only people she'd shared the truth with were the two EPA agents.

"Is there some kind of competition?" asked her mother.

Her mother had provided her the way out. "You're so smart. There's a national tournament with prizes. I thought, if I could win, there'd be extra money for college."

"On top of your scholarship, you mean?"

Kwashay nodded. There was still a possibility for some kind of scholarship or grant, if the Dean ignored her flaky behavior at the interview.

"At least you have a reason." She got off one knee but was stuck on the remaining one. "Help your mother up."

Kwashay stood and lent her mother a hand. Her mother came off the floor with a grunt and limped out of the line of sight.

Kwashay turned her head. "So can I stay home from school?"

Her mother spun around. "Certainly not! Get your homework done, at lunch or at study hall, and I'll give you time tonight to practice. But no skipping school."

Kwashay ran over and gave her mother a quick hug, bolted to the kitchen for cereal and milk, and returned to the living room to play while she ate breakfast.

73 – Selton (Kearney, NE)

The next morning, Selton was woken by something shaking him. *Not another communication! What additional bad news might Dissemination Oversight have to share?* Selton opened his eyes.

A tall man in jeans and a plaid corduroy shirt stood next to him brandishing a pitchfork. "You, bum, what in the hell are you doing?"

A hobo or a tramp, yes, but not a bum.

"Who's going to pay for this? You?"

Selton had enough presence to stick his hand in his pocket and retrieve his last five dollar bill, what he had planned to offer Tiny for the lemonade.

The man snatched the bill from Selton's grasp. "That's close enough, I guess. Now get off my property. And if I ever see you again, I'll call the police."

Selton stood, the back of his shirt and coat cascading down to cover his backroots. The torn fertilizer bags were a mess of useless pulp.

Selton's mind wasn't focusing. He felt granules chafing the inside of his body mass. *Are they my seeds, or remnants from a chemical reaction with alcohol, or a byproduct of the fertilizer feeding?* No matter the cause, Selton's inner materials were suffering from side effects. Fortunately, feeding off the fertilizer gave him enough energy to stand and walk despite the internal distress.

Selton attempted to flush his system of the contaminants at a public drinking fountain near the train station. Lacking a human digestive system, the liquid ran through his body spurting out of his faux navel.

In order to be presentable, Selton took a quick shower in the train yard before walking to the library. His clothes stunk of fertilizer.

Bernice saw the distress in his face as soon as he walked in. "What's wrong?"

"I drank something awful."

"Shame on you." A wagged finger supplemented the verbal scolding.

"No, you don't understand. I wanted to change my pH level."

"For what purpose, land sakes?" She tisked and dug into her purse. "Take a couple of these. It's what I take when my stomach is queasy."

Selton took the tube of Rolaids from her hand. "Do you have a glass for water?"

"To wash them down? I guess so, but I just chew them." She pawed through her lower desk drawer and came up with a clear plastic cup.

"Thank you. You have no idea how much this means to me."

The librarian scratched her head. The justification of Selton's gratitude must have been unclear.

Selton retreated to the men's bathroom and dissolved the tablets in the cup of water, held it behind him and dipped one of his backroots into the cup. The root thrashed at the force-feeding. Eventually, Selton's body absorbed the liquid. The internal distress waned. *It's working!*

Selton decided to leave the library before he became motivated to ingest another book. *I'm literally bursting at the seams with information and seeds.*

He made his way to his new favorite feeding ground, Centennial Park, sat under a tree and mentally reviewed snippets of his accumulated information while waiting until nightfall to plant himself for regeneration.

The topic areas were almost too many to enumerate: animals and astronomy, baseball and bicycles, Canada and chemistry, cooking and cowboys, dinosaurs and disease, education and elections, fish and fitness, fossils and French, games and gardening, insects and inventions, machines and magic, Mother Goose and music, plants and poetry, pregnancy and Presidents, rodents and Russia, scientists and songs, theater and trains, water and war.

Selton heaved a sigh. *Perhaps I've successfully evaded them.*

The sun was approaching the horizon when he felt the tree shake behind him.

Not another message!

"We will proceed with the megafeeding despite one incomplete portal. The risk is manageable."

The fact that the message reached him was clear evidence that the pH change hadn't worked. They could still pinpoint his location.

Selton wondered why the portal was incomplete. And what type of risk did they mean? Explosions? Meltdowns of a nuclear reactor?

Selton wandered back to the railroad underpass. He fumbled through his rucksack, looking for something that might inspire him. He came across the jelly jar and lifted it up. The lone filament was still bouncing, with as much vigor as that night when the others escaped. *I don't know the result of sending this last filament on its way, but it doesn't really matter. The portals are obviously established and operational without this one. As a living creature, it doesn't deserve to whither and die in a preserves jar.*

Selton walked from beneath the underpass into the setting sun. The filament glittered, dancing in the twilight, anticipating its release. Selton gripped the lid and unscrewed it. The filament bounced twice against the sides, then out into freedom, floated up on a gentle breeze, spun like a pinwheel, and rose skyward to the west even though the wind blew in the opposite direction. Selton felt a sense of loss while simultaneously understanding that he'd done the right thing.

As the filament flew away, Selton considered the seeds inside him. Thousands of them, if they were the textured bumps he'd previously discovered. *If I fail and the seeds germinate, they can't all grow inside me. For one thing, they won't fit.* The reality of his fate hit him. *They'll burst from my body and fly off in all directions.*

Selton lamented his imminent destruction. He took no pleasure that the gathered information would live on in thousands of his offspring.

74 – Charlie (Washington, DC)

Charlie snuck into the office just before noon. He didn't know what to say to Jane, so he avoided her desk. He got a cup of coffee from the break room, nodded to Lane who was conversing with his peers, and returned to his desk to nibble on a few ginger cookies, which resembled tree roots.

He checked his desk for a envelope. *No underground radar results.* Someone had placed a manila folder on his desk for an assignment that didn't involve travel. A Congressional subcommittee had requested yet another climate change summary, this time dealing with temperature across the planet, not just the United States. He'd done this before, plodding through various surveys, summarizing and bundling them into a synopsis digestible by Congress people whose attention span made a thirty second commercial feel like epic theater.

By their specification, Charlie was obligated to provide simplified prose to accompany the charts and graphs, never tables of raw data. *Too complex for the politicians' minds, unless the reports were campaign contributions or voting patterns. Those were numbers they understood well.* Except for a few specific technical references, which had been diluted down to one-syllable words and analogies, a skilled clerk could have easily created the report. Asking Jane to do it would have been an insult. Besides, it was above her pay grade.

He pushed the folder to the side. While checking his company voice mail, Director Stanton walked up. Charlie put down the receiver in the middle of listening to a recorded message from the testing laboratory.

"Welcome back, Charles. Quite a first field assignment, eh?"

"Yes, sir. Bigger than any of us thought." *And it's still going on without me.*

The Director leaned against the cubicle wall. "That one probably won't be the last. You got terrific feedback from the New York bureau."

Potter!

The Director continued. "But for now, there are things here that demand your attention. One of our unpaid interns has written an article instructing citizens about reducing their personal carbon footprint. Except he must have failed English Comp. I want you to edit the piece, make it readable, before we post it to our public web site. Under his byline."

Great, I won't even get credit for the final product. "About the dead grass assignment-"

"No longer your concern. When you identified electronic signals that interfered with communications, it was immediately escalated to Homeland Security based on the PATRIOT Act, Title II Section 201. Their investigators are probably there by now."

"They're certainly equipped to handle the security aspects of my case, but there are subtleties-"

The Director cut him off. "It's out of your hands. Topic closed."

"So that's it? Have they told you their plans for assessing the brown stripe? And what about the two students-"

The Director raised his flat palm almost in Charlie's face. "I'm not privy to Homeland Security methods. Come with me."

Charlie followed Director Stanton into his office, catching a brief glance at Jane whose desk was only a few feet away. She nodded an acknowledgement but was silent. Charlie was glad she hadn't said anything in the Director's presence.

"Have a seat." The Director closed the door before sitting down as a role model and folding his hands. "I was afraid this would happen. First field assignment syndrome. I've seen it too many time. Agent gets lured into the case so deep, they can't extract themselves when it's over."

"But it's not over. We still don't know why-"

"On top of that, you spent through my entire contingency fund, and it's only May."

Charlie attempted to speak but the Director again showed his palm. "It's over for you. If they're not there already, soon National Guard troops will be in place at each structure."

"But-"

"Actually, it isn't quite over. Homeland Security is a little understaffed at the moment so you'll prepare a detailed report for the consulting group they've brought onboard. Shouldn't take you more than a couple of hours, right? Then you can tackle that carbon footprint article. And I'm already looking through our pending work for a nice, juicy field assignment for you." He stood up so Charlie followed suit. "You did the best you could out there, Charles. Don't feel bad at all. In fact, Lane might need your help with North Carolina."

Hadn't Lane taken care of that by now? Charlie was halfway out the door before turning around. "The consulting company hired by Homeland, it wouldn't be Bates Corporation, would it?"

The Director opened a folder and flipped through a couple of pages. "No. Fencepost Consulting."

"Thanks."

"Charles?" The Director held out a two-inch thick manila folder. "When you've finished with those tasks, the Senate Environmental Pollution Subcommittee wants an updated set of reports on air quality."

Charlie let the folder hang in mid-air as he walked out, the Director's arm shaking at the prolonged extension.

Charlie was face-to-face with Jane when he stepped out of the Director's office. He didn't know what to say, out in public, so he smiled. She smiled back and batted her eyelashes. They needed to chat, but not then and there.

He returned to his desk and picked up a pen. *At least there will be a warm handoff.* All of the details, conversations, analysis, visits all swirled in his mind. *How can I effectively communicate all the complicated details and the loose ends in a digestible report summary? How can I describe the patterns I discovered?* Charlie dropped the pen and held his head in his hands. His phone rang, breaking his reverie. He answered "Keyson."

"Hey, partner, it's Potter. Long time, no see."

What had it been, forty-eight hours? "Something new with our case? How's Kwashay?"

"She's fine. I haven't seen her since my last visit to the portal in the park. I wanted to let you know that National Guard troops are onsite now. When I asked them, they said Homeland Security deployed them."

"My Director said Homeland Security took over when electromagnetic radiation was detected emanating from the portal." *Funny how easily we've become comfortable with that term.*

"So, does that mean you're officially off the case?"

"It sure looks that way. But that won't stop the portal operators. Since you're local, I think checking in with Kwashay occasionally is very much in her best interest."

"I agree. Well, take care, I guess. And next time you're in New York, I'm going to hold you to that dinner."

I don't remember making that promise. "Yeah, sure. And thanks for the good words. My Director was pleased." He hastily added, "And so was I."

"What are partners for? By the way, remember that preacher woman we saw in Brooklyn?"

"You mean Reverend Dogood?" *All too vividly.* "I sure do. Why?"

"An EPA colleague of mine from Pennsylvania contacted me that she's following the brown stripe. She's holding religious rallies about it. It looks like her next stop is somewhere in Ohio and then points west."

She's headed towards Kearney, the middle place! "She's an opportunist. Homeland Security can handle any trouble she makes."

"I'm sure they can. She doesn't matter now anyway, right? You're off the case." Potter let her comment sink in. "Catch you later." The line went silent.

She's provoking me, teasing me to stay involved. But my orders are clear.

As long he'd spoken with Potter, he owed Nachas the same conversation. He dialed Nachas' number.

"This is Gregory Nachas, EPA."

"Hi, it's Charlie Keyson. How are things?"

"The good news is, Dixon's guards are gone. The campus is open, so I have access to Matt if necessary. The last time I saw him, he seemed better, but he's since moved out of his room. At the moment, I don't know where he is."

"At least he didn't get worse. If you keep an eye on the portal, he'll show up eventually. What's the bad news?"

"Dixon's personal militia is gone, replaced by the National Guard that have surrounded the portal, like it's some kind of treasure."

"That might not be so bad. They're government, just like us. Maybe that's actually better."

"But they won't let anyone near the trellis. Or portal. Or whatever."

"That will frustrate Matt, when he needs to operate that thing. Homeland Security may be taking over the case and protecting the portal, but you still have local jurisdiction over the environmental issues."

"I do? Are you sure, because they're heavily armed-"

Charlie needed Nachas as his eyes and ears. "You represent California. You have a responsibility to California." He changed the tone of his voice from cheerleader to confidant. "And while you're performing that responsibility, you can keep me informed. Just updates every once in a while?"

Nachas clicked his tongue. "Sure. How can a few words with a friend hurt anything?"

Charlie hung up and turned his attention to the blank pad of legal paper. With pen in hand, he document the origins of the two portals. He knew both stories, about how the rods were found and the blueprints were flashed into Kwashay's and Matt's minds. *It sounds like science fiction, not an assignment report.* He even thought about including Reverend Dogood in the details.

Charlie's phone rang again. *I'll never get this damn summary done at this rate.* "Keyson."

"You bastard!"

Charlie didn't recognize the angry voice. "Who is this?"

"Trev Dixon. You sure know how to trump a guy. I put the portal under private security, so you send in the National Guard."

It's good that Dixon thinks I have that kind of authority. "If all you did was call to harass me, I have better things to do-"

"No, wait. I'm sorry. I can be a little controlling sometimes. I'm working on it. Actually, I'm calling for your help."

Interesting way to get someone's assistance, by name calling. "I thought Bates Corporation had everything well in hand."

Dixon's voice was softer, much more humble than Charlie had ever heard. "I've got a huge problem."

And he thinks I'm the solution? "I'm listening."

"My boss at the Foundation is expecting answers and deliverables. All I have are speculations."

"Why? What did you promise him?"

There was a long pause. "Alien technology."

Charlie nearly fell off his chair. "You didn't!"

"I was so sure-"

"You've really dug yourself a hole." Charlie adjusted his sitting position. "I don't know if there's anything I can do-"

"There's more. Matt is getting better, but slowly. His parents are threatening to sue. Me, Bates, the College."

Charlie felt sorry for Matt, much less so for Dixon, who'd caused all of his issues himself.

Dixon's voice was picking up steam. "And do you know who Matt Thready Senior is? A wealth manager whose clients have considerable positions in Bates Corporation. He's got the old man's personal cell phone number. Even I don't have that!"

Charlie smiled at Dixon's predicament. *Serves him right.* "Seems like you pissed off the wrong guy."

"Damn right. Thready's clients are liquidating, and the stock is plummeting. And besides that, the portal is sparking at the place where the missing rod goes. My best people didn't know what to do."

Was Dixon whimpering? "First thing, calm down. I'll help you, but you have to let me help you." Charlie didn't like the phrasing even when he was delivering it. "First thing, you won't do anything to get in the way of Agent Nachas' access to the portal or Matt. He'll be my eyes and ears." *He doesn't have to know I'm off the case.*

"Done. He has full access, with a personal bodyguard if desired."

Dixon couldn't promise full access with National Guard troops present, but his agreement was valuable anyway "No thanks, he can protect himself." *I don't need Nachas' every movement and communication observed.*

"You are going to help, aren't you? After all, this is your case."

I was pulled from it because of Dixon's clout, and now he wants help? "Give me your cell number and I'll call you back. Unlike some people, I have responsibilities." *For editing some interns essay.* "Just give me a few minutes."

Dixon's panic provided Charlie an opportunity. *If Director Stanton won't support my efforts, Dixon will.* He got up and approached Jane's desk. It felt awkward, because his first words to her after their dinner and a hug were about business. "Excuse me, Jane, how quickly can I fly to Kearney, Nebraska?"

"The middle place?" Her fingers moved at lightning speed. A travel web site provided the answer. "The shortest is eight hours. Two connections. The last flight is propeller plane."

Charlie had successfully avoided flying in such a craft in California. "I could barely stand the small jet.

How about a direct flight to somewhere nearby with a major airport?"

More key clicks. "That was, through Denver." She lowered her voice. "You going to the middle?"

Jane deserved the truth. "Yes, with or without the Director's permission."

"Oh my!" Her face glowed pink.

Charlie left Jane sitting there, her fingertips covering her lips. *If commercial flights aren't cooperating, there's a possible substitute.* He considered what resources Bates Corporation might have that could help.

He returned to his desk and dialed Dixon's number.

"Keyson, I thought for sure you were going to let me hang here."

Dixon sparked my motivation. Hopefully he'll provide the transportation. "I need one of your private jets."

"To come back out here? Done. We've got planes almost everywhere, including Washington. I'll contact our private flight control-"

"I'm not coming out to Eureka, at least not now. I need them to take me elsewhere."

"Who needs you more than I do? Please. Things are falling apart."

Charlie wasn't going to give Dixon any more information than necessary. *He still works for a company with enormous clout, and I don't want any interference.* "Trust me. What I'm doing will make everything right. Are you sure you have a plane in DC?"

"Let me check." Charlie heard Dixon typing. "Yes, I do."

"Great! Tell them to expect me."

"I will. The flight crew will meet you at the Landmark Aviation FBO at Dulles International."

"FBO?"

"Fixed Base Operator, it's the physical location for private jet flights. There's still security, so bring proper ID."

"Fine. I'm headed there right now." Charlie shoved the legal pad with one-half page of prose in his top drawer.

"I'll call so they can file a flight plan. Where are you headed?"

Charlie needed immediate departure, so he reluctantly gave up his destination. "Kearney, Nebraska. By the way, have you ever heard of Fencepost Consulting?"

Dixon's voice was brighter. "It's one of our subsidiaries. Why?"

"Nothing, just curious. I'll talk to you soon."

Charlie stood up and fingered the flip phone in his pocket. The device made him feel sad and unworthy. He jogged back to Jane's desk. "Everybody in the office seems to have a smart phone but me. Can you upgrade my device?"

"Of course." Jane dug into her bottom drawer and pulled out a colorful box. "This new model. The best for you. Give me old phone, please." Jane typed some numbers from the box into the carrier's web site, broke open the box and handed Charlie the smartphone. "Number transferred. All done."

Charlie was astonished at her capability. "Thank you so much. I'll keep in touch, I promise."

"Are you leaving again so soon? You just got back."

"I wouldn't go if it wasn't necessary. There are too many loose ends, and people who are depending on me."

"I watch AquaLung for you. I already packed." She pointed at her rolling bag, tucked in the corner behind her desk.

"One pinch a day." Charlie winked and dropped the duplicate apartment key into her waiting palm.

"Do you want me call you a limo?" Her hand was already on the telephone receiver.

"No, I'll catch a cab downstairs. And when I get back, we'll talk."

She stood. "Good. I like that." She touched his cheek with her fingertip.

Director Stanton stood in his office doorway, listening to their conversation. "Where are you going? You just got back, and you've got work to do."

"My dead grass case is a lot bigger than we thought, and it still hasn't run its course. Homeland Security does a great job, but they're ill-equipped. I already know the players and all of the loose ends. And I'm the best person to pursue them to a conclusion, whatever that is. That's what a field agent is supposed to do, right? Haven't you ever had an assignment that demanded your attention?"

The question caused the Director to reflect, during which Charlie grabbed his bag and marched toward the elevator.

The Director scuffled along behind. "You're prohibited from traveling to California. Homeland Security orders."

"Or Bates Corporation orders?" Charlie pressed the down button. "I'm not going to Eureka." The elevator door opened.

"And you can't go to New York either. You don't have the authority or the budget-"

Charlie entered the elevator. "I'm using a private jet, on my own time."

"You have a private jet?" The Director's face turned red. "If you leave, your job may not be waiting when you get back."

Charlie pressed the button for the lobby. "That's a risk I'm willing-" The elevator doors closed.

For someone who hated airplane travel, Charlie was racking up the miles.

75 – Matt (Eureka, CA)

Matt returned to Fred's room, now also his room, after confronting Dixon at the portal, now secured by National Guard. Before resuming his video game practice, he opened Fred's laptop to check email. Fred's desktop photo, a model in a skimpy bikini, was distracting, but Matt continued his login, expanding the window to full screen size. He was surprised to find an email message reply to his posting of the incomplete portal picture.

"Have you completed construction? Write back and share what you know so we can be successful together." It was signed "PortalPal."

Matt took more than a few minutes to compose a comprehensive response, mentioning the incomplete construction, the impact on him from Dixon's diamond-tipped saw, the messages from the portal to practice video games – everything that had occurred since that picture was taken. After he reread and edited a few typos in the message, he clicked send.

The screen showed a box: "Invalid email account – please contact campus I/T."

No! Now they cut off my email? After brief consideration, Matt calmed down. *If there are government troops on campus, they're probably intercepting communications, including email. I'd hate to get PortalPal in trouble.*

Matt tried to logout but that failed too. He closed the laptop, put his pillow on the chair to be more comfortable and booted up Space Fox.

Let's see how quickly I can get to expert level on this one.

76 – Kwashay (Brooklyn, NY)

After school, Kwashay was glued to the TV, her ship flying at full throttle through a distant unnamed star system filled with unknown hazards.

In the hallway, she heard the door of the apartment unlock, then some heavy breathing and footsteps. Her mother was home from work. "Are you still at that? What about your homework?"

"Done."

"And dinner?" Her mother moved from the foyer through the hall and into the living room behind her.

"Chicken legs in the oven, greens on the stove."

Kwashay glanced at the score. She was closing in on six digits, a new high. Her ship swooped down to avoid star debris with a flick of her wrist. Her skills were improving with every play. When she heard a beep, her instincts kicked in and she made a sharp left turn to avoid incoming fire. Her ship smashed into an orbiting moon.

"Your timer went off," said her mother.

Kwashay's score remained five digits, starting with an eight. She stood up and stretched her arms toward the ceiling. "I'm getting a lot better."

"Good for you. I hope it makes you good enough to win that tournament." Her mom donned oven mittens.

"It's already done good things." Kwashay sat at the kitchen table while her mother unloaded the oven. The chicken legs were golden brown and steaming hot. "My eye-hand coordination is so much better now. And my concentration has improved."

"Yes, and I'll feel very safe when you pilot me around the galaxy in your space ship. When did you do your homework?

"We had a study period when our history teacher called out sick."

"How are you supposed to get a high-quality education with teachers who slough off their responsibility? Tell me that."

"And I don't sit alone at lunch any more. Since I asked a couple of kids about video games, they became much friendlier. And they gave me helpful hints, and the names of some other games to try."

"I will not have you buying more of that junk. Use the games Vondell loaned you. They'll have to do."

Kwashay plucked a couple of legs from the baking sheet, a heaping spoonful of greens from the pot, and poured some dipping sauce onto her plate. She needed the nutrition before diving back in and pursuing that elusive six digit score.

77 – Selton (Kearney, NE)

The lights on Railroad Street in Kearney, Nebraska flickered on in sequence, east to west. Selton's energy level was at a historic low. *I have to chance a brief feeding or I won't have the strength to prevent the invasion.* Sheltered by the underpass, he surveyed possible locations. He'd feasted at the Parks and Recreation property across the street so many times, his brown body prints nearly covered the entire lawn. Any small grassy patches near the railroad had long since been depleted. For the past couple of weeks, he'd begun to roam south, judiciously choosing residential backyards where the owners had no lights or pets to expose his presence. His latest sojourns had been to Centennial Park, but that was quite a distance away.

He was about to repeat that exploration when a caravan of three buses pulled up to the Parks and Recreation building. They were all labeled identically: 'Reverend Billi Dogood's Mobile Morality Mission'. *She's here!* When the buses pulled out of the way, Selton saw the Reverend in the midst of a crowd of people scurrying around, assembling a fold-out stage platform, and erecting banners as a backdrop. Just like the photos in the local paper, she still wore the long white dress, a soiled choir robe. Even her dark hair had been bleached of all color. Organizers handed out signs to the passengers. Electronic torches that used LED lights illuminated the gathering.

In the midst of this tumult, two police squad cars pulled up, lights flashing but no sirens. Selton recognized the Chief of Police. Bernice the librarian had surreptitiously called him when Selton first arrived at the library. He didn't blame her for caution. She just wanted the other patrons to be safe, and wasn't comfortable with a shabbily dressed vagrant on the premises.

The Chief spoke with the Reverend for quite a while alongside the stage. Although Selton couldn't hear what they were saying, they were clearly arguing. After a short while, the Chief fetched a clipboard from his squad car and showed the woman its contents, pointing with his arm at the lawn at Parks and Recreation, and then in Selton's direction.

The woman nodded and took the stage with a megaphone. Videographers filmed her from two angles. "Believers," she shouted, "we are here to rid the besieged town of Kearney, Nebraska, our heartland, from the Devil incarnate." The audience cheered, on cue. "These patterns are a warning. First our lawns, then our children. The monster must be stopped, praise the Lord!"

More applause and cheering. *Patterns?*

"The Chief of Police has graciously shared with me the locations of the Devil's markings." *What does she mean?* Selton has seen no markings of the Devil. *Isn't that 666?* "It is our task to search out and destroy – I mean, capture the monster from Hell whose brown prints will lead to his destruction, uh, incarceration."

Lawns? Brown spots? She means me!

In the past, Marathon Man had coached Selton to recognize and take action in threatening circumstances. This was a real-life example. Selton ran from beneath the underpass straight south along a dirt alley between 1st Avenue and Central Street. When he glanced over his shoulder, he saw the crowd split in two, crossing Railroad Street, one group on his east flank, the other on his right.

Selton analyzed their offensive strategy based on historical battles as he continued south, across backyards of homes he'd previously visited. *Encirclement? They're on both sides, but not in front of me.* The groups were advancing on his increasingly southern position. *Can I get far enough ahead to break through their line of attack?*

"I found another one!" someone shouted.

Selton had left behind a series of brown spots from previous feedings, and the crowds were using them to track him down.

"He must be close by," hollered Reverend Dogood.

What have I ever done to these people, that I should be hunted down like an animal? Selton recalled the aggressive nature of human beings associated with battles he had studied. This episode was certainly predictable, except Selton had not predicted it.

He continued his review of offensive strategies, in search of an effective defense. *Blitzkrieg? No, I haven't established a position of defense.* Selton came across a fenced-in backyard. He couldn't circle around to either side lest he expose himself to the two groups. He struggled with the latch on the gate before scampering across the lush lawn. His backroots pulled at him, slowing his pace. *Not now! I'll feed when we've eluded them.*

A flanking maneuver? Yes, that was it, or something very close. The woman in white urged her followers on through loud proclamations.

Selton's energy level always waned as the day went on, so the crowds on either side were closing their distance. Selton was past his previous point of feeding exploration, so everything in front of him was unchartered. As he raced through the next yard, spotlights illuminated the patio and portions of the lawn.

"Who's out there?" a voice shouted from a sliding glass door.

A human wave attack! That's it. Selton was pleased to have identified the crowd's tactics but had no defensible position to withstand such an onslaught. It was a lopsided battle, hundreds against one.

His foot caught on a garden hose and he fell forward, face first. His fedora flew off, landing a few feet away. By the time he rolled face up, hiding his backroots, he found himself surrounded by shouting bus riders, chastising him, accusing him, berating him for unspeakable acts of horror. He tried to speak back in his own defense, pleading for a logical discussion, but the shouting was too loud.

The group parted to allow their leader to approach, Reverend Billi Dogood, grasping a megaphone. "I've got you now!" She scowled down at him, pointing a finger with one hand, the other a fist raised in the air. Someone snapped a picture of her standing over Selton, as if she was the successful hunter who'd bagged her prey. Humans with anger in their eyes swung their lantern-sticks like cudgels.

Selton was sure that his mission was over. He'd be pummeled to pulp by this mob of irrationally angry humans. *All of that reading and assimilating, and for what?*

A warning blasted over someone else's megaphone. "I order you to disperse." His tormenters froze in place. The order repeated, getting louder with each rendition. The police chief stepped forward flanked by several deputies, including the one who'd been keeping an eye on him at the library. "I said, this is an unlawful assembly. You don't have a permit, and besides, this is not hobo hunting season."

Reverend Dogood avoided the officer's attempts to grab hold of her, twisting and turning her upper body. "I've tracked this miscreant for years. And now that we can bring him to justice, you're arresting me?"

Two of the officers led her away as she implored her group to carry on without her. Selton didn't know what "carry on" meant, but was certain it would not be pleasant.

The group without their leader milled around, looking at each other more than him. None of them stepped up to prescribe their next action.

"Back to your buses," said the Chief.

Slowly, the group wandered away, leaving Selton on the ground surrounded by the Chief and the remaining police force. "I've been looking for you."

Selton didn't ask why. He was just happy to been found.

"I'm taking you into protective custody." The Chief waved his hands. "Stand up."

"Yes, sir." Selton didn't want his body touched so he pushed up with his arms. His backroots fought him, trying to snake out from his shirt and jacket. "I'm trying, sir." Once Selton got momentum by rolling to his side, the roots broke free and he shot erect. "Yes, sir."

"One of my men will drive you to the station, for your own safety."

Selton would have preferred to be left alone, so he could take in nutrition someplace nearby and green. Then he thought about the pending megafeeding, and lush grassy areas became a lot less tempting. Besides, the Chief's invitation had only one possible reply. "Yes, sir."

Two policemen asked Selton to raise his hands and did a gentle frisk of his sides, arms and legs. Finding and confiscating the pocket knife, they directed him toward one of the police cars on 1st Avenue, lights still flashing. "My hat, please?" One of the officers fetched it and returned it to Selton's possession after checking inside the liner.

As they opened the rear door, Selton glanced up. Against the dark sky stood a series of tall towers, Kearney's local power station.

Selton leaned forward and recognized the contents of the car's equipment console through the plastic suspect transport enclosure: a two-way radio, light and siren switches, a locking compartment for a spare firearm, a mobile data terminal, a vehicle tracking system, an evidence gathering video camera and an automatic number plate recognition system, with a radar gun on the front passenger seat. *Very high tech indeed.* The one-mile drive to the police station was short and silent. He'd never expected that a visit to the police station would be so comforting.

Two police officers escorted Selton into a small room near the back of the first floor of the police station. "Wait here," one ordered.

Selton sat at the table holding his hat facing an empty chair. Most of one sidewall was a mirror, which he knew was two-way. Was someone already watching him?

The Chief walked in, shut the door and pulled up the second chair. "We haven't been formally introduced. I'm Chief of Police Brick Rogers. Your name is Selton, right?"

"Selton Serulia, sir."

The Chief leaned the chair back so far, Selton thought he'd fall. "Me and my men got there just in time, hmm? Saved your butt from those bible thumpers. You have any idea why they were after you?"

Probably because I was running. "No sir." In retrospect, he regretted making himself a moving target.

"Well, Reverend Dogood and her followers are still in town, so for your safety, I'm going to keep you here overnight. Just to be sure, until they leave tomorrow morning."

Selton noticed that he wasn't being offered a choice. "Yes, sir."

"It's past supper, but I'll have one of my men roust up something for you to eat. Never let it be said I let one of my prisoners starve to death."

So I am a prisoner!

The Chief opened the door. The same two officers escorted Selton down the hall. As they passed a dish of potpourri on top of a row of file cabinets, Selton grabbed a handful and stuffed it into his jacket pocket. They proceeded down one flight of stairs to a row of jail cells. One officer held open the door of the first cell. After they'd locked Selton inside, one of them noticed that the clock above the door had the wrong time when compared to his watch.

"Damn!" He fetched a stepstool, climbed up and turned the bottom knob to advance the clock to the correct time. He smiled at his accomplishment, stepped down and departed.

There were no other prisoners, for which Selton was grateful. Answering questions from other incarcerated inmates would have been annoying. *I never thought I'd end up in the Big House, as Marathon Man would have called it.*

He sat on the lumpy bunk bed, useless for his physiology, as was the concrete floor. *I may starve to death anyway.* Selton picked bits of the dry potpourri from his pocket and rubbed it against his backroots. The dry bitter mixture was a poor substitute for a regular feeding, but neither the thin mattress or cement floor would provide what he really needed. Selton rubbed and then paced, time passing slowly.

An officer came down stairs. "Just checking. They deliver your meal?"

Selton lied. "Yes. It was delicious." He hoped the guard wouldn't notice the lack of a tray, plate and implements.

"Okay then, well, this is my last bed check. Best you get some sleep." He turned off the main lights and left the basement cell block. Dim EXIT signs cast sharp bar-shaped shadows on the floor and an eerie red tiny across the room.

In desperation for rest, he reluctantly curled up on the bed. His backroots surveyed the cinderblock walls and, finding no nutrition source, flopped uselessly to the side.

78 – Charlie (Washington, DC)

Charlie didn't bother going home to pack a change of clothes. *Things are coming to a head, I can just feel it.* He brought just what he had with him: the shoulder bag containing his case file, Potter's camera and his novel. Downstairs on 12th Street SW Street, he waved at cabs, all of which passed him by, even the empty ones. *What does it take to get a taxi?* A Red Top cab pulled up to the curb with its distinct black front and back, and a red middle. The driver rolled down his window. "Are you Mr. Charles Keyson?"

Charlie nodded.

"Get in. Dulles, right, the private jet terminal?"

He opened the rear door. "Yes, but -"

"Jane Yong called dispatch. You didn't know?"

"Nope." Charlie closed the door behind him. "She's very efficient."

As the cab battled morning traffic, Charlie imagined what might happen when the westbound and eastbound root systems met. Dixon expected a fissure in the space/time continuum, aliens streaming through to capture our planet. Instead, maybe a broadcast from a distant planet through the portals, demanding our surrender? Or maybe, just more dead grass.

The cab pulled up to Landmark Aviation FBO, the private jet facility at Dulles, a single story building about the size of a small strip mall opposite the commercial terminals.

Charlie reached for his wallet as he read the fare on the meter. "How much do I owe you?"

"Prepaid with a big tip. You know, Jane Yong is my best customer and I've never met her."

His loss.

Charlie jogged toward the flat brick building to escape the mind-rattling noise of small jets. Landmark Aviation was one of four private jet operators in the facility, on the near end. Heavy insulation and multilayer picture windows kept the noise and accelerated air outside.

On a board with changeable letters, he saw his flight: BATES/KEYSON KEARNEY, NE. Charlie approached the counter and pointed. "That's me."

The clerk spoke into her walkie-talkie, announcing Charlie's arrival. "Your plane is N-1701. It's waiting for you about fifty feet out. Follow the yellow path."

He thought about the brown stripe the same width, and Dorothy's yellow brick road leading to Oz as he walked out to the Bates jet.

A young man stood at the bottom of a short staircase. "Mr. Keyson? We're ready when you are. If I can see some identification." Charlie flashed his badge.

"No sir, a driver's license?"

Charlie complied.

"Thank you. You may come aboard. Take any seat."

Charlie jogged up the short staircase to the private jet doorway and ducked his head to enter. On his left, two pilots were reviewing their preflight checklist. On the right, he had his choice of four swivel captain's chairs, or two rows of bench seats facing each other near the rear. He took the front most captain's chair on the left.

The one flight attendant came by to be sure he was buckled in. "Our flight time should be approximately two hours and thirty minutes. After takeoff, you'll have your choice of beverage and several entrees."

I could get used to this. "Thank you." He pulled the novel from his bag and continued reading about Grissom's case.

Grissom was fast asleep when his phone rang. He checked the round silver analog alarm clock: 1:37 am. "Who's calling?"

"Yeah, hi, it's me, Arnie? I work the third shift at Indulge Financial? We just got a hit on the use of a suspect card-"

Grissom leaped from his bed. "You what?"

"We have a system that monitors suspected cards for fraud. Instructions say for this account, I'm supposed to call your number when I get a hit. So, I'm calling. Are you the right guy?"

"Yes, I'm exactly the right guy." Grissom stumbled into his study, flipped on the light and grabbed the Bainbridge case file with the list of compromised cards. "What's the name on the card?"

Arnie gave him the name and the card number.

Grissom scanned the list provided by Indulge Financial. *There it is, the only compromised card ever used outside of a single billing period! This is our break!* "Okay, give me the details, please." He swiped a pad of paper and pen closer.

"The card was used at Tailfeather Adult Dance Club, Baton Rouge, Louisiana. Five hundred and forty-nine dollars even, about fifteen minutes ago."

"And the transaction went through?"

"Yeah, our system flags the transaction but doesn't bounce it. No alerts."

"Perfect." *We wouldn't want the thief to know we'd identified him.* "Thank you so much. Please call your supervisor and let him know.

"I don't do that. Just you is what the instruction says."

Grissom used a father's tone. "You will this time, instructions or not. He'll want to know. Maybe even throw you a bonus." Grissom figured if this was important enough to wake him from a sound sleep, others deserved the same fate.

Adult Dance Club? Grissom wondered what kind of services and charges his client Bainbridge generated at Galileo's. As soon as he hung up on Indulge Financial Services, he called FBI Agent Clay.

Clay sounded groggy. "This better be good, Grissom."

"Indulge Financial just got a hit on one of the compromised cards in Baton Rouge, Louisiana. Tailfeather Adult Dance Club."

"At two in the morning?"

"That's probably when they do their best business. Besides, I thought you'd appreciate a hot lead, less than an hour old."

"Sure, of course." Clay groaned. "Okay, I'm on it."

"I'm going to alert one of my local Undergrads to meet you-"

Clay used a fully awake voice. "No, you won't. Things get more dangerous from here."

Grissom never wanted to put his Undergrads in harms way. Besides, his Undergrad might also be underage for an adult club. "All right but I expect to be informed."

Charlie looked up from the novel. *I wish my case had a transaction trail or an identifiable perpetrator.* They were aloft, and about a half hour had passed. The attendant asked for his choice of beverage and food.

A voice came over the PA system. "Mr. Keyson, this is the captain. We're making good time on our way to Kearney. I don't expect any problems. Good thing we're not flying into New York or northern California. They have some unusual weather conditions."

Brooklyn and Eureka? That can't be a coincidence.

The attendant returned shortly thereafter with a diet soda already poured into a chilled glass and a hot chicken sandwich with all the fixings. Charlie thanked him, took a big bite of the sandwich and rejoined his hero.

At a reasonable hour the same day, Grissom got a call from Agent Clay of the FBI. "I got those check images subpoenaed. Despite different company names, Mukhtar Aziz signed all of the checks."

"There's your link!"

"That still doesn't prove that the assessment and pawn shops captured the credit card information."

"What more do you need?" Grissom was running out of approaches to turn his patterns into indisputable evidence.

"Don't fall into a funk. The possibility of Aziz' illegal activity is enough for us to launch our own independent investigation. The Bureau thanks you for bringing these circumstances to our attention." Clay coughed.

"You're taking over, aren't you? You'll want me to cease and desist my efforts on behalf of my client and Indulge Financial. That is the implication, correct?"

"I'm afraid so. However-"

The word teased Grissom's expectations. "Yes?"

"Because your information was crucial in establishing the groundwork for our investigation-"

Grissom interrupted, "You'll keep me informed about your progress?"

"Yes, Quincy, I will."

"And if you need any assistance?"

"You'll be the first person I'll call. I promise."

"I guess that's all I can ask. Good hunting, Clay."

Charlie was pulled from the novel by the bodiless pilot's voice. "Please put your things away and buckle up. Low clouds have rolled in. I'm going to perform an instrument landing. Not to worry."

Charlie bookmarked his place and stuffed his novel into his bag. *Sounds like Grissom has almost wrapped up his case. Maybe for me, too.* The plane shook as it got swallowed by an infinite layer of translucent white. It bucked and dropped, the wind's play toy. They were barely out of the blanket when Charlie heard the screech of tires on the runway. The plane taxied for a few minutes, stopping and starting, likely because the ground crew had its hands full with the nasty weather. Finally, the plane came to a stop, and the seatbelt sign flickered off.

Charlie thanked the pilot and the flight attendant and deplaned. A short walk across the asphalt brought Charlie to the terminal. At the curb, one taxi labeled K-Cab waited for a fare.

Charlie leaned over into the open passenger window.

"You available?"

"Sure. Hop in. Where to?"

"The Kearney police station, please." *If anybody knows what's going on in Kearney, the police should.*

"You a member of law enforcement?"

"Nope." Charlie decided not to share. It would have been a long story.

Charlie saw the driver's eyes in the rear view mirror. "What brings you to our fair city?"

How could Charlie explain in simple terms? "I'm looking for something special." *The brown stripe, or a third portal, although there hadn't been any blight reports filed in the vicinity.*

"If you're here for the crane migration, you just missed it."

Charlie ignored the comment. He was looking for a conclusion, not birds on the move.

The driver twitched his head toward the back seat repeatedly. "You know, every year about this time, over half a million sandhill cranes migrate through here on their way north."

"That's nice."

"We get so many visitors who want to witness the spectacle, the town just about doubles in size."

"Good thing I didn't try to make a hotel reservation." Charlie didn't particularly want to stay in Kearney overnight.

"Like I said, they're all gone now. Birds and people. Plenty of space if you decide to stay over."

Charlie looked out the window, wondering when the cab driver would be quiet.

The voice from the front seat kept up a lopsided conversation. "Your first time in Kearney?" The cab driver's eyes remained fixed on the rear view mirror, not the road.

"My first time in Nebraska. And my last, if you don't pay attention to your driving."

The probing stopped. Evidently the cab driver finally took Charlie's short answers and driving feedback to indicate he didn't want to chat.

They rode in silence except for an occasional gust of wind that howled outside Charlie's window and the roar of three buses going in the opposite direction whose engines sounded like angry lions.

After only ten minutes, the density of buildings made it clear the cab was entering Kearney's downtown area. Charlie heard the ticking of the turn signal as the cab approached a corner labeled Avenue A, then continued up the street before stopping at a flat-faced brick and stone two-story building labeled City of Kearney/Buffalo County Law Enforcement Center.

"Here ya' go, pal," said the driver.

"Thanks." Charlie paid the cabbie, including a healthy tip to compensate for his harsh comment.

Before he could reach for the handle of the station's entrance, the glass door swung open. A man with a rough, bark-like complexion wearing disheveled clothes and a weathered fedora burst through, holding his thin tan jacket shut. Charlie got a glimpse of his glowing green eyes before he tottered south.

As Charlie extended his hand toward the handle a second time, his phone rang. The number indicated the area code and prefix of a phone line at EPA headquarters. "Keyson."

"Where are you?" The Director's voice was brusque.

"Why does it matter? You fired me, if I recall."

"I've done no such thing, Charles. You're a valued member of my team. Although, I think you've strayed from rational behavior."

"Did you call to harass me, because I have important things to do."

"I called because I expect you're still working the dead grass case. And to tell you not to stop. Suddenly I'm under tremendous pressure to get some results."

"This is not a 'do something to get results' kind of situation. In fact, we have very little control."

"You should know Washington by now. That's an unacceptable answer. The Committee on Energy and Commerce is banging on my door, inviting me to hearings with the threat of subpoena if I refuse, and they won't want to hear the phrase 'very little control.' They'll be looking for answers."

More likely a scapegoat, someone to blame. The implication was, either the Director or I would be held responsible. Charlie craned his head to watch the badly dressed man hobble across Railroad Street, stumble through an opening in the fence and vanish between train cars parked in the yard.

"Lane finally walked me through your findings and documentation, and now I understand why you couldn't stop. Charles, are you listening to me?"

Charlie's attention returned to the call. "Tell me, who did Congress blame for the last hurricane? Not our preparedness or lack thereof, but the hurricane itself?"

"Nobody. It was a natural disaster, an act of God if you prefer that phrase."

I don't. "Right. So the appearance of these unique rods and sticks from which the two young adults built the portals, those rods were an act of nature. As far as we can tell."

"What does that mean?"

"That no human being is responsible for the portals or the brown stripe or any of the damage." All Charlie had was Dixon's conjecture about alien origins.

It was a disservice to share such radical thoughts without evidence.

"Well, if you no one is to blame, we're in serious trouble. The situation is getting worse."

How did the Director know? I hadn't reported the last obstacles. "In what way?"

"That brown stripe of yours has damaged farms across the Midwest. More than a few governors have made formal requests for assistance. Lane told you that, right?"

Brown stripe of mine? The Director has already decided that I'm the fall guy. "Yes?"

"Farms owned by agriculture conglomerates invest in political candidates. The USDA, the FDA, and Homeland Security are considering reviving an old 2005 collaboration between states and private industry to protect the nation's food supply. By the way, I gave the FBI your name. They're considering this domestic terrorism."

"I'll cooperate with all of them. And they can collaborate all they want, those portals and brown stripes aren't going anywhere."

"Wrong, they're going everywhere! Shasta National Forest south of Big Bar, Lassen National Forest, Ashley National Forest just south of Salt Lake City, all cut in half by your brown stripe. And it's appeared in Steamboat Springs and Rocky Mountain National Park as well. The National Park Service is on my case for an explanation. They called it devastating!"

"What do they expect us to do?"

"Government agencies don't like to feel powerless. Including mine! You're my man in the field, whether I like it or not. Figure this out, identify a remedy, and I'll get you all the resources you need to implement. Got it?"

"Yes sir. Thank you for your support." Resources weren't the problem. It was patience. The portals had a game plan, and they weren't sharing.

79 – Matt (Eureka, CA)

Matt sat on the edge of Fred's bed, hunched over, the Y-Box controller in his hands. After beating Space Fox easily and racking up the best score nationally, he shuffled through the remainder of Fred's game collection. From previous experience, Matt knew none of them were challenging enough, so he searched the Y-Box online game store for something that would test his skills. He opted to download a copy of Smuggler's Dash, a top rated game with comments that supported its difficulty. The goal and style of the game seemed exactly right. Matt was tasked to pilot his cargo ship filled with exotic fruits and vegetables to the buyer's location, through many star systems and across multiple galaxies. Hazards lurked everywhere. And, if he didn't get to his destination quickly enough, his cargo would spoil.

Matt's left fingers caressed the directional pad while his right ones chose engine and shield settings. He was in the middle of a delivery campaign when he heard a knock on the half-open door.

"Go away!" *You'd think a college student could read my note.* Fred was bunking elsewhere, bothered so much by the game sounds during Matt's late night practicing he couldn't sleep. And Fred's roommate never showed up at all, allowing Matt to sleep in the second bed – assuming he chose to sleep. *Maybe Fred's roommate is back. But why would he knock?*

The light from the hallway cast a glare on the TV screen. "Shut the door!" Matt tilted his head to maintain his vigil at full throttle. From the freshness scale on the screen, the fruits and vegetables in the cargo bay were aging past edible, which in turn would reduce Matt's score. The numbers in the corner of the screen had passed a quarter of a million, but Matt was aiming for his first million score. He startled when the door slammed.

"Hey, Matty, you okay?" It was Fred.

Only my mother calls me Matty. "I'm fine." Matt smelled Fred getting closer.

"I haven't seen you around campus, in classes, or in the cafeteria. I even walked out to the botanic garden looking for you."

"Thanks." Matt performed a barrel roll around a meteor shower, which passed through by the time he'd finished the loop. "I'm still practicing."

Fred didn't leave. "You had anything to eat?"

"Don't need anything. Gotta get better." The portal expected a prepared operator, so that was Matt's objective.

"Whoa! I never get scores that high. Is that a new game?"

"Yeah, I bought it under your account. I hope you don't mind. My scores are under your ID."

"Great!" Fred's head cast a shadow on the screen. "But you gotta get some sleep, sometime. And you gotta eat to keep your strength up." Fred dangled a box in Matt's line of sight.

"Get that out of the way!" Matt slashed his arm at the box, knocking it to the floor. His ship tottered.

"Since when do you refuse pizza?"

"Since-" Matt took his eyes off the screen momentarily. A crash lit up the screen like fireworks. "Look what you made me do!" The controller fell from his hands. "Since the portal chose me to be its operator." *Who cares if Fred knows the truth?*

Fred moved closer. The game's menu screen with a floating fruit and vegetable animation illuminated Matt's face. "Your eyes are blood shot! How are you keeping them open?"

"By concentrating. Which you're not letting me do." Matt's fingers twitched even without a game in progress.

"So you're kicking me out of my own room? Fine." Fred slammed the door.

Good, now back to the task of delivering perishables.

80 – Kwashay (Brooklyn, NY)

The next morning, Kwashay checked in on her art project, the mysterious but beneficial portal for which she was the designated operator. She felt a growing anticipation that she'd be called upon at any moment, yet had no clue what operation involved. All she knew for fact was that her video game skills had vastly improved.

The National Guard was still in place, six soldiers within the dilapidated yellow tape, one at each vertex.

Off on the side by the path, a familiar woman sat: Potter, the female EPA agent.

Kwashay wandered closer, watching her devour a submarine sandwich. "Hi. Remember me?"

“Of course. Kwashay, the owner operator of Brooklyn’s only portal.”

Kwashay appreciated her choice of words. ”I’m not disturbing you, am I?”

“Oh no!” The female agent brushed debris from the bench. ”Please, have a seat.”

“Are you still working on my case? I mean, because I see you here a lot?”

“No, both Agent Keyson and I were pulled for other assignments. Why do you ask?”

“For a moment, I thought maybe you were staking out the portal, or following me.”

The agent smiled. “Agent Keyson and I had sandwiches here, and when I was looking for someplace to buy lunch for later, I remembered Cyber Cafe. Except, I decided to eat it now.”

“Oh.” Kwashay almost hoped that someone would help her make sense of the pieces. ”Can we talk, for just a little while?”

Potter put down the sandwich on its wrapping paper and wiped her fingers with a napkin. “Sure. What’s on your mind?”

“I’m trying to make sense of what the portal is telling me. I can’t talk to my mother or any of my classmates. They’d think I was loony. Maybe since you and your partner investigated it, you could help.”

“I’ll try.” Potter shifted her position, to face the young woman. “Is it still talking to you? What does it say?”

“It reminds me that I’m its operator, and that my mission, when it happens, will be very important. Critical.”

“It sure doesn’t look like it can be operated. Just a bunch of fat sticks.”

"Exactly. So why did it tell me to practice by playing video games?"

"Any particular kind of games?"

"You know, flying through space, avoiding planets and asteroids and debris. And I've gotten pretty good, even though my mother limits my playing time."

"She'd prefer you were studying, right?"

Kwashay nodded. "Sounds like you know her. So, do you think the portal is going to sprout wings and take off? It seems to be solidly planted in place."

"I don't think its going anywhere, which is why flying games make no sense." Agent Potter scratched her short brown hair. "Maybe the portal stays in place, but it controls something else that moves, like a drone or something."

"I hadn't thought of that. Maybe the portal is like the joystick for the video console." Kwashay smiled. "I guess I won't know for sure until it calls me to duty."

"It sounds like you feel obligated."

"Oh, I do! The portals are here for good, to help us. It's an honor to be an operator."

"I wonder how the other operator feels?"

"Maybe I shouldn't tell you, but I found him. He posted a photo on PictureNet."

"Then let me fill in a couple of missing pieces. It shouldn't hurt any. The other portal is in Eureka, California, on the campus of College of the Redwoods. The other operator is named Matt."

"Really? I wrote to him but he hasn't responded, even though I posted a picture of my portal to the same site."

"Don't take it personal. College students always have too much on their plates."

"Do you think I could meet him, to share our experiences?"

"I don't know. Maybe Agent Keyson can arrange that. Maybe after you two do whatever operators are supposed to do?"

"That would be perfect." Potter's relaxed demeanor put her mind at ease, for the first time in days. "I'd like that."

"I can see it on your face, it's obvious this operator obligation is getting to you. If you need to chat, here's my card. Call me anytime."

Kwashay took it even though she already had one at home. "I will." She stood and tucked the card into the slash pocket of her purse.

Kwashay walked back to her school building, feeling better. Agent Potter didn't have any answers. It seemed like nobody did. But their brief conversation made her feel like there was someone on her side, a confidant, a friend. She patted her purse.

Just when she'd crossed the street, she heard a voice call out from behind. "Hey, girly-girl." It was Sideways.

"Aren't you supposed to be working?"

"Even stiffs like me get a break. Looks like you been working overtime. Your eyes are really red."

"Kind of. I've been practicing your video games, and I finally got to a million!"

"Man, that's a wow. I never got a score that high."

"Really?"

Sideways made a crooked-finger Boy Scout sign. "For true." He relocated a curl that had flopped onto her forehead. "You doing okay?"

"I'm going non-stop, practicing video games and getting my school work done. I can't mess up my last semester."

"You shouldn't be burning yourself out. Nothing worth that." He glanced at his watch. "Oops, gotta go. Don't want no tardies."

"Go on, I'll be fine."

Sideways walked backwards. "You take care now, you hear!"

Maybe she had two friends.

81 – Selton (Kearney, NE)

A vibration under his bed woke Selton. Yet another communication. *What now?*

"Your seeds are ready. The megafeeding is nigh. We will initiate delivery to you."

Selton sighed in relief. *I'm safe from the megafeeding in here, unless it comes up through the floor.*

He heard his name being whispered. Was it the voice again? Bernice stuck her head past the door to the cellblock. "Selton?"

He stood and moved to the bars. "I'm here, Ms. Martin."

"You've known me long enough to call me Bernice." She walked towards the cell in slow motion. "Chief Rogers told me he had you in protective custody." Based on her tentative movement, she didn't like being down here any more than he did. "Your book came in. I thought you might want something to read while you're here." A tear dropped from her eye onto the dirty cement floor.

She handed Selton the book through the bars. "*The Day of the Triffids.*"

The last of the four alien invasion novels she recommended. "Thank you."

"Is there anything I can get you?"

A few square yards of sod? "No, I'll be fine." Selton didn't really believe that, but he wanted to spare his friend any additional pain and suffering.

"Well, all right. I hope to see you at the library tomorrow." She skulked out as stealthily as she'd arrived.

He sat down on the lumpy bunk and reached into his jacket pocket. Luckily, his rubber glove had survived the onslaught and chase. He only needed to read a few chapters to recognize the shocking similarities: tall plants capable of locomotion and communication, although Selton was not venomous or carnivorous, and in his case there had been only a single meteor, not a meteor shower.

Plants attacking Earthlings! Selton referred himself to Section 170, Ethics. *Earthlings have done nothing to Serulia that deserves an invasion.* He jumped to the bars. *I have to prevent this fictional account from coming true.*

Selton had failed at adjusting his pH to avoid detection. The megafeeding was sure to locate him and force its nutrients on him, causing his seeds to germinate. *I can't get away.*

Selton recalled the police officer on the step stool, which triggered the memory of Tiny washing the upper part of his front window, and Selton himself helping a shorter library patron get a book from a high shelf.

Even Bernice used a ladder to reach files stored high on the wall. *If the megafeeding is coming through the soil like every other feeding I've taken, than it won't reach me if I'm up high enough.* The tall power station transmission towers were fresh in his memory. *Perfect!*

Selton stood at the bars, listening intently for activity upstairs. There was no clatter of chairs on the floor, no idle chatter among police officers, no complaints from recently arrested suspects. Nothing.

He turned sideways. *I hope I'm soft enough to squeeze through.* Slowly and carefully, Selton extended one arm holding the book, one leg and half his torso including his backroots through the bars. *So far, so good.* He sucked in his stomach and pressed. He turned his head so it was facing the bars, a smaller depth than sideways. His ears flattened, but no harm since they were just for decoration anyway. His chest, back and butt were next, compressed. It was a tight fit, but doable. *Great!* His remaining arms and legs came through easily.

He stuffed the book into a big front pocket, his rubber glove in the other and tiptoed toward the door. He stumbled due to a relocated center of gravity, but he compensated as he climbed the stairs. The Chief was in his office near the back of the station, listening to the local news radio station. The remainder of the desks in the station were empty. With a few unhurried and light steps, Selton was at the door. On his way out, he almost collided with a suited human carrying a soft black bag. He muttered a whispered "Sorry" and plodded down the steps.

Pulling up his collar against the wind and his fedora tighter on his slightly compressed head, he trudged south towards the power station and his tower refuge.

82 - Charlie (Kearney, NE)

After his call with Director Stanton, Charlie finally walked through the doors and up a couple of steps into the police station. There should have been someone at the front desk to greet citizens, but the floor was empty of personnel. Charlie rang a desk bell instead of shouting out loud.

One person came out of a private room with a glass wall along the back, an officer in uniform but with an open collar. “Can I help you?”

“My name is Charlie Keyson, Environmental Protection from Washington, DC.

“So, you’re from Washington? Keyson, is it?”

Charlie nodded.

“Chief of Police Brick Rogers, at your service. Come on back.” He led Charlie to his office, pointed at a curved plastic chair and sat down in his leather swivel. “We don’t get visitors from Washington very often.” He turned off the desk radio. “What can I do for you?”

Charlie pointed through the glass. “Where’s the rest of your force?”

“We had a doozy of a situation last night. Most of my guys were up way past the end of their shifts, so I told them to sleep in. We’ll need them more in the evening than daytime. You still haven’t said, what brings you to Kearney?”

“Thanks for taking the time.” Charlie decided to keep his initial inquiry general. “I’m wondering if anything unusual has been going on.”

Rogers folded his hands behind his head and leaned back. "All towns have their quirks. Their unique citizens. Take Arnie for example. He goes to Bob's Barber Shop for a haircut every day like clockwork."

"Every day?" Charlie echoed.

"Bob just snaps his scissors around Arnie's head, pretending to cut his hair just to make him feel good." Roger's brought his hands down, playing with the folders on his desk. "Then there's our scholarly hobo. Think his name is Selton or Seldom, something like that. Comes to the library every day and reads books, one shelf at a time, in order. Been doing it for months. You need more examples?"

"No, that's plenty.'

"You see, we don't have the same problems you folks in big cities do. We don't wait for problems. We're proactive."

"I'm particularly interested in botanical anomalies." *And portals made of unusual materials.*

"EPA, huh? You interested in dead grass or The Second Coming?"

"Dead grass?" *I'm in the right spot after all!* "Tell me about it."

"Give me a second." The shuffled through the jumbled pile on his desk, extracting a specific manila folder filled with a stack of paper forms. "Citizens have been filing complaints about brown patches showing up on perfectly healthy lawns." He snuffled. "As if the police department can fix that. I've referred all of them to Kimball's Hardware or their favorite home and garden shop. Just look at these."

He handed Charlie a stack of 8 by 10 glossy photos with circles and arrows and a description on the back where each one was taken. Each picture documented a cluster of dark brown circles, each one with a hole in the middle, in the midst of an otherwise green lawn.

"We've got these all over. Municipal buildings, near the train station, and nearby homes, always the same thing. Have you ever seen anything like it?"

"No, I haven't." Charlie looked up. "Fascinating. Has anyone reported a fifty-foot brown stripe?" Charlie pulled out Potter's camera and showed the chief pictures of the east and west coast phenomena.

The chief shook his head. "Nope, just these splotches."

The chief's initial question bugged Charlie. "Did you say Second Coming?"

"Yep. Some damn televangelist caught wind of these brown spots. Went on the radio and preached that they foretell The End of Days, Apocalypse, something Biblical."

Sounds like Reverend Dogood. Charlie felt things were coming to a climax, but never conceived that the world might be ending.

The Chief continued, "She showed up last night with three buses full of her faithful, looking to search out The Devil himself. I deployed most of my force to keep them under control. You should have seen them, marching down the streets and sidewalks with torches and implements of destruction, hooting and hollering."

"Did they find him? The Devil, I mean?"

"Nah, just our scholarly hobo, working the residential garbage cans for scraps, I reckon. They were about to string him up if we hadn't taken him into protective custody."

"That's too bad." Charlie held the notion that Kearney was a peaceful little town.

"Over the top, in my book. I politely asked them to leave. Or else. I heard the buses roar past the office this morning."

Maybe those were the buses I saw on the way into town. "So what do you think is making those brown patches?"

He folded his arms. "I think it's a grub infestation."

"Really?" Although the edges weren't as sharp, the brown patches reminded Charlie of the brown stripe, which left other areas perfectly fine.

"Nasty critters." The Chief scratched his head. "Or dry rot. We're down on rain this spring."

Charlie handed back the photos. "Has anybody taken soil samples?"

"I don't know. Let's drive down to Parks and Recreation and find out."

The sky was exceptionally dark for midday. Charlie's suit jacket flapped in the breeze. The ride was two blocks, putting them directly across from the railroad tracks. *Why didn't we just walk?*

As they followed the cobblestone path to the front door, Charlie noticed the numerous clusters of brown circles on the green space surrounding the Parks and Recreation building. "Are these examples of what you mentioned?"

"Yep, here, and across the tracks in large numbers, and then they showed up in folks' backyards."

The brown clusters must be related to the brown stripe. It's a pattern, not a coincidence. Charlie walked closer to examine a sample. "They're all basically the same pattern. And look, the ground has been disturbed." He knelt down and ran his hands over a couple of the circles. "Are those holes in the middles? It almost looks drilled." *What would puncture the ground like that?*

"Told you. Grubs." The Chief pulled his jacket tight across his chest. "The grass is still there, just dead."

Charlie ran his hand over the brown lawn. "From lack of nutrients. Something sucked the life out of the soil."

"You know this?"

"Oh yes. From soil samples on both coasts."

Chief Rogers pushed his hat on his head and almost lost it to the wind. "Well I'll be damned."

Charlie's phone rang. Potter's name showed up on the display. *Jane must have transferred my contacts to the new phone.* "Hey, partner."

"No 'Keyson'? I thought you should know, I was hanging around Fort Greene Park, just in case Kwashay came by, and she did! Even approached me for a conversation."

"Was it productive?"

"For her, I think so. She needs somebody to talk to, and she's come to trust me."

"Great, because when this thing happens, we'll want to give her all the support we can. Who knows what kind of devastation the portals will do if unsupervised?"

"Got it!"

"Thanks for the update." He closed off her call. "Thanks for waiting, Chief. I've got multiple irons in the fire."

"Understood." The Chief led the way.

Inside, the pair was informed that no soil samples had been taken, and that the remedy had been liberal application of LawnGreen brand fertilizer. Shutters on the building clattered.

"Wind is kicking up." Rogers went to the window. The sky had darkened. "Looks like a storm is coming."

Charlie took a peek. "My pilot said the same thing just before landing."

Rogers asked the clerk to change the channel on the wall-mounted TV from a list of community events to local news.

The anchorman was handing the broadcast over to his weatherman colleague.

"I've never seen anything like this, Randy. California has seen its share of localized wind phenomena, like katabatic winds that carry dense air from higher to lower elevations due to gravity. Most of these have occurred in southern California and are known as Santa Ana. We never get straight-line winds like this in our neck of the woods."

The anchorman butted in. "And I heard that we're not the only area being affected by these uncommon winds."

The weatherman replied, "That's right, Dan. We've got the same situation spanning the country from California to New York in one almost perfectly straight line across the country. I've never seen anything like it."

Following the same path as the root system growing towards Kearney from both directions. "I knew it."

The police chief lifted one eyebrow. "Just what do you know?" His walkie-talkie rasped. "Chief, do you copy?"

"I'm here. What's up?" He didn't take his eyes off Charlie.

"The bum from the library escaped. His cell is still locked-"

"How in the hell did he do that?" He spat on the floor. "Never mind. He couldn't have gotten far. Put out an all-points-"

"Already done, Chief."

83 – Matt (Eureka, CA)

"Matt Thready, you in there?"

Matt opened his eyes and lifted his head. The controller was on the floor. The Smuggler's Dash screen saver showed various fruits and vegetables morphing from fresh to rotten, over and over. When his foot nudged the controller, the screen saver vanished. His score, three hundred ninety-nine thousand, four hundred and twenty-seven, and the words "New game?" flashed on the screen. *I must have dozed off in the middle of playing.*

The voice in the hallway asked, "Matt? It's Trev Dixon."

Matt shook his head. *That bastard?* "What do you want?"

Dixon stepped in, his movement tentative in the dark. "I haven't seen you down by the trellises – I mean, portal."

"Yeah, well, once I figured out that the portal can take care of itself, I didn't have to stand guard, did

I? The Feds are taking care of that." Matt promised himself not to share any more information.

Dixon pointed at the TV. "Getting in some relaxation before class?"

Matt checked his watch. *Ten fifteen A.M.. I wonder what time I dozed off?* "Don't you remember? I don't attend school here anymore. Just leave me alone." He reached for the pizza box on the floor.

"So, if you're not taking classes, what are you still doing here?"

"Practicing." Matt opened the box. Pepperoni, his favorite. He yanked out a triangular slice, folded the tip to the edge and took a bite. *Good even cold.*

"For what?" asked Dixon.

"Never mind." Matt's phone vibrated on the floor, generating a repetitive raspy thumping.

"You want to get that?" asked Dixon.

His phone was reminding him about a his collected voice mail messages. *Must not have heard them.* Last time he looked, they were all were from his folks'. "Nah."

Dixon cleared his throat. "The reason I stopped by, I managed to hang onto one of our measurement devices. The level of electrical transmission has significantly increased, day by day. Do you know what that means?"

The portal is getting ready for operation, as soon as the last stick is installed. "Nope. Want a slice?"

"Thanks." Dixon lifted a piece from the box and took a bite. "Not bad." He chewed a bit and then spoke with pizza still in his mouth. "You sure you don't know what that's about?"

"What do you think, that the portal is performing some sort of mental telepathy with me?

Well, it's not. It's just a bunch of dumb sticks." *That commanded me to be their operator.* Perhaps the portal was communicating with someone else. His partner operator?

"You won't be good to anybody in your current condition. Are you getting any sleep?"

"Listen, I already have two parents. Besides, you're in no position to give me any advice." Matt rubbed his eyes. *I did doze off while playing.* "Yeah. Sure." *As soon as I hit one million.* He shoved another cold slice into his mouth.

"I'm afraid the – portal – is going haywire, that's all. You need to be fit if you're going to help."

"Why do you care about help? You just want to destroy it."

"You've got me all wrong. Ever since I learned about its special properties, I want to understand it. How it works. What's it's here for."

Probably to make money off it. "You'll find out soon enough. And I'll be the one who shows you."

"You're the operator, right?

Matt jumped to his feet. "Who told you that?"

"My buddy Keyson from the EPA. He said his portal in New York City had a female operator, and mine would need one. My guess is, that's you."

Mine? The bastard still claims ownership? "You're making things up to trick me. Well, I won't fall for it. Get out!"

Dixon threw a chilling smile. "Okay, but I look forward to your performance. Keep practicing."

Matt plopped into his chair and pulled the controller into his hand by the cord. *That guy is dangerous.*

84 – Kwashay (Brooklyn, NY)

After her last class, Kwashay stood in the crowd gathered at the edge of the cordoned-off area. Soldiers with weapons guarded her portal. *At least no one can harm it this way. But I don't know how I'm going to do my part, when the time comes. I wonder if the other portal is being guarded?* She made her way through the crowd, to the sidewalk executing the short walk to the subway.

Kwashay rode the train with her nose in the Advanced Placement Biology textbook in her lap. She'd spent so much time practicing video games that she needed every minute of the ride to catch up with her schoolwork. She got off the train at Saratoga station and was halfway down to street level when the staircase shook. She grabbed the handrail and listened to her mother's voice advise: "The portal requires its operator."

Now? She crossed the street and headed up the stairs to the westbound platform, to catch the next train toward downtown and Fort Greene Park.

85 - Selton (Kearney, NE)

Selton stumbled haphazardly toward the power station under a quilted-grey blanket sky. Wind-blown debris hurled from both east and west pelted him, pummeling his softened torso. The power station was secure, with gated entrance and guards on duty. He couldn't just walk in.

Selton clutched his thin green jacket as he navigated the fence, putting himself at considerable distance from the guard shack. After looking both ways, he climbed the chain links, jabbing his toes into the gaps to hold his weight. Barbed wire along the top tore off a swatch of his pants as well as a piece of his thigh as he catapulted himself to the other side. He was over!

He tugged his fedora down hard as he ran for one of the towers. *Now, to get some distance between the ground and me.*

86 – Charlie (Kearney, NE)

Before they left Parks and Recreation, the Chief's walkie-talkie rasped again. "What is it now?"

"The power station called. Somebody breeched security and is climbing one of the towers."

"What's the fool trying to do, electrocute himself?"

"Looks that way. From their description, he might be our escaped bum."

"Damn it!" He bolted for the door.

"Can I come with?" asked Charlie.

"Damn right! I'm not done with you yet." The Chief called for backup from the fire department, but asked them to approach without sirens, lest the sound disturb the climber and cause him to fall. He also asked for police backup, with the same warning.

Then he led Charlie out to his car for the one-mile drive, almost directly south. They arrived on the scene before anyone else, pulling onto the grounds of the power station after the guard lifted the gate.

In an empty field across the street to the east, Charlie saw the brown stripe, still fifty feet wide. "See, that's what I was talking about. And if we drove around to the west side of the plant, we'd find another brown stripe, headed in this direction."

"What does that have to do with Kearney or that self-destructive vagrant?" Although it was early afternoon, clouds darkened the sky, and the wind had picked up. The chief aimed a high-powered spotlight at the climber. His clothes were raggedy. He was almost flopping from support to support, looking more like a giant beanbag than a human being.

The fire department arrived, one ladder truck, one ambulance and one rescue vehicle. A team of five first responders pulled a life net from their truck. A man with a distinct yellow fireman's hat came over. "Hey, Chief, what have we got here?"

"Our resident scholarly hobo has taken on a new hobby."

"Normally, I wouldn't think of using a life net, but there's no way I'm extending my ladder close to those power lines."

The Chief nodded. "See if you can get under him, in case he lets go. Damn, I hope he doesn't make it to the transmission wires."

The higher the climber went, the clearer it was that the wires were indeed his destination.

"Is there anything we can do to get him down?" asked Charlie.

"We? You're not suggesting I send one of my men up after him, are you?" asked the Chief. "Or are you volunteering?"

Charlie's phone rang. "Keyson." The connection was highly static. Charlie didn't know if it was the power station interference or the brown stripe, probably the latter. He backed off a dozen yards or so, close to the fence. "Keyson."

"Mr. Keyson, it's Jane."

Still not calling me Charlie. He hadn't checked in to the office. *Without the call from the Director, I would have expected they'd written me off.*

"Hi." The vagrant was still climbing, slower. "What's up?"

"I saw your voice message light blinking. I thought it might be important."

"Who was it from?"

"Mrs. Williams-Jackson. She sounded really upset. Her daughter didn't come home after school. Is that serious?"

I'd provided Kwashay my card, and her mother used it to call my office. "Maybe. Thanks for letting me know. I think I know where her daughter is. Did she leave a number?"

"I not speak to her. I just open your voice mail."

That wasn't what I'd asked. "Okay. Are you still caring for AquaLung?"

"Oh yes. And I not overfeeding him, like you told me. Will you be back soon? We miss you."

Charlie wasn't convinced that was true for anyone in the office except her. "Pretty soon."

"Oh, I almost forgot. Someone from underground radar company called. They finished their survey and have results."

Too little, too late. "I'll call them when I get back."

"Pretty soon you said?"

"Yes." Charlie took a deep breath, an image of Jane's sweet face in his mind. "We'll talk when I get back. About us."

"I like that." Her voice was a bird's warble.

"Bye."

As soon as Charlie disconnected, before he could tuck his emotions neatly away, his phone rang again. "Keyson."

"Hey, partner, it's Stephanie. You told me to keep an eye on Kwashay? Well, I just got a call from her mother, who says she's missing. Sorry, I screwed up."

Charlie didn't share Jane's news. "No, you didn't. She'll be at her portal in Fort Greene Park."

"Of course, I should have thought of that!"

"And I want you to do everything you can to assist her as operator."

There a pause on Potter's end. "Everything?" She audibly sighed. "Okay, I'll call you when I get there."

If Kwashay was headed to her portal, then Matt was surely doing the same thing at his end. He dialed Nachas' number.

"Gregory Nachas, EPA."

"This is Keyson. How's Matt?"

"Good news. I talked to his best friend, Fred. Says he's fully recovered, playing video games like his life depended on it. Why, what's up?"

I wish Nachas had seen Matt in person instead of relying on a third-party. "Get over to the College as quick as you can. I need you there to protect him." Charlie didn't say from what.

"From Dixon?"

Smart man. "Yes, and maybe more. Do what you can to help him operate that portal."

"Are you sure? We don't know what it's going to do."

Charlie stared at the climber. "Especially if they're weapons, I'd rather have human beings at the trigger."

"Got it. I'll do everything I can."

Charlie was convinced that the climbing hobo and the two students were connected. *Patterns.* After all, the brown stripe was common to them all. And their locations were all lined up across the continent.

The Chief came over. "I've sent officers to bring the librarian here. She knows him best. Maybe she can talk him down."

Charlie was skeptical but nodded.

87 – Matt (Eureka, CA)

Matt was laying on Fred's bed, taking a break after reaching a new personal best that put his game score within the top five nationally, when he heard his father's voice in his head: "The portal requires its operator."

It was time! *I'm prepared as I'm going to be.* Matt slid his legs to the floor and staggered out of Fred's room. He ran as fast as he could, down the stairs of the dorm, along the sidewalk and across the ball field. Dixon's motor home was still on the goal line. *He's going to be the audience while I go in for the score.* He trampled through the brush to the woods. The sky was overcast, as if a storm was coming.

The wind gusted at his back, urging him forward. He stomped past a few trees to reach the clearing. Artificial lights had been erected on three sides of the boundary. The portal was still surrounded by red tape and protected by four guards. But the portal didn't have to be protected from him. He was the operator.

There was a commotion in progress. A small crowd had gathered at one end of the red-taped area, interacting with National Guard soldiers. Two Guardsmen stood sentinel, keeping a few portal groupies on the outside of the barrier. As news of the strange structure had spread around campus, a small group of hexagonists – that's what they called themselves – took up residence at the secured boundary. *With their hexagon-decorated t-shirts and poems, do they think it's some kind of religious artifact?*

At the bare connection points for the missing stick, the portal was sparking. *Maybe I can do something to fix the problem. If only I had the last stick!* He reached the tape barrier and lifted it, preparing to enter.

"Oh no! Not him! Keep him away!" Dixon, the one who'd shaken and threatened him, remained a threat to the mission.

"He's not in charge." Matt fought the soldier. "Let me through!" He was holding his own, almost breaking free, but then there were two. The National Guardsmen held Matt's arms tight, preventing him from moving despite his thrashing legs.

Then a familiar touch on his shoulder: his mother beside him, urging him with a single word to be calm, not to fight. "Please?".

He continued to struggle, attempting to meet the portal's expectations, despite her request. It was no use. Two trained soldiers had enough strength to incapacitate him. He stood, helpless, each arm still gripped by a guard on each side, watching the portal try in vain to achieve full power. But without the last stick, it would fail, and so would the mission.

Matt wasn't concerned about Dixon's presence. *Even if they let him through, it won't do him any good because I'm the operator.*

"He won't make a fuss," said Mrs. Thready. "I promise."

The guards let go of Matt. He shook off their latent contact, then paced along the red plastic BATES barrier. *I can't make my mother out to be a liar.* The rods had grown so thick that the spaces between them had shrunk to little more than a foot. *How can I operate the portal if I can't get inside? The soldiers won't let me near the structure anyway.*

The only upside was, they were also keeping Dixon at bay, but just barely. Soldiers were having friendly chats with him, smiling and laughing. He was their friend. Matt was just another pesky student. *Who knows? The soldiers are probably being funded by Bates Industries.*

88 - Kwashay (Brooklyn, NY)

Kwashay stood a foot behind the dirty, tattered yellow police tape in Fort Greene Park, staring at the portal. She had to hold down her skirt to prevent it from flapping in the breeze. Her locket whipped around to her back. Six state militia stood guard at the circumference, matching the vertices of the structures. The rods had grown since the portal's construction, and even thicker than her last visit. *As skinny as I am, I don't think I can squeeze through. But I'm supposed to be inside.*

Wind swirled dust and debris around the portal. Military guards staggered but held their ground. Kwashay also fought against the wind, which had become a hazard to pedestrians and drivers alike. Trees, which, if healthy, would have bent instead broke off, their trunks and branches carried along the ground.

She jumped at the touch on her shoulder.

"Hey, girly-girl, what's up?" Sideways stood behind her in his construction clothes and hardhat, which was positioned brim-forward.

"Oh, hi. I didn't expect to see you here."

"I stop by every chance I get. You know, to keep an eye on our thing." He pointed in the direction of the portal.

The crowd was considerable and growing, as passersby seemed to be drawn by the assembled crowd as much as the portal itself.

"I have to get inside," she whispered.

"What? Inside the thing? How you gonna do that?"

"Maybe there's a button or a latch. I have to get closer."

"There weren't no doors when we built it." Sideways' head turned, surveying the situation. "If you wants to get closer, me and my crew can make a fuss, you know, a distraction."

She put her hand on Sideways' chest. "No, you can't. You're on probation. Just imagine what a judge will say if you're involved in a scuffle, especially with soldiers."

"You right." He adjusted his hardhat, pushing it back a bit on his head.

Another tap on the other shoulder. "Kwashay, are you all right?"

It was the female agent from the EPA. *Potter?* "Yes, of course." *What did she want?* She felt like she had to introduce her to Sideways. "This is Agent Potter from the New York EPA. She interviewed me about my art project."

"You must be the young man Kwashay mentioned." Potter extended her hand.

His face got red. "You said you didn't rat me out."

"I didn't. I never told them your name." *Not even now.*

"Well, okay then." Sideways folded his arms on his chest.

Potter withdrew her offer to shake. "I spoke to Agent Keyson. Your mother is looking for you." Potter glanced at the portal, her eyes returning to Kwashay. "He thinks the time has come. You're supposed to operate that thing now, right?"

Kwashay nodded. "I have to get inside."

"Inside the portal?" Agent Potter took another look. "Although there might be room inside the inner hexagon for a person, there's no way to climb in. Unless you're a contortionist."

"The soldiers will grab me before I can get close enough to look for a way in."

Agent Potter looked around, scratching her head. She smiled and put one arm on each of their shoulders, like a miniature football huddle. "We'll need a series of distractions."

Sideways popped to vertical. "See, just what I said!"

Potter pulled him back down. "You're working on a construction project near here?"

"Yes, ma'am. Over on Flatbush."

"And there are scaffolds?"

He nodded.

That's what got Sideways into trouble in the first place.

"Well, in this fierce wind, there might be a public hazard. And the soldiers should be notified, right?"

Sideways smiled. "I can do that."

"Then, when some of them go off to investigate – you'll lead them there, and take the long route – I'll introduce myself to one of the remaining guards. And I might argue with him a bit. Maybe even raise my voice. Which should get the attention of the other guards. With some guards paying attention to an irate government official, that'll be your opportunity. Got it?"

Kwashay was flabbergasted that someone from the EPA was going to help distract the soldiers so she could get to the portal. She just hoped there was a control to open it up.

Potter patted Sideways' shoulder. "Okay, you're on."

They watched as Sideways made his way through the crowd to the soldier on the west side of the sculpture. Kwashay handed Potter her backpack and headed in the opposite direction. In front of the soldier, Sideways pointed a waving arm, making the most of his acting debut. The soldier he spoke with tried to use a radio, unsuccessfully. With hand gestures, he ordered three of his squad to follow Sideways towards Flatbush Avenue.

Evidently, that soldier was in charge. Agent Potter approached and flashed her badge. She pointed at the portal and stepped forward, as if to cross the barrier. He put his gun across his chest, to block her advance. She shouted at him, flung her arms in random directions, making a big fuss over something

Kwashay couldn't hear. The other guards crept slowly from their positions toward Potter in support of their colleague. Potter escalated, shouting directly into his face while stomping her foot and flailing her arms.

Kwashay saw her chance. She broke through the yellow plastic tape and ran for the portal. The guards saw her movement, but they were out of position. Besides, with the tape gone, the psychological barrier restraining the crowd vanished. Curious citizens advanced towards the portal, effectively preventing the soldiers from intercepting her. When Kwashay was within two steps of the structure, a section of the outer hexagon slid back, followed by a similar gap in the inner one. As soon as she was inside, the bars slid closed. She was the operator, trapped inside an absolutely quiet cage with nary a breath of moving air.

Kwashay looked out between the fat rods. The soldiers struggled to push the crowd back. In the distance, she saw her mother, standing with Agent Potter's arm around her.

89 – Selton (Kearney, NE)

Selton folded his fedora and tucked it into his back pocket. *It'll never stay on my head with this heavy wind.* He found the tower climb exhausting. His last recuperation opportunity had been the previous night, and it was now early afternoon, a normally sluggish period. The potpourri had provided scant nutrition. Attempting a climb to distance himself from the imminent megafeeding was a struggle. *If the seeds within me get a dose of that potent nutrition, I will effectively have orchestrated an invasion. I can't be party to that.*

From his vantage point, the convergence of two brown stripes below him was evident. *That's how the Reverend found me! Brown, like the patches I've left behind after my nightly feedings. But why two, from opposite directions?*

90 – Charlie (Kearney, NE)

A police squad car pulled through the gated entrance to the power plant. An officer opened the back door and escorted a woman from the vehicle.

"Thank you for coming," said the Chief. "Mr. Keyson, this is Bernice Martin, our public librarian. Mr. Keyson is from the EPA in Washington."

Bernice wasn't looking at Charlie. Her head tilted back, fingertips covered her mouth. "Oh my goodness! That's Selton, isn't it?"

"We believe so," said the Chief.

"Ms. Martin, can you tell us about him?" Charlie wasn't sure he had her attention. "He visits your library frequently, I take it."

Bernice gazed at Selton, unblinking. "Mercy, yes. When he first arrived in town, he was in the library from open to close, maybe even a bit longer. I'd let him in early and we'd stay late if it wasn't my bridge or yoga nights." She finally made eye contact with Charlie. "What is he doing up there?"

"That's why we asked you to come. Perhaps something in his recent behavior will shed light on-"

"But he's such a peaceful and gentle soul. Why would he bring this upon us?"

She'd obviously developed a close relationship, if she viewed herself as being hurt by his actions. "Maybe he's not the cause. Maybe he's the victim."

"You're on to something there, Mr. Keyson." She forced a half smile. "You know, he hasn't been the same for a while now. Even before the Bible thumpers came and hunted him down like an animal. They should have been ashamed!" The smile melted as her eyes shifted away from Charlie to her daily patron, clinging to the tower braces.

"Does he do anything at the library besides read? Does he talk with you or anyone else?"

Her eyes connected with Charlie. "He practically lives there. I've never met a more dedicated or voracious reader. Books are his life."

She'd been unresponsive to the question. "Has he exhibited any unusual behavior lately? Anything out of the ordinary?"

"No, not really." She scratched her head but didn't disturb a single grey hair or the precise bun on the top of her head. She took another glance at Selton, high on the tower but then pulled her eyes away. "Lately, he's been leaving well before closing. He doesn't seem to have the same energy. I was worried, but I didn't want to pry. He's a very private individual."

"Okay, that's something. Do you two talk much?"

"Just simple pleasantries when he arrives and departs." Her fingertips touched her forehead. "Until a few days ago, when he asked me the strangest question. He wanted a recommendation for the best science fiction books about alien invasions."

Trev Dixon's prediction reverberated in Charlie's head. "What did you say?"

"I got him the books, three in stock and one I had to transfer in."

Charlie swallowed hard. Could he have used them as a how-to manual? "Did he read them?"

"Oh yes, that same day. He wasn't very happy with them, I'm afraid." She paused. "Oh, and the last time he was in the library, I gave him a tube of Rolaids from my purse. Is that important?" Her eyes returned to her patron.

People who have gastric distress don't climb transmission towers for relief. "When's the last time you saw him?"

"Last night. I brought him the fourth book to read while he was in jail."

Charlie looked at the Chief for an explanation.

"Protective custody, that's all."

"The book had just come in from another facility. *The Day of the Triffids.*"

Isn't that about an invasion of Earth by plants? "Dixon!" he muttered.

"No, John Wyndham, 1951," said the librarian. "His best-known novel." She kept glancing up at the hobo, then averting her eyes. "Is there something I can do? Maybe if he hears my voice, he'll climb down."

The Chief threw Charlie a glance. "Couldn't hurt." He fetched a megaphone from his squad car trunk. "Here."

Bernice took the megaphone in hand, squeezed the trigger and spoke in a soft but amplified voice. "Selton, it's Bernice. I've just received a batch of new releases. They're waiting just for you. I won't let anyone else check them out. Please come down."

Selton didn't move.

"Oh, how horrible!" She almost dropped the megaphone but the Chief caught it.

The Chief called the driver over. "Escort Ms. Martin home." She cried as the officer, arm around her shoulder, led her to his vehicle.

"It was worth a shot. I'd really like to speak with him." Charlie wondered if the police chief felt as helpless as he did.

The wind got even stronger.

"I'm sure glad they're not using a ladder." The police chief held his hand in front of his face to deflect dust. "It'd blow over for sure."

Charlie's phone rang. "Sorry, I need to take this."

"Busy fella, aren't ya'?" The chief walked away towards the fire commander and the security fence.

Charlie backed up. "Keyson."

"It's Potter. You were right, Kwashay was at the portal, but now she's inside."

"Makes sense. How could she operate it from the outside? How did she get in?"

"I helped, per your instructions. By distracting the soldiers, she had an opportunity. When she got close, it slid open, as if it was expecting her. Her lips are moving, but it's like a muted TV. Oh, and her mother is here with me. She's very upset."

"I'm not surprised." Charlie's phone registered an incoming call. "Hold on." The screen showed touchable buttons, one of which was HOLD AND ACCEPT CALL. He tapped it. "Keyson."

"It's Greg Nachas. I'm here at the College with Matt."

Charlie was expecting a pattern. "Is he inside the portal?"

"No, the National Guard has the portal pretty well secure. Nobody's going to get close to it. Man, the wind has really picked up."

"Listen carefully. Matt is bonded to the structure. He's the operator."

"What's to operate?" asked Nachas. "It's gotten really dark, and we're being pelted by twigs and leaves."

Charlie heard a side conversation. "Nachas?"

The voice on the other end changed. "It's Matt. You know me, the operator?"

"Yes, Matt, just like Kwashay is the operator in Brooklyn's portal."

"Is that her name? She called herself PortalPal. I've seen her face, in my head I mean. Can you order the soldiers to let me get to the portal?"

"Outside my jurisdiction, I'm afraid. But the portal should open up when you get close. That's what happened for Kwashay."

"Okay, thanks."

There was a faint side conversation before Nachas' voice returned. "I'll see if the National Guard will listen to me, but I doubt it. They seem to have a better working relationship with Dixon."

Dixon? I thought we were done with him. "Maybe he can convince them to let Matt close."

"I'll ask."

"Don't hang up, I'm going to try to conference you in. I'm on the line with an EPA agent in Brooklyn."

Charlie found an ADD CALL TO EXISTING button. "Are you there, Potter?"

"Yes."

"And you, Nachas?"

"Still here."

Charlie made quick introductions.

"Are either of Matt's parent's there?" asked Charlie.

Nachas paused before replying. "His mother showed up a while ago. No sign of his father."

"I'm glad she's there, for support. He'll need it." *Or maybe she can provide a distraction like Potter did.*

91 – Matt (Eureka, CA)

Matt had been prepared to physically assault a guard to get to the portal until his mother promised he'd behave. He pressed hard against the red plastic barrier, which stretched but didn't break. One of the guards laughed at him. *I'm pathetic, a mama's boy.*

He kept one eye on the portal as he spoke to his mother. "What are you doing here?"

"We were worried, leaving you behind, so I didn't drive back with your father. Then Fred called and told me you were playing video games non-stop."

"Great, my best friend rats me out again. Where's Dad?"

"Your father was called away on business, but he's just as concerned as I am." She ran her hand up and down his arm.

The local EPA agent was chatting with one of the National Guard soldiers, pointing in Matt's direction. Matt looked at his mother. "They won't let me through, I just know it."

She took him by both shoulders and stood face-to-face. "Now there, don't be pessimistic. Threadys are winners."

Nachas came back after his consultation. "They said no one gets closer."

"What did Dixon say? Did he speak up on my behalf?" Matt bounced on the balls of his feet, hands jammed into the front pockets of his jeans.

Nachas shook his head. "He didn't weigh in on the topic."

Asshole. "Figures." Matt considered his options: violating his mother's promise and fighting his way through, bribing the guards, or distracting them with something more important.

The voice in Matt's head announced it just before he saw the missing stick, leaning against a nearby tree, outside the guarded perimeter.

Matt bolted from his position at the red tape. He saw Dixon's eyes follow him, but Matt had a first mover advantage. He swiped the rod from the ground and held it aloft, the last component the portal needed. Matt ran to the barrier and shook the stick. "I have to install it!"

The soldier yanked the stick from Matt's grasp. "Don't you know better than to threaten a soldier with a weapon?"

Matt clenched his fists. "It's not a weapon. It's the missing piece."

Dixon sauntered over. "I'll take that. It's Bates Enterprises property." The soldier handed Dixon the two-foot long rod. "Just like that trellis."

"Give it back!" Matt reached for the stick but Dixon held it away, beyond Matt's grasp. "I'm the operator."

"And I'm the owner. Don't you get that?" Dixon addressed the soldier. "May I please install this in its rightful location? You're supposed to be protecting this structure. How better to protect it than let me add a missing component?"

"I have my orders. No one goes near that thing." He brought his rifle up to his chest.

Dixon glared at the soldier. "You can't believe that having it sit there and spark is better than having it repaired! What if those sparks start a forest fire? Then what? You'll be responsible." He poked the soldier's chest. "Why don't you check with your superiors?"

The guard tried to use his radio. "All I get is static."

"The portal gives off electromagnetic radiation. Try again at a distance."

The guard called another soldier over. "Keep these two apart, and away from the trellis thing." He ducked under the red plastic tape and marched out of the clearing.

The soldier jogged back into position after a few minutes of Matt staring at Dixon and Dixon ignoring the student. He swiveled his head, from Dixon to the animated student and back. "Okay, go ahead and install it. After all, it's yours."

Matt tilted his head back. "Nooo!"

Dixon wore a self-satisfied grin. "You be quiet or I'll have you removed from the vicinity. You got that?"

"You can make the fix, but you're not in charge. Got it?" asked the soldier.

Dixon saluted. "Yes, sir."

Matt's mother led her son away from the escalating confrontation. "It'll be okay."

"No it won't, not if he fixes the portal." Matt stood by, helpless, as Dixon walked directly to the proper side of the portal and lifted the thin stick into the precisely correct position. "Now, let's see what you can do when you're complete."

After the stick snapped into place, with it still in his grasp, Dixon stood frozen, his body stiff. An aura formed around the man's body. He stood stone rigid, as if glued to the structure.

Matt felt the portal abandoning its connection to him. The urgency to act, to take his rightful place as the operator, faded. His legs felt like rubber. As he collapsed, his mother and a guard held him up. Matt knew what was happening to Dixon, the same thing that happened to him. Dixon was being probed, his memories examined. He knew personally Dixon's experience of bonding with the portal, becoming its operator. The missing stick bulked up, becoming as thick as the others. The portal was complete.

Dixon's head wobbled. Matt felt his connection with the portal fading away. By connecting the fresh rod to the portal, Dixon had become the operator. And Dixon's obligation was at hand.

Matt crushed the red plastic barrier in his fists, his mother's arm around his shoulders. Feelings of urgent action had faded, replaced with pure jealousy.

An area in the outer hexagon slid open. Dixon looked in both directions and pivoted, slipping into the opening before any of the soldiers noticed.

"Look!" Matt pointed at the portal. "See what you did? He's inside."

Once Dixon breeched the inner hexagon, the bars slid shut.

The soldiers converged on the structure, hitting it with the butts of their guns, shouting at Dixon to come out. But the portal had its operator and wasn't going to give him up until he'd completed his task.

The wind kicked up, blowing dust around. Some of the military men put on goggles. Others held up gloved hands to ward off the gritty air.

The wind got even stronger. Neighboring trees swayed. One entire stand of trees creaked, groaned, and fell in an awkward pile. The portal stood immovable against the wind.

Dixon turned inside, examining his cage. One horizontal stick on the east side of the structure at waist height lit up, a throbbing blue. Dixon faced east and put his hands on the stick.

His mother stood back while Matt shook his fists above his head. "Damn, that was my job!"

'Was', because Matt's bond with the portal was gone.

92 – Kwashay (Brooklyn, NY)

Kwashay stood prisoner in a space too small to pace. *Nothing is happening. Maybe it isn't ready.* There were no sounds except her heartbeat, which was faster than normal. *This is the right time, I just feel it.* She adjusted her locket and then wiggled her fingers as a limbering exercise.

Without warning, two glowing handprints appeared in the horizontal bar at waist height on the west side of the portal. She placed her hands, palms down, on the bright areas.

Voices coaxed Kwashay to close her eyes. Instantly she felt the ground drop out from under her while her hands were still on the rod. She peeked through her mostly-shut eyes momentarily. Nothing had changed.

When she closed her eyes again, she seemed to be below ground, twelve tubes surrounding her, merging into six thicker ones, curving off into the distance. A long way away, a object appeared, a miniature version of her portal. This wasn't a reflection or a mirage. She was seeing the portal's mate, the one she'd sensed before. As her hands slipped along the surface of the rod in front of her, she felt movement. Just like a game controller, manipulating the bar was an acceleration and aiming mechanism. She knew instinctively that her job as operator was to traverse the distance, keeping both portals aligned.

She sampled the responses with a variety of gestures. The crossbar responded with forward movement when she rolled her hands forward. Sliding her hands left and right could modify her horizontal orientation. *Just like a flat joystick! I can do this!* Kwashay had played enough video games to be very comfortable with hand controllers although she'd never had great skill in zapping aliens.

Beside the six main tunnels, there were dozens of smaller offshoots, all leading away from her position in various directions. The voice in her head directed her to fly through the thickest tunnels, delivering an unspecified cargo that pushed at her from behind. She thrust her arms forward, fingers extended against the bar. With agile wrist movement, she zoomed through the largest tunnel, which formed from the merging of the six big ones. The shape and texture of the smaller tunnels looked root-like. *These aren't tunnels! I'm traveling through the portal root system! I wonder what's at the end?*

93 – Selton (Kearney, NE)

Selton's heart would have broken at Bernice's pleas, if he had a heart. Instead, he felt very bad. More shaking, this time the tower itself, interrupted his reverie. He held on tight as the resonance translated to sounds in his head.

"You are our designated ambassador. Make yourself available for the megafeeding."

Ambassador? Attack force commander is more like it.

Selton felt confident that if he maintained sufficient distance above the ground, the megafeeding would come and go. He could dismount the tower and walk away, probably into the arms of a police officer. *How many laws have I broken? Escaping from custody. Trespassing. Endangering private property. All while preventing an invasion.*

The megafeeding arrived, showing itself as a bulge in the grass below Selton's aerial position at the point where the brown stripes merged. The mound sat there, expecting a prone Serulian ready to absorb the excessive nutrition.

Since I'm not down there, the nutritive soil has no one to absorb it. The mound might grow for a while, but it's useless. Sorry, you'll just have to be content making that hill of very green grass.

Selton wrapped his arms around a crossbeam and hung there, waiting for the mound to settle. But it didn't. A cracking sound announced the fissure. The mound split open. Rich, black soil oozed out.

He felt relieved as the nutrient-laden soil bubbled from the fissure. *No problem, it's a simple mound of dirt, no harm to me. So what if some of the megafeeding breaks through? I can spend my last days comfortably reading, rotting away in the public library. Or a jail cell.*

A second sound punctuated the howl of the wind. The tower shook again, this time from the rumbling quake. Beneath him, the ground split wide open, accompanied by a dirt fountain spurting from the crevice, jumping to several feet. The firemen abandoned their position below him. *No threat.* Just in case, Selton stretched his arm up to the next beam and dragged himself higher.

No reason to take chances.

94 – Charlie (Kearney, NE)

Charlie watched the firemen holding the life net scatter as dirt accumulated at the fissure beneath the climber. "I've got something happening here," he announced to the other participants of his conference call. Glistening dirt bubbled up from the crack, forming a mound of sparkly soil.

He stared at the growing pile while holding the cellphone to his ear. Potter and Nachas took turns describing what they were seeing at the portals.

"You won't believe it, but Dixon is inside the Eureka portal," said Nachas.

"How'd he manage that?" asked Charlie. "I thought Matt was bonded to it."

"The missing stick showed up, and Dixon installed it."

Given their previous conversation, Charlie was certain the loss of responsibility would weigh heavy on the young man. "Damn! The portal must have decided that Dixon's now the operator."

"You talk like these structures are intelligent, making decisions," said Potter.

"They put words and images inside Kwashay and Matt's heads – most likely now Dixon's. That's pretty unbelievable, but what's the old saying? Perception is reality."

"To Kwashay, that portal is alive, and communicating with her. She's leaning against the horizontal bar, like she was pushing a lawn mower."

"I don't know what Dixon is doing. Maybe dancing with an invisible partner?"

Charlie heard Matt holler "Jerk!" in the background.

All the while, he watched Selton climb the tower, moving one level higher. Selton's jacket snapped in the wind.

Charlie considered the underlying theme common to the Grissom novels. *There's always one bad guy, the kingpin of the operation, that Grissom has to identify. In this situation, everything points to Selton, but he's the most reluctant antagonist I've ever seen.*

"I wish I could get a sample of that dirt. It's darker and richer than any soil I've ever seen." Charlie startled that he spoke his thoughts out loud.

Potter interrupted. "Kwashay's mother is here. Right now, she's peppering one of the National Guard with questions. She asked me if this is the game tournament, and how well her daughter is doing. What do I say?"

Must have been a story Kwashay fabricated. "Tell her that Kwashay is doing just fine." Charlie remembered Dixon's promise of a scholarship for Matt. *Why not one for her as well?* "Tell her I'm confident she'll come away a winner."

"If you say so."

"This isn't a tournament, is it?" asked Nachas.

"No, Greg, it's something much more serious."

"Kwashay changed her stance. She was upright, but now she's leaning forward, hanging onto one of the sticks for dear life. Or maybe she's pushing it. I can't tell."

"Is the structure moving?" asked Charlie.

"Oh no. It's solidly in place. But given the apparent wind in her face, it must feel like she's going eighty miles an hour."

"Dixon looks like the portal is dragging him along for the ride."

"She's doing something. I don't know if I'd call it operating. More like driving, except her portal is still in place. Wait, I just noticed, the bars are getting thinner."

"Same here. They're nowhere near as thick as before Dixon got in. He's really struggling. It's obvious he's in way over his head."

Charlie heard Matt's voice in the background. "Darn right he is!"

"Kwashay is facing west, just like you'd expect-"

"-and Dixon is facing east-"

"I wonder if they can see each other?" asked Charlie.

"You must be kidding. They're hundreds of miles apart," said Nachas.

"In a world where sculptures and trellises communicate, anything is possible," replied Charlie.

"What's going on where you are?" asked Potter.

"I've got a vagrant who used to visit the library for hours on end, climbing up a power station tower. The ground below him split open and there's a growing pile of the richest soil I've ever seen, maybe six or seven feet tall and getting taller. Don't ask me why this is relevant, except the split is precisely where the brown stripes have joined up, from east and west. And I'd bet anything there's going to be an eruption."

His compatriots were silent.

95 – Matt (Eureka, CA)

Matt leaned against the red BATES security tape, his mother's arm around his shoulder. They both stood within earshot of Nachas, the EPA guy, who was on his cellphone.

Matt was desperate to let his mother know how much more competent an operator he would have been, if only they'd given him the chance. Failing that, he was determined to share his perspective on Dixon's performance within the portal.

He elbowed his mother as Dixon's shoes slipped on the grass. "See that? He's not controlling the portal. It's practically dragging him along." He hoped his mother wouldn't look down at his shoes, whose rubber soles wouldn't have done any better than Dixon's leather loafers. *In retrospect, an operator should be wearing cleats.* Matt switched topics. "He'll never succeed that way. He didn't practice like I did."

"Is this really that important?" she asked. "It looks like he's performing an exercise routine."

"Yes, oh God, yes! If he doesn't coordinate with the other operator-"

His mother pulled back. "There's another one?"

"Yes, a pretty girl in Brooklyn who calls herself PortalPal. She and I were chosen to operate the portals."

"Do you know this girl? We've never been to Brooklyn. You know how distracting girls were at Dartmouth."

"I've only seen her here." He pointed to his head. Matt kept his eyes on Dixon, hanging from the control bar. "I never figured out why I was chosen, let alone somebody else. Maybe because we both love nature?" It wasn't the right time to mention what kind of work he wanted to do long-term.

"This is all so confusing, sticks and portals. I don't understand what he's doing." Matt's mother clutched her purse even tighter.

"He doesn't either. Dixon is a dangerous novice. He's going to mess it up, I just know it. Why didn't they let me do it?" He looked deep into his mother's eyes. He found empathy but no answers.

Dixon's body thrashed like a towel being shaken.

He's going to ruin the opportunity for the whole planet.

96 – Kwashay (Brooklyn, NY)

Manipulating the directional controls of the portal was familiar to Kwashay, much like the video game controller. In fact, her video game practice had been so rigorous that navigating the payload through the portal root system was easy in comparison.

She was so comfortable that she decided to experiment. When she lifted her hands from the control rod, her forward momentum slowed and sparkly specks rushed into her field of view from behind. Most of the speckles flowed into smaller roots that branched off the main run. Pressure behind her eased.

Now I know why I'm guiding the payload. If it flowed on it's own, it would distribute to every root branch, big or small, throughout the entire system. I'm here to direct the flow forward to the target location.

Kwashay returned her hands to the control rod and pushed forward with greater urgency. In the far distance, she viewed the faint image, almost a shadow, of her operator partner who was working in concert with her to deliver his payload from the West Coast. *We need to be coordinated.* He was surrounded, almost overtaken, by glittery specks.

Clearly, NeedleAndThready is not in control.

97 – Selton (Kearney, NE)

Selton watched the fountain of nutritive-rich soil percolate higher in spurts. It loomed successively taller as if reaching up for him, desperate to deliver its healthy payload to the seeds within his body. *I can't let it touch me.* Selton shimmied higher, to the next crossbeam, one step closer to the power cable itself. At this range, he heard the buzzing of electricity.

Selton noticed the two brown stripes coming together at the fissure and the lean of the fountain at a westerly angle. *The pressure from the east is stronger.*

Selton felt the seeds inside wiggling in anticipation, seeking their germination potential.

Thousands of future invaders wanted instinctively to be fed. At the same time, Selton's pulpy mass was softening in response to the nearby exposed power conductors. *I'm being cooked from the inside!*

Selton hung on with both arms, fighting the wind and fatigue. To prevent sliding down, he snaked one leg around the support beam. His fedora escaped from his back pocket and sailed off in the wind. He saw a stranger on the ground nab it in mid-air.

98 – Charlie (Kearney, NE)

Charlie snatched the airborne hat, rolled it up and stuck it in his jacket pocket for safekeeping. *I'll return it to the climber, assuming he makes it out of this alive.*

The dirt spurts at the fissure grew into a miniature pulsing volcano. "It's getting bigger," he shouted into his phone.

"What is?" asked Potter.

"What's happening?" asked Nachas.

Glistening dirt shot up from the crack, spraying black soil into the air. "I've got a dirt version of Old Faithful. The fountain of soil keeps getting taller."

"What in the hell is that?" asked the Chief.

Charlie paid attention to his coastal colleagues, not local law enforcement. "The two portals are causing this, I'm sure of it."

"Portals?" asked the Chief. "It's got to be a broken water main. Yep, I'm sure that's what it is."

Charlie reported what he saw to his colleagues. "The dirt is so full of chemicals it looks like glitter is mixed in. The fountain is sparkling!"

The Chief grabbed Charlie's shoulder. "I don't care if you're from Washington, DC. I've got some questions that need answering."

99 – Matt (Eureka, CA)

Matt watched Dixon's body, thrashing, clinging to the portal's control bar. *He's not steering at all.*

"What is he doing?" asked Matt's mother.

"Not what he's supposed to." Dixon's body bounced from side to side, bumping into the inner hexagonal structure. Matt pointed. "There's some stuff, a valuable payload, here and in New York." Matt struggled to take faded feelings and turn them into understandable language. "And it has to be delivered to – I don't know – some place in-between. But it needs to be guided, otherwise it goes off in all directions."

"Like water?" she asked.

"Yes! Just like water. PortalPal and I were supposed to keep the water in the hose, instead of it spraying all over the place."

Matt liked the analogy just as much as he hated Dixon's execution. "Dixon is using too much body English, wasting his energy."

Matt tried to be a role model, leaning left and right, pulling up and then leaning forward, to demonstrate the proper techniques to Dixon. But Dixon wasn't looking for assistance. He barely hung onto the control handle.

Dixon could never deliver exotic fruits and vegetables across the galaxy. Never in a hundred parsecs.

100 – Kwashay (Brooklyn, NY)

Using subtle flicks of her wrist, Kwashay kept her payload on target while focusing on the image in front of her. *I can feel it. The target isn't in position. The payload is not being received.*

The image in her mind panned up. *There! It's a person, or what looks like a person, up in the air. That's the target.* She twisted her wrists hard, calculating an optimal path for the nutrients and minerals through the root system. *I have to accelerate the flow so it reaches him. And my partner operator needs to as well. I hope he sees the problem.*

101 – Selton (Kearney, NE)

The fountain of soil spurted skyward from the center of the dirt mound at the fissure, aiming for Selton. His backroots pushed against his ragged shirt, desperate for nutrition. He couldn't suppress his body's physiological needs. *I'm fighting myself, and it's a losing cause. I can't let the seeds germinate.*

The only tactic available to him was pushing onward and upward to the next, and highest, cross-brace on the tower. He was within arms reach of the insulating cap and the bare power cables.

If the megafeeding gets any higher -. He stared at the bare cables filled with a fatal dose of electricity.

102 – Charlie (Kearney, NE)

Charlie listened to Potter's report from Brooklyn while the Chief of Police pressed a heavy hand on his shoulder. "Kwashay's body language and posture has changed. She's leaning into the bar hard, like she's pushing something. Maybe operating a lawn mower over really tall grass, jerky like."

Nachas chimed in. "Dixon is running in place, like he's being dragged along, even though his portal is still anchored. And the sticks of Dixon's portal have shrunk to the diameter of pencils."

"Same here," said Potter. "They're so skinny, I don't know how much longer they'll support her body weight."

Charlie took a cleansing breath. This was the end, one way or another. "It's almost over."

The Chief pushed back his hat, which promptly flew off. "What is?"

103 – Matt (Eureka, CA)

It looked like an illusion to Matt, a trick done on stage by a professional magician. The sticks from which he'd constructed the portal were originally about three-quarters of an inch in diameter. Over time, they'd grown thick and fat, over five inches at least.

But ever since Dixon got inside, they'd shrunk. Slowly at first, but then accelerating in their diet. Now, they were thinner than toothpicks, almost all used up.

It was a miracle the portal was still standing, and still in Dixon's grip.

A soldier came over and leaned close. "Do you know what's happening?"

"Yeah, you let the wrong man inside, and the whole thing is going to fail." Matt stared, eye to eye. "And it's all your fault!"

104 – Kwashay (Brooklyn, NY)

Time was running out for Kwashay and the portal. The payload was almost gone. The rods were draining. They were harder to manipulate as they got thinner. Less responsive.

Kwashay glanced over at her mother, hands in prayer, being comforted by Potter, the EPA agent.

I have to make Mama proud.

She put all of her weight behind her legs and leaned forward as hard as she could. One last push, to deliver the nutrition to the individual hanging suspended in the air before the portal disappeared around her.

105 – Selton (Kearney, NE)

Selton looked down at the megafeeding stream. Instead of percolating spurts, the lurching gurgle of soil became a roar, a rushing, rising torrent, an eruption of sparkling loam. It bent at an angle, leaning west, in his direction.

He clamored higher, to the top of the transmission tower lattice, within easy reach of the ceramic insulator.

The geyser of nutritive soil was just high enough to reach the bottoms of his threadbare shoes, where a couple of toes stuck out. He'd lost the structure within his legs. They dangled soft and useless. Every part of his body was pleading with him to succumb to the megafeeding.

But Selton couldn't do that to a planet he'd grown to love through its flora and its literature. It became a choice between saving the planet or his own limited existence.

The choice was simple.

Selton reached past the ceramic insulator and grabbed hold of the bare power cable wires just as the dirt fountain brushed the soles of his well-worn shoes. His body experienced the extreme voltage from the city's power system a moment before the massive nutrition brushed against his feet. His body went stiff, as much as a pulpy mass could stiffen.

Streetlights flickered and the throbbing noise of the generators deepened as they slowed, but the power station withstood the disruption.

Selton felt the caress of his adopted people, a sense of calm within a storm of power. His seeds fed momentarily, absorbing nutrients but their fate was sealed. Electricity fried them black. It was only a matter of milliseconds, and Selton too would depart. As a mineral-rich conduit, electricity flowed through his body directly down the soil cascade and into the fissure. His last thoughts were Maxwell's equations.

106 – Charlie (Kearney, NE)

Charlie couldn't have predicted the result when the soil geyser and the power lines assaulted the vagrant's body simultaneously. The moment the eruption touched Selton, he exploded.

Hundreds, maybe thousands, of small pods escaped from Selton's body in all directions, propelled by the energy of the blast and steered by the wind. Several fell within feet of Charlie's position. The winds subsided and the ominous clouds vanished as quickly as they had arrived.

Power surged down the diminishing geyser into the ground, a swirling combination of sparkling particles with flickering electrical charges.

Dixon and Kwashay are at opposite ends of that soil stream!

"The portals are dissolving," reported Nachas.

"Mine is almost completely gone!" yelled Potter.

Charlie hollered, "Quick, tell Dixon and Kwashay to step back. There's a short circuit."

Potter answered, "She can't hear me. My God, she's down!"

Nachas moaned. "Oh my God!"

107 – Matt (Eureka, CA)

Just before the portal's sticks disintegrated, Matt saw Dixon get zapped as if he'd stuck his finger into a wall socket. Miniature lightning jumped from the control stick to Dixon's fingertips. His tongue shot out, his eyes bulged, his body lurched, kicking his feet off the ground, but he didn't let go. Sawdust remnants of the portal fell as Dixon's body hit the ground.

Matt grabbed his head with both hands, the pain debilitating, as his legs collapsed beneath him. The red plastic barrier broke under his weight. His mother screamed. With his meager energy, Matt crawled past two soldiers and scooted forward to Dixon, prone on the ground. "Did you do it?" he shouted.

Dixon was unresponsive. His arms and legs twitched.

The clouds drifted off and the wind dialed back to a gentle breeze.

A soldier was on his knees next to Matt. "His breathing is uneven. Call for a medic."

The guards pulled Matt to his feet. "Give him some air!" said one.

To Dixon, the other said, "We've got an EMT team en route."

Matt stood only with the support of two guards, silent, watching what could have been his fate if he'd remained the operator.

108 – Kwashay (Brooklyn, NY)

Kwashay's hands slipped from the control bar. She fell face first onto the dead grass. The remaining toothpick-thin remnants of the portal fizzed and sparked around her and then vanished.

She blinked her eyes and wiped the dirt from her face. Her mother and the EPA agent were kneeling alongside. Sideways stood behind them.

Kwashay rolled to her side, facing the threesome. "What happened?"

"You okay, girly-girl?" asked Sideways.

"Honey, are you all right?" asked her mother.

She nodded, waiting for an answer to her question.

"The portal rods kept getting thinner and thinner until they disintegrated while you were inside," said Potter. "It looked like lightning hit it from the inside-"

"Sounds like an electric shock." Kwashay sat up, legs crossed under her, breathing quickly. "Wow, that was amazing!"

One of the National Guard jogged over. "We've got an ambulance en route."

Kwashay heard the shouts of firemen and ambulance workers before she saw them, clearing the crowd.

Two paramedics rolled a gurney up to Kwashay's position. "We'll take it from here," the first paramedic said. "Any family here?"

"I'm her mother."

"Good. Young lady, I need to ask you a series of questions to assess your situation. Are you having any trouble breathing?"

"No."

"Are you suffering any back pain?"

"I could probably stand up if you want-"

He held out his palm. "Don't!"

"My back is fine. My knees hurt."

"She fell face forward." Potter flashed her badge, but the EMT ignored her.

"Got it." He checked her arms. "I don't see any obvious bleeding. A few scrapes."

"Like she said, she fell on her face." Her mother eased hair from Kwashay's forehead.

"Lay back."

Kwashay complied. She reached for her locket, still securely around her neck.

The paramedic palpated her arms and legs. "Any pain?"

"Just around my knees."

"Do you have any existing medical conditions?"

"Not that I know of."

"She's a very healthy girl," said her mother. "Gets regular check-ups. Eats the right kinds of-"

"Good. Just to be sure, we're going to run a few tests en route to Brooklyn Hospital Center next door."

"Oh no, you don't! She goes to Brookdale University Hospital or nowhere."

The paramedics exchanged glances. One pointed across the street to the west. "We're right here. Why would we drive half an hour-"

"Two reasons. One, I'm on staff there." Kwashay noticed her mother left out the fact that she was on administrative staff, not a physician. "Second, it's a block from where we live."

"It's not standard procedure," said the first.

"We'll make the exception," said the second.

With Kwashay's assistance, the two paramedics eased her onto a stretcher.

"I'm going with." Potter flashed her badge again. This time, the paramedic nodded.

Kwashay glanced at Sideways, holding his hard hat against his chest. "Vondell comes too, or I'm not going."

"Mom, you're up front with me," said the second paramedic. "The rest of you, squeeze in back, on the bench seat. It'll be cozy."

Potter put her arm around Sideways and escorted him to the rear of the waiting ambulance.

It was the worst possible circumstance but at Kwashay was finally getting her ride in an ambulance.

"I hope they use the siren," Sideways said.

"Me, too." Kwashay couldn't wipe the smile from her face.

109 – Charlie (Kearney, NE)

"Hello? Hello?" Charlie's connection to his two coastal associates had been lost. He was anxious to redial them, but when the Chief came over he slid his phone into his pocket.

"Poor man." The Chief shook his head. "What did he think would happen if he climbed a transmission tower?

Charlie knew it was a combination of circumstances linked to Matt and Kwashay and their portals that led to the vagrant's demise. He just couldn't prove it. And the one person who held the secrets had just exploded in front of him. "Yeah, poor man."

The Chief hung his head. "I don't know how I'm going to tell Ms. Martin that one of her favorite patrons committed suicide."

"Do you think that's what happened?" asked Charlie.

"You saw it just like me, plain as day."

Charlie was flummoxed at the Chief's lack of perception. "And what about that dirt geyser? What was that?"

The Chief gave a hesitant answer. "An earthquake."

"Really?" Charlie had to hold back a laugh.

The Chief must have sensed Charlie's disbelief and scowled. "We get earthquakes all the time out here. A 3.3 back in '81. A 2.8 back in '79 less than 50 miles from here. All around, down in McCook and up in Broken Bow. It could happen."

To Charlie, it sounded like the Chief was trying to convince himself. "So that's what you'll tell the Mayor and city council when they ask?"

"Unless you got something more scientific to share, yes."

Charlie chose to ignore the challenge. "I think you've got it nailed, Chief." He pulled out his phone and dialed Potter's number. *No interference but all trunks busy. Not surprising.* He decided to walk the power plant grounds and took only a few steps before he was halted by the Chief's fingers hooking his elbow. "Hang on a minute, pal. This is a crime scene. I don't want it compromised."

"What crime?" asked Charlie.

"Suicide is illegal in Nebraska." He walked about ten yards and retrieved his hat.

Charlie followed. "But there's no victim except the perpetrator himself."

The Chief whipped his hat back and forth against his leg, knocking off dust and debris. He plucked a small dark sphere from the hat and tossed it over his shoulder. "Still gotta investigate."

"I'll be careful." Charlie approached the fissure, staying clear of the dark rich soil pile lest he disturb evidence. Bits of fruit rinds and goopy strands decorated the top of the pile, what Charlie would have expected if a pumpkin exploded. Fabric scraps from a scorched shirt and burnt pants, and bits of well-worn toasted leather shoes. Here and there, twisted snake-like roots. No chunks of a corpse. Not even a hint of bodily remnants. Charlie caught the eye of one of the officers carrying a sample bag similar to Potter's. "Can I get an evidence bag, please?"

The police officer reached for his belt and handed Charlie two. "Don't touch anything important."

"I won't. Thanks." He shoveled a sample of the rich earth into the bag with his fingers, sealed it tight and put it in his jacket pocket. He picked up a couple of burnt pods, each the size of a walnut. They were charred black, lifeless. No good for anything, especially not growing. He stuck them in a different bag and tucked it away.

He pulled out his phone and tried again to call his compatriots one at a time and reestablish the conference call. This time, he was successful.

"Sorry, things blew up here." *Potter was right. I make puns subconsciously.* "Potter, what happened in Brooklyn? How is Kwashay?"

"She seems to be okay. Maybe a couple of skinned knees. We're on our way to the hospital, just to be sure."

"Great! And how about Matt and Dixon?"

"Matt is healthy, just really disappointed," said Nachas. "He's with his mother. It sounds like she's going to take him home. No point staying around campus now that he's no longer enrolled. Dixon didn't fare too well. His hands got burned pretty bad. Paramedics have transported him to a local hospital."

"By the way, our portal is gone. Evaporated," said Potter.

"This one is gone too," said Nachas. "I would have said dissolved."

They must have been used up, enriching the soil that erupted in Kearney. "Are the National Guard still there?" asked Charlie.

"Ours are packing up to go," said Potter. "Nothing here to protect."

"My group is still here, awaiting orders I guess. Or maybe they just like hanging around a college campus."

"So, what happened in Nebraska?" asked Potter.

"Yeah, tell us," said Nachas.

How could Charlie explain what he saw? “A person the Chief of Police and the town librarian identified as the local hobo made the mistake of climbing a power company transmission tower. He must have touched a live cable. We’re still looking for the body.” Charlie had never seen anything like the charred pulp and pods scattered around the power company grounds. “At the same time, we had a dirt geyser that originated at the junction of the two brown stripes.”

“The ones that originated at the portals?” asked Potter.

“Precisely. I’m certain the geyser and the portals are related. I haven’t a clue why, even if it is cause and effect. It’s the hobo I’m having trouble tying into the solution.”

Charlie was certain in his gut that the immolated stranger was at the center of the puzzle, but he had zero proof. “It almost looked like he was climbing the tower to avoid the rich soil, no matter how high it spurted.” Charlie shook his head. “That makes no sense. I need more time to gather evidence before I can make any conclusions. Any remnants at all from the structures?”

“No, all gone. The sticks got thin and then turned essentially to dust, and that blew away,” said Nachas.

“None here either,” said Potter.

“Okay, well, make sure Kwashay and Dixon are cared for.” Interviews with Kwashay, Matt, and Dixon about their experiences were vital for his assignment field report. “When they are stable and able to talk, get detailed statements and forward them to me.” How these phenomena eventually got reported popped up as a concern. "I've changed my mind. Potter, you interview Kwashay. Hang onto the transcript. I'll fly back to California to debrief both Matt and Dixon. No offense, Nachas, but he'll be a handful."

"None taken. I'm happy to leave him to you."

The Chief came back around from checking in with his officers. Charlie closed off the call and made a list of things to do in his notepad. He was about to bid farewell to the Chief when one of the evidence officers came running over. "You gotta see this."

Charlie followed the forensic officer and the Chief to a spot ten yards away from the fissure. On the ground lay a blue rubber glove whose fingers had been blown off.

"Strange, huh?" he said. "And we also found this."

He led the Chief and Charlie another five yards to a smoldering copy of a book. Using a meter stick, he flipped the book over. The edges were scorched but the cover was mostly intact. "*The Day of the Triffids*?"

Vegetable pulp. Burnt seeds. The novel Bernice the librarian gave the hobo about an alien plant invasion. Can this be just a coincidence? Charlie fought off a mental Grissom lecture about patterns and experienced an involuntary tremble. "I'm done here. Can you provide me with a ride to the airport, or at least call me a cab."

"That's it? You're leaving?" The Chief put his hands behind his back.

"No point in me sticking around." A team of police was wandering the power station grounds, taking photos and putting down markers. "Looks like you've got things under control."

The Chief stuck his hands in his pockets. “So, are you going to produce some kind of report for your boss?”

“I expect so.”

“You gonna say something different from what I said?”

“No sir.” *No point in disputing the Chief’s rationale.*

“And you’ll send me a copy?”

“Sorry, it’s classified.”

The Chief slapped his hat against his thigh. “Bullshit!”

“Think about it from my perspective for a minute. You’ve had a vagrant living here for weeks, maybe months, reading every book in your library. One day, after asking about alien invasion novels, he decides to electrocute himself. You’ve got brown splotches on lawns all over town, including at government buildings, plus wide brown stripes you’ve never noticed. You’re the chief of police. I’m just a recent visitor to your fair city. So who’s in a better position to know what’s going on here, hmm?”

The chief scratched his head silently and then placed his hat back on his head.

Charlie continued. “I’ll give you some advice. Stick with your story about how tectonic plates shifted under Nebraska – again - and caused a small earthquake that kicked up a bunch of dirt. That pile of soil is especially rich, and if your citizens spread it on those brown patches, their lawns will recover nicely.”

“What about Selton?”

“The hobo? You heard the librarian. He was in bad physical shape. Maybe he discovered he had a fatal illness and couldn't deal with it. Write it up as a suicide, an intelligent but perhaps ill migrant who decided to end his life."

"I'll take your suggestions under advisement. You willing to put anything in writing? Like what you just said?"

"I apologize for rambling. We've all had a very long and stressful day." He checked his watch. It was mid-afternoon. "Now, how about that lift?"

The Chief called over a police officer. "Take this Washington bureaucrat to the airport."

"Thanks, Chief." Charlie knew that everything he'd suggested to the Chief was bogus and wouldn't survive scrutiny. Then again, no one would likely take the effort.

He and the officer rode in silence to the airport. He thanked his uniformed chauffeur and entered the terminal building. Nestled in between some fast food venues and a newspaper stand, Charlie came across a Buy Nebraska store with trinkets and mementos for visitors. *Maybe I should get something as a gift for Potter, for her assistance. And Jane, for watching AquaLung.*

Prominent in the window display was a female mannequin wearing a blue shirt with slanted white lettering that read "Lopers."

"What's a loper?" he asked the clerk.

"That's the nickname for the University of Nebraska Kearney teams," she replied. "It's a local animal, the North American Antelope. It's also known as a Pronghorn."

"Really?"

"Did you know that the antelope is the second fastest mammal in the world? It can run at speeds of more than sixty miles per hour. Only the cheetah is faster!"

"Well then, how can I pass this up?" He made a short list in his head. "One large, one medium, one small." *That'll take care of me, Potter and Jane.* "Oh and one more large." *For Nachas.*

The clerk folded the shirts and slid them into a BUY NEBRASKA bag decorated with the state flag, the state seal, antelopes running across the plain, and flocks of flying birds, cranes if he wasn't mistaken.

Charlie took the opportunity to pack the gifts, the fedora, the soil sample and the burnt pods into his shoulder bag.

In the private plane terminal, Dixon's jet was waiting with crew aboard, playing cards in the passenger area.

"Ready to depart?" The pilot shuffled the deck while the other players waited for the deal. "Where to?"

Charlie thought for a moment. He didn't have Matt's home location. "Hang on and I'll find out."

Charlie wandered into the private terminal building and dialed Nachas' number.

"This is Gregory Nachas, EPA."

"Hi, it's Charlie Keyson. Did you get Matt's home address before he left campus?"

"Sure did. Hang on." There was a few minute gap before Nachas returned to the phone. "His folks live up in Marin County, a town called Tiburon, across Richardson Bay from Sausalito." He gave Charlie the address of the development.

Charlie wrote it down. "Thanks. I'm flying out to interview him. Wish you could be there."

“Me too. You should have seen him, when Dixon took over operation of the portal. He was absolutely heartbroken.”

“You know what he’s going to do now?” Charlie remembered Dixon’s commitment to fund Matt’s education.

“He needs some time to deal with everything that’s happened. We had quite a chat before he left campus with his mother, and I gave him my card. I hope he decides to go back to school.”

Charlie remembered that he had a shirt for Nachas, and that he needed local transportation in Eureka. “Listen, after I interview Matt, I’m flying up to Eureka to debrief Dixon. Why don’t you pick me up and join me for that interview?”

“I’d love to.”

“I’ll let you know when my flight will land in Eureka.”

“Great! I’ll meet you at the airport, same place as last time. Then you can tell me just what in the hell went on in Nebraska.

Charlie completed the call and reentered the plane. The crew were still seated, tossing their cards into the middle of the table. “We’re headed to San Francisco.”

The pilot stood up while the flight attendant raked in all of the cards. “Not Eureka?”

“No, that’ll be our second stop.” He wanted to speak with Matt before tackling Dixon.

“We’re all fueled up, so I’ll file a flight plan and we’ll be on our way.”

Charlie stood near the door to the cockpit. “I really appreciate this. I’ll rent a car and drive up to Marin County-”

"Marin?" The pilot turned around. "We'd be better off flying into their County Airport. A lot easier and quicker than driving up from South San Francisco, and through all that traffic."

"Great suggestion! Let's do it."

The flight attendant put his hand on Charlie's shoulder. "Why don't you make yourself comfortable?" He reached for Charlie's bag but he refused the offer. "Would you like something to eat or drink?"

Charlie loved the level of flexibility and personal service. "Maybe when we reach altitude." *I'm getting used to this. Too bad I'll have to go back to commercial flights.*

While the pilot filed a revised flight plan, Charlie took his Grissom novel out of his stowed bag, picked his usual seat and resumed reading where he'd left off.

> Grissom didn't get a call from Agent Clay of the FBI for a couple of weeks.
>
> "Quincy, it's Clay. I'm in Louisiana and I have some status to share."
>
> "Good to hear from you. What have you learned?"
>
> "That college helper of yours who got us access to the car rental security video? We got a facial recognition match. And with a little help from other government agencies, we tracked him down."
>
> "Great! What have you learned from him?" Grissom expected that there had been some form of interrogation.
>
> "He was quite cooperative. He was recruited for what his boss called "a

demonstration of strength." He was sent a package with an Indulge Financial Tanzanite card, matching identity documents including a driver's license and one thousand dollars in cash. His instructions were to make his way to New Orleans, take a one-way flight to Baton Rouge, rent a full-sized car, get a hotel room and then lie low to await further orders. Oh, and to stop using the Tanzanite card once he'd returned the car and checked into the hotel."

"That matches the pattern of illegal transactions for many of Indulge Financial's clients."

"I know. But for this one, we have first-person testimony. You see, our man got bored just sitting around, so he went looking for entertainment."

"Word is the Tailfeather Adult Dance Club is quite entertaining." Grissom had no knowledge of the establishment, but teasing Clay was almost expected.

"Bingo. He became a regular look-and-tip patron of the club. Until that fateful night when he decided to buy his first lap dance. The dancer did her thing, and then hung around his table. He bought her drinks, made small talk, and in short order his tab exceeded the cash in his wallet. He tried to negotiate terms for a payment later that week, when he could get some more money, but the club owner insisted on payment before he left the premises."

"So, he used the Tanzanite card to avoid bodily injury?" Grissom expected places like that would extract compensation one way or another. They had reputations to maintain.

"Something like that."

"You've taken him into custody, I assume."

"Never assume, my friend. This recruitee had a change of heart. For a lesser charge, he's going to cooperate with law enforcement. We've placed an FBI agent with him, seven by twenty-four, monitoring all communications. He says he doesn't know the identity of his boss, and I believe him. God, you should have seen him, shaking in fear when we apprehended him. He's probably the same age as some of your college helpers."

"How unfortunate! So, how will you proceed?"

"He agreed to use an emergency communication technique, a social media post, to contact his boss, admitting that he'd misbehaved and spent his cash allowance on women and alcohol. He prayed for forgiveness, another chance, and additional funds."

"Did his boss take the bait?"

"We weren't sure at first, because the response took a long time. We thought we'd been made. But his boss finally agreed to wire him additional money. We traced the funds transfer in real-time to a local currency exchange. One guess who it led back to?"

"Mukhtar Aziz in London?"

"Give the lucky man a stuffed animal! We've asked Scotland Yard to issue a warrant for a search of Aziz' business and residence. Requests like this have a lot of paperwork associated with them, so it won't happen immediately. Hopefully, soon. I'll let you know."

Charlie was startled by the screech of tires on the runway.

"We've landed in Marin." The flight attendant's message was tardy and redundant.

110 – Matt (Tiburon, CA)

Matt lay on his bed, winding the game controller cord around his hand. The game console wasn't connected or turned on. *I'm not in the mood.* He looked around the room, searching for something to take his mind off the portal and Dixon.

His mother called up from the main floor, "Matt, that nice man from the EPA is here to see you."

What does he want with a loser like me?" Matt unwound the cord, dropped the controller on his unmade bed and clomped down the steps.

Matt's mother stood with Agent Dixon at the door. "I remember how you protected Matty from that horrid man from Bates." She turned and acknowledged Matt's arrival. "Here he is."

The EPA guy seemed to be wearing the same suit as last time, and it had been days. "Didn't think I'd ever see you again. What's up?"

The agent spoke to both of them, turning his head. "If it's okay, I'd like to talk with Matt in private."

"That's fine with me." Matt put his hand on his mother's shoulder "If I need you, I'll holler."

She nodded and scurried off toward the basement door and out of sight.

Matt led Charlie into the living room section of an open floor plan with large picture windows. Even with only torchlights, the view of water was spectacular. They took positions on opposite sides of a long off-white sofa.

Charlie pulled out his notepad. "So, how does it feel to be home?"

"Terrific, although I miss campus. And even Fred, a little." He smiled. "I miss the gardens and forest more."

"I'm here to chat about what happened at the portal. I heard what you and Agent Nachas told me over the phone, but I'd like to get your fresh recollections directly, if that's okay."

Matt folded his arms across his chest. "You mean, after the portal rejected me?"

Charlie leaned forward, elbows on his knees. "The portal did not reject you." He closed his notepad. "I understand that Dixon put in the missing rod, and the portal accepted him as the operator."

And after all that work, preparing. "Sounds like you have a pretty good handle on things." He interlaced his fingers, his hands on his head. "Why do you need me?"

"I'm trying to figure out the operator's mission."

So, maybe I am valuable after all. "I was pretty close to figuring it out, until the portal abandoned me." Matt's feelings hadn't come close to healing.

"How close, exactly?" The agent's notepad was open, his pen poised to take notes.

Matt brought his hands down, his fingers fidgeting. "You see, the portal told me to practice videogames, especially flying simulators."

"But the portals stayed where they were, rooted to the ground."

He doesn't have a clue. "The portals weren't going to fly. Something else, some kind of payload, needed direction. That's why a flying simulator was the right kind. Keeping the payload on track, from Eureka to someplace east."

The agent made more notes.

I wonder what he's writing?

"So that's what Dixon had to do?"

"Yeah, but the jerk screwed it up, I'm sure of it."

The agent's face reddened. "Given how you were feeling, you might not have had the strength to operate the portal."

"Yeah, and that was Dixon's fault too. Him and his damn diamond saw. I would have succeeded. I just know it. I practiced my ass off, preparing, and he just waltzed in. If only they'd let me put the last stick in."

Charlie changed his questions to that subject. "Tell me about that. I thought the National Guard were supposed to protect the portals from interference."

"So did I." Matt dropped his hands in his lap. "I don't know how he got the soldier to let him do it. At first, the soldier said no way."

"Of course. The National Guard protected the Brooklyn portal as well."

Matt thought about the other operator. *I'd sure like to meet her.* "Dixon told the guard in charge to check with his superiors, and bang, he had access."

The agent scribbled yet another note. "At least, Dixon will be paying for the rest of your college experience, at a four-year school of your choice."

Matt shrugged.

The agent seemed surprised. "What's the matter? I thought you'd be thrilled."

"I wasn't at College of the Redwoods because of cost. My dad makes enough that he could send me to Princeton or Harvard or wherever." Matt's eyes scanned their surroundings. "After my failure at Dartmouth, he insisted I step up. You know, get high grades as a return on his investment. That's how he described it. Now, after this, I expect he'll apprentice me at his company."

The agent scratched his head, his face scrunched up as if concentrating. "Maybe there's something I can do to help. With your Dad, that is." He stood up.

"That's it? No more questions?"

"I trust you've told me everything you know. I can't ask for more than that."

"Cool." Matt remembered his conversation with Agent Nachas. "Tell me, do you enjoy your work at the EPA?"

The agent hesitated before answering. "Yes, I do. I feel like I'm making a difference."

"Cool."

Mrs. Thready came up from the basement and met them at the door. "Did you learn what you needed to know?"

"Quite a bit, actually." Charlie turned to Matt. "You provided some important pieces to the puzzle."

"Are you going to interview the other operator? The girl?"

"One of my colleagues has probably already done that in Brooklyn."

I bet he compares my account to hers. Except, she was inside her portal and I was just an observer. Damn!

The agent offered his hand. "The best of luck in whatever you decide to do. Thanks for seeing me." They shook, and then the agent departed.

Mrs. Thready closed the door behind their visitor. "He seems like a nice man. Did you tell him what he needed to know?"

"I think so. Yeah. And he said something about helping me out with Dad."

She shook her head. "You know your father. He'd have to work a miracle." She wandered off to the kitchen.

Matt considered the agent's comments about working at the EPA, plus what Nachas had told him, then took the stairs two at a time to look up the agency on his computer.

111 – Kwashay (Brooklyn, NY)

Kwashay sat with perfect posture across from Agent Potter in her mother's apartment, her hands folded on the kitchen table.

"I'm going to record our conversation, so Agent Keyson can hear it verbatim. Is that okay?"

"Sure." She'd be sharing not only with a New York agent, but one from Washington, DC!

Potter pressed the record button and nodded.

With perfect articulation, Kwashay announced, "I figured it out." She felt rightly proud.

"Go on." Agent Potter had a laptop, prepared to take additional notes.

Kwashay felt special, providing valuable information to government officials. "When we first met, you said the portal was the origin for what you called a brown stripe, soil that was dead. Well, the nutritives and minerals had to go somewhere, right?"

"Of course. They didn't just evaporate."

"Precisely. The portals pulled chemicals from the ground and stored them in the rods. That's why the grass and stuff died, and why the rods got so thick."

Potter typed as she spoke. "Makes perfect sense. But why was the portal storing all of those chemicals?"

Kwashay sensed from Potter's tone that she was anxious. "It took a while for me to understand that part. The chemicals were nutrition. You know, to make things grow."

"Okay, so the rods grew. The roots grew longer and more grass died. So what?"

Kwashay was deliberately holding back some of the information. She was enjoying her celebrity too much for the interview to end quickly. "The nutrition wasn't to make fat rods or longer roots. It was storing the nutrition for another purpose."

"You're going to make me ask every little thing, aren't you?" Potter closed the laptop lid and laid her arms on top. "Do you remember who engineered the distraction that allowed you into your portal?" The agent leaned back and folded her arms. "It's time you told me the story."

Kwashay regretted her teasing. Potter's actions were crucial in allowing her to be the operator she was tasked to be. She pulled her locket chain tight. "Sorry. I like being the one who knows things." She relaxed her posture a bit, without slumping. "As the operator, my job was to direct that nutrition to the target."

"Who or what was the target?"

"I'm not really certain. I think it was a person. At least it looked like a person." Kwashay hoped Potter wouldn't ask why a person would need soil nutrition, because she didn't have an answer.

"Agent Keyson was in Nebraska, and he told me by phone that there was a huge spurt of mineral-rich dirt."

"Is that where it came out? I kind of saw a place, and the other operator, but I couldn't tell the geography. I felt the pressure reduce but didn't know why. It must have been when the nutrition broke the surface."

"Agent Keyson said it looked like a geyser."

"I pushed really hard, especially at the end."

Potter leaned forward. "So let me get this straight. You pushed the nutrition that was stored in the rods to Nebraska, to somebody that was going to use it, for some purpose we don't know."

"Oh, I know the purpose. He needed a megafeeding. That's what the portal called it."

"And after you directed the megafeeding to this person, the nutrition in the rods was depleted."

"Exactly. That's why the portal vanished. Because it was used up."

Potter shook her head. "Wow! That's some story."

"I was afraid you wouldn't understand. Mom doesn't, and I've explained it to her three times." Kwashay glanced sideways at the agent. "You believe me, don't you?"

"Every word! And after all of that, are you okay?"

"I have some blisters on my fingers and skinned knees, but otherwise I'm fine. It was really fun." Kwashay's buoyant feelings faded. "Too bad I'll never get s chance to do it again."

"Why are you so sure?"

"Because just after my partner operator and I sent the last big push, the voices told me so. There was one opportunity, and I messed up. I guess we missed the target." She wiped a bit of moisture from her eyes. "And I'd practiced so hard. It's tough, living with failure."

Potter put one hand on Kwashay's. "According to Agent Keyson, the target may have been avoiding your delivery."

"Really? Because I knew the person was supposed to be on the ground, but instead he was up in the air."

"Hanging onto a power station transmission tower."

"Really? But why? The nutrition was vital. The megafeeding was supposed to help us all. Everybody on the planet."

"Any speculation on my part is way past my salary grade." Potter slipped her laptop into a shoulder bag. "All I know is, you did precisely what you were asked to do, and you did it well. You can't be blamed if you shot an arrow perfectly and someone moved the target after you released."

"I guess." Potter's comments made Kwashay feel a little better, that parts of the situation were outside of her control.

Agent Potter picked up her recorder and stood up. "So I guess that's it."

"That's all? Don't you have more questions?" Kwashay wanted Potter to stay. She was smart, nice and good company.

"Agent Keyson may have some after he listens to this tape." She pressed the STOP button and slipped it into her bag.

"Oh, okay, well he can call anytime or stop by. Anything to help." He was kind of cute, for an older guy.

Potter walked to the foyer. "Thank you for your cooperation. I expect Agent Keyson will be in touch, if only to deliver his thanks. And send my regards to your mother."

"I will." She wanted to hug Potter but instead thrust out her arm for a vigorous handshake.

The memories from her adventure faded quickly as Kwashay sat alone on her sofa. She turned on the TV and picked up the game controller. *This is nowhere near as exciting, but maybe I can beat my high score.*

112 – Charlie (Tiburon, CA)

After meeting with Matt, Charlie drove back to Marin County Airport where the Bates plane was waiting, an idea percolating in his mind about how to set Matt up for success with his father.

"Where to now?" asked the pilot.

"Now we fly to Eureka. Arcata/Eureka Airport, that is."

"I've been there before. Flew Mr. Dixon there at least once." He tipped his cap back. "Nice place. Beautiful scenery. Probably take us a little over two hours."

Charlie called Nachas and gave him the approximate arrival time.

"You ready for this?" Nachas asked.

"I will be." Dixon was a powerful individual, more adversary than partner. *I'll have to maintain control of the conversation.*

Before the plane took off, Charlie called Lane's office number. It was after hours, so he got an expected recorded message. He waited until the message ended, then left his own. "Brad, this is Charlie Keyson. I need a big favor. There's a young man out in California who could make better use of your EPA Gold Medal for Exceptional Service than as a dust collector. You'd be doing something special if you'd overnight it." He read Matt's name and home address from his notes. "You won't be sorry." Charlie knew that, at Washington speed, any request for Matt's own medal would take months, and Matt needed support now.

Charlie buckled into his seat and reviewed the notes about what information he needed from Dixon. He anticipated that Dixon wouldn't be quite so cooperative as last time, when he was in trouble. The question was, would Dixon remember how Charlie had helped?

It was a stable flight and more than quiet enough for Charlie to squeeze in a bit more of his novel. Both stories were moving toward conclusions.

Grissom met with his clients, Harrison Bainbridge and the executive at Indulge Financial's office. "I've solved the case." *With the assistance of Homeland Security and Scotland Yard, but they don't have to know that.*

"I expected no less." Bainbridge smoothed his tie.

"I uncovered a plot by a group of terrorists to bomb a large number of state capitals simultaneously on our nation's birthday."

Bainbridge squinted. "Excuse me?"

The Indulge Financial executive looked at his watch. "That's only a few weeks from now. That's what these fraudulent transactions were about?"

"Indeed. Their system was quite effective in obtaining operational funds for their large-scale attack. Individually, Indulge Financial was willing and able to cover the fraudulent transactions, to maintain their customer loyalty. The terrorists' approach was much more cost effective than taking out a loan."

The Indulge Financial executive mopped his forehead with a white handkerchief.

Grissom continued, “And the bad transactions were timed to avoid being detected too early. By the way, did you ever locate the mole in your organization?”

“It was pretty obvious when she stopped showing up for work. We called, even sent our security personnel to her apartment, but she’s vanished.”

“She will turn up, like bad pennies always do. I suggest you increase your scrutiny of your clients’ transactions, especially if they’re out of state.”

“Our clients are quite mobile.” The Indulge Financial executive glanced at Bainbridge. “I wouldn’t want to inconvenience them.”

Bainbridge glared at the Indulge Financial representative. “Like this fiasco didn’t?”

The Indulge Financial executive slumped. “We’ll take a look at tightening that up.”

Grissom stood. “You’ll both be getting my bills in the mail. Registered with signature required.”

Handshakes all around, Bainbridge’s enthusiastic, the Indulge Financial executives reluctant, capped the quick meeting. Grissom strutted out of the Indulge Financial building, planning to stop at the local pawnshop to buy himself a gift for solving the case.

With two paying clients, I can afford an indulgence.

As Charlie deplaned, jealous of Grissom's success, Nachas was at the curb, as promised. "Welcome back."

Charlie got in and buckled. "Where's Dixon?"

"St. Joseph Hospital, downtown. So tell me, does Nebraska make any more sense after talking to Matt? I couldn't understand what you were describing over the phone. A hobo climbing a transmission tower, a dirt geyser, an explosion?"

"Those were all true. I'm still muddling through the relationships, the causes and effects. Matt was an observer, just like you. His bond with the portal was long gone by the time the dirt erupted." Charlie didn't divulge the details Matt had shared. "After we talk to Dixon, maybe it'll be clearer."

After a short drive, Nachas parked in a visitor space at the hospital.

"By the way, I brought you a souvenir." Charlie pulled a Lopers t-shirt from his bag. "I hope I got you the right size."

"Large, perfect." He examined the front of the shirt. "What's a Loper?" He placed it on the back seat.

Charlie explained as they entered the building. They got Dixon's room number from the reception desk and took the elevator to the third floor.

A floor nurse at a counter, evidently the arbiter of who was allowed access to the Burn Unit, greeted them. She checked her charts, all filed vertically in a floor stand. "You can have a few minutes with Mr. Dixon, but he needs his rest. Both his mind and body were subjected to significant stress. Maybe after your visit, you can explain to me what happened so we can treat him more effectively."

"That's what we're hoping to find out," said Charlie.

Charlie and Nachas entered the private room. A half dozen large 'Get Well' flower arrangements filled every flat counter. A dozen boxes of unopened candy were stacked precariously on the floor near the window.

Dixon lay back, the bed raised to an angle, with heavily bandaged hands on his chest. His eyes were closed.

"I heard you had quite an adventure," said Charlie.

Dixon opened his eyes. "Agent Nachas, nice to see you again. Agent Keyson, finally. Where have you been?"

I had told Dixon I was going to Nebraska when he arranged for his company jet. Given what he's been through, I'm not surprised he forgot. Charlie ignored the direct question, which would have put Dixon in control. "Nice to see you too."

Nachas leaned against the wall near the window.

Charlie took a side chair and sat down near the bed. "Agent Nachas described to me what he saw at the portal. But I need to know what you experienced on the inside, as part of my investigation."

"And I need to know if I was right. Was it aliens?" Dixon was wiggling on the bed, like an expectant child on Christmas morning.

"You have it backwards. I'm here to debrief you."

"Come on, I've been through hell." He held up his useless white-wrapped hands. "I deserve to know."

Charlie remembered their previous arrangement. "I'll trade you. A complete description of your experience inside the portal for an answer to your question. Plus, I'm going to hold Bates Foundation to your promise that Matt Thready Jr. gets a full scholarship to the four-year school of his choice."

Dixon repositioned him self in his bed by bouncing. "No problem. I submitted the paperwork for that back when he was in the infirmary."

It was ironic that by bullying Matt out of being the portal operator, Dixon put himself in a medical facility. "And one for Kwashay Williams-Jackson as well."

"Who?" Dixon scratched at his head with a bandaged mitt.

"Your portal operator partner? The young lady at the East Coast portal?"

He brightened up, eyes wide and almost a smile. "Her? We connected, her and me, through the portals. The girl was exceptional. She even compensated for when my aim strayed. Which wasn't often, mind you. Can you arrange for me to meet her?"

"That'll be up to her and her mother." Charlie thought about Mrs. Williams-Jackson and Dixon in the same room. *Pheeew.* "I'll let them know you're interested. But your money won't be wasted on her, I guarantee."

"Good. I'll initiate the scholarship funding request from here. Maybe I can do one better."

"Glad to hear it." Her scholarship was more critical then Matt's given their disparate family situations. Charlie wondered what Dixon meant by "one better" but decided not to ask. *Another opportunity to stray from my agenda.* "So, we have a deal?"

"Yes, yes. Was it aliens?"

Charlie crossed his legs, his notepad open. "I haven't heard your story yet. Tell me what happened when you were inside the portal."

"I did fine. Better than fine, despite what anybody says." He glanced at Naches. "I did great."

Nachas' and Matt's assessments of his performance hadn't been as positive. Charlie waited for Dixon to continue. *He's going to make me work for every detail.* "I'm glad you performed well. Doing what?"

"Operating the portal. It seemed to expect that I was prepared, except I wasn't. And when it figured that out, it pushed the instructions to me, all in one blast."

"What were you asked to do?" Charlie refrained from asking 'What did they ask you to do?' because it raised the question of who 'they' were.

"First thing, they throw this hypnosis or astral projection or three-dimensional virtual-reality at me, like I'm underground." His voice got louder the more he spoke. "It must have been aliens. Who else could do that?"

"I'd be careful if I were you. This hospital has a psychiatric ward, and the floor supervisor has been watching you."

Dixon glanced around perhaps the see if there was surveillance equipment in the room. "They won't think I'm nuts once you confirm it."

"Back to business, shall we? What went on while you were operating the portal? What did you see and hear?"

Dixon couldn't lay still, repositioning himself often. "It was like I was flying, moving through some sort of tunnel. In my mind, not in reality. Or maybe like a roller coaster. And something was pushing at my back. But I hung on for dear life."

Hanging on wasn't the goal, according to Matt. "You still haven't told me what you were supposed to do as the operator."

Dixon leaned forward from his back pillow. "You know Star Wars, the original movie?"

Is this another stalling tactic? Charlie nodded. "I'm familiar."

"Okay." Dixon's waving bandaged hands illustrated his explanation. "Near the end, Luke was flying an X-wing fighter through the trench, preparing to fire his proton torpedoes at the exhaust port of the Death Star, right?"

"Yes."

"So, the best I can figure, they wanted me to be Luke."

Charlie accepted Dixon's interpretation. "Aiming at what?"

"See, that's what I don't know. Sometimes it felt like a single thing, and sometimes a whole bunch of things. You were in Kearney, Nebraska. Was that the destination for the energy surge? Did I succeed?"

Dixon deserved a morsel of information. "You and Kwashay delivered all right."

"Great! So maybe you can tell me what we were aiming at?"

"I'm sorry, that's classified."

Dixon scowled. "What? I thought we were sharing."

"Last time, we shared. This time, you're talking and I'm listening. There are some things reserved for only folks above my pay grade. How did it feel inside the portal?"

"At first, cramped and silent. No noise from the outside. I wondered how they did that, because there were openings between the rods. Then, I felt claustrophobic, and had trouble breathing. There was this energy behind me, trying to bury me alive. I wanted no part of that. When I pushed the rod in front of me, the only one that lit up, I moved forward. I thought maybe I could outrun it. Some voice in my head kept telling me to follow a course and steer the energy, but all I could think about was getting away."

"So it wasn't easy?"

"Hell no. A few times, I reconsidered what I'd done."

Charlie had never witnessed Dixon showing regret. "What, specifically?"

"Like maybe I should have let the kid be the operator. Somehow, after I installed the missing stick, I didn't have a choice. Was I being manipulated?"

A technique Dixon is probably very familiar with. "Something like that."

"By an alien?"

Charlie sat silent.

"This is just like UFOs sighted by Air Force pilots and astronauts, isn't it? You government guys will stamp the information CLASSIFIED and the public will never hear about it again.

Dixon was probably right. "We'll share when we have facts, not theories." Which would probably be never. Charlie didn't contradict Dixon's account. He scanned his pending question list. "By the way, how did you get the National Guard troops to let you install the last rod?"

Dixon grinned. "You helped. Remember when you asked about Fencepost Consulting? I figured you asked because they were involved in your assignment. So I called in a favor from the guys who were managing the local troop deployment, just in case. When the final stick showed up, I told the guardsman to call his superiors. That was my guys at Fencepost. They told the guardsman to make an exception for me. Pretty slick, huh?"

Charlie was angry at himself for giving Dixon the leverage he needed to squeeze Matt out of his role as operator. *Yet, maybe I saved Matt from physical harm.* "Yes, very slick indeed. And probably in violation of some Federal law. I'll have to do some research."

Dixon looked uncomfortable, like he'd wet the bed.

"What happened to your hands?"

"Doctor says third degree burns. Lots of nerve damage, or I'd be in worse pain."

"It looked like you were being electrocuted," said Nachas.

"I was not going to let go of the controls, come hell or high water. Damn electrical malfunction of the portal, my best guess."

Charlie knew what caused the power to flow to the portal. The hobo's body acted as a conduit between the transmission line and the mineral-rich stream of soil that led back to the portals. "Sorry to hear. They'll heal."

"Yeah, eventually. I've asked to be transported to a hospital down in Austin near my home. Speaking of transportation, I'm going to need my company jet back. You'll have to fly commercial from now on."

The grin on Dixon's face made it clear he enjoyed pulling the private jet away. Charlie didn't look forward to another redeye, but he'd appreciated the favor nonetheless. "Now that the portals are gone, what's the status of the construction project at the college?"

"Don't know. My boss is threatening to reassign me to customer service after I'm healed up. Bates operates it's own call center."

"Managing the Center?" asked Nachas.

"Nope. Customer service rep."

"You're going to be answering 1-800 calls?" *Quite the fall, from portal operator to phone operator.*

Dixon attempted to sit straight despite the tilt of the bed. "Listen, whatever doesn't kill you makes you stronger."

Charlie couldn't picture Dixon taking customer service phone calls with his high and mighty attitude. *He has no empathy.* Maybe this was Bates' way of easing him out of the company. *He'd better arrange for Kwashay's scholarship before he gets busted down to phone operator.*

"Okay, I've told you my story, at least everything I remember. So what were those voices in my head?"

Charlie took a deep breath. *I can't believe I'm going to say this out loud.* "You were right all along. Aliens were communicating with you and Kwashay. And Matt, before you became operator."

Nachas came off the wall, his head leaning forward. "Aliens? Really?"

"I knew it!" Dixon's were wide with excitement or fear. "And the invasion? Have the authorities been warned?"

"There won't be any invasion." *The hobo short-circuited it.* "Your only problem is, where's the proof? The portals are gone and your aliens didn't leave anything behind." Charlie remembered the burnt seed nodules in his shoulder bag. *None of Dixon's business.*

"No big deal, my friend. You know the truth. You can vouch for me." Dixon paused. "Won't you?"

"I told you before, all of this is classified."

"So I can't tell anyone?"

Charlie nodded. "Or you'll be arrested."

"So you've given me nothing." Dixon slumped back. "It's really too bad. Alien technology could've been a big moneymaker."

Just what I'd expect from a Bates employee. "Tell you what. I'll leave something with the floor nurse."

"Really?" He sat up straight for the first time. "What is it?"

An attending nurse stuck her head in. "I'm sorry, you'll have to go now."

Dixon waved his arms "Wait-"

"Gotta go. Doctor's orders," said Charlie.

"I hope you feel better," added Nachas.

Charlie thought for a moment about gifting his Lopers t-shirt to Dixon, and then reconsidered it. *He wouldn't appreciate the gesture. Besides, he's probably not size large - except for his ego.*

"One last thing." Dixon waved a blanketed white fist. "If you ever get tired of government service, come see me. I can always use a good man."

Like I could ever work for someone like Dixon? "Thanks for the offer." In his new customer service position, he wouldn't have hiring authority.

On their way past the floor station nurse, Charlie paused. "You asked about Mr. Dixon? He's suffering with delusions about aliens. Very sad. The man used to have a keen mind. You should probably put him through some tests-"

Her eyes went wide. "There are many psychological screening tests. Depression, anxiety, bipolar." She scribbled notes on his chart. "Even a Post Traumatic Stress Disorder screen for those who've had a traumatic life event."

Charlie leaned his head near hers and whispered, "Mr. Dixon was trapped in a confined space and then almost electrocuted."

The nurse matched his volume. "Oh my, I had no idea! Maybe I should request them all, just to be sure."

Charlie nodded in agreement. Nachas' lips sputtered as he tried to constrain his laughter.

They walked out to the car. "You are a nasty man, Charlie Keyson."

"You'd agree that Trev Dixon has some interpersonal issues, wouldn't you? Those screens will do him good – in the long run."

"And feeding his obsession about little green men from outer space? That was priceless!" Nachas unlocked the car.

Charlie had finally accepted Dixon's explanation about aliens. *No need to confuse Nachas.*

They made their way back to 101 and headed north toward the airport. "So are you clearer now about what happened?" asked Nachas.

"A little. But before I write up an official report, I want to review Potter's interview of Kwashay. Then I'll have what I need."

"Any chance I can get a copy?"

"Sure. You were part of this. I'll provide both you and Agent Potter copies after my director reviews it." Charlie remembered that Dixon had removed the Bates company jet from his disposal. "I guess I'll have to catch one of those blender flights."

Nachas looked puzzled as he pulled up to the curb at the airport.

"You know, the ones that shake up your insides?"

Nachas and Charlie shook hands before Charlie went into the terminal.

"We always seem to be saying good bye," said Nachas.

"If you ever get to Washington, look me up. And you can count on me as a reference, for what it's worth."

"That's priceless." Nachas shook Charlie's hand hard, and then got into his car and drove away.

I'd like to thank the Bates jet crew before I go.

Familiar faces stood near the private jet desk in the terminal. "We just got word that we're to return to Austin as soon as possible," said one of the pilots.

"I heard. I was just stopping by to thank you for your hospitality and efficiency. I couldn't have attended to my case without you." Charlie turned, prepared to walk away.

"So, where are you going?" the pilot asked.

"I need to catch a short flight to San Francisco, and then cross-country to the East Coast. Why?"

"Well, SFO is on our way to Austin. At least, we can make it on our way for refueling. Can't take you all the way to DC, but we can drop you off on our way south. No trouble."

"Really?" Charlie checked his watch again. "Because the only commercial flight isn't for a while, and it always runs late."

"Maybe we can even get you to SFO quick enough that you can take an earlier flight. At least, we can try."

Charlie's tension about the shuttle plane evaporated. "What are we waiting for?"

The Bates flight crew led Charlie out to their plane.

"You know the drill," said the pilot.

The flight attendant took Charlie's bag, this time with his permission, and stowed it in an overhead compartments while he buckled himself in.

During the short but smooth flight, Charlie made notes from his conversation with Dixon, adding them to those he'd already documented from his chat with Matt and his parents.

When he got to SFO, he thanked the Bates crew again and found his way to a ticket counter.

"Your destination, please?" asked the agent.

By instinct, Charlie almost told her Washington, DC. After all, that was home. But he knew a chat with his partner to review Kwashay's interview was mandatory. "Make it New York City, LaGuardia please."

He pulled out his smartphone, to let Potter know he was New York bound and needed to be picked up.

Now I just have to decide how much to share..

113 – Matt (Tiburon, CA)

Matt waited to have the discussion until his father came home from his business trip. That night, after dinner, he invited his folks to the living room. They sat on the sofa.

He sat in one of the two padded chairs that faced them, a small box wedged in alongside his thigh. "We have to talk about my future."

"You make it sound so serious," said his mother.

"He's right, dear," said his father. "This is a crucial decision point. It should be taken seriously. After two disastrous college experiences, maybe you've come around. I can bring you into the business, teach you everything I've learned about financial planning-"

"Dad, I don't want to be stuck behind a desk."

"You won't be." His father crossed his legs, making sweeping gestures with his hands. "You'll get out, see clients at their homes and offices. I'll lease you a nice car, to maintain the image of success from day one."

"I didn't mean that literally. I don't have any interest in pushing numbers around on spreadsheets."

His father's hand gripped the arm of the sofa. "Is that what you think I do? The job is a whole lot more than just formulas-"

"Dear, what are you interested in doing?" asked his mother.

"While at Redwoods, I came to enjoy nature. The splendor and majesty of living things."

"You became a tree hugger?" asked his father. "That doesn't pay very well. And if you think I'm going to fund your chosen life style while you sit on your ass-"

"Bates Foundation offered me a full four-year scholarship to the school of my choice."

"You're kidding! That's marvelous." His mother turned to her husband. "Isn't that marvelous?"

"You'd take money from Bates after what that asshole Dixon did to you?" His father folded his arms on his chest. "It's never been about the money. We can afford to do that ourselves. We always have."

"I know. You wanted me to prove myself. And maybe, with this portal incident, you don't think I have, that it was just another distraction from getting my head on straight. Isn't that what you said?"

His father nodded.

Matt pulled the box from his side and took off the lid. "Well, the Federal government thinks I have." He tilted the box so they could see. "I've been awarded the EPA Gold Medal for Exceptional Service."

"Oh my goodness." His mother stood up and took the box from his hand. "I'm so proud of you." She moved it closer so her husband could see it.

His father grunted. "Okay, I guess that proves something."

"According to Agent Keyson from the EPA, the Bates Foundation has also offered me a paid summer internship down in Austin. Seems they offered one to Kwashay-

"Who?" asked his mother.

"The other portal operator. From Brooklyn? I'd be working with Dixon on some special project-"

His father uncrossed his legs and almost came off the sofa. "Seriously, you aren't considering that, are you?"

"Hang on. I've already rejected the internship offer. I never want to spend another minute in the same room with that jerk."

"Good choice." His father sat back and relaxed. "At least that part of your brain is working properly."

"But, money is money, right? So I am going to accept the scholarship offer."

"Where will you go, dear? Back to Dartmouth?" asked his mother. "I loved that school."

"I'm postponing that decision for a year. The Bates Foundation said I didn't have to enroll immediately."

"Then what are you going to do?" His father's voice sharpened. "Hang out around the house playing video games? Sail on the lagoon with your latest paramour?"

"We could remodel the basement into your own private apartment," said his mother.

"I called Agent Nachas from the California EPA to see if he can arrange an internship with his agency. It doesn't even have to be paid, since Bates will pick up my college tab. He was optimistic, especially because of that." Matt pointed to the medal his mother was clutching to her chest.

"Well, I'll say one thing." His father stood up, crossed the room and held out his hand. "You've taken charge of your life, which is all I ever really wanted."

Matt stood, ignored the potential handshake, and put his arms around his father. His mother quickly joined in for a family hug.

114 – Kwashay (Brooklyn, NY)

Kwashay hung up the phone just as their front door opened. She rushed to the foyer and grabbed her mother's arms above the elbow. "Mama, you'll never guess who just called!" She was practically dancing, spinning her mother around. Her locket flew with her momentum.

"I'm a terrible guesser with my coat on."

Kwashay unbuttoned the coat, leapt behind and ripped it from her mother's arms. "I can't believe it!" She jammed the garment onto a wall hook and pulled her mother into the living room. "Sit down and I'll tell you all about it."

They both plopped down on the couch. Her mother took both of her daughter's hands in hers. "What's got you all jangled up?"

"I just got a call from Trevor Dixon from the Bates Foundation. Do you know who they are?"

Her mother shook her head. "Should I?"

"They're just the biggest and wealthiest philanthropists on the planet! They fund colleges and universities, research in all kinds of scientific areas of study-"

"Okay, I get the picture. Big money." Her mother leaned forward. "So?"

Kwashay couldn't disclose that Trevor was her portal operation partner. *Mama thinks the whole portal story was fiction, and that I was competing in a contest.* "Bates was the sponsor, and he called to tell me I won."

"That's marvelous, dear. It was nice of him to call. We'll make a place on the shelf for your trophy." She stood up. "What's for dinner?"

I thought she'd be more excited. Kwashay looked up at her. "We're going out to celebrate tonight. Where would you like to go?"

"Honey, we can't afford to be splurging like that, on a weeknight. We eat out on special occasions-"

'But this is a special occasion. Trevor offered me a full four-year scholarship to the school of my choice! Anyplace!"

One eyebrow lifted on her mother's face. "That's the prize? Really? What's the catch? Because you survived a horrible experience, he's going to gift you hundreds of thousands of dollars? What about the financial aid you interviewed for?"

Kwashay didn't want to share the story of messing up that interview. "That doesn't matter now. I don't need their money. Now, I can choose whatever school I want."

"We agreed that NYU Polytechnic School of Engineering was the best. You know the school and some of their professors, and you can keep living at home."

"But that's the whole point. With a full boat scholarship anywhere, Bates Foundation will pay for tuition, room, board, books, everything. I can have the complete college experience, living in a dorm, making new friends for the rest of my life-"

Her mother plopped down on the couch. "And I'll be all alone."

Kwashay put her arm around her mother and tugged gently. "You knew I'd grow up and leave some day."

Her mother nodded. "I just hoped it would be later, not sooner. At least we'll have the summer together, before you go off on your college adventure. I'll take some vacation time-"

Kwashay leaned away. "Well, see, there's this other thing."

"What?" Her mother's jaw jutted forward. "Lord almighty, I knew there was a catch. Nobody gives away that kind of money without wanting something in return. What is it? What are they forcing you to do?"

"Trevor – Mr. Dixon - invited me to come down to Houston, Texas for an internship this summer. A paid internship."

"Oh." Her mother collapsed back on the sofa.

"So, instead of working for minimum wage in some service position, I'll get a full researcher's salary. And free housing near the Bates corporate campus. Trevor said they'd rent an apartment for me. I'll have money left over after food and miscellaneous expenses that I can save." She paused. "Or you can use it for whatever you want."

"What I want is my daughter at home, with me." Her mother stood up and threw her shoulders back. "I can take care of myself, thank you very much. And it sounds like I'll have to, starting after your graduation." She headed for the kitchen. "I'm going to start dinner or we'll never eat."

Kwashay followed after, fingering her locket, wondering how she could engage her mother in the process of college selection. *There are so many to choose from.*

115 – Charlie (New York City, NY)

By the time his plane landed, Charlie had decided to share everything with Potter. He saw her hybrid with the New York insignia on the side at the curb waiting for him. He ducked his head as he got in. "Thanks for picking me up."

“That’s okay.” She glanced at her wrist. “I wasn’t doing anything at 5:30 in the morning anyway.” She smiled and patted his hand. “Good to see you.”

He buckled up before she pulled away. “Where are we headed? Your office?” Charlie expected that Potter’s superiors would want a post-incident briefing after all the time she’d spent on the case. He was prepared to deliver a Grissom-style end-of-novel summary.

“Nope, there’s this little café on Central Park named Kerbs Boathouse. I’m taking you to breakfast. I want all the dirty details about Nebraska.”

“And I want to hear about Kwashay’s debriefing.”

“Fair trade. I have it all recorded, so you can hear her words without interpretation. Besides, you can give me feedback on my interviewing skills.”

“It’s a deal.” Charlie’s eyes closed as the movement of the car rocked him.

“You’re not falling asleep on me, are you? Am I that boring?”

Charlie blinked, then rubbed his eyes. “Sorry, it’s not you. I didn’t get much sleep on the plane.”

“That damn novel?” she asked.

He nodded.

“You’re so predictable. How is Matt doing?”

“He’s facing a difficult time, reconciling with his folks. They still don’t understand.”

“Just like me. By the way, I checked with the groundskeepers on Governors Island and Liberty Island. They both did heavy root feedings and they seem to have taken. The grass is coming back.”

“Great! I expect the remnants of the portals’ root system will deteriorate slowly.”

Potter speculated, "The remaining roots might even put nutrients back into the soil as they decay."

Charlie was happy with the subsequent silence, but evidently Potter wasn't. "How's Jane?"

"She's fine." Charlie reminded himself to give Jane her Loper t-shirt when he got back to DC. "Taking care of my goldfish while I'm away."

"Goldfish? I loved them in college." She exited the expressway. "I probably swallowed over a dozen in my freshman year."

Charlie sat up straight, straining against the seatbelt. "You did what?"

"Just kidding." She tapped his shoulder with her fist. "Awake now?"

"Quite."

"I figured a guy like you, always making quips, would have a sense of humor."

"I do. Really. Just not on that topic."

Potter pulled up to the corner of 5th Avenue and 74th Street. There was half a parking space at the corner. Potter pulled the car in, blocked the pedestrian crosswalk, and turned on the car's flashers. "It's on the water, just across the street.

They crossed against the light and followed a path into the park. Charlie marveled at the copper-roofed building with green patina located on the edge of a quiet pond. "This is lovely."

"The pond is called Conservatory Water, Central Park's model boat pond. Folks come here to sail and race." It was way too early for any of them to be out, so the water was smooth and silent. "I come here often for a hot cup of coffee and to think things out."

Charlie took in the panorama. "I can see why."

“Come on, they’ve got homemade muffins.” Potter tapped on the wooden shutters that sealed the food stand counter. Someone from behind unlocked and pulled them open. “You’re a little early.”

“We’ll wait at one of your tables. Let us know when you’re open for business.”

The man nodded.

Potter pointed to the pond. “You have a place like this, a get-away?”

“I guess my novels are the place I escape.” Charlie wondered if Selton used the library as his escape. *He couldn’t escape that loam geyser. It seemed to reach out for him.*

“Afterwards, we can walk over and see the Alice in Wonderland statue. It’s just down the path.”

Charlie appreciated the clean, crisp morning air. “You know, this case has been a bit ‘down the rabbit hole’, if you know what I mean.”

Potter nodded and led Charlie to one of the tables along the pond’s edge.

Charlie reached into his bag. “I got you a gift.” He handed her a Lopers t-shirt in size medium. “As a souvenir, since you weren’t in Kearney.”

“I could have been.” Potter pressed the shirt against her chest. “Nice color.” She moved closer and delivered a hug, leading with her shoulder, which prevented body-to-body contact. Charlie breathed a sigh of relief. He didn’t want his relationship with Potter to get complicated. Partners – colleagues in work – was clear and comfortable. *Besides, long distance relationships are doomed to failure.* “Did your EPA guy in California get one?”

“Yes, I bought one for Nachas.”

“And one for Jane?” Potter smiled.

What was Potter's obsession with Jane? "Yes, and one for Jane, as if it's any of your business." Charlie regretted the words as he spoke them.

"Partners should share, right? Well, I have a gift for you. The underground radar company sent me their results. Want to guess what they found?"

If Potter got the East Coast report, there should be a West Coast version waiting back at my desk. "A root system starting at Kwashay's portal extending almost directly west for hundreds of miles?"

"Give the man a stuffed loper. Or how about a world-class muffin instead, my treat?"

"Thanks. Speaking of sharing, how about you share your debrief of Kwashay?"

"Sure." She pulled out her recorder and put it on the table. "She was completely forthcoming, after we cleared the air.

"Was there a problem?" asked Charlie.

The man behind the counter called out, "We're open for business."

"How about coffee and a muffin first?" Potter stood up. "Their blueberry is to die for."

"Banana nut if they have it. And coffee-"

"Black. Yes, I know."

Potter trotted over to the counter, placed and paid for the order, and returned with their food and drink on a plastic tray. "Here you go."

"So why did the air need clearing?" Charlie peeled the paper back on his muffin and took a bite.

"She enjoyed the spotlight a little too much. I'll use the speaker so we can both hear. Press pause if you'd like some clarification."

"Mmm. You're right, this is delicious. Go ahead."

Charlie sipped his coffee as he listened intently to Potter's conversation with Kwashay, staring at the device, only occasionally looking up at Potter when he heard her recorded voice. After a little while, Charlie pressed PAUSE. "Initially, she held back. How come?"

"This was a big deal for her, giving testimony. I can't really blame her. Now here's where it gets interesting."

Charlie munched his muffin and listened to the part where Kwashay described her job: to direct nutrition stored in the portal to a target – a person – who was supposed to get a megafeeding. He pressed STOP. "She used different words than Dixon - nutrition instead of energy - but the underlying scenario matches perfectly."

Potter had consumed her muffin half as fast as Charlie. "Kwashay has a different reference set, a more technical and whole lot more biological perspective than Dixon."

"That means the messages they both got were functional in nature and consistent, but not explicit."

"That's why they each put their own spin on them, even though they were supposedly doing the same thing." Potter wiped crumbs from the corners of her mouth.

It's time to share, but gently. "I'm not a betting man, but I'd bet anything that the hobo was the target."

"Why him?" She cupped the recorder with both hands.

"Who else? But he wasn't cooperative. In fact, exactly the opposite. He wanted nothing to do with that nutrition-rich soil. So much so, he was willing to climb a transmission tower to avoid it. The higher he climbed, the higher it spurted."

"I told her that. Listen to the next part." Potter pressed PLAY.

They listened to Kwashay's consistent proclamation: "The nutrition was vital. The megafeeding was supposed to help us all. Everybody on the planet."

The tape ended. Potter pressed STOP and pulled it to her side of the table. "How was the megafeeding – whatever that was – supposed to help everybody on the planet?"

"We'll never know. What matters is, the hobo didn't agree. You should have seen him climb, almost in fear for his life."

"Didn't help any." She gestured an explosion with her fingers.

"Speaking of Kwashay, how is Ms. Williams-Jackson taking things?"

"I spoke with her yesterday, after you told me you were coming. She has a lot of faith and trust in Kwashay. That government citation you mentioned will be icing on the muffin." She took another bite.

Charlie had convinced Lane to donate his EPA medal for Matt. He made a note to have one issued for Kwashay as soon as he was back in the office. "I'm sure she'll be thrilled."

"They both agree that Kwashay will enter college this fall. Somewhere. Although her mother didn't react well about Dixon's offer of a summer internship in Austin."

Dixon's comment echoed in Charlie's mind. "That's what the 'even better' was. Crafty bastard.

Probably wants to dissect Kwashay's brain for residual alien traces."

"Charlie Keyson, that's not funny!" Potter scratched her head. "So is that what Dixon thought this was? Aliens?"

"I'm afraid so." *Since he was the other operator, he should have the procedure done on himself first. If his brain is in any shape for it after all of those psych screenings.*

"The internship he offered her was really tempting. Do you think there's a residual bond between Kwashay and Dixon, as joint portal operators? Is that why he invited her down to Houston?"

Charlie's coffee was almost cold. He wondered if there were free refills. "I think he's looking for proof of alien involvement, and hopes Kwashay can help him produce some. Between us, I think his chances are between slim and none."

"And you certainly don't have any, with the portals gone." She patted Charlie's hand. Through her chewing, she mumbled, "Your turn, partner. Tell me about Kearney."

Charlie considered the burnt pods in his bag. "You heard most of it on the phone."

Potter swallowed. "Like that was sufficient. Did that vagrant really explode?"

"Yes, without a trace." Charlie remembered the stringy pumpkin guts laying scattered on the ground, a few tendrils, the melted rubber glove and the scorched science fiction novel. "All that was left were hundreds, maybe thousands, of these things." He pulled the burnt pods from his shoulder bag and put one on the table between them.

Potter picked it up. "You do have evidence!" She examined it closely. "It looks like a seed."

"He must have been carrying them in his pockets."

"Hundreds of them? Thousands? Not likely." She held it up on the flat of her palm. "Think about how much space they'd take up.

Charlie channeled Grissom's analytical skills. He recalled how the hobo's jacket whipped in the wind. *These seeds were not in his pockets.* They stared at each other. Charlie was afraid to put his thoughts into words. *Who better to talk this out than my partner?* "If Selton wasn't carrying them in his pockets, then where were they?"

Potter became the interviewer. "Was he carrying a backpack or shoulder bag? A briefcase?"

"None of the above." The only other possibility chilled Charlie's blood. "If they weren't on him, they had to be inside him." *Inside his body? Nutrition is what Kwashay had said. Megafeeding a target.*

"What kind of person has seeds like this inside them?"

"Dixon was confused about whether there was one target or many." Charlie plucked the burnt seed from Potter's palm and rolled it around on the table. "These must have been the target for the megafeeding." He gingerly placed the dead nugget on the table and stared at it.

"These?" Potter leaned in and focused on the rough sphere. "They were supposed to grow? Into what?"

"I have no idea, but Selton refused to be a participant. His actions made it very clear he was trying to avoid the megafeeding, eventually at the cost of his own life." Charlie thought about all of the burnt pods collected at the power station. *How did the Chief dispose of them?* "The only thing I'm sure of is that Selton got what he wanted, and put an end to whatever was supposed to happen."

"That Dixon guy said this was aliens." She poked at the seed with her finger. It didn't move. "Is this a creature from outer space?"

"One we'd never expect." Charlie reviewed the catalog of strange images: the literate hobo climbing the power tower, the eruption of enriched dirt, the two portals and their corresponding brown stripes. "So much of this case is not natural."

"Just plain weird, you mean." Potter leaned back, coffee cup in hand near her chin. "So, Dixon was right after all? We were dealing with aliens?"

Charlie decided not to mention the scorched copy of *The Day of the Triffids* found after the explosion. "I'm not willing to publically endorse that conclusion, or even put it into my official report. All I know is, the vegetation is coming back all along the brown stripe. Governors Island is reopened."

"Case solved. So, will your bosses in DC be suitably impressed?"

"Probably not. I didn't really figure out the cause. I came off as an observer, not a problem solver."

"That's a shame. You did much more than watch." She took a sip. "Speaking of cases, how did the novel turn out? Did Grissom solve his case, or was he just an observer too?"

"Grissom saved the day, as expected. The credit card scam was the tip of an iceberg. He identified a group of terrorists who'd planned coordinated attacks of state capitals on the Fourth of July. Grissom and his team uncovered the plot and notified the authorities.

"Grissom has a team? You mean even Grissom needs partners?"

There was that smile of hers again. "College undergrads, not day-to-day partners. But it's always harder to go it alone." Charlie recalled the progress he made talking the case over with both Potter and Jane. "Of course, the FBI and Scotland Yard couldn't publicly acknowledge his contribution, or the attack at all for that matter."

"Well, I think you were a behind-the-scenes hero, in a similar way."

Charlie thought about terrorists from other countries, who might have been called aliens, and Dixon's theory of an alien invasion. "Maybe so." He wadded the muffin wrapper and napkins into the empty coffee cup and pushed it away."

"Watching out for Matt and Kwashay was very admirable." Potter finally put down her cup. "I guess that wraps things up. So, what do you do now?"

"You won't believe it, but Dixon offered me a job at Bates. After all he put me through!"

"You're not going to accept, are you?" Potter put her hand on Charlie's.

"Hell no. The man has no integrity. His boss threatened to demote him to a customer service rep. Given his personality, he'll be lucky to hold onto his own job if that happens."

"How the mighty fall."

"A pure example of over-promising and under-delivering. He didn't come through with alien technology like he promised. The portals disintegrated, so he had nothing to demonstrate. Even the scholarly hobo was blown to bits." Charlie pulled his hand away, plucked the burnt pod from the table and rolled it around in his palm. "I expect Director Stanton will welcome me back, maybe just not with open arms or a parade."

"Well, I can't order up a parade on short notice, but I can be your personal tour guide." Before he could pick up the second pod and put it in his bag, Potter snatched it. "I'll keep this as a souvenir. You still have one."

"No harm, I guess." Charlie folded his hand around hers. Her eyes were wide, focused on his face. He felt compelled to ask. "Why are you attracted to me?"

"Don't you know, super sleuth?" She pursed her lips. "It's your boyish charm."

Charlie didn't buy her answer, but didn't object. He liked the feeling.

Potter stacked her hand on top of his. "I've got the day off. There are some great places to see while you're in New York, besides Governors Island and Fort Greene Park."

Charlie remembered Jane's suggestions. "I've got time." When Charlie gently slid his hand from between hers, she pocketed her burnt pod in her jacket. He pulled his itinerary from his jacket pocket. "I'm on the Amtrak 4:04 p.m. Northeast Regional back to Washington. After the tour, you can give me a lift to the station."

"Hell no!" She hit the table so hard that the last drops of coffee in her cup splashed on the table.

He tucked the bag with his one seed back into his tote. "Why not?"

"Because if you take that train, I'll never get that dinner you promised.

Charlie wracked his memory. Had he promised her a dinner? "You're serious."

"After your perfect sightseeing tour of New York, we'll have a leisurely dinner. We don't even have to talk work."

Given the duration of the trip, if he took a later train, he'd arrive home between eleven o'clock and midnight. Jane would be in his bed. "Where will I sleep?" He realized too late he'd said that out loud.

Potter blushed. "Oooh, that was unexpected."

"No, I didn't mean-"

"That's all right. I've got a couch where you can crash."

Sleeping over at Potter's? Charlie knew instinctively that was a bad idea. "You've already done so much."

"Nonsense, partner. You've been flying all over the country, back and forth. That'll take its toll. You almost fell asleep in my car. You need a day off, one free from stress. I'll show you the best parts of New York. And I'll take you to the train station myself personally tomorrow morning."

The two of them, alone in her apartment overnight? "You're being very hospitable, but I couldn't impose."

"Even if you don't stay over, we'll have to stop at my place anyway, so I can change for dinner. I have a dress that'll be perfect." Potter stood and put her hand on Charlie's shoulder. "So it's settled. Let's walk over to the Alice in Wonderland statue and plan our day."

"One call first, to the office. To let them know I'll be back a day late." Charlie trailed behind Potter as he dialed the Director's number, expecting to hear Jane's voice. The Director himself answered.

"It's Charlie Keyson, sir. It looks like the situation is back to normal."

"Not clean and not simple, but you got the job done. Better than Lane, who's still dawdling with that spill. Maybe I should give you a crack at it."

Lane told me it was nearly wrapped up. "If it's all the same, I'd like a chance to catch up with things at home, get back to normal."

"Sure, you've earned it. Take a day, two if you need it. Getting you back will make my assistant more productive as well."

"Why, what's wrong?"

"Jane's been just sitting at her desk, wound up like a clock since you've been gone. Evidently you mean a lot to her, but that's your business to sort out."

I'd already promised Jane a chat. "We'll work that out when I get back."

"Good. I can't stand it, seeing her sitting there with that pathetic expression. In the meantime, I sent her home early."

To my apartment. Charlie looked hard at Potter. "Good idea." He said goodbye and put his phone away.

As the sun rose above the trees that bordered the park, Charlie shielded his eyes. Then he remembered the hobo's hat. He took the fedora out of his shoulder bag, thwacked it against the table, picked a few splinters out of the liner and put it on.

Potter stopped and turned around. "You look like a '30s detective. But not bad. All you need is a trench coat."

"It's too warm for that."

She glanced at his hand. "And you've got a new phone! Show me the videos you shot in Kearney."

Charlie's shoulders slumped. "I was so busy talking to you and Agent Nachas, I didn't think to shoot photos or videos." He shook his head, internally chastising himself.

"Maybe someone else did." She put her arm through his. "By the way, it's about time you stopped referring to me as Agent Potter. We know each other well enough for you to use my nickname - Steffi."

"Okay, Steffi." It didn't roll easily off his tongue.

"So, what cuisine would you prefer for dinner? I'll make a reservation." Her cell phone was poised in her hand.

###

80211332R00280

Made in the USA
Columbia, SC
14 November 2017